A STAND
for
TIR na nÓg

THE FENIANS

This is a work of fiction. Names, characters, places and incidents are either the product of the author's imagination or are used fictitiously, and any resemblance to any persons, living or dead, or events is entirely coincidental.

A STAND FOR TIR NA NÓG: THE FENIANS

First printing: October, 2016

ISBN: 1537433598
ISBN-13: 978-1537433592

Acknowledgements

I am greatly indebted to my Great-grandmother and Great-grandfather, whose story this is. These are just two of the giants upon whose shoulders I stand.

They were flawed people who loved too deeply and took on much more than they could handle.

Because they survived, my husband and I have three *super-kids* who produced nine amazing grandchildren who, I pray, will look back on my life and say that I had the strength of my convictions and courage enough to write the unvarnished truth, as told to me, about their ancestry.

My gratitude extends also to my great-great-grandmother whose gold wedding band I wear today.

And to my first grandson, Nathan Young, who always picks up the slack for me and sees that my work is properly published, my undying devotion.

Words You Need to Know to Read This Work

Aye
yes

Ave
prayer

Auld
old

Banshee
death spirit

Brogue
shoe

Buachaillí
/Boo-chill-ee/
Boys

Bulls
English Policeman

Byre
barn

Cadger
crook

Clúrachán
A sprite who brings speedy ruin

Colleen
girl

Coor
hitch

Da
daddy

Divil
devil

Eireann
Ireland

Fadge
bread

Fae
magic qualities

Faeries
magical creatures

Flannel
wash cloth

Gaol
jail

Ha'penny
½ cent

Hie
hurry

Houligan
trouble maker

Jumper/Wooly
sweater

Lay in
sleep longer

Loy
turf shovel

Maire
Mary

Nae
no

Niamh
Neeve

Oisin
O'sh-een

Padraig
Patrick

Poteen */pah-cheen/*
homemade liquor

Pradies
potatoes

Prody
Protestant

Punt
Irish currency

Quay */key/*
dock, pier

Quid
English money

Raggins
shredds

Scroggins
food

Shenanigans
tricks

Shillelaghs
weapon

Siobhan
/Sha-von/

Smoor
rousing the fire

Stone
14 pounds (lb)

Stranrer */Stran-rah/*
Scottish port city

Tinker
Gypsy

TIR na nÓg
/Cheer-na-noge/

Turf
Land that burns

Truncheon
night stick

Wane
boy

Wee
tiny, little

Queen Victoria's small hand lay heavy on the neck of Ireland. Only one band of men stood between her and total subjugation. They were ill equipped and undermanned. They had only two advantages: An inherent hatred of British Rule and the dream of another TIR na nÓg.

TIR na nÓg was the mythical land where no one grew old and no one went hungry and no one ever had to go to war. It was ruled by Queen Niamh who married Oisin, the son of Finn MacCool, the legendary Irish giant.

Finn MacCool was a giant not only because of his size but also because of his gallantry as the leader of Ireland's Grand Fianna. With the sword of justice, he slew all of Ireland's dragons and then led the Grand Fianna in banishing all invaders who set their blades of conquest against Eireann, the Emerald Isle.

The legend of Finn MacCool was emblazoned on the mind of every child as tales of his bravery were told around the turf fires of home. It was the bedtime story, the subject chosen for themes by schoolboys, the name picked by shop owners to paint on their windows.

But Queen Victoria had her heart and all her royal crowns set on the beautiful Emerald of the Sea known as Ireland. Someone had to hold her off, turn her back. Someone, like the legendary giant who had taken a stand for TIR na nÓg.

It was from Finn MacCool that the little band of outlaws took their name and their cause. They called themselves:

The Fenians!

A STAND
for
TIR na nÓg

THE FENIANS

a personal novel

by

MIDGE SHUSTA

1

"A salmon in the sea cannot fill an empty plate."

MI EANAR (January, 1848)

Young Egan O'Shea pulled himself to his full three feet seven inches. The wind swept down the face of the mountain with a force that brought tears to his eyes. But the tears would have been there anyway. They were burying Grandfar. He clung to the calloused hand of his mother, unconsciously feeling the bones beneath the thin, pale skin. He looked up at her face. There was nothing written there unless you counted anger. No. Maddness; maddess drawn from hunger, stained with the blood of her family, sealed and bound by the suffocating laws of Victoria's Royal decrees.

Heavy gray clouds curled up against the green hills, soiling the sky. It would soon rain again. Perhaps the pradie crop would be good this year.

The long black box that held Grandfar's frail body rested unevenly on the rocky ground and tilted back and forth as gusts of wind tried vainly to move it from where Finn and Hugh had placed it.

Egan's father, Finn, a man of huge proportions, now somewhat round at the shoulders and dull of eye, bent his back with his oldest son over their loys, creating another hole for another coffin. As hungry as they all were, the ground seemed to be the hungriest, for it ate the very heart of Ireland, her people.

Ten-year-old Marian rolled rocks into a pile to place on the grave later. Her thinning hair, loose from her bonnet, flew like a shredded flag in brown and grey wisps. Her gaze roamed slowly as she tried to focus on the work her father had given her. No matter if she blinked or concentrated, her vision was blurry. She saw less every day. But prehaps the pradie crop would be good this year.

There were no mourners this time. No wake at the house with family and friends. There were no tears, except for Egan's and the hushed wails from his grieving mother as she had tied her father's two big toes together with a piece of candle string to keep the fairies away. Everyone knew that fairies would come to cause havoc around the place and try to steal Gandfar's soul if they found out he was dead before the priest got there. When Father MacConree had left after giving last right to the corpse, Egan was assured that Grandfar was the lucky one for he would never have an empty belly again.

At the grave site the tap, tap, tap of rain struck against the coffin's top, as if God were dropping the prayers of the Irish Catholic back to earth, ignoring the pleas that were sent up daily for relief. Even so, Atty O'Shea fingered her rosary beads with a knowing touch never letting go of Egan's little fingers.

Hail, Maire, full of grace. The Lord is with thee. Blessed art thou amongst women and blessed is the fruit of thy womb, Jesus . . . Hail, Maire, full of grace . . . Bead after bead, her prayers went on in her head, becoming meaningless banter. Her mind slipped into the hidden memories of dancing to the pipes, full larders and smiles on now dead faces as bowls of steaming food were passed around her table. But now their tables were bare and their lips and teeth were green from eating grass every other day. At least they still had their home. The O'Brien's and Byrne's, the Cahill's and the MacPartland's homes had been tumbled and they were gone, living in caves or ditches or . . . maybe not living at all. The English lords, having their own way swept across the countryside waving eviction notices with men and muskets to back them up. The O'Shea's were the lucky ones. Though they were Catholic, they had managed to keep control of their own land through Atty's cousin, Morrin, who was married to John Newhall, an Engishman. No one could evict them. The land was in John's name, though he had promised Morrin he'd never assume it. "Let the croppies have it," he'd said. "We'll take their rent and leave it at that." He hated Ireland and in particular, County Cork though he had never said why. But what good was the land any how? Not even an English lord would have it . . . it was poison. Not that Finn would sell so much as a square foot of it. "'Tis life in the land, Atty," he'd said. "The land will always come back. We'll not be sellin' it. When it comes back, the O'Shea's will be here."

"Aye," she'd said, her head nodding, her heart breaking. "'Tis the land."

The dull thunk . . . thunk of spades full of thick, black dirt struck the wooden casket waking Atty from her memories. She led Egan to the grave where, after the dirt was packed down, they all placed rocks on top, knelt, crossed themselves and said their individual prayers over her daddy.

"He should be lyin' in the church yard, Atty, not out here in the wind. I'm sorry," Finn apologized softly, helping his wife to her feet.

"Aye." She shrugged her shawl-draped shoulders beneath his broad hand, looked up at him and smiled wryly. "He just couldn't seem to die soon enough to be getting' the last place there, could he?"

Hugh lifted Marian and Egan into the cart beside the potato loys. Finn grasped one long cart handle and Hugh took the other and they started back down the dirt road that led home.

The cart bumped and creaked over the roadway through shallow, brown puddles. The two children gripped the edges and huddled together. Marian spread her shawl over both of them as the rain pelted down on their heads.

Hugh had been wet before. He didn't bother sheilding himself from the water that pasted his auburn hair to his skull. Other thoughts passed through his young mind. It was time he left home. He was already thirteen and big for his age. He could get a job on the docks and send money home by way of traveling priests . . . when he could find them. If he slept in crates and ate once a day he could get by on next to nothing. He'd tell his plan to ma and daddy when they got home. He knew they'd agree. Even with the packages received from cousin Morrin once a month, one less mouth to feed would be a blessing. He'd come home again when things got better. And perhaps the pradie crop would be good this year.

"After you put the cart in the byre, Hugh," Finn directed, "you've got to be diggin' out the trench. I'll not be having rain water in the house again for your ma to clean up. Egan help your sister stack the fireplace with turf bricks, bein' sure they're truly dry now."

"Aye, daddy."

Atty hung her shawl on the wooden peg beside the door and took up her broom. The hard packed dirt floor of the cottage needed sweeping badly. Then she stopped, her gaze wandering around the shadowy room to the mat where her father had died barely two days ago. She leaned the broom against the table and lifted the stained goose down quilt from the straw mattress. "Tis a good washin' you need if . . ." She said not finishing her thought.

Outside, she flung the quilt over the stone fence and straghtened it, staying only a moment to see the growing dark spotches left by the rain.

As Hugh took up his loy and cleared the rain trench that ran in front of the cottage door, his plan for leaving began to take on a more exciting aspect. He would get a job on a boat going to England. From there he would try to find . . . nae, he *would* find Morrin and John. They would care for him and see to it that he found work that would pay enough so he could send plenty of money home. Everyone knew that there was food in Ireland for those who could buy it. His job was to earn the money. A bright smile filled his blue-gray eyes. It would be easy as falling out of the byre loft. Nae, easier!

The turf glowed a bright orange behind the white-washed stone hearth. Though the rest of the family was used to it, even enjoyed the faint, sweet aroma that the burning turf gave off, the fumes made Marian's eyes water profusely and she rubbed them constantly with the tip ends of her wooly.

"Daughter, be not touchin' your eyes like that," Atty said in the poor light as she fashioned the last of Morrin's gift flour into round, tasteless scones.

"But they itch, Ma. Sure'n you know what turf smoke does to me eyes."

Atty nodded uselessly. There was nothing, short of binding her eyes, that she could do for the girl. "Where's your daddy?"

Marian shrugged and shuffled around the table. She hated that question and her ma always seemed to ask it of her. "You know where he is, Ma," she managed uneasily. "It bein' the end of the month and all."

"Aye," Atty sighed. "I'd forgotten with the burying of your Grandfar."

Quietly she placed the scones in the oven beside the fireplace. She cleared her throat of the ache that had settled there. "Don't be lettin' those burn, Marian. I'll be in the byre for a time. Egan, love, peel the wax off that fruit, will you now? And, be careful not to lose any."

The little boy smiled and lifted his small, skinny frame from the warm harth. "Aye, Ma," he said.

The barn was dark. Old straw still cluttered the main floor and the stalls, though the cows had been long since eaten. Atty wondered which booth she would find her husband in this time.

"Finn?" she called softly. "Where are you, darlin'?"

"Go back in the house, Atty. There'll be nothing out here for you . . ."

She followed the sound of his sinking voice. "Your bein' out here is worth the comin'."

He chuckled without humor. "Why do you keep followin' after me, Atty? I'm not good enough for you. I never was . . ."

She smelled the strong odor of poteen as he swirrled the jug for another swallow. Every month as time came to go from their home in the Boggeragh Mountains to the docks at Cork Harbour to pick up the crate from Morrin, Finn thickened himself with the illictly distilled spirits. Ireland was not a place for a proud man anymore.

Ever since the feverish death of their tiny son, Francis, in the fall of 1845, Finn had found it hard to cope with life as it came to him. It was easier for him to lose himself in the jug of poteen made in the shadows by the widow Shirra who lived near the turf bog beyond the mill.

"I've put scones in the oven," Atty attempted softly. Her voice trembled and she pulled her damp shawl closer around her shoulders. "Marian's wonderin' why we're not inside what with the weather . . ."

The wind-driven rain pressed in from the west and dripped through the high knot holes of the old, leaning barn, tapping a monotonous tune on the sodden straw. Decaying leather tappings draped the worn white-washed walls. Remnants of cow hair and manure fused together with the dank, moss-greened wood of the barn and reminded Atty of her childhood. Once again she could hear her ma and daddy singing tunes after supper in the light of the coal oil lamp. All the faces . . . smiling faces and bright eyes lost to time and hunger. Who would have guessed the year after Egan turned three the pradie crop would blacken into poison before their very eyes.

Though the blight didn't touch the corn or the cabbages or any of the above ground crops they grew, Lord knew they couldn't be eating those things. For those were the things that paid the rent. They couldn't eat themselves out of a home to live in, though Atty did take and hide the dirty, outer cabbage leaves and she had learned to boil the stems and corn stalks to give flavor to the flavorless. John Newhall, like the other landlords, demanded his due and the other crops were what he wanted.

The jug sloshed again.

"Will you be comin', Finn?"

"Nae. Tis later I'll be in . . . or not. Now's me thinkin' time."

Atty turned to leave. Thinkin' and drinkin' seems to be the same thing anymore, she thought. She stood a moment silhouetted against the slanting rain before the barn door. "Finn?"

"Aye?"

Her hands moved slowly up and down her own thin arms. Her voice was as thin as her body. "I'm needin' you tonight. With me own dear daddy barely cold and buried, I . . . I'm needin' you fiercely, Finn." She hadn't meant to cry.

She heard a rustlng in the straw as Finn corked the jug and stood. "Scones is it?" he said lightly, brushing straw pods from his trousers. "I could be havin' a go at it." He appeared in front of her, a great show of a man getting old before his time.

Atty loved Finn, though she knew little about him still. In their fourteen years as man and wife she only knew that he'd come from the province of Ulster, County Tyrone in particular, and his mother had been an O'Neill. She knew too that she'd captured his big heart for he'd stayed and married her. She'd given him four children. And to stay in the Boggeragh Mountains of Cork, never to go north again was both the hardest and the easiest thing he'd ever done. Finn was a fighting man. He was a strong bull-of-a-man with a hatred for the English lords that ate at his insides like wood worms in a dead stump. And it was dead he felt. Now the only way he could protect his family was to accept the food sent every month from the wife of a bloody Englishman!

Day after tomorrow, he and Hugh would trek down the mountains with the cart through the labyrinth of gateless rock walls that made a comic patchwork of the Irish countryside, taking time to restack the rocks behind them. They would cross the miles of heather moorlands and travel down through more miles of graceful larch and juniper trees that could catch morning fog thick enough to slice. They would then move on past the massive old Norman keep called Blarney Castle down into the boggy lowlands of the Lee river. From there they'd follow the sparkling waters of the Lee to the docks at Cork Harbour, just as they had done the first day of every month for the past three years.

Finn drew Atty into his arms. There was hardly enough to hold onto anymore. The famine that began with the harvest of 1845 was suriving as if it had a life of its own and its biggest ally and benefactor was the British government and their Prody landlords! He looked up at the dark sky through the spilling rain. Maybe it was time to leave Ireland forever . . . take his wife and children and go on to America. Lots of families had done so; bought passage on ships and . . . With what would he be buying passage? He hadn't in years had so much as a ha'penny in his pocket. Leave Ireland . . . Bite your tongue, Finn O'Shea! The very thought should curdle your brain . . . what there is left of that!

"Atty, darlin'," he ventured. "Have you ever thought of leavin'?"

She leaned away from his shoulder. "Leavin'? And where is it we'd be goin'?"

"To Morrin maybe or America . . ."

"Ahhh! What a thing to be sayin'. Wasn't it you who said that the land would be comin' back? Did I not hear you say that we'd be here when it did? This is the ground where I've buried a mother and a son and only today . . ." Her voiced cracked as if she could finally weep over the passing of her father, Milo MacLoughlin. But she choked it back and went on irately. "This bit of land has been in our family since the grand days of the Fianna and it won't be me that gives it up!"

Finn clasped her face between his calloused hands and brought hard lips down on hers. His mouth softened from its fierceness as she returned his passion with a warm eager kiss. Wordlessly he lifted her into his arms and carried her back into the darkness of the barn where he laid her in the straw. Her shawl fell away and he groped with the buttons of her short gray blouse.

Again she felt the roughness of his hands and the smoothness of his kisses on her flesh.

He knelt above her and unbuttoned his shirt to feel her body against his own. This is what made it easy to stay. Atty MacLoughlin O'Shea. There was nothing in Ireland stronger than his love for Atty . . . not the blight, not the starving, not even the British.

Marian pulled the scones from the oven and placed them in a towel on the table.

"Why would cousin Morrin be dippin' the apples in wax?" Egan asked as his small fingers removed strips and chunks of wax from the fruit to be carefully made into candles by his mother later.

The girl shrugged. "I'd not be knowin' that, Egan. Maybe tis the law. Daddy says the English have nonsense laws for everything.

Hugh turned in front of the fireplace where he stood to dry off. "Tis to keep the doxies and the others at Cork Harbour from smellin' the fruit and breakin' into our crate. If they knew what it was, believe me, they'd have it in a minute and we'd have nothin'." His voice was deep for his age and he spoke with the authority of one who knew.

"Aye," Egan replied and kept peeling the wax from the fruit, dropping the fingertips of precious wax into a bowl. Egan was old for his age, too. Soon he'd be four.

Marian went to the door and peeked out. The rain was savage, though it wasn't cold. "I wonder what could be keepin' them?"

"Tis the end of the month, Marian," Hugh stated flattly. "You know that daddy keeps his jug in the byre. He can't seem to go to the harbour if he can see straight. Come back from the door. They'll be in when they're good and ready."

Marian slammed the door at Hugh's unmistakable command and gave him a look that could have soured milk, had there been any.

Finn slipped from the warm cradle of Atty's body. "You'd best be goin' in," he whispered. "They'll be comin' out here next."

"Aye. They've taken to slammin' the door." Her tone was light as she rebuttoned her blouse and dropped her skirt over her drawers. "Are you comin' then?"

"I'll be in later . . . Soon. I love you, you know," he said.

"I know."

"'Tis a promise, Atty; a true promise."

Lifting her straw-littered shawl to cover her head, she stepped out into the rain.

Finn watched her go then settled himself in the corner of the stall. His hand fell on the jug and he pulled it into his lap, cradled it like a baby. It sloshed with his movement. Near-silent tears of self-abasement and rage-filled frustration flooded his eyes and crept unchecked down the rugged contours of his face. Atty could never understand the meaning of the pain of depending on the enemy for one's own life, even the lives of those you love most. How could she?

Finn squinted into the nonexistent light to see his miserable, useless hands. Those hands that had plowed and planted, dug and hefted and stacked sacks of pradies in the cool, underground storage sheds; hands, now nearly idle, fit only to lift a jug. How was a woman to know? How could she hope to understand the tarnished pride of a strong man?

Ahhh! What's the use, Finn thought. I'll do as I've done for years . . . toddle down that damned hill to the sea, pick up a fortnight's worth of food from Morrin Newhall . . . He chuckled through the pain. "I wonder if that pinch-faced blister of a husband of hers knows what she's been doin' for us?" He laughed to keep from crying and pulled the cork from the poteen. Oh, well. Perhaps the pradie crop will be good this year.

"Lift a leg, lad!" Finn encouraged Hugh who was knee deep in mud behind the cabbage crates on the cart.

A rock-splitting rain bore down on them, soaking them to the skin. The cart seemed twice as heavy. The Lee had sprung a leak and the lowlands were flooded. The spongy bogs had accepted all the water they could and the cart wheels caught and stuck in the mire. The rain had pounded away at them every day of their trip down the mountain. Now, only hours from Cork, the cart had lost a wheel.

"Unload the crates, Hugh!" Finn shouted above the downpour, letting the long handles flop into the muck.

"But Da, the crates will fill with mud."

"Aye," Finn smiled. "An Irish present for our dear cousin, John."

Hugh smiled in spite of himself as he hefted the heavy crates from the cart and dropped them in the filthy ooze.

Finn's big hands grasped the muddy wheel and reattached it in minutes and fastened it tightly, then he checked the other wheel. "That'll have done with it, lad," he said holding out his hands for the rain to clean.

Hugh lifted one crate of the tightly packed, apple-sized winter cabbages into the cart and reached for another.

"Hand that one to me, Hugh."

"But Da they're heavier than you think." Hugh's voice had an astonished tone.

"Do I look that auld and feeble, lad?"

"Oh no, Da. I didn't mean that, . . . I . . ."

Finn grinned at the boy and hauled the crate to his shoulder. The cart rolled much easier with only two crates to burden it. With each one grasping a handle, they pulled the cart side by side the rest of the way to the cobbled streets of Cork. The hardest part of the journey was ignoring, as best they could, the milky blue corpses that lay in the water-clogged ditches beside the road as they headed for the docks at the southern end of the Irish sea.

They supposed that the deluge had emptied most of the city. At least this time most of the lifeless bodies of the starved had been picked up and taken out of the streets. Even more than accepting food from cousin Morrin, what bothered Finn most was having to deal with the death that swarmed around him and his son.

Men with running, bleeding sores, who had never begged for anything in their lives had thrown themselves at his feet, begging for pennies to feed their fever-ridden children. Carts had been turned over and were used as shelter for entire families. And, where there was no wagon or cart, there was no shelter. Suffering was everywhere. The best thing about coming to Cork was the going home again.

They pulled the cart over the uneven stones. It clattered behind them, the rain making as much racket as the wheels. The road to the docks looked longer somehow. The two story whitewashed buildings on either side of them loomed like huge, scaly dragons ready to snatch them into their black door mouths. Lace curtain eyes moved aside as the two of them passed then blinked back into place as they vanished from sight.

"Tis a bit spooky this time through," Hugh said, his lips barely moving.

"Aye. I wonder what's happened. Even the stink is gone."

Hugh had noticed that, too. The smell of grog from the ale shops, the rotting corpses of man and beast, even the perfume of the doxies was gone. "Is it the rain then?" Hugh asked, looking up at his father.

Finn shrugged. He grimaced as the edge of the crate dug into his shoulder.

A few people moved about the streets in ragged clothing as drenched as theirs carrying everything they owned on their backs and under their arms, but no one begged and no one spoke.

They turned the corner at MacTredhorn street where Finn stopped and looked down the long row to the sea. He shifted the crate from his shoulder to the cart.

"Where's the boat, Da?"

"I'd not be knowin' that, Hugh," Finn said as he put a firm hand on the boy's shoulder. "But I think that we'll be havin' us a good look."

They dragged the cart over the worn, rain thickened boards of the dock. The usual loud bump and push for the jobs of loading and unloading the ships from England, France and America was nonexistent. No one was waiting to board what was coming to be called, *Death Ships* for America and Canada.

Finn rapped on the door of the Dock Master's shack. The top half of the door opened to reveal a gruff walrus-of-a-man with pinched red eyes and wide nose under which a bush of gray whiskers sprouted in every direction.

"Aye!" he bellowed as if his sleep had been interrupted. "Ahhh, tis you, Finn O'Shea. I was expectin' you yesterday. Come in . . . come in."

"What about the cart?" Hugh asked, shivering with cold as he yanked on Finn's coat sleeve.

"Aye," the man roared, "best drag that in, too. If you leave it out there, you'll find nothin' left when you go. Most of our beggars are off to Skibbereen but there are still those who would steal it all and leave you nothin' for your rent."

The bottom of the door swung wide and the warmth of the small room sucked them in.

"Good day, to you, Mr. Cummins," Hugh said.

"And to you, lad. Not much room with your cart in here but tis better in than out."

Finn held his hands down to the tiny fireplace. "Is that where the world's gone then. To Skibbereen."

"Aye. Rumors are that the British mean to supply emergency relief to the skeletons that live there," Cummins said as he turned to take two walrus-sized shirts from the wall pegs. "Here, you can wear these while you dry."

"You don't sound convinced, Tom, about the British, I mean."

"I'm not. Have you been there lately, Finn . . . to Skibbereen?"

Finn shook his head. "Nae. Tis too far south for me. When did they leave?"

"Most left . . . maybe a week ago, now. Just before the rains come anyway. Nearly every man, woman and child dragged out of here in the most miserable parade I've ever had the discomfort to see. Cork's been like a tomb since."

"But Mr. Cummins," Hugh put in, "where are the boats? Have they come and gone?"

"Aye, lad . . . the boats." Tom Cummins aided young Hugh in taking off his drenched coat and boots. "You too, Finn. You need to be dryin' out."

Slowly, Finn removed his coat and hat. Something in Tom's voice bothered him. "Where are the boats, Tom?"

Cummins hoisted his trousers with his forearms and tucked his thumbs behind the thick leather belt. The folds of his breeches told the story of a man who had lost much of himself to the famine. But he'd lost more than himself. He'd lost Jenny and Nora, too; his wife and daughter.

Finn had met Tom Cummins and his family when he'd first arrived in Counnty Cork, fifteen years ago. They'd shared a pint at the Brown Bull Inn on Brian Boramha street. The next day as he wandered through the market place, he laid eyes on sweet Atty MacLoughlin.

"Well, Tom?" Finn pressed.

"They'll not be in for a while . . ."

"What does that mean, Da?" Hugh's eyes were round with dread.

Finn hushed the boy with an uplifted hand. "How long a while?"

"Of that, I'm not sure." Tom spread the wet clothes over the sparce furniture. The ceiling fluttered with cobwebs made fat by months, perhaps years of hanging untouched except by steam, grease and dust. "There was a wreck at sea and the British are holdin' up all the boats at Holyhead and Pembroke. All the ships that put in here are them that come down the coast from Dublin or Rosslare and the English have put a hold on every one. I'll know they're comin' when I see them."

"And when was this wreck?"

"The middle of last month."

Finn ran a rough hand over the stubble on his chin. "Then, 'tis possible they're bein' held up by this new storm . . ."

"Aye, 'tis possible."

"Would you mind if we waited the time out here with you, Tom?"

A brisk, easy smile crept around the corners of the Dock Master's eyes. "If you hadn't asked, I'da offered. I've been savin' this for an occasion and I'm thinkin' this must be it!" He dug through a deep wooden box of trash and brought forth a brown paper-wrapped loaf of bread and, in digging deeper, found the familiar jug of poteen.

"I could use some warmin' up," Finn said with a broad smile, rubbing his hands together.

"And for you, lad," Tom whispered as if there were others in the room who might hear, "A cup of peppermint tea with a *real* peppermint stick!"

Hugh's eye's lit up at the sight of the slim white piece of candy. He'd not had candy in two years.

"Now, where in the world did you come upon the likes of that?" Finn asked.

Tom Cummins smiled sadly, shook his head. "Those who want to leave our fair land will beg you to take almost anythin' to see that they have passage . . ."

"I understand."

"I don't like it for one minute, Finn. Not for a minute but I don't have a choice . . ." he sighed. "I'm not makin' five pence a day. All I have is this." His arms spread wide as he indicated the leaking shack he lived in.

"I've heard of work gangs who . . ."

"Who make six pence a day," Tom interrupted angrily. "They build roads that go from nowhere to no place and grand bridges that span puddles and bushes. They work their guts out and drop dead at the end of the day, leavin' families to die without their men. The overseer's wouldn't think of hirin' a woman. Oh no, they leave them to die slowly with their wee ones!"

Hugh swallowed hard and shuddered at the older man's anger. If the boats don't come in soon, he thought, Mr. Cummins could be talkin' about us.

Tom stuffed another turf brick into the fireplace. His breathing was hard, sharp as if he'd run a mile and back.

Finn patted his friend's shoulder. "Are we drinkin' from glasses or the jug?"

"Ahhh!" Tom shrugged, realizing he couldn't mend any part of what he'd said. "For you, Finn, I'll drag out me best!" Two short, thick, cut crystal tumblers were drawn from an overhead shelf. Tom ran his fingers around the insides of the glasses, blew out anything that might remain then filled them.

"To you, auld friend," said Finn raising his glass.

"Don't be wastin' toasts on me," Tom said as he raised his glass. "Here's to 1849 and a decent crop of pradies!"

"Aye!"

The kettle whistled for Hugh's tea.

The drinking and talking dawdled well into the night. Hugh curled up on the floor by the fireplace. Tom covered him with a ragged quilt. With the fading murmur of voices in his head and the rain that assaulted the shack and the constant drip, drip of the leaking roof into a bucket that would soon be splashed over the swollen pier, Hugh drifted into a paralyzing dream.

He saw his da's body at the end of a road that led nowhere. There were piles of potatoes and cabbages along the roadway and people dancing to a fiddler who smiled a grizzly smile. The only thing he would remember from the dream was the scratchy voice of a whirling woman who glared at him and sang:

> *My son went off to England and sent back all this food.*
> *You should've done the same, lad. You should've done the same . . .*

Hugh's eyes snapped open. The fire was nearly out and the dim, colorless room was bleakly cold. He knelt and tucked another turf brick in the fireplace and blew on it until it flared and began to burn. One good thing about the famine, he thought as he shivered under the frayed quilt, it hasn't slipped into the bogs yet. For without the turf bricks, cut from the bogs and dried in the sun, they would freeze as well as go hungry.

Looking about, he saw his daddy and Tom still at the table, their heads resting on their arms, snoring away, dead to the world from the poteen and a bone-tired weariness.

His dream had been so real, Hugh was relieved to see Finn sitting there. Sober or with a head full of poteen faeries, he was the best father God had ever made.

For the next three days they waited with Tom and shared his meager food supply with a trip once a day to the soup kitchen in the city's center that had been set up two days ago by the British Asociation for the Relief of Extreme Distress.

The rain stopped the morning of the third day and a warm bright sun bore down through the banner-like clouds that streaked the eastern sky. The air was fresh with the clean scent of washed wood and wild budding rhododendrons.

Hugh meandered along the wide dock in the afternoon, his dream a constant companon as he stepped over the moss-peppered boards. The tall pilings sprouted squealing gulls and song birds, denied the right of song for days, warbled in unlimited glee.

Hugh sat, dangling his long legs over the edge of the pier. A golden path of sunlight spread out before him on the whispering black ripples of water and drew his eyes down the harbour to the wide expanse of ocean. His legs swung lazily back and forth as his blue-gray eyes scanned the horizon. He blinked, sat up straighter. It was truly there. Sails. The sails of a British Merchantman rounded the point and headed into Cork Harbour.

"Da! Mr. Cummins! The boats are back! They're back!"

The boy ran toward the shack. He slipped on the damp wood and struggled to keep from sprawling along the slippery boards. Reaching the door, he thrust it open and yelled, "Mr. Cummins, the boats are back! Come and see!"

Finn and Tom grabbed their hats and ran down the dock.

"Run into town, Hugh," Tom ordered. "Knock on doors. Tell the men we've got a ship to off-load!"

"Aye, Mr.Cummins!"

Finn's smile broadened as the sails grew larger. Atty would be worried half sick about them. Now, the only thing left was to collect the crate from Morrin . . . if this was the right ship.

The dock filled with men eager to work the rest of the day for a measure of free corn.

"Shore the lines!" Tom shouted to the rough, shaggy men who waited at the ship's bow.

They obeyed, grasping the thick ropes thrown by the sailors from the foreward and stern decks of the tall three masted Merchantman.

Sails dropped, whopping against the decks. Men moved up and down the riggings like great white clad monkeys in a jungle of hemp braces that connected the masts.

Planks were lowered onto the pier. The unloading began.

Morrin's crate was there along with a hundred barrels of dried corn. Though the cost of the corn was minimal, there wasn't an Irishman in the land with enough punt to buy a cupful.

Finn lifted the crate of food and took it into Tom Cummins's shack where he tapped it open and scooped out a handful of flour, a small chunk of salt, some beans and wax-wrapped fruit. At least, this way he could repay Tom's generosity.

"Da," Hugh said softly as Finn resealed the crate.

"Aye, lad?"

"Do you remember me tellin' you and ma how I'd like to go to cousin Morrin and work to send money home?"

Finn straightened his back and looked his son in the eye. "I do," he said cautiously. "Are you thinkin' up somethin' else now?"

Hugh shook his head. "Nae, Da . . . except . . ."

"Except?"

"I talked to the ship's Captain. He said that I could earn me passage from here to Pemroke and from there tis an easy jog to Bristol." Hugh's thin anxious face begged permission.

"Gettin' to Bristol won't be so easy, lad . . . not easy at all."

The boy's face brightened. "But sure now, you know that I could do it."

Finn sat at the table. "I have no doubt of that. You're a fine, strong lad with a good head on your shoulders."

"Then tis all right? I can go?"

"I didn't say that, Hugh. Your ma would have me peeled, you can be sure of that."

"But, Da . . ." The brilliance in his eyes faded.

"The pradies are poisoned everywhere, Hugh, not just in Ireland. I can't let you run away from it because we're hungry from time to time."

"That's not it at all, Da. I want to work and send back money to you and ma for Marian and Egan. I can do it. I know I can!"

Finn looked lovingly at the eager, pleading child. He sensed the urgency the boy felt and understood. The same yearning had crossed his mind hundreds of times but word had always come from over the water that there were too many Irishmen and not enough work to send anything home but broken bodies and dashed dreams.

"I have no doubt that you could do it, Hugh," Finn said earnestly. "But you'll not be goin' this day. Perhaps the pradie crop will be good this year."

Hugh sank into a chair. "We'll be goin' home now, then?"

"In the mornin'." His father's voice was warm in its words but firm in its tone.

"Aye, Da," he said.

A paltry meal of one stolen winter cabbage and mashed beans was consumed in the light of burning turf bricks. Tom and Finn talked of the waste of the corn stored in the wharf warehouses. The food was there and still hundreds of thousands of people died of hunger.

"Protecting the rights of British private property, you know." Hugh heard Tom say with disgust.

"Aye," Finn replied. "We're a starving nation that exports food from our own gardens. Tis a pure crime it is. Who could imagine that we'd be growin' corn for the English to feed their anmals," he said with the slightest sign of laughter in his voice. "And they dry what's left over and ship it back here to sell to them that's got no money to buy it." He shook his head and ran a hand across his face. "I don't think the Irish who live through the famine will soon forget. Especially the Catholics."

Tom nodded. "Tis worse in the north where you come from, Finn."

"So it is, Tom. So it is . . ." Finn's forehead furrowed as unwelcome memories overtook him. Again he saw his own father standing with other men of Dungannon and he heard their bitterness as they were forced to recite once more the laws laid upon them by the British Parliament headquartered in the city of Dublin.

~An Irish Catholic is not permitted to own property.

~An Irish Catholic can not hold public office or work in the civil service, practice law or medicine, or anything else of a professional nature.

~An Irish Catholic is not permitted any formal education, in or out of Ireland.

~An Irish Catholic can not earn more money than a third of the value of the crops he grows and cannot own personal property above the value of 5 pounds.

~An Irish Catholic who owns a weapon faces a prison sentence.

~The practice of the Catholic faith is forbidden.

Finn placed his head in his hands as the memory tormented him. He recalled the secret masses, the hidden rosary beads and how the priests were forced underground. Finn rememered what happened to Catholic priests who were hunted down as if they were rabid dogs. In the town diamond of Dungannon, in the south of County Tyrone, a captured priest had been stripped to the waist. His hands were tied together in front of him and he was lifted up so that just his toes touched the ground. If the priest had said anything before he was whipped sensless and left hanging in bloody torment, Finn couldn't hear for the weeping of the Catholics and the cheering of the English soldiers and the Orange Prodies. The final ceremony came at midnight when he and the other children were carefully tucked away in sleep, a special team of soldiers would come again to the diamond with long knives where the priest was drawn and quartered and ultimately decapitated as a sign to the others that obedience to Britain was the only way to survive. It was especially a sign to the O'Neill Clan who had led rebellion after rebellion against British rule starting as early as the year 1600.

May God damn them all to hell, he thought in his bitterness. The faces of the men with the whips who took turns beating the priest sprang up again in the vivid eye of his memory. "And them that made the rules and them that hunted him down," he said under his breath.

"Did you say somethin', Finn?" Tom asked yawning.

Finn drew a deep breath. "Nothin' that matters a whole hell of a lot anymore."

Hugh lay again on the floor before the fire. His eyes were shut but he couldn't sleep. The scratchy song of his dream turned over and over in his brain . . . *My son went off to England and sent back all this food . . .*

The bosun's whistle wailed announcing the pending departure of the ship.

Oh, Da, Hugh thought, his heart aching, I'm sorry but I have to go now . . .

The amplified sounds of deep sleep filled the little shack when Hugh tiptoed out the door. He crept down the dock. The massive ship had been turned in the night and it was lit within and without by swinging oil lanterns. Barefooted men scrambled again, quickly, silently setting sails making ready to move away from the dock at Cork Harbour.

"So, mate, you've come," the Captain said as he raised one eyebrow.

"Aye," Hugh replied.

The Captain motioned at the gang plank. "Welcome aboard."

Hugh's heart drummed in his chest as he watched men haul the gang planks on board the ship and the great anchor chain scraped against the timbers as the huge metal claw gave up the ground and dripped into place. The wheel was turned. The rudder creaked and the breeze caught the luffing sails, snapping them full. With a deep inner groan the Merchantman slipped away from the dock. Hugh gripped the rail. He watched the tall pilings shrink in the last of the moonlight. But a sudden movement on the dock drew his attention.

"Hugh!" the frightened voice of Finn cried. "Come back, lad! Hugh!"

Finn sank to his knees. Tears rushed to gorge his disbelieving eyes. So the famine had now taken the second son. How long before he lost Egan, too?

2

"Forgetting a debt doesn't mean it's paid."

MI Na BEALTAINE (May, 1866)

The funeral procession wound through the streets of Dublin like a wailing, disjointed, black serpent and Liam O'Neill was its head.

It should be a crime to die so young; to have your last breath choked out by a rope. And worse, to die dangling from the gallows over the front door of Dublin's Kilmainham gaol.

"Looks like it'll be rainin' soon again," said Egan O'Shea glancing at the heavily bruised clouds that crouched against the high hills. He shifted the sharp edge of the coffin to a less sore spot on his shoulder.

"Aye," Rory Kilcullen answered from behind him.

The path to the cemetery left the main roadway to curve up the hill. The casket turned and the long serpent followed. At every cross-road, Father Kenyon creaked to his knees for a short prayer and caps were doffed, heads were bowed.

Two men walking toward the procession turned and, as tradition required, joined them for a half-dozen steps before going their own way.

Thick blossoms decked the apple trees making even this day lovely. Pale green shoots jutted from other trees and bushes as a quiet reminder that life did go on. But not for Liam O'Neill, who had been captured by Queen

Victoria's hounding Constabulary under suspicion of harbouring and/or being himself an outlaw Fenian. The boy carried nothing more dangerous than a bundle of the banned Irish People Newspapers and was going nowhere more suspicious than home. Not much to hang a lad of sixteen for.

"They'll pay for this," Egan muttered under his breath. "Jimmy will see to that."

They passed through the cemetery gates and Father Kenyon lifted his long cassock to climb the hill to the grave-site. He reached down and took a handful of newly turned earth while family and friends encircled the coffin. With a simple gesture the dirt was blessed and the coffin was placed on the rocky soil for a final word before being lowered into the ground. A low growl of thunder rumbled from the west, behind the clouds that bumped portentously across the sky. Women clutched their dark shawls closer about their heads as gusting winds sent their rosaries tapping against their dress buttons.

"Hail, Maire full of grace, the Lord is with thee. Blessed art thou amongst women and blessed is the fruit of thy womb, Jesus. Hail Maire full of grace . . ." Father Kenyon's scratchy voice led the rosary.

Egan tried but he couldn't speak. Instead, he took the tin whistle from his back pocket and held it in his open palm. Liam had wanted to learn to play. "I'll have you playin' in no time," he remembered saying to the boy. Now Liam had no time left. "Our Father who art in Heaven . . ."

At the end of the prayer each mourner scooped up handfuls of dirt.

The muted staccato tapping of rain struck the coffin as it was lowered into the deep hole. Father Kenyon dropped the first handful of earth onto the top of Liam's final resting place. It was followed by a shower of dirt and field flowers from the others. Liam's mother wailed in the arms of her eldest son.

"The sun hides its face for shame this day."

"Aye, Egan," Rory agreed, patting his friend on the shoulder. "Let's get on to the house for some scroggins. Me belly thinks me throats been cut. For a time there, I thought you was goin' to throw your tin whistle in the grave with wee Liam."

"I thought about it," Egan said softly. "He did love to hear the tunes."

The clouds opened and rain fell in earnest, pasting Egan's auburn hair to his skull as around him, the long black serpent silently fragmented.

3

"A trout in the pot is better than a salmon in the sea."

MI na NOLLAG (December, 1867)

Egan O'Shea stood on the bluff above Drogheda Bay, his fists in the pockets of his brown woolen trousers. A cold wind surged up the shallow gullies. Tall grass whipped around him. Ocean waves, as if timed by a metronome, collided with the rocks below.

Gratefully, he breathed in the wintery air remembering how close he'd come to being fruit for the gallows above Kilmainham's front door, himself. Months had passed since Liam O'Neill was hanged and over a year since John O'Leary, Tom Luby and Charles Kickham had been gaoled for urging Home Rule in The Irish Republican newspaper, The Irish People.

Besides counting on Gladstone becoming Prime Minister of England, the greatest hope for a 'Saorstat Eireann', Irish Free State, was the end of the Civil War in America. Irish soldiers who had swelled the ranks of the Union's "Fighting 69th" New York battalion were coming home in droves. Real soldiers, experienced and self-confident, were stepping onto Irish soil shouting, "Dublin next!" But there was no "Appomatox" for Ireland . . . not yet anyway.

James Stephens, founder and leader of The Irish Republican Brotherhood, awaited trial in Richmond gaol and Tom Kelly hovered, like a vulture, over Jimmy's bones. Who was to lead the masses of eager patriots willing to fight and die for a free Ireland? Egan O'Shea was just one of many who wondered.

Sharp-eyed gulls soared above him. He watched, as effortlessly, they hung on the wind. "You have the freedom that should be mine, you great stupid birds. You have no reason in your head and no loves but food. You just have all the world with nobody lookin' to hang you."

The growth of auburn stubble and the crimson rims of his eyes were telling. He hadn't slept since he'd learned of Stephens's arrest last month. Sitting in the grass, he pulled the tin whistle from his coat pocket and began to play mournfully.

"Egan! Egan O'Shea!"

He turned, not surprised by the voice. Keelin Bonner ran toward him, her cropped black hair flouncing about her head. Strong, stocky legs flashed beneath her gray woolen skirt.

"He's here!" she gasped and bent from the waist to recover her breath.

"Keelin, love. What are you sayin'? Who's here, girl?"

She grasped his shoulders for support. "I run all the way to tell you, Egan. He's here . . . at Rory's now. Get up! You've got to come. You're the first one he asked to see."

Egan slid the tin whistle back into his pocket. He stood and gripped her hands. "Who's come, Keelin? Who?"

"Jimmy. He's escaped."

"Jaysus, Maire 'n Joseph! You've seen him yourself?"

"That I have. He's been drivin' the Constabulary nuts. He thinks they think he went back to Dublin," she puffed, grinned, "to . . . to the paper, but he didn't. He's here!" Her pale blue eyes glistened and the burned blush of her cheeks seemed to glow in the late morning light.

"Well, come on, girl, don't be standin' there!" He yanked her behind him down the slope toward Rory Kilcullen's house.

Rory had become a member of the Irish Republican Brotherhood a year before Egan joined. He was a master at the use of blasting powder, a genius with disguise and was slippery as a wriggling eel when it came to the law. His boyish face and wide, innocent, eyes made trusting souls of nearly everyone . . . everyone but Keelin. She knew exactly what Rory was and she loved him, even so. He had taught her how to make bombs and she was good at it. In his four years with the Brotherhood, Egan had seen Keelin snuggle up to Victoria's soldiers like an insistent doxie while he and Rory slipped past to steal rifles or set fires, shred saddle cinches, loosen carriage wheels or simply escape. How the girl had never been ravished, Egan couldn't guess.

The door to the Kilcullen home was wide open.

"Rory!" Egan shouted. "Where . . ."

"Drop your voice to a dull roar, Egan, if you please," Rory whispered hoarsely, putting a finger to his lips. "You'll be havin' all the angels of Heaven droppin' by . . . and us unprepared."

"In here," Keelin said, casting a playful eye at Rory as she led Egan to the small pantry room where Jimmy sat in candlelight at a small table.

"Ahhh, Jimmy," Egan said in a strained whisper, "you look like somethin' the gulls threw back. When did you get away?"

"Yesterday mornin' . . . maybe the day before, I can't recall." Jimmy's deep voice was worn. "I overheard some guards say that O'Leary, Luby and Kickham are goin' to be retried soon."

"When?" Keelin asked. "What can we do?"

"I don't know, and that's the truth." Jimmy twitched with exhaustion. He ran dirty fingers through his long straight hair and over his beard.

Egan could hardly believe this was the same person he had first known. Jimmy Stephens was a strong man in his early forties then, with eyes of blue fire that stirred passion for Irish Home Rule even in the breasts of Protestants. For the past eight years he had led the Fenian movement, nicknamed The Brotherhood, through The Irish People publication. He promised that no one was exempt from the written word and proved it by attacking every Orangeman of consequence he could find. "Roman Catholic bishops are more dangerous than British control or British guns," he had said, and wrote: "If the people were submissive to the clergy in politics, there would be no Fenian Brotherhood. Ireland would be allowed to perish without a hand being raised to help her."

Now Egan wondered if Jimmy could raise a hand even to help himself. He looked used up, like a once bright candle becoming a puddle of wax.

"What are we to be doin' then?" Egan asked, repeating Keelin's question.

"Go for them! Get them out!" Rory growled from behind him.

"Go for them?" Keelin said incredulously. "Jaysus, Rory, you told me yourself that J.J. Corydon said they was in Chester. Tis a by God miracle Jimmy escaped from Richmond, but Chester Castle . . . Have you lost what little mind you come with?"

Jimmy looked from the girl to Rory's dark expression. "Sure'n she's right . . . for now."

"Are you sayin' that even knowin' where they are, you intend to be doin' nothin'?" Rory snapped with a blazing glance at Keelin.

"Soon," Jimmy said. "We'll be doin' somethin' . . . soon."

"The sooner the better. I'll call a meetin' of the lads for two days from now," Rory said with authority.

"All right. Now I have need to be talkin' with Egan . . . alone."

"Aye," Keelin said, pushing flat hands against Rory's chest. "I can find somethin' for this great fool to be doin'," she said, and winked at Egan.

Jimmy slouched in the chair, rubbed his eyes. "Pull the curtain, Egan, and sit," he said, his voice sounding powdery and feeble.

The curtain bumped along the rough wooden rod and the cramped, little room became swamped in shadow. Egan pulled up a milking stool and waited for Jimmy to speak. The familiar odors of apples, onions, soured milk, burlap, earth and tallow that filled the pantry mingled with the scents of unwashed skin and damp woolens that smelled faintly of fish.

"I'll not be keepin' you long, lad," Jimmy said. "But you bein' the one with a head on your shoulders and all . . ." His fingers scraped through his untrimmed beard. "I want you to be pullin' the reins on Rory. He's liable to botch things. We can't be movin' too quickly now . . ." Jimmy's voice trailed away as if his mind had turned a corner. He shook his head to keep his eyes open.

"What about O'Leary and them? Are we to leave them to the hangman?"

"They won't hang, lad. The British court has dished out handsome prison sentences. But you know all about that."

"Aye, I know. But they've done nothin' wrong. Tis not right, lettin' them rot in British gaols for printin' the truth!"

"Don't be workin' yourself into a lather, Egan. The time's not right. I'll let you know when and what after I have a word with that divil, Tom Kelly." His eyes narrowed, latched onto Egan's. "Now keep an eye on our friend out there."

Egan sighed. "Aye, Jimmy, but it won't be easy."

Stephens laid his head on his arms. He was asleep before he drew another breath.

What's wrong with Jimmy? Egan wondered. Had prison taken the fight out of him? Why was he so against attempting a quick rescue of the others? Quietly, Egan left the room.

"Well?" Keelin whispered, jumping up from Rory's lap. "What are we to do and when?"

"Nothin'. We're to do nothin' for the time bein'."

Rory's chair crashed into the corner. "What the bloody hell does that mean? Are we to sit and twiddle our thumbs then? Maybe we should all take up knittin' so's we can send O'Leary and them woollies to keep them from the cold!"

"Ahhh, hush, Rory," Keelin said. "Can't you see, Egan don't like it anymore'n you do? Jimmy's leader, not us. Sure'n he knows what's best."

"Sounds to me he's lost his nerve!"

Egan set hard eyes on his friend. "I'll not be listenin' to that, Rory; not from you nor anyone. You've got no right. Jimmy's done well by us all these years and if he's gone a little bats . . . well, it could happen to any one of us. And I don't want you droppin' off the short end because of it. He counts on you and so do I. We have to stay together or they'll pull us apart like sticky buns at breakfast." Egan's gaze offered no quarter. Then he walked out.

"And where is it you're goin', Egan?" Keelin called.

"To Maire," he called over his shoulder. "I'll be back in time for the meetin'."

Keelin grinned. "Late, no doubt!" It was twenty-five miles to the Martin farm just north and west of Dublin. "Best not let her da see you!" she yelled playfully. "He'll scrape off your top layer!"

Egan waved. Keelin was right.

Maire Martin's father took Egan O'Shea for a scoundrel and though "The Brotherhood" had never been mentioned, Egan knew that Martin felt he was involved somehow and made no bones about wanting his daughter out of the company of such a houligan. But staying away from the warm arms of the copper-haired Maire was more than Egan could bear and the reflection of her in his mind drove him southward at a near lung-bursting pace.

Thanks to the farmer who offered him a ride, Egan arrived at the Martin farm before dark. He didn't knock. He waited. A pallid light shown from the windows and rumpled images passed behind the curtains.

"Come out Maire, darlin'," he whispered, his fingertips whitening against the rough bark of the gnarled oak. Had he half the boldness her father gave him credit for, he'd have walked up to the door and pounded away. But he didn't go and the door didn't open and the lanterns went out.

Rejecting the protection of the barn or the rocky hollow farther down the hill, he hiked his collar and drew up his knees to sleep in the crisp, brown leaves beneath the tree. The cold night left dew on his clothing and as morning rimmed the hills he shivered awake. His shoulders were stiff and his legs ached from walking.

"Tis a miracle you was ever found, Egan O'Shea. What is it you're doin' here in the wet leaves?" Maire's green eyes danced as she teased him.

He sat up, rubbed the leaves from his jacket, cleared the sleep from his voice. "Waitin' for you."

She tossed her head, the long copper waves falling over one shoulder. "And did you think I'd be under the leaves then?"

"Nae. But I thought your da might put you under lock and key if he seen the likes of me again."

She smiled sadly, knelt and caressed his whiskered face. "Where've you been, Egan? I've worried for you these many months."

Answering her question was impossible. He simply reached for her and, pulling her into his arms, he kissed her, losing himself in the warmth of her body.

She nestled against his shoulder. Somehow he knew just how to kiss her, where to touch her to set her afire. The agony of the days, sometimes weeks or more of waiting between their meetings under the great oak vanished when she was in his hands.

"Ahhh," she sighed, "I've missed you sorely . . ."

He pressed kisses down her throat and opened the first two buttons of her blouse. Her breaths came rapidly as his tongue made warm circles on her skin, inching toward the peaked nipple he felt in his cupped palm.

"Ahhh, Egan, I wish . . ." She stopped unable to speak.

"Tell me what you wish, Maire, darlin'."

The cool morning turned his moist kisses cold on her bare flesh. "Why don't you marry me? I want you so badly . . ." she pled with him through liquid eyes and began to rebutton her blouse.

"Don't," he whispered, placing a hand on hers. "Don't be takin' it from me now . . ."

Her hand slipped helplessly into her lap and she wondered how she had refused him all these months. Closing her eyes, she felt the morning touch her skin as the rest of the buttons on her short blouse were opened and she was re-clothed with his rough hands. "Marry me, Egan," she whispered breathlessly.

He raised his head from the creamy pillow of her breasts. "You know what your father would be sayin' to such as that."

"I don't care! Not for a minute! Not forever!" She slid down in the damp leaves and drew his mouth over hers.

His hand moved down her hip, rubbing her skirt, lifting it quietly out of place until he felt the warm flesh. No one else could have this . . . no one.

"Maire Martin! Where are you girl?" Her mother's crisp voice shocked the morning.

"Damn!" Maire whispered. Her fingers worked furiously at refastening the buttons. "If you'd marry me, Egan, you great stubborn fool, you could tell her to go polish shillelaghs and she'd do it!"

"I can't marry yet," he said thickly, watching her pull leaves from her hair.

"Shhhh! Lie down!" she ordered.

His silvery-blue eyes followed her as she straightened her skirt and settled the heavy woolen shawl around her shoulders again. His gaze stopped at her pouting mouth. "I love you, Maire Martin. I love you with me whole self!" he said softly.

Her eyes shimmered like emeralds underwater. "Fine way of showin' it you have, Egan O'Shea, fondlin' me in a bed of leaves!"

"There are things you can't be knowin' yet. Things . . ." His eyes dropped away from hers, unable to contend with the love he saw there. "I've too many things left to do . . ."

"And I'm not one!" she snapped, getting to her feet. "Thanks to you, the saints'll have me doin' penance in purgatory!"

"Maire! Get yourself up here, girl. Breakfast's gettin' cold and there's work to be done. I swear you get more muddle-headed as time goes on!"

"Comin', Ma!" she called.

"Will you be back?" Egan grasped her ankle.

"Maybe . . ."

"Please . . . We'll talk about a weddin'."

She looked away, gripped a rough limb. "You don't have to be sayin' such as that to make me come back you know. I come every mornin' anyhow."

Egan's expression paled and he swallowed the guilt he felt. "I know. Might you be bringin' back a scone or two?" His wide, tilted grin appeared.

"Aye." She smiled and ran up the slope to the house.

Egan lay on his stomach, watching the flow of her hair in the breeze then, shifting positions, he tried to ease the throbbing in his groin.

4

"Even a tin knocker will shine on a dirty door."

MARTA (March)

"And where is it you've been again so early in the mornin'?" her father demanded from his place at the breakfast table.

"Just out past the oak," came Maire's winded reply as she slid into her chair. "The hills are beautiful now and I truly love the look of them."

"And just what is it *about the hills* that you love, Maire?" Bobby teased.

She stamped her foot then smiled nastily at her younger brother. "Why, Eireann, of course," she said, her green eyes narrowing in a threat he readily recognized.

"That'll be enough, you two," Peg said and wrapped her apron around the handle of a steaming pan of fried potatoes and onions. She didn't look at her daughter as she placed the pan on the trivet in the middle of the table. "Seems to me a girl who's old enough to enjoy Eireann in the mornin', could learn how to button her blouse."

Maire gasped as she looked down the botched row of buttons. A flash of color reddened her cheeks. "You . . . you'd think so wouldn't you now?"

Ten-year-old Bobby giggled and pointed as her fumbling fingers corrected the mistakes. A sharp kick under the table made him yowl.

"Enough!" Kean Martin said. "You'll be after wakin' Kate before it's time and your ma has enough to be doin' today."

"Aye, Daddy," Maire and Bobby replied together.

The late winter sun streaked through the faded blue linen curtains. Kean pushed his chair back and reached for his hat.

"We'll be goin' into Dublin this mornin'," he said abruptly. "After your chores are done."

Bobby bounced from his chair. "Ahhh, Daddy," he cried. "Why didn't you tell us before now?"

"You wouldn't have slept a wink nor eaten a bite now, would you?"

Maire's heart pounded in her temples. "Do I have to go, Daddy?"

"You mean you don't want to be goin' with us?" Peg asked.

"Course she does," her father put in with a pleased smile and a sound hug. "After you finish the milkin' help Bobby with the goats and the pigs. We'll be leavin' in a bug's wink."

"Aye, Daddy!" Bobby was out the door, turned he said, "I've got the milk pails for you Maire!"

The girl found it hard to breathe and couldn't understand exactly what had been said. "But . . ."

"But what, Maire child?" her mother asked.

"Well, in the first place, I'm not a child anymore and . . ."

Kean turned in his chair. "And?" he inquired.

Suddenly Maire couldn't think of a thing to say.

"How old are you now, Maire?" Kean asked facetiously.

"Seventeen . . . almost."

"Well then, Peg," he said to his wife. "I think we should be tellin' her the main reason for goin', don't you?"

Her mother's pretty, round face glowed. "Aye. Tell her then," she said with a nod.

Kean motioned Maire to sit again at the table. "I've met a man in Dublin. A man of means he is . . . owns a stable and a store. He's a fine fellow to boot." His tone was definite as his eyes fastened on hers.

She blinked his gaze away. "Tis glad I am for you, Daddy . . . to have found a friend in Dublin. But what has that to do with me?"

Kean leaned back in his chair and laughed. Then he rocked forward and clasped Maire's face in his big, wide hands, looked cheerily into her eyes. "He's got a son, Maire, girl; a good lad with a fine, level head on his shoulders, not like that O'Shea houligan. This lad's just the sort of man your ma and I hoped you'd marry one day. We want you to come, meet him. You'll see."

His words echoed through her and she thought the scream in her mind could be heard through the pores of her skin. It was true enough . . . she was the oldest spinster she knew. Even uncomely Molly MacDermott had married Tim Foley's boy, Ross, almost a year ago. She was already burstin' at the seams with child. Every time they passed the MacDermott farm someone ran out to say, "And have you seen Molly lately? She's big as a byre. Twins I'd be sayin'."

"Well?" her father asked.

Maire fidgeted with the lace on her sleeve. "Aye," she said softly.

"Well then! When you've finished the milkin' tell Bobby to get the next to the biggest piglet washed and sacked after he feeds them. We'll take him to MacSweeny as a gift!"

Maire drew a breath and offered her father a wan smile. "Will we be leavin' soon then?"

"Work fast, girl. I'm coorin' the horse already. Oh, take the pig bucket to Bobby when you go to the byre."

"Aye, Daddy," she said and tied her work apron over her skirt. When her mother left to care for Kate, she stuffed her pocket with scones and hefted the bucket of corn and scraps for the pigs.

Hurriedly, Maire placed the bucket in front of the barn door, then, looking around and seeing no one, she raced again to the oak.

"Egan!" she called in a hoarse whisper. "I'm back!"

He came from the brush farther down the hill. "Can you stay?"

She shook her head. "We're bound for Dublin this mornin'. Me da's found a man there. He says he wants me to marry him. Here are your scones."

The smile on Egan's face melted into rage. "What?" he said, letting the food remain in her outstretched hands.

"Well," she said, toying with his fury, "you don't have time to be marryin' me yourself so . . ."

Egan jerked her into his arms with a force that jarred her. "You're mine, Maire Martin. And I'll kill anyone who puts a hand on you. Do you understand that?"

She stared at him, frightened for the first time, then encircled his neck with her arms. "Aye." She sighed and pressed warm lips against his, the hardness of his mouth softening at her touch.

"Will you be here when I get back?" she asked, her eyes searching the silver-blue of his eyes.

He shook his head.

"Then I'll come every mornin' and every night till you're back."

"Aye." He crushed her against his body to fill his memory with her every curve and then he let her go.

Peg watched her daughter run up the hill from the ancient oak and rush to the barn where the cow lowed to be milked. She stood in the veiled darkness of the opened door. A wrenching sigh brushed passed her lips as the shadowy figure of a man vanished from sight.

Keelin Bonner watched Egan pace. He paid no attention to the hushed zeal of the conversation among the ten Fenian leaders. Pipe smoke and the scent of ale clung to the walls of Rory's small house in the Drogheda hills.

Jimmy Stephens, now cleaned and brushed, held the floor. His was the only voice to preach patience. "You don't understand, lads!" he protested. "I've been in their stinkin' prison and I'm tellin' you, if we don't put a lock on it for now, we'll prick a seepin' hole that we'll not be able to plug if we're not careful as a shepherd at sheerin' time! There are plenty of British citizens who'll soon put enough pressure on the Members of Parliament to give Ireland back to us on a silver plate. But if you go runnin' off causin' damage we'll be startin' at the beginnin' again. I'm warnin' you!"

The strained high-pitched voice of Kevin Burke broke through. "If we take the push off them now, they'll think we've gone soft. They respect us truly. It'll not be me who lets them forget it!"

"Aye!"

"Aye!"

Jimmy dropped his hands in disgust and turned on them. "If you had the sense of a suckin' lamb you'd know what I've been sayin' is the only way to get what we want. You'll blunder into some grand show of force and march us years backwards. The bloody Orangemen are just hopin' you'll do somethin' stupid then they'll pluck you like apples for their crates and ship you off, separate and helpless!"

"Ahhh, Jimmy," a lively voice boomed. "You're getting' auld."

The men's laughter seared Stephens's mouth shut. Thoughts of the stark Richmond prison cell came back to life like a dragon to be slain all over again. Perhaps that was the reason. Outliving one's usefulness had never been a concern before, and age had nothing to do with love for Ireland . . . did it? He pressed his back against the rough plastered wall. The laughter came in waves like vulture's wings, flapping in the face of his abilities, or lack of them. With a tightened jaw, he blocked the bile that rose in his throat. He looked around the room and saw that of all the men there, over half he had recruited himself. It made him feel as if he were dying in front of his own children. Is it time to be leavin' already, Jim? he asked himself.

Keelin grabbed Egan's arm. "Look what they're doin', Egan. Do somethin', . . . before it's too late!"

Egan stared at the sturdy young woman as if he'd just seen her. "And what is it you'd like me to do, Keelin?"

"Talk sense into them!" Her eyes were round and her voice had a desperate edge to it. "They'll listen to you."

Egan sighed. "And why should they listen to me?"

"Because they do!" She shoved him into the center of the room.

"Well, lads," he began, regaining his balance and the spirit of the meeting. "It would appear that we have sympathizers for British Rule in the room." His words caused an abrupt silence. "Anyone who'd disrupt the Fenians from within might want that, don't you think?"

"And just who would you be pointin' a finger at, Egan O'Shea?"

Egan shoved his hands into his pants pockets. "Ahhh, no one in particular, everyone in general. Seems to me, what Jimmy had to say slipped into your empty heads through one ear and you didn't bother to stop up the other one."

"All right, Egan," Rory said, "if you've got somethin' to say, out with it."

"Aye!" others said, their voices tinged with more than a little anger.

"I do. You've been talkin' about bustin' in on Chester Castle. That's all fine and good to be puttin' England in the cannon's mouth for a change."

There was a rustling of approval.

"I agree," Egan went on. "But, the timin' must be right. And the right place will be wherever they take O'Leary, Luby and Kickham after they're retried . . . not before. If we strike before the trial, and fail, they could get the rope. If it was you there would you want us to chance that?"

Eyes darted about the room. No one spoke.

"Well, then," Egan said, turning his attention to J.J. Corydon, who sat quietly in a corner. "When did you say they'd be retried?"

"That's anybody's guess, Egan. As far as I know now, they're all three in Chester Castle's gaol. But for how long?" He shrugged.

Egan turned again to the group. "All right then. J.J.'s done his job. But we still need to know if they're in Chester Castle or if they're goin' to be moved; when and where. As long as one of us is in Chester he might as well check Manchester courthouse as well. Then we can plan a raid for the right place. Are we agreed, lads?"

"Aye, Egan," Rory stated, urging those around him to do likewise. "Who's to go then?"

The question swept the room and, as with a single thought, all eyes settled on Rory Kilcullen.

"Me? Why me? I'm a bomber, not a spy!"

Egan smiled and placed an arm around Rory's shoulder. "Don't worry, lad. You'll do fine. We'll send someone with you; someone to take good care of you . . . keep you out of trouble, so to speak."

"And who do you have in mind, may I ask?"

"Why Keelin, of course."

"Keelin? It'll be me watchin' out for the likes of her, you mean."

Keelin stood in front of him, hands on her hips. "I never needed your watchin' over me, you great fool . . . just you're watchin'!" she teased, rucking up her skirt to just below her knees.

"Keelin Bonner, you tart!" Rory scooped her off the floor and swung her around.

"Now when you go, which should've been an hour past," Egan said, a crooked smile on his face, "look respectable . . . not like a pair of Brotherhood houligans!"

"Aye!" A low chuckle filled the room.

Jimmy Stephens didn't laugh. He was making plans to leave Ireland for good.

An hour later Rory and Keelin were ready. Rory looked through a pair of small square spectacles. A cap covered his black curly hair and he carried a worn copy of Dickens's "David Copperfield."

Keelin had draped a ragged black shawl over her head and shoulders. A long gray sweater hid her figure and she wore black stockings. "And when I talk to someone," she said, "I'll squint. Like this." Her nose wrinkled and her forehead creased. "How's that?"

"I'd not know you," Egan said with genuine admiration. "Now off with you. If you hurry you might get the last boat from Drogheda and be in England by mornin'."

He watched them from the threshold of the little thatch-roofed house. The others left, too, slapping him on the back, congratulating him for his excellent plan.

"'Twas Jimmy's plan all along," he told them. "You just wasn't listenin', that's all."

When the last man had gone, Jimmy came to him. "Nae, Egan. 'Twas my plan to do nothin'. Yours is better. Keepin' good men on their guard is best. I knew you was the one all along."

Egan O'Shea had not turned to his friend. His eyes were yet on the empty road. "The one for what, Jimmy?" he asked absently.

"To take me place, of course."

"Don't talk like that. I'm takin' nobody's place."

"Then who'll lead the Brotherhood when I'm gone? Tom Kelly? He won't leave London. He thinks he can do it all from there. Watch out for him, Egan. Sure as God's in heaven, Kelly's the wolf in granny's gown."

Egan came back into the room. "And where is it you're goin', then?"

"America, I think. 'Tis been on me mind for a long time."

"Ahhh, Jaysus, Jimmy. America's half full of starvin' Irishmen. There's nothin' there for you. You belong here, in the green hills of Eire."

"Egan, me lad." Jimmy sighed, trying to smile. "Tis a poet you are and t'would be me greatest pleasure to stay on, but now, tis goin' time. John O'Mahony in New York City heads the biggest bunch of Fenians that side of here. He might be needin' some help. Besides, I'm told that parts of America look a lot like Eireann."

Egan's expression faded. "You can't be serious about goin' . . . I mean, about *leavin'* us."

"Aye, serious as another famine. And I'm askin' you to remember the oath you took and obey the commands of a superior. I wrote a note," he said, nodding toward the table. "It says what I have in mind for you. I'll do me best to keep your name out of this. I don't want you bein' fruit for the gallows at Kilmainham's front door. But be a good lad and do as your told. Without you to lead them, I fear for this bunch of Fenians."

"Well then . . ." Egan hesitated, not quite grasping the full impact of Jimmy's words. "I'll . . . I'll do me best . . . till you get back, of course."

"That's a good lad but I'm not lookin' to come back so . . ." Jimmy patted Egan's shoulder and retrieved his coat as his voice vanished in a deep sigh. "You know that I had to give over the leadership I hold to Tom Kelly but…" Jimmy shook his head in frustration. "You're the better man I'm thinkin' so give it all you got. It'll mean meetin' with Tom in London and that's goin' to be dicey business.

"I wish I could disguise meself as well as Rory does." Jimmy looked at Egan, the thin smile fading from his bearded face. "This whole thing's a damned game to him, isn't it?"

"Rory?" Egan shrugged. "I think so," he said sadly.

Jimmy pulled his cap down on his head as he walked past his young replacement and started down the road that would take him to America. "Tis a deadly game he plays, God help him. He'll wind up dead if he don't take it more serious."

Egan watched his leader and friend walk out of his life. "Keep a good watch Jimmy," he warned, his eyes stinging with sudden, fear-filled tears. "They're lookin' for us all."

Jimmy turned. "And you as well, me young friend. And may God take you out of the peril I've surely put you in. Blessin's on you, Egan O'Shea!"

Jimmy's solid frame shrank and disappeared as he rounded the far hedge. "And you too, Jimmy Stephens . . ." Egan brushed at the tear and reached for the note.

5

"In Dublin's fair city . . ."

Kean Martin drew the reins back on old Winnie and the cart creaked to a stop. In another hour they would be in Dublin. Bobby slid to the ground and reached for Kate.

"I'll take her, Ma," he said.

Peg handed him the little girl. She was glad Kean had stopped to check the foreleg of the mare. It gave her time to get down and stretch.

An unseasonable sun climbed steadily toward the line of trees to the west. Peg rubbed her eyes. Maire walked slowly back to the cart from a necessary trip into the roadside bushes. She straightened her skirt and pushed her hair back over her shoulder. She's truly a pretty thing, Peg thought. No wonder that O'Shea lad keeps sniffin' round.

"Well, then," Kean called, "are you ready to get goin'? It'll be near noon when we get there if we don't get a move on."

"Maire and I want to walk a little, if you don't mind," Peg said, putting an arm around Maire's shoulder.

"A wee walk'll be good for you. Just be keepin' up now." Kean's click and whistle sounded and the cart lurched forward.

"Why are we walkin', Ma?"

"I thought we should be doin' some talkin'. We don't talk much, you and me. Tis time."

Maire looked quizzically at her mother. "What are you wantin' to talk about, Ma?"

"Egan O'Shea," Peg stated, training her own green eyes on the sudden glow of Maire's cheeks.

The girl wished the ground would swallow her, but it didn't and she matched her mother's long strides, finding it impossible to do otherwise.

"Do you love him?"

Maire's eyes went wide with astonishment but she could see no reason to lie. "Aye," she said softly.

"Is he a member of the Brotherhood?"

"I . . . I'm not sure of that." Her voice slipped away and her eyes found other things to see.

"Your daddy thinks he is. And you know how he feels about them."

"Aye." Maire cringed. "But it don't matter. Egan's a fine man, and he loves me."

Peg nodded. "Them in the Brotherhood, I'm told, are commanded not to marry. They take an oath that weds them to Ireland till all the Orangemen are gone for good. Has he told you that, Maire child?"

She shook her head and squinted into the bright sky. Is that why he hasn't asked for me hand? she thought, making an effort to remove any picture of her thoughts from her face.

"Well, then," Peg went on, "meetin' young Luke MacSweeny may be a tall fence, but you can climb it, can't you, girl?"

"Aye . . . I can."

Peg smiled at Bobby whose legs dangled over the back of the cart as he struggled with his little sister to keep her from falling.

Maire swallowed hard and bit her lower lip wondering where her mother's talk would go next.

"I want to ask you a tender question," Peg said.

Maire nodded, trying not to appear as weak as she felt.

"I'm assumin' that if your da was to ask, I could tell him his daughter is yet unspoiled." She noticed the blush on Maire's white skin.

"You mean has Egan ever . . ." She nearly choked on the thought.

"Well?"

"Course not, Ma! I mean o'couse I'm . . ." Maire stopped walking and stared at her mother through wide, wet eyes, her breaths surging and retreating in rigid gasps. "Why would you be askin' such a thing?"

"Well, tis truly glad I am to be hearin' that," she said and smiled before she went on. "I know you understand about virginity, with the blessed Mother and all." She crossed herself.

"Aye, Ma."

"Do you know how much yours should cost the man who takes it?"

"Cost?" Maire's jaw dropped in surprise. "Sure and you don't mean I should be sellin' it?"

Peg grinned and shook her head. "It costs more'n money, darlin'. How much is your virginity worth to you?"

"Why, everythin', I suppose."

"Aye." Peg nodded. "Everythin'. And the man who takes it, must offer his life, for that's what it costs. The very life of the man . . . that's what he owes you. Not a quick kiss and see you next month. Is Egan O'Shea willin' to give his every breath for you? To work and die for you and the children he'll father? Or is he so in love with Ireland, God help him, that the Church and what he'll owe to you won't enter his curly head?"

Maire couldn't answer. She knew Egan so well, didn't she?

"Ahhh, by the way," Peg added offhandedly, "tell Mr. O'Shea, the next time he comes callin', he's to come to the house, like a gentleman. I'll not be havin' guests stay the night out by the oak."

Astonished, Maire couldn't move and her mother walked on without her. "Aye, Ma . . ." Her voice vanished in the breeze.

Kean stopped the cart at Peg's call and glanced over his shoulder at Maire while Peg climbed onto the cart seat. "Come on, girl! You're laggin' too far behind."

Maire ran and jumped on. Bobby thrust Kate into her arms.

"Your turn," he said brightly. "What was Ma tellin' you?"

"She wasn't tellin' me anythin'. We was talkin'."

"About what?"

Maire glared at her brother. "None of your nosy business."

"Ha! Bet she was talkin about that fella . . . The one who looks like *Eireann in the mornin'.*"

"Bobby Martin!" she whispered. "You're a fat worm! And I've no desire to be speakin' to you again as long as you live, you ugly toad!" She pushed him from the cart.

"Daddy!" he cried. "Wait for me!"

"What happened?" Peg asked, turning abruptly in her seat as Kean pulled Winnie to an impatient stop.

Maire glanced from Bobby's dirty clothes to the faces of her parents. "He fell off," she said.

The cart bumped along the road following an ancient path that cut through the maze of high and low rock walls that made a unique jumble of the Irish countryside. Tufts of spiny grasses grew along the road's edge and every so often the wagon splashed through giant puddles.

Kean adjusted his cap and squinted into the distance. The spires of Trinity College rose like sentinels through the clear air. "Always wanted to have one of me kids go there," he said. "Don't suppose that'll ever happen though . . . do you?"

"I don't know," she said. "Bobby's doin' real well in the National School . . . and there's always Kate."

"Ahhh! Tis boys need schoolin', Peg darlin'," he said, patting her hand. "Girls need a good husband to look after. The hand that rocks the cradle rules the world."

A defeated sigh left Peg's lips as inwardly she threw a silent fit.

Winnie's hooves clicked over the cobblestones as they entered the city. Gulls swooped and squawked overhead. Kean turned Winnie down Fishamble Street just so he could pass by the Music Hall. If the doors were open, they might be able to hear the musicians practicing. Each time he would remind Peg: "Handel gave the "Messiah" there, the first time it played anywhere . . . more'n a hundred years ago now."

"Aye," she replied again.

But there was no music this time and they continued toward the MacSweeny store and stable.

Bobby's eyes couldn't dart fast enough to catch all there was to see.

He loved the sights, the smells, the pace of the city. The children of Dublin paid no attention to him as they ran, rolling cart and larger wagon wheel rims over the damp cobblestones followed by barking dogs and more children. The red uniforms of British soldiers caught his eye as a squad drilled down by the quay.

The city was noisy with carts, horses, sheep, fishmongers, street-side clothing markets, open-air butcher shops and dirty children. Pigeons squabbled with fat gulls for food scraps. And the aromas of bake shops were lost in the smells of manure, fish pots and bales of pungent wool being offloaded by muscular stevadors from a ship that had arrived, no doubt from America.

"How much farther, Daddy?" Bobby asked.

"Patience, lad," Kean replied. "Tis up ahead round the corner."

Maire couldn't help turning to look at the young men hefting the heavy bundles of wool, buckets of tar or water, wondering which one might be Luke MacSweeny. Perhaps he was the one with the bulging muscles who turned the corner ahead of them with the anvil resting on his forearms.

"Well, Kean Martin! Tis good to be seein' you again!" a stout man in a bloody apron shouted as he wiped his fingers across his chest. His untidy graying hair had once been dark and still had a trace of black to it. His waxed mustache was curled so high that it threatened to put out his lively blue eyes. When he spoke, Maire noticed that two of his top side teeth were missing. "And you done what I asked; brought the whole family! Tis pleased as punch I am!" He slapped Kean on the back and, walking around the cart, reached for Kate who held her chubby arms out as if she knew him. "Luke! Roddy! Company!"

Peg shuddered as the large blood-sticky hands seized her eighteen-month-old baby from Maire's arms and vanished through the dark doorway of the butcher store. She glanced at Kean.

"Don't go to worrin', Peg. MacSweeny's a bull but Kate's as safe now as she would be with me."

"Somehow that don't ease me mind, Kean Martin! I don't know the man!"

Maire dropped to the ground from the back of the cart. "Well," she sighed, "best be getting' on with it." She rubbed her palms down the sides of her skirt and straightened the lace collar of her round-necked blouse.

Bobby grasped the sack that held the piglet and went into the store behind his mother and father.

"Maire!" Kean called from the doorway. "Get in here, girl."

Raising her skirt above her ankles, Maire stepped gingerly over the puddles that ran pink with blood.

Young Roddy MacSweeny squirmed with excitement. "Would you like to be goin' to the docks?" he asked Bobby in an animated whisper.

Bobby shrugged and looked at his father. "I guess so."

"Maire," Kean said proudly, "I want you to meet Luke MacSweeny."

Her eyes hadn't grown accustomed to the dim interior. "Pleased to meet you, Luke MacSweeny," she said and held out her hand to the shadow that walked toward her.

"And you Miss Martin," came a deep reply as he took her hand.

Roddy tugged on his father's apron. "All right, lads," MacSweeny said. "Be gone with you. But be back when the tower bell rings three. We'll have just enough time then for some scroggins."

"Aye, Daddy!" Roddy exclaimed and yanked Bobby after him. "Wait till you see it! There's crabs and dead fish all over the place and when we're done there we can go see me good friend, Manus!" Roddy's voice emptied into the sunlight and just as suddenly they were gone.

"Luke, lad," MacSweeny said from between the sides of meat that hung from the ceiling on giant hooks. "Show young Maire round. She don't get to Dublin much and t'would be shameful to be wastin' weather such as this. Show her *The Pair*. She'll like that."

"Aye, Da," he said and took her gently by the elbow.

"Ma?" Maire called over her shoulder.

"Mind what I told Roddy about the time," Luke's father warned. "Martin wants to be home before dark."

"Aye."

"Ma?" Maire's plea went unanswered as Luke made for the door.

"Let go of me!" Maire hissed and jerked free of his grasp. "I've no need of the likes of you holdin' me up!"

"Luke," his father called, "stop at Feeney's and get young Livie. Bring her back with you. I promised she'd make the boat to Liverpool tonight."

"Aye, Da." At the door, Luke dropped Maire's arm and stepped over a large bloody puddle.

"Damn! You did that on purpose, didn't you!" she snapped, standing in the water.

"Aye," he said through a widening smile. "I was under the information that that's what you wanted."

With her eyes adjusting back to the light, she saw him; tall, lean, broad shouldered with a wide, even smile and his father's eyes. His dark curly hair was short at the sides but sank into the collar of his blue cotton shirt. A curl fell down his forehead and Maire felt herself wanting to brush it back.

Luke MacSweeny was a full head taller than Egan O'Shea and in the depths of his eyes there burned a cooler fire.

"Let me help you, Miss Martin," Luke said, reaching for her shoe.

"I've no need of help, *Mister* MacSweeny," she said, more annoyed with herself than him.

He stood back while she hopped on one foot, shoe in hand, toward the cart. As she reached the back of the small wagon, Winnie readjusted her stance and Maire found herself sitting on the street.

"Damn!"

"You have a limited use of the language, don't you?"

"Oh, get away, you great fool!"

Luke watched Maire right herself and place the wet shoe on her wet foot. "Somethin' tells me, I'm not goin' to enjoy Dublin this day," he said, folding his arms.

Maire dusted her skirt and rubbed her backside, looked up at him through narrowed green eyes. "This may come as wee shock, *Mister* MacSweeny, but I'm findin' it hard to care!"

Luke shrugged. "Would you like to see Da's Matched Pair, then? They're the most beautiful horses round here. Natural twins, you know. Sometimes I think he loves them more'n Roddy and me."

"No, I would not!"

Luke turned away, walked down the street toward the harbour, his hands locked behind him. "So, Maire Martin," he said, making conversation, "when was the last time you was in Dublin?"

"Last summer. I hate it. Tis hot and everythin' is dirty."

They neared the pier in silence. Gulls squawked, resting effortlessly on wafts of cool salty air, their stark eyes scanning the ground for scraps. Waves struck the rocks and the surrounding pilings of the dock.

"Do you like the sea?" Luke asked, tossing a pebble into the dark depths.

Maire shrugged. "I suppose. Why?"

"One day, I'll cross over . . . travel England maybe or go to France or Spain." He turned to her, his eyes bluer than his shirt. "Don't you ever wonder what's out there?"

"Nae. Ireland's all I need."

Luke sighed, nodding at her witless remark. "Don't you ever wish to have your own freedom?"

"Freedom from what?"

He shrugged. "From havin' to answer to everybody; to do what you like and not have to say why."

Maire smiled. How often had she wished that? Not having to milk the cow or help with the washing, the mending, the cooking . . . Freedom to do as you please. She looked out again across the dark waves. Is that where freedom was? The idea had never had a name before, now it did . . . *freedom.*

"Would you like to be goin' into town then?"

A cautious smirk crossed her face and as she brought her thoughts back in order. "You know what they're doin', of course."

"Who?"

"Your da and mine." She tossed her head, the copper waves settling around her shoulders.

"Aye. I'm still figurin' how they let Roddy and your brother slip away instead of sendin' them with us. Maybe they thought Livie would be enough."

"To chaperone? You're bats!" She looked at the tall, handsome young man. "I don't even like you."

Luke laughed. His blue eyes flashed.

Maire took an unsteady step back. "What's so funny?"

Luke tried to stop, but the laugh stayed in his eyes and voice. "I don't like you either."

"Well then," she said, brightening and crossing herself as if to be sheilded from anything he might say or do, "let Heaven be praised for that much! Who's Livie anyway?"

"Livie? She's our cousin. Her da and mine are brothers. She's been here on a visit, that's all."

"She's English?"

Luke grinned. "Nae. Uncle Dooley works on the ferries and he gets free passage sometimes. Livie was born here on the day his job came through."

"She's named for Liverpool, then?" Maire asked, astounded.

"Aye," he laughed. "'Tis mad, I know. But she's all right, if you like harp-playin' girl cousins."

"What about our brothers? Ma'll skin me if somethin' happens to Bobby."

"Roddy's just showin' him round, that's all. They'll be fine. Now, then, are you ready to be seein' Dublin, Maire Martin?"

"Aye, Luke MacSweeny."

"Don't mind the smell," Roddy said and knocked on the door of the old, crippled shack. Without the tree to lean against, the building would have been a pile of rubble long ago. A gruff voice from within bade them enter. Except for streams of light that crept through cracks in the weathered boards, the room was dark.

"That you, Roddy?"

"Aye. I brought a friend, Manus. His name's Bobby Martin. Lives to the north of here."

A palsied hand reached for the newcomer's face.

"Don't be scared," Roddy said. "Manus sees you through his hands."

Bobby stood, holding his breath, as the bony fingers skimmed his head and shoulders like living cobwebs.

"Don't he talk?" Manus asked roughly.

"Aye," Roddy laughed. "Say somethin', Bobby."

"Do . . . do you *live* here?" the youngster stammered.

Manus snorted. "Does he always say stupid things like that?"

"Nae. Sometimes he's even fun."

The room came to shadowy life in the light of a single candle. Bobby saw a drawerless dresser, strewn with wadded blankets and a tilting cupboard housing two plates, a bowl, two cups, a jug and a handful of used candles. The lower shelf held jars of flour and oats and a pot of honey encrusted with dead flies.

"I brought you a fish, Manus," Roddy said, holding out a dead mackerel.

Manus grasped the fish, smelled it and laid it across his lap. "Aye. And where'd you get money to be buyin' fishes?"

"Buyin'? I promised old Feena you'd marry her for it. She near swooned in her rush to be givin' it up."

"Roddy, you're a damned scoundrel!" Manus laughed. "Light me pipe, lad."

Roddy went to the dresser, brushed the blankets aside and got two white clay pipes. From the shelf he lifted a jar marked *meal*, reached in and stuffed both pipes with tobacco.

While Bobby's eyes widened, Roddy lit one and sucked the smoke through the barrel several times before handing it to the old man. As Manus leaned back blowing long streams of smoke, Roddy lit the other. "I'll share mine with you," he said, sitting cross-legged on the floor next to Bobby. "You smoke, don't you?"

"Well," Bobby swallowed a strangling fear. "N-not for a good long time." His heart beat faster than a runaway team—even faster than the time when he watched the O'Donnell's stud mount the Toolis's mare.

"Well, don't just be starin' at it. Puff."

Bobby cleared his throat. Sweat suddenly beaded his upper lip. "Aye," he said, his mouth twitching. Wordlessly he crossed himself, spoke a prayer that he'd not be sent to hell for what he was about to do and drew smoke through the long stem and filled his mouth, but didn't know what to do with it and thinking he was going to suffocate, he swallowed.

Roddy sat stunned. "I've not seen that done before. You smoke the best pipe I ever seen!"

Bobby smiled painfully. "That's the way real smokers do it," he grunted, smoke pulsing from his mouth with every word.

"Manus, would you have a story that's achin' to be set free? Bobby here deserves a good one."

The old man scowled. "I might . . . if me whistle was oiled."

Roddy got the jug and handed it to Manus.

Somehow the old man pulled the cork with what was left of his teeth and Roddy filled the cups. "You can share mine," he told Bobby who thought a sincere but hasty 'Our Father . . .' at the sight of the whiskey punch.

"You know about Finn MacCool," Manus said, stroking the limp fish.

"I heard the name," Bobby said. "Does he live in Dublin?"

Roddy roared with laughter and rolled around the floor.

"Ahhh, this lad's education's been sorely abused," Manus growled.

"And why are you laughin'?" Bobby demanded.

"Finn MacCool is Ireland's grandest hero. He lived 2000 years ago and he won't be back in Dublin till next week!" Roddy could hardly breathe.

"Well, I was knowin' he was someone important. Now shut up and let Manus tell the tale." Bobby snatched the pipe from the table and puffed. He choked and coughed cleared his throat and straightened his back then settled himself against the wall. "I'm waitin'," he rasped, blinking through the smoky drifts.

"Here." Manus groaned, shifted the fish to the floor and held out his cup. "Sip this. It'll clear your pipes. Here," he repeated, thrusting the cup, sloshing it over the boy's legs.

Bobby took it and drank. It built a fire in his mouth that scorched his brain. He thought the whiskey was leaving his body through the tears that scalded his eyes. The room was dim and he was glad.

"Finn MacCool was a fightin' man, "Manus told him. "He was the son of Cool MacTredhorn, leader of the Grand Fianna who guarded our shores and protected our king, Conn-of-the-hundred-battles.

"But a druid, one of them fearsome creatures who looks like men but that's all, wanted MacTredhorn out of the way, so to speak, so he put a dark spell . . ."

Bobby saw Roddy pour more liquor into the cups then his vision wavered. His stomach rolled. He watched Manus's mouth move but the words no longer made sense. In the flickering light, the mackerel grew and smelled like a barrel of fish. He couldn't understand how Roddy kept sipping from the cup and sucking the pipe. The stuffiness of the place closed in on him. Manus's flinty voice droned on. Bobby felt his shirt collar try to choke him. He wanted to unbutton it but his fingers were attached to a hand that was far too heavy to lift and soon he fell over, unable to move.

"You like Dublin, then?" Luke asked, running his hand over the early shamrocks in the high meadow where they sat on the outskirts, overlooking the city.

Maire shrugged. "'Tis all right, I suppose . . . for them that likes big cities. I like the quiet of the farm where you can think and walk forever, if you like."

"So you still don't like Dublin at all, then?"

"Ahhh, nae! I like the theaters in Smock Alley and Aungier Street. They was me favorite and, of course, Trinity College." She touched his hand to reassure him. "Your city's beautiful, Luke. I'm just a country girl in me heart. Don't be angry." She glanced around the meadow at the black-faced sheep then back at him. "How old are you?"

"Twenty, almost."

"Where's your ma? I didn't see her at the store."

"Dead."

"I'm sorry. I didn't know."

"'Tis all right. She died when Roddy was a tyke. We're used to livin' alone now. Are you cold?"

She shook her head and picked at the tiny shamrocks in the grass.

Somehow Luke could not take his eyes from her. He hated to think that his father had been right about this strong willed vixen-of-a-girl but she was nothing like he'd imagined. There was a tenderness in the way her touch lingered on his hand, a warmth in her voice. Even her profanity had an innocence about it. He became aware that she hadn't fastened the top button of her blouse and he glanced around, glad none of his friends were there to see how clumsy he felt. Her presence overwhelmed him as she sat, unencumbered by proprieties, making a silly bouquet of shamrocks and budding wild flowers.

He dragged his eyes away to look beyond the city, across the high meadow, past the sheep and out to sea, his confusion not allowing him to speak.

"Is somethin' wrong, Luke?" she asked.

He shook his head. Suddenly the sound of her voice was the loveliest song he'd ever heard. He shivered.

"Are you all right?" Her voice betrayed a sudden concern.

"I . . ." He cleared his throat. "Tis time we went to the Feeneys for Livie. We don't want to be late." Standing, he offered his hand.

"Are you not feelin' well?"

"I'm fine." He smiled.

"Nae. You're not fine. We've plenty of time. What's wrong?"

Luke turned away, trying vainly to stop the flutter that started in his chest and sent a shock throughout his body.

She moved in front of him. "I'll not be goin' till you tell me!"

He looked down at her. "You," he said.

Me? she mouthed. "Have I talked out of turn, then? I didn't mean to be sayin' anythin' wrong. Dublin's a fair city, truly. And I didn't know about your ma. And about your da's horses? I'll see them. I promise . . . and . . . and I'll tell him how grand they are. Ahhh, please forgive me, Luke. Please?" She was plainly flustered and completely confused by his one word answer.

"It has nothin' to do with that," he said, his eyes searching her face, hoping to see something, anything to encourage him.

"What then? I don't understand."

Luke looked away as he spoke. "I think our fathers were right."

"About what?"

"Wantin' us to meet."

"What? Are you bats? I have a gentleman friend, you know. . ."

"I feel like I've known you for the longest time," he said, ignoring her words, his brow wrinkled in honest bewilderment.

"Sure'n you can't be thinkin' what I think you're . . ."

Luke's gaze stopped her remarks. He placed his hands on her shoulders, stared into the depths of her emerald eyes. Her heart began to pound and she tried to tell him not to look at her lips like that, but no sound came.

Egan had said . . . What had Egan said? Would Luke kiss her like Egan did? I won't encourage him, she thought. I won't . . . She watched Luke's mouth come closer to hers and she didn't move as he approached.

"I don't think you should be doin' that . . . again . . . No . . .no . . ." she gasped weakly, surprised by her own reaction.

Suddenly it didn't matter to him if they were seen or not. "Again," he whispered and pulling her to him, covered her mouth once more with his soft, eager lips.

Luke's kiss was different. It was gentle, filled with the same need, but peaceful. Certainly not polite, but not harsh either. I like it, she thought as her arms crept over the muscles of his arms and shoulders and, one by one the shamrocks slipped from her fingers. "Damn you, Luke MacSweeny . . ." she moaned. "What is it you think you're doin'? I don't know you . . ." she said, still wondering why she responded to him the way she had and why her feelings for Egan seemed to diminish in the power of Luke MacSweeny's tender kiss.

Customers came and went in the small butcher shop and feed store. They glanced at the strangers in the corner then greeted MacSweeny and watched as he cut chunks of beef, pork or mutton from the hanging carcasses. His rich laughter filled the shop as easily as did the light from the burning lanterns and two open doors.

Peg's face glowed with perspiration. For winter it was warm as June. Everyone had commented that there hadn't been enough rain. They had already begun rationing themselves and the animals. She dabbed her throat with the hem of her skirt. Even with the opened doors at front and back, the place was stuffy. She pushed her shoe through the floor's thick layer of wood chips that was not able to totally absorb the rotting smell of old blood. And the seeping, wooden bucket of entrails behind the counter, meant as a fly-catcher, gave off its own stench.

"I don't like lettin' Maire and Bobby go off like that," Peg whispered as she watched MacSweeny wrap another chunk of meat in newsprint. "And them boys; I hardly seen their faces."

Kean shifted in his chair. "I'm thankin' you to be keepin' your voice down," he whispered with a side long glance at their host. "MacSweeny's a gentleman and no doubt raised his sons in like manner. You've no cause to go worrin' and less to be speakin' so."

Peg sighed and adjusted Kate's clothing, thankful the child slept for the time being. Her green eyes drilled Kean's. "He's no gentleman," she hissed. "He's a butcher!" She stared out the front door, her fingers drumming the table as she wondered where her children were, wishing there was a breeze.

Kean covered her hand. "No reason for that now. The boys'll be comin' through the door soon enough. If they wasn't havin' a good time, do you think they'd be gone still?" He watched her face soften. "Why, they'd be here clammorin' to be goin' home."

"I suppose so," she murmured. "It's just that . . ."

"What, Peg darlin'?"

"Nothin'." She smiled at him. How could she tell him that Egan O'Shea had been back, knowing how he felt about the man? Perhaps they were right to bring Maire here. But as she wondered, she doubted anything would come of Maire and the young MacSweeny. She knew what it was to love a man and lose him. Long ago she'd convinced herself that marrying Kean had been the best thing. He was a kind, decent man. He had everything a woman could want in a husband except . . . the inner flame that stirred her. The spark that had seared her blood, made it hard to catch her breath when Conor O'Gill held her in his arms and. . . . She looked across the table at Kean and smiled. The breeze quickened, picking up her skirt, blowing her hair. She shivered. The memory of Conor had returned so clearly when she saw Egan O'Shea's shadow under the oak. But . . . She sighed deeply, that was all so very long ago, more'n seventeen years.

"Never have I seen heat like this in winter," MacSweeny said, mopping his neck with a handkerchief and plopping down in the third chair. "If it wasn't for that, Martin, I'd be lockin' the shop in your honor. But I don't dare. I'd have a cart full of rotten meat by mornin'."

"Aye," Kean said, understanding.

The butcher scooped water from a small pail with a crockery cup and it swirled down his throat. "I want to thank you for the wee pig. Tis a beauty. Sure'n you didn't have to bring it."

"'Tis for the hospitality you've shown me and mine."

"*Cead Mile Failte*," the butcher said in Irish, telling Kean that he was welcome a hundred-thousand times over. "Have you seen that young houligan you was tellin' me about last time you was here?"

"Not hide nor hair," Kean said with assurance. "I told him already what I think of him and the Brotherhood. He'll not be back to bother me Maire. Not for an age, he won't!"

"Well," MacSweeny said, mopping his brow again and shaking his head. "I've no use for them either. They may be doin' a fine job but, I have to admit they scare me. Only last month a girl was tarred and feathered, right here in Dublin. I didn't know her of course, but talk says that one of the Brotherhood saw her walkin' with a British soldier. The next day," he snapped his fingers, "the Constable found her—her head shaved. Tarred and feathered she was and naked as the day she was born. There can't be good reason for doin' a thing like that. None."

Peg shuddered.

"Don't be mistakin' me meanin'," the butcher went on, "I got no use for the bloody British and their buggerin' of Ireland either." He paused, seeing Peg's distress. "Pardon me language, ma'am but don't you go to worrin' now," he said as he stood to greet a new customer. "Your daughter's safe enough with Luke." He smiled, gave a twist to his mustache and turned away.

"I think I'll be havin' a look at old Winnie," Kean said. "She may be needin' some water."

"Take her out to the yard," MacSweeny called from the counter. "If the trough's not full, would you help me out by pumpin' some?"

"Aye." Kean's chair scraped through the wood shavings. "Would you like to be comin' along, Peg darlin'?" he asked, loud enough for MacSweeny to hear.

"I would, that."

Kean took Kate and walked out into the busy street. The sky was filled with clumped, useless clouds that partially obscured the sun, leaving a heaviness in the air. A strip of darkness nudged the horizon.

"Saints be praised," she said, pointing.

"Aye," he smiled. "Tis coolin' off. Come Winnie," Kean clicked. The mare picked up her ears and followed him like an obedient pup.

The yard was full of freshly shorn sheep. The watering trough was nearly dry. Kean pumped it full and Winnie stretched her neck over the rail to drink. Kate reached across his chest to touch the horse's thick red-brown coat.

"Drink up," Kean said to the horse, patting her neck.

From the corner of her eye, Peg saw Roddy MacSweeny run into the shop alone.

"Kean," she said anxiously. "The boy's come back but Bobby's not with him." There was a desperate edge to her voice as she ran back to the shop, not waiting for her husband.

MacSweeny saw her face as she stood in the doorway. "Your lad's all right, Mrs. Martin," he assured her.

"Where is he?" she asked coldly.

"Not far. It seems that he and Roddy shared a pipe and a wee drop of punch with old Manus."

Roddy stared at the woman, terrified. "He told me he'd smoked before, but I've not seen anyone who ever turned that color . . . and he did it while I was lookin'! It scared me sorely, it did." He glanced up at his father, a look of terror in his eyes.

MacSweeny curled his big arm around the boy. "Don't go worryin', lad," he said with a broad smile. "We'll go fetch him."

"Thanks, Daddy," the boy said, his voice strengthening, his eyes still on Peg.

"Lads haven't changed a lick over time, have they now?" the butcher said with a light chuckle.

"Where is me son, Mr. MacSweeny?" Peg demanded. "Tis now I'll be goin' for him." She stood with her hands on her hips, feet apart.

"Aye," the butcher sighed and pulled his apron off over his head. "Watch the shop, lad."

"Aye, Daddy."

"And don't go givin' the meat away this time. Use the hook. Weigh it proper."

The boy nodded. "I know how," he assured his father with a sidelong glance at Peg.

"What's goin' on?" Kean asked, coming through the door.

"Bobby's missin'," Peg said flatly. "We're goin' after him now." She turned on MacSweeny. "You are knowin' where it is we're goin'," she stated flattly.

"Aye," MacSweeny said. "There's a shack on the bluff. A blind old man lives there. Roddy goes to take him food now and again and listen to his nonsense. Your boy'll be there, no doubt."

"Are you sure, MacSweeny?" Kean asked, suddenly alarmed.

"Aye."

"I'll be comin' with you." He thrust Kate at Peg. "I don't want you to be walkin' all that way. I'll go fetchin' Bobby."

Peg watched the two men stride away leaving her no place to put her anger but behind the thin, hard line of her lips.

Luke and Maire walked hand in hand to the rock fence. Luke stopped, turned Maire in his arms and looked down into her face. "The sun's goin' behind the clouds. Are you getting' cold?"

She shook her head. "Are you just goin' to look then?" she asked coyly.

He nodded. "I'd like to be doin' more than lookin', Maire. You've moved me, truly. I don't know why. I've not been so forward with a colleen, ever. Will you forgive me?"

She pressed two fingers over his lips. "There's no forgivin' necessary. Besides, the day you know why you care, I'll probably be gone."

"Gone where?"

She turned out of his arms and continued toward the fence. "Ahhh, I don't know." She turned a shy gaze on him. "Maybe tis you who'll be gone. Out there . . . over the water to England."

"I'm thinkin' that's all changed." He stood watching the gentle sway of her hips as she walked.

"Ahhh! Don't go changin' your plans on account of me, Luke MacSweeny. You know nothin' of me." She faced him. "*Nothin'*."

"Would it be proper then, Maire Martin, to ask if I call on you . . . in a gallant way, of course, just to know you better?"

Her eyes grew wide with surprise. "Are you serious? Tis a very long way. More'n two hours by cart."

"Then I'll come by horse," he said lightly. "Or run. I want to know you, Maire"

"Well then," she said with a bright, easy smile. "I suppose it would be all right." Suddenly Egan O'Shea's words riveted her; *I'll kill anyone who lays a hand on you.* "Perhaps you should wait till we come back to Dublin one more time. You wouldn't want our da's thinkin' they was right now, would you?"

Luke laughed. He walked down the slope toward her. "Does that matter so much to you?"

"Aye. Don't it to you? Have you no pride?"

"Course I do. But when Da's right, he's right."

"Ahhh!" She tossed her head. If I tell him about Egan, she thought, it would only hurt him and perhaps he'll lose interest in me. What if Egan loses interest or never comes back? At least there'd be Luke, then. But, what if Egan does come back and Luke is there? Did he really mean what he said? Ahhh! That's silly. He'd not kill anyone . . . not Egan.

Luke leaped to the top of the rock fence. "Give me your hand," he said and lifted her up in a rush of laughter. He turned her around so she could see the ocean and he held her, her back against his chest. "Isn't it lovely?"

"It is, that."

He moved her hair aside and kissed her neck.

A quiver arced through her at the touch of his lips. She drew in a sharp breath and started to turn. "Are you sure you should be doin' that on the top of a . . . *wall?!*"

The rock that broke away from under Maire's foot sent the two of them to the ground and they rolled down the easy slope toward Dublin. When they came to a stop, Maire's blouse was torn, her ankle ached.

"Maire! Maire, are you all right?" Luke asked, jumping to his feet.

She shoved her hair out of her face. "Damn!" she fumed. "Me ankle! And look at me blouse! Ma'll be takin' a switch to me, sure." She started to cry.

"Nae, she won't. I'll explain."

"You'll explain? She'll think you done it! She thinks all the boy's want is me virginity and nothin' else!"

Luke blushed. Never had he heard a girl speak as this one did. He pulled the kerchief from his back pocket and rubbed the tears and dirt from her face then slowly pulled shamrocks and grass from her hair. "Your virginity's safe, Maire Martin. For now, all I'd like from you . . . is your heart."

Blankly, Maire stared up at him. Egan always wanted more than she could give him. Maybe Luke was different. Maybe she could . . . no. The thought in her mind was quickly dismissed.

"Can you walk?" he asked, helping her to her feet.

She nodded dumbly, inwardly ashamed, outwardly confused.

"We have to be getting' Livie from the Feeney's. Tis not far. Here, let me help you."

Maire felt the hard muscles of his arm come against her back. Perhaps Dublin wasn't so bad, after all. She would have to make a choice and make it quickly.

Peg balanced Kate on one hip as she ran toward Kean and MacSweeny who carried Bobby in his huge arms. "What's wrong with him?" she cried.

Kean smiled through a deep sigh. "Well, by the smell of him, too much punch, I'd be sayin'."

"Kean Martin! You get that cart over here, now! I'm not one to be tellin' you what to do, but if we're not gone from this . . . this establishment in five minutes, I'll . . . I'll . . ."

Peg's attention changed sharply as MacSweeny turned. He stared up the street and mumbled: "Ahhh, thunderin' Jaysus!"

Peg thrust Kate into Kean's unsuspecting arms. She ran passed a girl with wispy gold hair and wide blue eyes, who clasped a small harp to her breast. "Maire! What's he done to you, girl?" she called, racing toward her daughter whose head lay on Luke's shoulder.

Secretly, Maire pressed a kiss on Luke's cheek then lowered her arms from around his neck. "Nothin' Ma, really. I fell. We fell from a wall. I hurt me ankle and . . ." Her eyes darted from Luke to her mother to her father to her brother. "What's ailin' him?"

"We'll talk about that later. You're sure you're all right now?"

"Aye, Ma."

"Put her down!" Peg ordered. "Kean Martin!" she cried, "the cart!"

Luke walked into the middle of the street as the Martins pulled away. He wanted one more glimpse of Maire as she sat on the back of the cart, her brother's head in her lap.

"Is she special to you, Luke?" the blond girl asked.

"Aye, Livie. She's more'n special, I'm thinking'," he said, placing a hand on her narrow shoulder. "Would you play your harp at our weddin'?"

Livie's enormous eyes filled with astonishment. "Have you known her that long? I've not seen her here be . . . Luke, are you listenin' to me?"

"I only just met her, Livie, and aye, she's pretty . . . pretty as a rainbow at midnight. Have you never been in love, girl?"

Livie blushed, hugged her harp tightly. "I'm but thirteen. How would . . . You're teasin' me again, aren't you, Luke?"

"Nae, cousin, I'm not teasin'." Luke could barely see Maire's torn blouse, but the afternoon sun gleamed on her coppery hair leaving a vivid picture his mind he would long remember. He waved. She didn't. Perhaps she hadn't seen.

The tower bell rang three.

6

"There is often the look of an angel on the Devil himself."

AIBREAN (April 1867)

Egan stirred restlessly on the hard bed, the blankets twisting around his legs and torso. Rory and Keelin had been in England for two weeks without a word about the times or places of the impending trials of O'Leary, Luby or Kickham. And worse, every night since Jimmy's departure, Egan suffered the same dream. Each time he'd awakened cold, lonely, desperate.

He lay there, staring at the dark underbelly of the roof's thatch. Then, sitting, hunched over on the edge of the bed, he shoveled tired fingers through his thick auburn hair and sighed not understanding the dream or the silence from England. Night sounds seeped through the walls and Egan felt a heaviness settle around him.

He lit the bedside candle and picked up Jimmy Stephens's note, now torn in the fold from the many times of reading. He didn't know why he took it up again, the words were memorized.

To All The Fenian Brotherhood-

Be it known that I, James Stephens, have given over the power that was mine to Egan O'Shea. His loyalty goes unquestioned and he is worthy of the command. Follow him.

-J. Stephens, Past Commander

Egan crumpled the note in his hand, but the oath he had taken kept repeating itself:

I, Egan O'Shea, in the presence of Almighty God, do solemnly swear allegiance to the Irish Republic now virtually established; and that I will do my utmost, at every risk, while life lasts, to defend its independence and integrity; and finally, that I will yield implicit obedience in all things, not contrary to the laws of God, to the commands of my superior officer.

So help me God.

Amen.

"I'll not be showin' this note to the lads," he whispered. "They'd not follow the likes of me anyhow. I'll just tell them that Jimmy left special orders. That'll do it. It'll not be me splittin' the ranks of the Fenians." He shook his head. "Not this mother's son. That'll have to be done by another. When Jimmy comes back . . . well, I'll not stand in his way."

He pulled his trousers on, buttoning them as he moved about the dark house. He added turf bricks to the smoldering ashes in the fireplace and drew some water for tea then filled the basin to wash. As he soaped his face and hands a sudden eeriness startled him. The crickets were silent. His heart beat quickened. He reached for the towel and the handgun simultaneously. Toweling his face and chest, he inched toward the door and leaned an ear against the cold wood. There was a sound of footsteps crunching frosty grass. Egan waited, the revolver gripped tightly in both hands, pointed toward the ceiling. Cautiously, he moved a curtain aside. Stars glinted through dark, moving clouds. Daylight was a long time away. The footsteps rounded the house again and stopped at the front. Egan's fingers tightened. His jaw clenched as he spurned the fear inside him.

A light tap on the door sent Egan a step backward in surprise. He said nothing. Another knock sounded. He flattened himself against the wall. The handle turned. Egan slipped the lock. Slowly the door creaked open. The figure of a man entered, outlined by the starlight.

Silently, Egan tipped the cold nose of the pistol against the intruder's neck. The man froze.

"To be movin's to die," Egan said coldly. "Who are you? What are you doin' here?"

"Kevin Burke. I'm . . ."

Egan dropped the weapon to his side. "For the sake of all that's holy, Kevin, what are you doin' sneakin' round in the dark? You scared the spit from me mouth, you fool. You could've gotten yourself killed and me cursed! Damn you!"

"Egan?"

"And who the bloody hell do you think I am . . . Queen Victoria come for a visit in the country?"

"I'm sorry, Egan, I wasn't told who'd be here, if anybody."

Kevin watched as Egan paced. The gun in his hand swung aimlessly as he walked off his anxiety and anger. "Who didn't tell you? Damn! I could have killed you, you great fool. Next time walk up to the door and knock. Don't be creepin' round a house before you finally do somethin'!" He slammed the pistol onto the table. "Well?"

"Well, what?"

"What are you doin' here in the middle of the night, scarin' me out of two years growin'?" His breath charged in irratic waves, his hand shook as he lit the candle.

"Oh!" Kevin said as if he'd just awakened. Sitting in a chair, he pulled his shoe and sock off. "There," he said plopping his foot onto the table top.

"Am I supposed to be countin' your toes then?"

Kevin laughed. "You're supposed to be readin' the bottom of me foot."

Egan dropped into a chair. "Wasn't this a bit more difficult than writin' on paper?"

"Aye, and harder for the Constabulary to find. Read. Tis a message from Rory."

At last. Egan grasped Kevin's toes and tipped the candle to read the faint words.

"What does it say?" Kevin asked.

"You've almost walked it off, I can tell you that!" He turned Kevin's foot in his hand.

"Ouch! Move the candle back a bit and don't be unscrewin' me toes. Tell me what it says."

"You mean you truly don't know? You let Rory write all over the bottom of your foot and you didn't ask him what it says?"

Kevin shrugged. "He was in a hurry. Besides, if I didn't know, I couldn't tell. Does it say where O'Leary and them are? Can we break them out?"

Egan shook his head as he studied the writing on Kevin's foot. "Nae. The bloody English parliament has suspended Habeas Corpus. They're goin' to be holdin' them longer. O'Leary's trial's to be held next month."

"And Luby and Kickham?"

"Aye. The same."

"What's this, habies . . . corset . . ."

"Corpus. It means they don't have to be tellin' us why we've been arrested anymore. They just sock us away and forget us."

Kevin's foot hit the floor. "That's illegal! They can't be doin' a thing like that. There are rules to be followed here!"

"Aye," Egan sighed weakly. "They make the rules and we follow them." His eyes flashed in the candlelight. "We have to learn their damnable rules well so we can fight them well . . . and win!"

"Damn!" The candle rocked as Kevin's fist struck the table.

Egan held his hands out to the glowing turf. "Did Rory say when he and Keelin was comin' back?"

"He said he wanted to stay on for a while. You know, check out the courthouse and things. Make a holiday of it he said."

"He's got puddin' for brains that one! If he gets caught . . ."

"He'll not be caught," Kevin said with as much persuasion as he could put into his voice. "You know Rory."

"That I do, and I know there's cause to be worryin'." He shook his head in disgust. "With him out there . . ." He swallowed his words, turned and smiled at Kevin hoping his thoughts were hidden behind the forced glint in his eye. "There's not an Englishman safe in his own bed."

Kevin laughed and yawned.

"Go in there and get some sleep." Egan motioned toward the bedroom. "I'll not be sleepin' anyhow."

"The faeries crawlin' in, are they?"

Egan smiled behind tired eyes. "I suppose."

Kevin stood and stretched but he didn't move toward the door. His face was a question mark.

"A dream . . . that's all." Egan put tea leaves in the hot kettle and stirred, capped it and took a cup from the cupboard.

"Maire Martin?" Kevin guessed, his lips teased by a wry grin.

Egan shook his head. "Nae." He looked up. "Me grandfar. He died when I was a tyke. The famine took him. I didn't know what he was doin' then but I remember him takin' food from his plate and puttin' it on mine . . . such as it was. Tis like he's askin' me to come home." He poured the tea.

"Why not go? Rory and Keelin are takin' a holiday . . ."

"Ahhh! Don't talk nonsense. There's too much to be doin' here."

"Like what?"

"Plannin' how to break O'Leary and them out, that's what."

Kevin waved Egan's words away. "Look who's talkin' nonsense now. Just which prison are you plannin' on breakin' them out of? I mean since we don't know which one they'll be puttin' them in."

Egan smiled. "True enough, but . . ."

"I'm not one to be tellin' you what to do, Egan. But, if you've had the dream more times than one, well . . . I'd not be askin' trouble from the faeries." Kevin shook his head to emphasize his words and the power of the little people as he left the room.

"Faeries," Egan said under his breath, irritated at his friend's childishness. He took his cup and sat beside the small fire. Memories danced before him in the leaping, smoky flames. Flashes of family faces appeared and he blinked them away only to find them replaced by others. "Damn! I don't have time for the likes of this!" he whispered. The cupboard door squeaked open and a cup smashed on the floor.

"I'd not be askin' trouble from the faeries," Kevin had said. Trouble . . .

"Kevin!" Egan called, staring at the broken pieces. "I'll be goin' south. To the Boggeraghs." He drained his teacup and stuffed his pack, strapped his handgun to his ankle, grabbed his cap and coat. The door slammed behind him as a bright streak of sun crowned the hills to the east smearing the lavender sky with gold.

"Egan!"

Egan squinted through the patches of light and shadow, down the long dirt road to see J.J. Corydon running toward him.

"I don't think I ever seen you run, Corydon. What's the rush?"

"Tis glad I am to have found you so quick, Egan," he said, trying to catch his breath. "You've got to call a meetin' of the lads. Tis a sure thing that O'Leary, Luby and Kickham are in Chester Castle gaol and will be till their retrials on the twelfth of May. I've looked it over and except for the gate, the place is an easy nut to crack. Tom Kelly's for takin' it, if you are."

"You've talked to Kelly?" Egan asked suspiciously, remembering how Jimmy Stephens felt about him.

"Aye. He's closer to Chester than we are, him bein' in London and all. Is somethin' wrong?"

Egan shook his head. Something was out of joint but he couldn't put his finger on it. Still, Corydon's news was in tune with Kevin's message from Rory. The only thing he knew for sure was that there was no time to see his family in the Boggeragh Mountains of Cork, especially now with Rory and Keelin across the water.

Keelin rolled over and nestled against Rory's shoulder. As dawn crept through the yellowed lace curtains of their rented room, she lifted her left hand and gazed at the third finger. The gold band gleamed. She let her hand fall lightly on his chest and closed her eyes again, reveling in the warmth of the bed and the man beside her. Someday, she thought, he'll be puttin' the ring on in earnest. Someday it'll be for me and not for silent lies . . . someday. Keelin sighed and watched the room brightened. Such a stupid rule; not lettin' the Fenian's marry. How many times had Jimmy Stephens scoffed at her for saying that an unmarried Irishman was a sure target for a British bullet! He was just as unshakable when he said he wanted no widows to care for.

Rory stirred. "You awake?" he asked thickly, his eyes closed.

"Aye."

"Hungry?"

"Nae."

Rory encircled her with his arms. "Well, I am . . ." He buried his face in her neck and pulled her over on top of him.

She giggled. "Rory darlin', you great fool!"

"Now, don't be tellin' me you're unhappy we're here."

"Nae. I'd not be sayin' that." Her laughter and smile faded as she bent to kiss him. She silenced his wit with the warmth of her lips, leaving him empty of words and filled with the need of her.

Keelin and Rory crowded the morning with each other. They ate hot bangers and scones with honey in the refectory across the street. They shared tea and kisses and walked around the city. In the afternoon Rory bought her a pink shawl with a long fringe.

"How much money's left?" she asked.

"Why do you ask?"

Keelin picked up a red scarf. "Can we get this? 'Tis not expensive and was you to wear it, I'd find you anywhere."

Rory handed the fifteen pence to the vender. Smiling, he folded the scarf and put it in his pocket.

"Are we out of money now?" she asked.

"Don't you go to worryin' now," he assured her, patting his pocket. "Come on. There's even enough to be sharin' a pint."

She grinned as he led her into a pub, crowded with noisy patrons. He sat her down at a newly vacated table near a stained glass window and ordered cakes and ale.

"Are you havin' a good time?" Rory asked, his eyes shining.

"Aye. I am, but . . ."

"But?"

"What made you decide on doin' this? I mean, we never . . ."

"Had never gone away together . . . alone?" he said.

She blushed and looked toward the tricolored window.

"You know that I want to be marryin' you, Keelin Bonner," he said softly, gently turning her chin to peer into her pale blue eyes. "You're the one that makes me more than I am. There'll be no one else beside me in the comin' years." He sucked back a breath and his tone changed. "But rules are rules. The day after this is all over and we have Home Rule in Ireland, the first thing I'll be doin', I promise you, is draggin' you off to the nearest priest and force you to marry me."

"*Force?*"

"Aye. You can't be thinkin' that your ma has a soft spot in her heart for me, can you now?" He winked.

She laughed and sipped at her ale. "Nae. I don't think that."

"I have a brilliant idea! Give me the ring," Rory said in an excited whisper. "Let's be doin' it now!"

Keelin's eyes widened. "Be doin' what?" she asked, reluctantly placing the ring in his palm.

"Marry me. Now."

She looked around her. 'Where?"

"Here. Now." Without stopping to explain, he said, "I, Rory Kilcullen, take thee, Keelin Bonner, as me wife. To have and to hold and (make love to)," he winked. "For as long as I live. Now you" He gripped her hands, looked into her confused face. "Go on. I, Keelin—"

"I . . . I, Keelin Bonner, take thee, Rory Kilcullen, to be me one and only husband. To have and to hold . . ."

"And make love to," he inserted.

"Aye" she said softly, a blush pinking her cheeks. "Forever and ever, Amen." She crossed herself quickly.

He took her hand and slipped the ring on her finger. "I now pronounce us man and wife," he whispered and leaned across the table to kiss her.

"Have we done it then?" Her expression was hopeful, cautious. "I . . . I mean without a priest or a church full of people?"

Rory took a large gulp of ale, the tankard thudded against the table top and he leaned back in his chair, released a quick breath. "I feel married," he said, nodding. "Do you?"

She looked down at the ring on her finger. "I do."

"I do, too . . ."

The better part of an hour was spent sipping ale and talking of nothing more pressing than planning their lives together.

Finally, Keelin smiled and took his hand. "Shall we go on to the courthouse, Lord Kilcullen?" she teased in her best British accent.

"Best be keepin' your mouth shut, Lady Kilcullen," he chided. "Your English'll get us arrested!"

She laughed and drew her new shawl up over her dark hair, brushing her fingers over the ring. "To the courthouse," she whispered and tugged on his arm. "Egan will be needin' all we can find out."

They walked slowly down the street taking the turn that led to the center of the city. A huge building loomed before them and they ambled up the broad steps of the courthouse as if they belonged there. Only one English Bobby glanced in their direction and Rory tipped his hat as the heavy oak doors opened. They weren't ready for what lay beyond the second set of giant doors.

"Jaysus, Maire and Joseph," Keelin whispered and hurriedly crossed herself.

Manchester courthouse was a massive hall of dark polished wood and wrought iron. The judge's bench was like a tall, hooded throne at the far end with polished tables on either side. To its left was a long balcony for the jurors, they supposed. In the center of the hall stood a large circular witness box rimmed with iron railings, as high as a man's head. The barrister's table faced the witness box in front of the Judge's bench and there were seats for the nobility and standing room for others. Rory guessed the ceiling to be twenty-five feet high or more. The room was lit by several long windows at the top of the walls and huge chandeliers of crystal with at least fifty candles each.

"I've not felt so small since I was a child in Saint Padraig's Cathedral in Dublin," Keelin whispered.

"Aye." Above his square spectacles Rory scanned the empty space, checking the doors; all the places that could be guard stations. He made mental pictures of everything he thought important.

"Here! Here now! What do you think you're doing?" roared a voice from the dais. "Who let you in here?"

"Oh," Rory said looking up, squinting through the square lenses. "It is good to see someone. The name's . . . Pierce, John and Priscilla. Dreadfully sorry if we've wondered into a wrong spot. We're here on holiday from London you know. Heard so much about the place, thought we'd take a peek for ourselves. Hope we've not caused an inconvenience." He smiled. "Come Pris." He offered his arm.

They exited slowly, hardly able to contain their laughter as they walked hurriedly through the streets to their rented room.

"Priscilla?" Keelin howled as the door shut behind them. "And where in the names of all the Saints did that come from?"

"I don't know," Rory chuckled. "It just fell out of me mouth as if it were God's own truth!"

"Ahhh! Tis a bad one you are, Rory Kilcullen. To think lyin' should come so quick and easy. I should be havin' nothin' to do with you."

Rory moved toward her, forcing her backward. Her knees struck the edge of the bed and she sat abruptly. He loomed above her, then pushing her down, he pinned her hands above her head. "And you don't mean a word of it . . . do you now, Mrs. Kilcullen?" He covered her mouth with his.

She could feel the hardness of him through his trousers. "Oh, you are a wicked, wonderful man . . . husband . . ."

Egan set an emergency meeting for the evening of May second. He and J.J. Corydon managed to contact Tully Linnehan in Dunleer and Colin Tyrrell at Clogherhead. They would see that the rest were told.

When Egan was finally alone in the house at Drogheda, he set his mind to preparing a plan of escape for O'Leary, Luby and Kickham from the gaol inside Chester Castle. He worked for hours, but in every plan he saw major flaws. He placed both hands on his forehead, closed his eyes and sighed. Ahhh, Jimmy Stephens, he thought, why did you have to leave? You always knew what to do.

Egan rubbed his eyes and yawned. He felt little left inside him with which to plan. What had kept Jimmy working at this for so long?

Egan stretched. He walked to the window, pushed the curtain aside. A pale setting sun streamed in unbroken fingers of light through the clotted clouds to the west. The hills and fields were checkered in unending shades of green and the trace of a rainbow remained in the sky. Egan smiled. It was so simple. Jimmy had persevered for only one reason: "Eireann . . ." he said.

Smiling, he ladled water from the bucket into the teakettle, smoored the fire and hung the kettle over the flame, then he sat at the table with a pen and ink and as he scribbled notes in his crude hand, he half-sang, half-hummed:

"There was a wild colonial boy, Jack Duggan was his name
He was born and raised in Ireland in a place called Castlemaine
He was his father's only son, his mother's pride and joy
And dearly did his parents love their Wild Colonial Boy.

"Surrender now, Jack Duggan, for you see we're three to one
Surrender in the Queen's high name for you're a plundering son."
Jack drew two pistols from his belt and proudly waved them high
"I'll fight, but not surrender" said the Wild Colonial Boy.

Suddenly the plan came. It was so simple even Kevin Burke would have no trouble with it. The teakettle hissed and Egan chuckled as he filled his cup. It was growing late, but with the plan outlined, perhaps he could get some sleep after all. *"I'll fight, but not surrender," said the Wild Colonial Boy!"* He blew out the light.

Had he not had the same nagging dream, Egan might have rested. Kevin had said it was the faeries. Egan was afraid he was beginning to believe him.

Before the midnight meeting time, the windows in Rory's house were blacked out with blankets and most of the men had arrived, including one Egan had never seen. He turned to J.J. Corydon.

"Would you be knowin' that wee one?"

J.J. shook his head. "From the looks of him, I suppose he's full grown. Anyone vouched for him?"

"We'd best find out before we start. He's too small to shoot."

Michael Davitt, from County Mayo was the last to arrive.

Egan raised his hands for silence. He looked straight at the stranger. "And who might you be?" he asked.

The small, dark man leaned against the wall by the fireplace. His eyes glittered in the light of the turf flame. "I might be Prince Albert," he said. "But I'm not. I'm Dob Quinn from Ballyshannon."

"Who's vouched for you, Dob Quinn from Ballyshannon?"

"Why, me good friend Michael here." He bounded onto a chair with acrobatic ease.

"Aye, Egan," Michael Davitt said. "He's queer as fish feathers but he can do things the rest of us can't."

Dob Quinn grinned and nodded. He whistled through his lone front tooth. When he pulled the tall hat from his dirty hair, his ears wiggled.

The men laughed.

"Are you simple then, Dob Quinn?" Egan asked.

"Nae," he said, eyes flashing in his leathery face. "Are you?"

"Don't be tryin' to best him, Egan," Michael warned, smiling. "He'll tie your words in knots. Why don't you tell us why we're here. Does it have to do with O'Leary?"

Egan nodded. "Corydon, tell them what you told me."

J.J. Corydon took the floor. "I was in England lookin' to see what they intended for O'Leary and them. I learned that all three are for sure in Chester Castle gaol and will be till their retrial on the twelfth. If we want to get them out and gone, it'll have to be before then. I'm lookin' at the time of the new moon when the night is at its darkest."

Egan took over. "With the new moon as the target, that gives us just nine days to agree on a plan, get to Chester and get it done."

"What do you have in mind, Egan?" Kevin Burke asked.

"Well, it won't be easy, what with Rory and Keelin still over the water, but what I've planned might work if there's enough of us."

"Wait," Colin interrupted. "Where's Jimmy and what does he have to say about all this?"

Egan drew in a deep breath. He was afraid of someone asking about Jimmy and what he would say. "Jimmy's gone for a while. He said that if you all agreed, I'd be in charge until he returned. Does anyone want to make a challenge of it?"

The room was quiet with one man looking at the next and shrugging.

Tully Linnehan stepped up. "Looks like you're the one till Jim comes back, Egan. Let's hear what you've come up with."

With just the flash of a smile, Egan nodded. "When we get through the iron gates, which is a whole problem of its own, we bomb two places; the Half-Moon Tower and Shire Hall. They're far enough apart to force Her Majesty's soldiers to separate to protect them that live there. The trouble is that the gaol is in between. The guards'll have to be taken out quick and quiet. That's your job Colin. Tully, when the bombs go off, you take ten men to the officer's quarters and when they come out, you keep them busy so they can't give any orders. Colin and I will take whose left and storm the guardroom where O'Leary and them are bein' held." Egan turned to Colin. "Get all the keys from the guards. We don't know if the men are latched inside a room or padlocked to a post."

"Aye, Egan."

"Can anyone think of somethin' better?"

Dob Quinn cleared his throat noisily. "I'd not be goin' into Chester Castle without seein' a map of the place . . . if I was you." He doft his cap and bowed as if he'd just finished a fine preformance.

"We don't need one," Egan assured him. "I've been there and so has Rory and Colin."

"I can get you a *new* map . . ." Dob sang.

Egan bit the corner of his mouth thoughtfully. "Can you get it in the next four days?"

Dob's face crinkled into a smug grin. He nodded.

"How?"

"Ahhh, now," Dob said, looking up, shaking his finger in Egan's face. "I'll not be tellin' you that, lad. No sense clutterin' up your mind with useless information. Just you be knowin' that I'll have your map to you in no more than four days. Where am I to bring it?"

"To the next meetin'," Egan said.

"Aye."

For safetys sake, the next gathering of the Fenian Brotherhood would take place four days hence at Colin Tyrrell's house in Clogherhead on the Irish Sea.

7

"Wild goose ne'er reared tame gosling."

Kevin Burke stayed with Egan at Drogheda, though he often felt himself alone because Egan's mind wandered most of the time.

"I know you haven't the time to see your folks, Egan, but for the sake of all the nerves in me body and the boards on the floor, take a day and go to Maire. I'm goin' bats with all your pacin'."

Egan offered a tired smile. "Am I that bad, then, Kevin?"

"I'm believin' you're worse, but I wouldn't want to say so."

"Maybe you're right."

"Course I am," Kevin said smoothly. "Maire's the salve for your own wounded nerves. Go on with you now, so I can have a wee bit of peace before marchin' all the way to Clogherhead."

Egan shifted from one foot to the other; he grinned and chuckled softly as he nodded, offering Kevin an almost shy glance. "I'll be back in a couple of days," he promised, grabbing his coat and cap.

"For the love of Saint Brigid, take your time!" Kevin shouted after him. He stood in the open doorway grinning as spiraling notes from Egan's tin whistle echoed back to him.

The road to the Martin farm south of Drogheda was long and lonely but Egan's mind was set on Maire and with every step bringing him closer, the miles seemed to vanish. He passed the old farm where, in bad weather and dark nights, he had stayed undiscovered in the barn. The only person he had ever seen working the place was an old woman.

As he neared the Martin house in the late afternoon, he skirted the road and made his way to the old oak. He looked for Maire but her ma and brother were the only people he saw. The cart was gone and her father didn't seem to be there either. In a rare fit of prudence, Egan decided to make certain before announcing himself.

After he was sure Kean Martin was gone, he circled back to come up the road, his tin whistle singing.

Bobby ran up to him. "You're Egan, Maire's beau," he said.

Egan smiled. "And where might she be?"

"She's with Daddy. He took her into Dublin this mornin'. What are you doin' here?"

Egan placed a hand on Bobby's shoulder and started walking toward the house. "I was thinkin' I'd like to be seein' her, that's all." His stomach growled.

"Sounds like you're hungry."

"Aye, lad." Egan ruffled Bobby's hair and laughed. "Is your ma one to be feedin' a pipe playin' traveler like meself?"

"She might. Come on. Can you not smell the scroggins?" Bobby tugged on Egan's hand and pulled him into the house. "Ma? Can you spare a scone or two? Maire's friend, Egan's here."

Peg turned from the oven, the hot pan in her hand. "Ahhh, God," she said under her breath and managed a feeble smile of welcome. "Course. Please," she stammered, "sit yourself." She gestured toward a chair then dropped the pan, the scones skittering over the tabletop.

"Good catch!" Egan said to Bobby.

Peg smiled. Her embarrassment and fear lessened. In her kitchen, Egan O'Shea didn't seem near the ruffian Kean made him out to be. He didn't have the dangerous look of a Fenian. "Would you care for butter, Mr. O'Shea?"

"Me too, Ma?" Bobby said and sat optimistically in his own chair.

Peg gave him an irritated look but scooped a knob of rich, yellow butter onto a plate for him. "Just be eatin' your supper when your da gets home."

Egan ate one scone and licked his fingers. "Ahhh, you're a better cook than me own ma, I swear," he said.

"Have another," Peg said, smiling. "There's plenty."

Bobby reached for another but Peg's dark look made him drop his hand back into his lap.

"Sorry you come so far," Peg said, "just to find Maire gone."

"Tis not all that far. I'm down from Drogheda is all. I don't often get time from me work but when I do, I try to see her," he grinned, "though your husband makes me feel welcome as a fly on one of them lovely scones." He licked the melting butter from his finger.

"Tis sorry I am for that," Peg said. "He just . . ."

Egan swallowed. "I know. He wants the best for Maire and he thinks that I dance to a Fenian fiddler."

"Somethin' like that," Peg said. "And do you?"

Egan raised his brows. "Do I what?"

"*Dance* . . .with the Fenians?"

Egan smiled. "I dance to me own tune, Mrs. Martin. Sometimes I can't help wishin' I was a Fenian, what with our own sweet land bein' the emerald in the crown jewels . . . so to speak."

"Why would you wish that?" Bobby asked. "We don't hold with killin'. Da says . . ."

"Killin'? Is that what you think Fenians do? Not that I could take the time from me printin' business to help anyway."

Bobby shrugged. "But, Da says . . ."

Peg glared at her son. "Go feed the stock, lad, before your tongue burns a hole in your manners."

"Tis all right," Egan said, mussing Bobby's hair again. "I'll help him. I should be goin' anyway and tis the least I can do for them fine scones."

Peg wrapped two more in a towel. "Take these with you."

Egan smiled, genuinely pleased. "Thank you," he said and followed Bobby outside.

The barn was dim. The cows had moved inside and the sheep bleated in the pen. Egan took a bucket and the milking stool to the only milker he saw while Bobby hauled buckets of turnips and potatoes to the pigs and the sheep pen and filled the mangers with hay.

Mounds of foam topped the milk as Egan's strong hands forced the streams against each other. The rich smell of fresh, warm milk was another reminder of home.

Bobby came up behind the cow and pushed her busy tail through a noose attached to the wall. "Would you know anythin' about Finn MacCool?" he asked suddenly.

"Aye, lad. I do. Why?"

"Well," the boy hesitated. "When we was in Dublin a time back, I met an auld man who was goin' to tell me, but I got frightful sick on whiskey-punch and never heard the end. Besides, Daddy said that Finn MacCool was a Fenian and I didn't need to know about him."

"Come here and sit. I'll tell you about Finn. Not that your da's wrong mind you, but Finn MacCool was Ireland's first great hero. He knew nothin' about the Fenians of today. He just knew he had to protect Ireland from all them who wanted to rule and spoil her. That's why the Fenians named themselves for him. To the north, where the British are stompin' about, killin' as many of us as they dare, there are giant steps that lead out to sea. Did you know that?"

Bobby shook his head, fascinated. "And who built them?"

"Finn MacCool."

"Well, who walked on them?"

"Why, the giant, Finn MacCool did o'course. It was a long time ago when he went to Scotland to fight the fearsome Finn Gall."

"They had the same name?"

"Aye, lad. Some people have another name for the Scotsman but I'm not sure of what it was," Egan said through a near soundless laugh. "But, *Finn*, you see, is the name of heroes and champions." Egan spoke as he finished milking. He turned from the cow and looked at Bobby. "'Tis me own da's name." The beautiful Boggeragh Mountains flashed before him. He'd come to see Maire because time didn't permit him a trip to Cork. But Maire wasn't here and the dreams of home hadn't stopped.

"Did he beat the Scotsman, then?" Bobby asked.

"Aye. He wasn't as big as the Scotsman but he was smarter," Egan forced himself to go on. He took the bucket of milk to the bench by the barn door and patted the wood, smoothed by years of use, for Bobby to sit beside him. "Finn MacCool's da, Cool MacTredhorn, leader of the Grand Fianna, had been killed by the Clan MacMorna on the say-so of a druid by the name of Tadg. MacTredhorn is said to have died the same instant that Finn was born. His ma was warned that the MacMorna's were now lookin' to kill her and her new son. She had two friends deep in the forest and she took the wee boy to them and ran away, drawin' the MacMorna's after her; them thinkin' that a mother wouldn't leave her just born son."

"Did they get her, then?" Bobby asked, his blue eyes round with angst.

"Nae. They thought they did a time or two but . . ."

"What happened to Finn?"

"He was hid in the forest by the women his ma gave him to. They raised him up, all the while tellin' him who he was and trainin' him to be quick and smart. Men followed him because he was brave and they all loved Ireland just the way God made her."

Bobby watched Egan's face and listened as much to the tone of his voice as to the story he told. "The MacMorna's never got him, did they," Bobby said with certainty.

"Nae, lad. They never did."

"Have you ever walked the giant steps to Scotland?" the boy asked.

Egan shook his head. "They don't reach Scotland anymore, lad, but there's plenty of steps left for you to climb, if you should go. And speakin' of goin', I should get started. The sun's fast fadin'."

"You could stay here," Bobby offered.

Egan chuckled. "You'd just love to see your da break me bones, wouldn't you?"

"Ahhh, nae! He don't come into the byre except for chores. I'm the one puts Winnie up," the boy said. "You can stay. . . truly. I won't even tell Ma."

"Could you be findin' it in your wee heart to tell Maire?"

Bobby shrugged. "Do you think I should? I mean, Da . . ."

"I come a long way to see her and . . . talk to her."

"After supper, then." Bobby stopped at the barn door. "I'm thankin' you for doin' the milkin' and tellin' me about Finn MacCool."

Egan smiled. "Don't go drinkin' so much whiskey-punch next time. There's an auld sayin' that says, drink is the curse of the land. It makes you fight with your neighbour. It makes you shoot at your landlord and worst of all, it makes you miss him!"

"I'll remember," Bobby said as he turned and struggled, under the weight of the milk bucket, to the house.

Egan looked around the barn. He found an empty stall in a back corner and made himself comfortable on the pile of clean straw. He took a scone from his pocket. When he finished it, he laid back, his head on his arms and waited for Maire.

MacSweeny lifted the jug and poured.

"One more and that's all," Kean said, slurring over words he had said before. "I got to be getting' home. Peg'll skin me sure for havin' Maire gone so long."

"There's always time for another tune. Livie!" MacSweeny ordered. "Play a sweet, leavin' song, girl."

"Aye, Uncle," the youngster said and picked up her harp again.

Maire and Luke stood on the back stoop with the door open, glad that their work was done while Roddy was relegated to cleaning up the butcher store.

"So," Luke said. "How do you like Da's horses?"

Maire shrugged. "They're big."

"Aye."

"And perfectly matched."

"Aye."

"How do you like Livie . . . the way she plays and sings, I mean?"

"Fine," she said and took a step back. He stood much too close to her.

"Livie don't get here much," Luke said, looking somewhere beyond the coming twilight. "If her da didn't have work on one of the ferry's here, she'd be home in Liverpool. "I'm glad you got to meet her. She's a good girl, for a cousin . . ." He turned toward her, his hands locked behind him. "Not as pretty as you, but I know of no one that is."

Maire smiled shyly. "I like Livie. She has lovely hands. Does she take her harp everywhere she goes, then?"

"Aye. 'I'm thinkin' she sleeps with it."

Maire gave a soft laugh. "I love to hear her play. Tis like her fingers was born to it."

"Did you get everythin' you needed today?" Luke asked, trying to keep his words light, meaningless, fearing Roddy or his father would walk through the open door at any moment.

"Aye. I'm thinkin' so."

"I was surprised to see you again so soon," Luke said as he watched the sun in the withering sky turn Maire's hair a burnished gold.

"I know," said Maire. "I thought Ma'd never let me come again what with me takin' a tumble down the hill and Bobby getting' sloshed. If it hadn't been for needin' the linen and Kate ailin', she'd have come herself." She turned to face him. "Tis not good of me, bein' glad a wee colleen is sick . . . is it?"

Luke searched her eyes. "And are you glad, then?"

She felt it suddenly hard to breathe and in answering he might hear her pounding heart sound from her open mouth.

The strains of Livie's harp drifted around them like thistle down. She was playing the new song she had sung for them earlier. Her gentle voice filled the empty space between them.

> *"Oh, Danny Boy the pipes the pipes are calling,*
> *from glen to glen and down the mountain side*
> *The Summer's gone and all the roses falling,*
> *tis you, tis you must go and I must bide . . ."*

Luke leaned toward her and when his hands settled on her shoulders, she felt a shock that left her light-headed. She found herself looking from his deep blue eyes to his lips. The music of the harp seeped through them into the mottled twilight. "I waited all day," Maire said, hardly recognizing her own voice. "Are . . . are you not goin' to kiss me?"

Luke nodded, his gaze intense. "I wanted you to ask."

"But come ye back when Summer's in the meadow,
or when the valley's hushed and white with snow.
Tis I'll be there in sunshine or in shadow,
Oh Danny Boy, Oh Danny Boy, I love you so . . ."

Suddenly she found her arms around his neck and, as he kissed her, she crowded against him to feel the hard muscles of his chest, his legs. His wide hands pressed against her back, holding her to him. He whispered her name as his lips moved fervently over her cheek. What was there about this young man that she couldn't resist? He seemed to tempt her without trying and his nearness now was enough to make her disgrace herself. What would Egan say? she thought. I don't know . . . I can't think of Egan right now. I can't.

"Touch me, Luke," she whispered softly as if she might crumble if he didn't. "Touch me skin . . ."

His lips lingered on hers as his hand slid up the side of her hip beneath her bodice at the waist, his flesh tingling when her breath caught. God help me! his thoughts rang. What manner of girl is this? She'll lead me straight to hell! And, God forgive me, I'll go . . .

The sun dipped below the horizon sending long violet fingers to encircle them while sooty clouds blotted the coming stars.

"And when ye come and all the flowers are dying.
If I am dead, as dead I well may be . . ."

She left him weak as a new born fool and he knew but one thing; Maire would stay in his arms no matter who came through the door.

"You'll come and find the place where I am lying,
and kneel and say an Ave there for me . . ."

Luke's kisses confused her, left her wanting him to the exclusion of all reason. She opened his shirt to the waist and ran the flat of her hand over his rippled skin.

Blood pounded through his veins. He wanted to sweep her up and take her to his bed. He wanted to feel her lying next to him. He wanted to do all the things he had heard about but had never done for fear of hell and purgatory. Now! Now! "Maire!" he sighed as Livie's lilting voice lingered around them, becoming part of the air they breathed:

"And I shall hear tho' soft you tread above me
And all my grave will warmer sweeter be
If you will bend and tell me that you love me
Then I shall sleep in peace until you come to me . . ."

Luke scooped her into his arms and stepped off the porch toward the barn.

"Maire! Maire, girl!"

He stopped in mid-stride at the discordant bellow of Kean Martin's voice. It plowed into him like a runaway team through a rose garden.

"Maire! Be gettin' your coat, girl! 'Tis time to go."

Luke held her tightly. His eyes filled with a strange, sad mixture of love and defeat. She tried to smile but her lips trembled. She kissed him. Then, wordlessly, he put her down and she walked into the house without looking back.

"Good night to you, MacSweeny," Kean said, slurring over the words. "Thanks for your usual hospitality."

The butcher stood unsteadily in the road and waved.

The night was dark and cold and Kean was drunk. The light mist turned to rain. Maire fidgeted on the hard seat of the cart. The way was long and she was tired, but more than that, she was confused by her own response to Luke MacSweeny.

For miles Kean sang, "*Danny Boy*" with all the wrong words and then he cried. He put his head on her shoulder and she pushed him away. "If you don't sit up and behave yourself, I'm goin' to tell Ma!" she threatened and was relieved to finally see a dim light in the kitchen window.

"Shhh!" Kean whispered. "I'm thinkin' we missed supper."

"You know Ma's waitin' up, Daddy. She'll have somethin' hot and handy for you when you get inside," Maire said stiffly, hoping it was a well-aimed kettle.

"Take Winnie to the byre and bed her down."

"But that's Bobby's job," Maire complained.

"Tonight, girl, tis yours." Kean placed one foot carefully in front of the other. Even so, he tripped on the worn step and burst through the door.

Maire trudged toward the barn, pulling Winnie with the wagon still coored behind her. A cold breeze lifted off the hillside. In the darkness of the barn she unhitched the mare and pushed the cart to one side. "Well, go on," she said and smacked the horse on the rear. Winnie nickered and wandered toward her stall but stopped short. "What is it now, you silly auld thing?"

Winnie nickered again. "All right, all right. I'm comin'. No beddin' for your stall again, I suppose. Damn Bobby anyway for makin' such a mess of me life." She skimmed the wall for the pitchfork. "Not doin' his own jobs and never leavin' things where they go."

There was a rustle in Winnie's stall. "You weren't thinkin' of takin' the pitchfork to me now, were you, me darlin'?"

"Egan?" she cried. "What the bloody hell are you doin' here?"

He sat up, brushed the straw from his head and shoulders. "Well, don't sound so happy to see me. I don't think me poor auld heart can stand it."

Maire knelt at his feet. "Course I'm happy but I can't see you at all."

"Didn't Bobby tell you I was here?" he yawned.

"Nae. Daddy and me, we only just got home."

"Come here," Egan said and pulled her onto his lap. "You're wet."

She nestled against him. "Tis rainin'."

He tipped her chin and kissed her. "I have to leave before first light. Will you stay with me?"

"And how would I be explainin' that in the mornin'?"

Egan offered a small shrug. "You could say there was somethin' wrong with the horse and you stayed to see her through the night."

"Bobby knows you're here. And, you should know somethin'. Bobby can't keep his mouth shut about anythin'. He'll tell Daddy and you'll be a Dingle Fair gallery duck for the rest of your life."

"Stay for just a little while, then?" he pleaded.

"Well, maybe a little while," she said.

Egan pulled her down next to him. "Tell me about that man in Dublin."

Maire's heart skipped. "What man" she asked cautiously.

"The one you said your da found for you to marry. I'm bettin' he's older'n air and fat as a hog at slaughterin' time. Does he have lots of money?"

Maire giggled. "I don't want to talk about him," she said. "I want to talk about you and me . . . and gettin' you out of here before Daddy shoots you for a cadger."

"Ahhh, Maire," Egan said, his voice tender. "Lie here with me. I want to feel you next to me without one of us havin' to run off . . . just for a wee time."

Maire lay back against his chest. What Egan asked was simple enough and she could stay . . . for a while.

"I was goin' mad without you," Egan whispered. "Me friends said, 'go see Maire, for God's own sake!'"

"They know about me? Your friends, I mean?" Maire asked, turning to look at him in the darkness.

"'Course they do. I tell them *almost* everythin'."

She could feel his teasing smile. "Do you have any . . . women friends?" she asked.

"Aye. One. Her name's Keelin. You'd like her."

"If . . . if somethin' was to happen . . . to me, would you marry her?"

"Nae. She's just a friend. Besides, she loves another."

Maire nodded as if she understood. "I don't have any women friends," she said sadly. "Well, except Ma . . . maybe."

Egan pulled her close, kissed her warmly. In the darkness, she felt him release the buttons of her coat. Then her blouse fell away and he caressed her skin. She never had to ask Egan to touch her; it seemed that he always wanted to. Was there something wrong with him . . . or Luke? Right now it didn't matter. She was far too tired and with Egan's lips pressing against her, teasing her, she didn't want to think about their differences at all.

The rain had stopped and it was nearing the high moon when Egan kissed Maire at the front door of her house and left. She had always been loving toward him but tonight, had he pressed it, he felt she would have given all she had.

"Not in a bed of straw," he remembered saying. In truth he feared Bobby being sent for her. "There must be a name for the kind of fool I am," he said under his breath with a shake of his head.

The sodden sky turned milky in the east and a cold wind whined through the tree branches. Egan shivered. "Thunderin' Jaysus, the birds aren't even awake yet," he mumbled as he hiked his collar up to his ears.

He shoved his hands into his coat pockets and found the second scone Mrs. Martin had given him. He ate it slowly.

Three hours into his journey to Drogheda the skys opened again. He was drenched and tired and when the shabby, familiar barn came in sight, he headed for it like a nesting swallow. The old woman was no where to be seen. Probably in the house, Egan thought as he slipped between the worn barn doors to find a place for himself out of the weather. A cow lowed in one of the dilapidated stalls. She was down, heavy with calf and moved no more than her head as he passed. He took off his drenched coat and cap and hung them out of sight. An hour or two of sleep in the sweet, musty straw was exactly what he needed. He lay down and covered himself with straw, folded his arms behind his head and closed his eyes. The wind whistled a silken song through the old, uneven, boards of the barn and Egan slept, unmoving through the night.

An old, gnarled hand put Egan's coat and cap back in place before he woke. When he put them on, he only thought a moment about them being dry and warm.

Sunshine split the gray sky and by noon the coat was slung over his shoulder on his thumb.

The little thatched house in Drogheda was a welcome sight and Rory met him at the door.

"Kevin said you'd not be back till evenin'."

Egan draped his coat over a chair. "How was your holiday?"

Rory grinned. "Eventful. How was yours?"

"Short. Did Kevin tell you we take Chester Castle on the eleventh?"

"Aye. He'll meet us at Clogherhead tomorrow night."

Egan nodded. "Anythin' round here to eat?"

Rory sliced some soda bread and put it on the table beside the bowl of butter, poured Egan some tea before reheating a pan of mutton stew.

"Where's Keelin?" Egan asked, his mouth full of bread.

"At her folks. We'll pick her up on the way." Rory filled a plate with mutton and cabbage.

Egan ate. It tasted like it always tasted but it filled him up. "I'm goin' to use the bed for a bit," he said, yawning, pushing away from the table. "We'll talk about the project tomorrow."

"God willin'. . . may we die in Ireland!"

The pasture behind Colin Tyrrell's house at Clogherhead swept up to a rocky ridge that looked out over the sea. Egan, Rory and Keelin arrived ahead of schedule.

The house was empty and silent but warm. The turf bricks in the small fire place were covered in ash. Rory took two bricks from the basket to lay over the embers and watched as they smoked into flame. Keelin filled the kettle, reached for the tea tin on the open shelf above the basin and set three cups on the counter.

Something scraped across the floor from somewhere in the house and they stood still as if rooted to the spot. Egan quickly put a finger to his lips. Rory reached for his sidearm. Egan shook his head and pointed at Keelin.

"Hello? Somebody here?" she called. "Tis me, Keelin Bonner. Hello?"

A door at the rear of the room opened and a dark, diminutive figure, back lit by a lantern, entered. She looked startled at the sight of the three people standing there.

Keelin reached out. "Mrs. Tyrrell?" she asked. "We're Colin's friends. We thought there was no one here. We're sorry if we gave you a start."

"Colin's friends?" the woman asked her.

"Aye, we are."

The older woman smiled and nodded as she drew her shawl up over her shoulders. "I'll make the tea, miss," she said as she took the kettle from Keelin. "I recall now. Colin said you'd be comin'. Me and Siobhan will wait in the bedroom till your meetin's done. We've got mendin' to be doin' and this'll give us time." She cocked her head. "Colin's friends you said?"

"Aye, Misses," Keelin repeated.

"We're thankin' you," Rory inserted. "We won't keep you in there long, Misses."

Colin's mother was a pretty woman in her mid-fifties with a pleasant way about her and an easy smile that made her faded blue-green eyes sparkle. Her black hair was streaked with gray, her hands and broken nails showed a life of toil. "Colin tells me what you're doin' is good so tis glad I am that you're here." She studied Keelin's face for a moment. "When the water boils do you mind bringin' cups of tea for me and Siobhan in there?" She said acknowledging the open door. "The cream's in the larder." She nodded at the small, waist high door on the room's north side.

"I will."

Mrs. Tyrrell closed the bedroom door behind her.

Keelin sighed, bowed her head and crossed herself. "May God protect her," she whispered.

"From what?" Rory said.

Keelin lifted teary eyes to him. "From us."

The room fell silent again. "I'm goin' for a walk," Egan announced.

"Jaysus, Egan," Rory said, "we just come ten bloody miles. Wasn't that far enough for you?"

"I've got some thinkin' to do, that's all."

"Well, do it quick. What am I to tell the lads when they come?"

Egan grabbed his coat. "Nothin'. Not to worry. I'll be back."

Keelin sent a worried look at Rory. He shook his head.

Egan rounded the house and began to climb. Rory's reckless attitude bothered him but he envied it too. Rory never took himself or Brotherhood activities seriously. But Chester Castle was serious business. Someone could get killed, or worse, maimed and captured. The plans for the project, as it was coming to be called, seemed perfect enough but Egan knew that human error was a constant threat and nothing was infallible, especially if there was a traitor in their company.

He stood alone in the wind with the responsibility that Jimmy Stephens had left for him, his coat and knobby sweater were unable to shut out the cold that seemed to come from within, or the salty blasts of air from without. He crested the ridge and sat in the shelter of a rock outcropping. Egan threaded his fingers through his hair, trying to rid himself of the thoughts that haunted him. He side-armed a stone. It clacked over the shale of the cliff and the wind carried it off course, out of sight. Would the others feel the same as he did, or would they be eager to get on with it? Who would back out at the last minute? Who would die from going on?

A big red Setter lumbered toward the shelter and stopped short.

"Have I got your favorite place, then?" Egan said, smiling. He coaxed him and the dog inched closer.

"That's a good boy," Egan murmured, reaching a hand out for the animal to sniff. "And where is it you've come from?"

His voice was soothing and the dog whined, laid his head on Egan's feet to be petted. The man didn't disappoint him.

"That little man has me worried," Egan told the dog of Dob Quinn. "What if he's an English spy or maybe worse . . . an Irish traitor? Many a rebellion's been lost for the likes of them two." He sighed heavily. "Still, Michael said . . ."

The dog cocked his head, whined as if in sympathy.

"'Tis an army of poets we are. We've no trainin' to go blowin' up castles. We're outdistanced, outmanned, outgunned and out of our minds. If some of us die over there, no one'll know. Only them who get away will tell, but who'd believe that a wee band of Fenians tried to smash a place like Chester Castle?" He lifted the dogs chin. "Would you?" He helped the dog shake his head. "I didn't think so."

Again he went over the simple plan; when to get there, where to wait, when to strike, who to kill. Lord have mercy. Christ have mercy. Lord have mercy. Holy Maire, Mother of God . . . Pray for us sinners now . . .

"Egan!" Rory's voice called above the wind. "Egan!"

Stiffly, Egan stood, rubbed his legs. "Time for me to be goin', lad," he said, patting the dog's head. "You can have your place back now." He walked down the hill and the dog followed. "Go home, now," he ordered. The dog wagged his tail. "All right, then have it your way. When it gets darker, your empty belly'll take you home."

Rory met Egan half way. "Some of the men are here now. I've had the windows blanketed except for the back of the house where Colin's Ma and sister are."

"Are Ned and them in place?"

"Aye."

"Good. The moon's a puddle tonight. I want no surprises."

"Who's this," Rory asked, looking at the dog.

Egan shrugged. "He just showed up. He'll go home when he gets hungry . . . I'm hopin'."

Rory laughed. "From the looks of him, he thinks he is home."

Thirty minutes later, Colin Tyrrell's house fairly bulged with Fenians. Egan met each man as he entered. At the appointed time, he stood on a chair. "'Tis glad I am to be seein' all of you," he said in a soft voice that quieted the men instantly. "Anyone know of somebody who might still be comin'?"

"Aye, Egan. Terry Biggins said he'd be late. His mare's time's come early. He can't leave till he's sure about the foal."

Egan spoke quietly to Rory. "Send someone to Ned's bunch, if any man sees Terry, send him home. He's out." He turned back to the men. "Anyone else?"

"Anybody heard from Dylan Delaney?" came a voice from the rear.

Tully Linnehan answered. "He's still in Wexford. He's out for this one."

"Any more?"

No one answered. "Good," Egan said. "I got news that some of you aren't goin' to be takin' too well." Briefly, he mulled over the words he was about to speak. "Some of you know that Jimmy Stephens will be gone for a while. Truth be told, he's gone to America and we don't know when he'll be back, if he's able to come back at all." He listened to the muffled surprise, trying to hear some of the comments then he went on. "Jimmy's gone to John O'Mahony in New York . . . to raise money for us here in Ireland.

Unless you have other ideas, he left me in charge of this bunch of Fenians. If you don't like it, let me know now and we'll put it to a vote if there's someone else want's the job."

The men divided themselves into separate groups. The discussion was short. J.J. Corydon took it upon himself to bring the consensus. "Looks like you're the choice, Egan," he said, smiling. "So, let's get on with it."

Egan nodded soberly, trying to keep the pride he felt from showing. "What we say here tonight, don't leave this room. We can't be takin' chances that might be dangerous to the success of the project. If you're not used for this one, there'll be plenty more times to be strikin' England in her sore spots."

"Who'll be doin' the deed, then?" someone asked.

Egan raised a piece of paper, blank except for his own name at the top. "If you can be gone from your homes for the next week, startin' tonight, sign your name here. If you can't sign this time, even though you've come far, I'll be askin' you to leave now. If you're thinkin' of signin', I want you to know it could mean your death. There's not room for anyone who don't love freedom more'n his own life. If we're successful in bringin' O'Leary and them home, tis a good bet that the people of Ireland will rise up behind us. This could be the start of the Irish Republic." He handed the paper to Rory who signed his name below Egan's and handed it to Keelin. She signed and passed it on.

Egan watched the faces of the men. "Your loyalty's not on the line here. If you can't get away this time, there'll be others. We're needin' your support, even if it's just a lock on your tongue and a prayer in your heart. If the British find out any part of what we're doin' here, the project will be lost . . . and most likely, us with it."

The paper rustled through the men's hands. Some signed. Some shook their heads and left. Soon those who would be involved in the raid on Chester Castle gathered around the table with Egan O'Shea.

"Count the names, Rory," Egan instructed.

Leaning the paper to the light, Rory counted. "Twenty-seven."

"Call them off."

"Keelin Bonner."

"Aye," she said firmly.

"Michael Davitt."

"Aye!"

"Tully Linnehan."

"Aye, Egan."

"Kevin Burke."

"I'm in all the way, Egan."

"J.J. Corydon."

"Aye."

"Colin Tyrrell."

"Aye."

All of the names and most of the faces were familiar to Egan and he looked into the eyes of those who answered. Twenty-six men and one woman; hardly enough to bring a castle to its knees. Michael Davitt had made the long trip from Lancashire. He was young, strong, eager to see Ireland a free republic. Even with but one arm, he was a match for any. If he lives through this, Egan thought, he'll make a fine leader. His gaze settled upon Dob Quinn, perched on the sideboard like Zacchaeus, to get a better view. Egan studied the leathery face, the baggy clothing, the stubby fingers locked across the narrow chest. Why had Dob Quinn chosen this section of Fenians when there were others closer to Ballyshannon?

"I didn't hear your name on the list, Dob Quinn," Egan said.

Dob grinned, his one front tooth catching the flicker of candle light. "Sure'n you don't expect the likes of me to go punchin' holes in castles, do you now? And me riskin' me skin to be getting' this scrap for you." He waved the promised map.

"Let's have it, then."

Dob bounced to the floor. Impressed with his own importance, he pushed his way through the forest of larger bodies and stood beside the seated leader. The map was unfolded slowly and placed on the table. "There it is, lads," Dob said eerily. "All the ins and outs of Chester Castle. All ready for the takin'."

The map had everything; perspectives, room positions, depths and heights, even the ages of buildings inside the seven-foot-thick castle walls. "There's the guardroom, Colin," Egan said. "You'll find the guards here and here," he went on, pointing.

"That's all well and good, Egan," Colin said, "but how are we to be gettin' inside the iron gates? We can't go blastin' through seven feet of outer wall."

"That'll be a job for me," Dob Quinn said firmly. "The gates'll be open."

Rory glanced from the little man to Egan. "How can we be sure of him? I don't want to be caught flatfooted with our fingers in the puddin', so to speak, or have the gates locked up behind us."

"Won't happen," Dob vowed. "I'll be at the gates the whole time with me wee pistol. It shoots as true as yours and is just as deadly. Should someone try to lock the gates, he'll feel me lead."

"And how am I to know that, when I don't know you from Adam's fig leaf?"

Michael Davitt pushed his way toward Rory. "If Dob says he'll stay, he'll be there till we're all out or he's dead. Count on it."

"Aye," Dob sang. "I crack the nut, you eat the kernal."

"All right, Rory," Egan said. "Tis settled."

Keelin squeezed in front of Rory. "What about the bombs, Egan?"

"We bomb the Half-Moon Tower, here," he pointed, "then the Forbishers and Shire Hall. We'll not be able to take them down, but we don't need too. I'm thinkin' six or seven bombs a piece should put enough crack in them big enough to worry the soldiers. What do you think, Rory?"

"Aye," he said, his left hand moving thoughtfully over his whiskered chin. "*If* Tom Kelly does what you say."

"He'll be there," J.J. said with certainty. "How do you feel about the auld abandoned cottage at the end of Sizemore Street, Egan? I can get the key and tis close as we can get to the target."

Egan glanced around the room. "Any objections to J.J.'s suggestion, lads?"

Most shook their heads, others shrugged.

"Do it," he said to Corydon.

"Who gets the key?"

"Give it to Tully."

J.J. nodded.

"How many men will Kelly bring?" Rory asked.

"Fifteen for sure, maybe twenty. He and his lads'll cross the Dee and place their bombs outside, at the base of the wall on the city side"

Egan looked hard at Corydon. "Do you believe him?"

"Course. I've talked to him. He'll be ready when you are."

Egan nodded without conviction. "I hope so, for we've no time to go changin' things now. Without his bombs goin' off, might none of us get out alive."

"When everythin' is set here," said Corydon, "I'll hie meself to London and make sure he don't make a mistake. You've got enough to worry you, Egan. Don't go agonizin' over Kelly."

By early morning, all plans were finalized. They would leave at sunset, arrive in England separately or in twos and threes and gather at an old abandoned house on the outskirts of Chester to await the early morning raid time together. Smuggling gunpowder into England for the bombs was the riskiest part, but Keelin said she would take care of it. Only one man questioned Keelin's abilities and was laughed to shame. She left shortly afterward, saying that she would see them all at the meeting place. Rory took over, explaining the timing and positions of the bombs. The teams and leaders went over their parts, acting them out, mentally sliding along the castle's inner walls and buildings, careful to stay off the broad parade grounds where they might be seen by the guards on the walls. The only men to have a single job was J.J. Corydon and Dob Quinn.

The men left the room to spend what was left of the night in the Tyrrell's barn. Tomorrow they would take the day to plant the widow Tyrrell's garden, whitewash the windward side of her house, patch the drafty door and clean the barn. Other than that, the only thing different about the cottage was the large red dog, lying peacefully along side the fireplace.

An hour before dawn, Colin Tyrrell's mother and sister removed the blankets from the windows and had set about smooring the breakfast fire.

Siobhan finished grating potatoes and went to slice pieces of ham from the slab that hung in the larder. She gave the dog a small fatty chunk of ham and let him outside.

"I was listenin' to what went on out here last night. I want to go with you, Colin," she said.

Colin stared at her, disbelief overlaid his face. "Siobhan, you're but fifteen years old. You have no experience in . . . Do you even understand what we're fightin' for?"

She turned her back on the ham, the knife in her hand. "You fight for a free Ireland. That's what I want, too, and where do I get *experience*? When? Who'll teach me?"

"Hush, girl! Ma'll be havin' a stroke hearin' you say such a thing," Colin whispered. "You've not mentioned this before. Why the sudden interest now?"

"I want to help. I know what's goin' on. You're goin' to break O'Leary, Luby and Kickham out of Chester Castle. I'm not a child anymore, Colin. You can't keep me locked up in the house forever."

"What about Ma? She needs you, you know. She can't work like she used to. Her eyes and hearin' are gettin' worse all the time. Since Da died she's not been the same."

Siobhan's shoulders drooped. "I know," she said softly, her tone betraying her disappointment and frustration. She raised her head and looked directly into her brother's eyes. "But there will come a time when I'll not listen to your explanations. Just like Keelin Bonner, I will make a difference someday . . . somewhere. You'll see."

"I know you will. But let it come to you," he said. "Don't go lookin' for trouble, Siobhan, for it will surely find you and the difference you make could be deadly . . . maybe to one of us.

"Get to cookin' breakfast now. The lads will be in from the byre soon."

Siobhan did as she was told but inside her frustration sparked a surge of anger and quiet revenge.

The tug released the ferry into the open sea just as a cold sun split the clouds. The sails snapped loudly in the wind and the ship pushed easily through the black waters toward Liverpool.

Egan paced the outer deck. Every detail of the raid on Chester Castle surfaced and with it the same nagging questions: Could Keelin get enough gunpowder? Would the bombs provide enough diversion? Would Tully

Linnehan's team be able to hold off the men from the officer's quarters? Could Colin take out both guards without being seen or heard? Would they be able to find O'Leary, Luby and Kickham once they entered the guardroom? Would Tom Kelly do his part? "Ahhh, God! Jimmy," Egan sighed. "Why did you go and leave me this?" He shivered and went inside where he found an empty seat in the shadows. He folded his arms and closed his eyes, pulled his cap down over his brow. Maire appeared. One day, he thought, when there's no Orangemen left in Ireland, you'll be mine forever. We'll marry and be like Ma and Daddy . . . workin' the farm . . . havin' kids. He laughed to himself. It was hard to think of his ma and da touching each other, loving like he wanted to love Maire but he supposed it had to be so. There was only one way to have babies and his ma had had four: Hugh, the oldest, gone these many years. He had run away to England to send money home during the long famine. No money came and Hugh had never come home. Marian lost her sight completely during that hard time. She died an old woman just after her fifteenth birthday. Then came himself. The only child to have lived through the famine. Probably with thanks to Grandfar who continued to call him home in his dreams. And the last baby, Francis, who Ma adored. Francis lived only three or four months. Ma had said that her milk was weak. Come home, Egan, lad . . . Tis time to come home . . .

Egan shifted in his seat, yawned, massaged his eyes with his fingertips. Daylight sparkled through the water-sprayed windows. The ferry's bell clanged telling everyone the pier was in sight. Egan stood in the stuffy cabin that was nearly empty. He rolled his shoulders, stretched. The odor of unwashed bodies was cleansed by the fresh air that rushed past him when he opened the door to go on deck.

A tug towed the old vessel down the Mersey toward Liverpool. The piers were a noisy glut of people, most of whom were dockers who hoisted bales of damp cotton onto horse drawn lorries bound for the textile mills at Manchester and Leeds.

The passenger plank struck the pier. Dirty children begged for pennies from those who left the boat. Egan watched a Police Constable help a pregnant woman across the slippery stones to safety. For a moment he imagined he saw Dob Quinn dash behind a rug vendor's cart. He shrugged. It was most likely another dirty child.

Egan caught a ride on a cart to Northwich. It was farther east than he wanted to go but he had the time and going directly to Chester might draw unwanted attention.

"Who d'ya know in Northwich, young feller?" the weathered old man asked, smacking the reins on the mule's back.

Egan grinned at the man's long, slow drawl and said, "Me aunt lives there. Morrin Newhall's her name."

The man scratched the white stubble on his chin with crooked fingers. "New'all," he muttered. "Don't know that nyme."

Egan shrugged. "Well, Northwich is a big place."

On the outskirts of the city Egan said good-bye and turned west. He had not gone a mile before another cart driver called, "Goin' far, are ya?"

"Birmingham," Egan lied.

"A long way," the man said in heavy, slow tones. "Hop on."

Egan nodded and settled himself among the sacks of wool on the back of the cart. "The ride's welcome," he said over his shoulder.

The driver clicked to the horse and they jerked ahead. "Can't take you to Birmin'am but I can get ya as far as Chesta."

Egan thanked him and laid back on the sacks, his heart pounding, his cap covering the smile on his face.

The late afternoon turned cold and Egan buttoned his coat, raised his collar. He'd seen no one he knew. That was good . . . and bad.

Until then he hadn't noticed the Police Constables. They walked in pairs and seemed to be everywhere. He felt their eyes on him and, with an effort, slowed his pace, looked into shop windows, talked to venders.

It always comes down to this stupid game, he thought. They snatch and hide our freedom like it was no more'n an interestin' pebble they found in their shoes and they'll keep it hid till they grind it to powder. Freedom! Tis our treasure and rare as an Irish Elk these days, so we go scratchin' after it like a dog scratchin' fleas to get it back. The trouble is, there's always more fleas. And if I'm killed tomorrow . . . absently, he crossed himself and willed the image away. What of Maire and Ma and Da? Am I the last O'Shea of our strain? By savin' O'Leary and them, will the fightin' be done or will it begin all over again? Was the truth he sought to be found anywhere in England . . . or in Ireland?

Egan glanced quickly behind him. The Police Constables were still there. His palms were sweaty. His stomach tightened. As long as they were behind him he couldn't go to the house so he turned the corner where he saw the nearly completed Town Hall. He had heard that its design was the work of an Irish architect from Belfast but he couldn't remember his name. Across the street, scaffolding was up around the old, disintegrating Chester Cathedral. He walked on down Bridge Street toward the River Dee. His first opportunity to elude the P.C.'s came at St. Michael's Church on Pepper Street where he slipped through a side door to await the dark. Worriedly, Egan marked the time, trying to lose himself among the candles and the worshippers and the trappings in the sanctuary. When he finally felt he could look outside, the street, as far as he could tell, was vacant. An eerie wind blew close to the ground swirling the fog around his feet as he walked briskly, hands deep in his pant's pockets around the final corner. The deserted cottage loomed before him through the mist and profuse wildness of the long abandoned garden.

A dove cooed.

Egan moved quickly to the rear of the small house and tapped the signal on the crooked door.

Tully Linnehan greeted him in the light of a single candle. "Rory and Keelin with you?" he asked.

"Nae," Egan replied. "I was hopin' everybody got here ahead of me."

"Not yet. You make twenty-five."

Other faces took shape before the covered windows. The house was dank and tangled in spider webs. Egan accepted a cup of tea, laced with whiskey. "Who's lookout?" he asked.

"Pat Harrigan. One of the men on my team."

Egan drained his cup.

The dove cooed.

One knock then four sounded. Tully, key in hand, unlocked the door.

"God Almighty," Rory swore and brushed a clutch of spiders from his forearm. "How do you expect a man to be seein' in this dreary place?"

A cup of tea was given to him. He took a gulp. "Ahhh, that's better, now. Things are startin' to brighten up. Where's Keelin?"

Egan shook his head. "Not here yet."

"Damnit! I wish she'd have let me go with her. I looked for her all the long way but . . ." He finished the tea. "Is there more of this mother's milk?"

Rory drank and paced.

Without the blasting powder, there would be no raid. Egan's stomach churned. *I should never have trusted her with somethin' as important as this! Jimmy might have. Tom Kelly never would. If she's caught . . .* He brushed a hand across the back of his neck. The muscles were kinked. *If Keelin leads the police to the house, the crown'll put our necks in nooses before we can scratch!*

"Where is she?" Rory asked, his voice low, grieving.

"She'll be along," Kevin Burke said optimistically. "You shouldn't drink no more, Rory. It won't do no good and Keelin'll be fierce with you."

"Ahhh, shut up, you bloody simpleton! What do you know of it anyway?"

"Rory!" Egan snapped. "There's no need of that."

They heard the cooing of a dove.

One rap was followed by four quick ones. Tully snatched a glance at Egan who held Rory back.

The door opened and the pregnant woman Egan had seen on the pier entered. "You?" he said.

"Aye," she replied from behind her spectacles. "I saw you lookin' my way on the pier. Thanks for not givin' me up. Rory, love, help a poor girl out of this harness."

She lifted her outer skirt. Suspended from her shoulders was a large drooping bag of blasting powder.

Rory's eyes gleamed. "Pregnant with gunpowder. Now that's a new one I'd be sayin'." He put his cup down and went to her rescue. The wide straps slid down her arms and the heavy canvas bag was eased to the floor.

Egan secured the door. Tully handed him the key to the padlock. "Will it hold?" Egan asked.

"Truth, I don't know," Tully said. "When we leave I'll ground the key . . . just in case I don't come back."

Egan slapped Tully's shoulder. ""You'll come back," he said. "We'll all come back."

Keelin rolled her shoulders, rubbed them. "Ahhh, Rory darlin', hold me down! I could fly away with that gone," she said with a great sigh.

Rory bent to kiss her. "Twas a big chance you took, Keelin," he said. "That bag must weigh more'n three stone. What would you've done if the Constables had found you out?"

She accepted a cup of tea and sipped. "That had occured to me. I'm thinkin' I would have cried a lot and told them the Brotherhood was keepin' me poor auld ma prisoner till I come with proof that I'd been where they wanted me to drop this bundle off." She shrugged and looked innocently into Rory's face. "You see, sir, they didn't tell me what it was. All I know is that I'm the first of many."

"You charmin' divil," Egan grinned.

"Me?"

"Might not be a bad idea to be doin' just for the mischief of it," Rory said and grinned. "Imagine them copper buttoned bullies askin' to check all the bellies of every lady in waitin' they see. There'd be more blood shed by angry husbands than we'll see in a lifetime!"

Stifled laughter drifted around the room.

"All right, lads" Egan began. "Now that we're all here, we'd best be puttin' the bombs together and getting' ourselves set. Who brought the extra clothes for the prisoners?"

"I got them all taken care of, Egan," Darby Callaghan said.

"Good. Rory, Keelin. Let go of each other and make the damned bombs."

"We'll be needin' more light," Rory said.

Tully handed two candles to him. "It'll have to be enough."

"Anybody hear somethin'?" a man asked.

Two groups of three sharp dove calls sounded.

"Shhh!" Egan ordered.

The door rattled. No one breathed. Every eye was on the padlock. The house shook as a shoulder bumped against the door. Egan nodded at Michael Davitt and they lifted pistols from their belts. No one else moved. It seemed an eternity before the all clear was heard.

"Jaysus, Maire and Joseph," Egan breathed, crossing himself and slipping the weapon back in place. "Where were we?"

"Makin' bombs," Rory said huskily, taking a long drink from the bottle of whiskey that passed from man to man.

"Put that away," Egan ordered. "I want no fuzzy heads in this."

The bottle was corked, set on a sideboard.

"Get to them bombs you two, but be listenin'." Egan gathered the men into a tight circle. "Dob Quinn will have the castle gates open. We'll all need to be inside by half three. The guards are the sleepiest then. Get to your places quick. Who's got the armory?"

Five raised their hands.

"Good. The Forbishers?"

Three hands.

"The Half-Moon Tower and Shire Hall?"

Eight hands.

"Now, soon as you're there, plant the bombs and run the fuses. The guards may be a limp bunch but count on the one closest to you bein' the only one to have snatched a wink or two.

"Michael," he said. "You get the weapons for the team guards?"

"Aye, Egan. And plenty of ammunition."

"Colin," Egan said, searching the shadows. "I found out there are four guards: Two out, two in. Them outside have got to be taken out quick and quiet, before the bombs, if you can. How'll you do it?"

In one hand Colin held out a short, thin garrote. In the other hand, a knife with a wide blade. "I'll go in first."

"Good. Now, Tom Kelly's team'll draw the guards by settin' his bombs off outside the north wall. When that goes up, that's the signal to blow the Forbisher's workshop."

"I don't like havin' Kelly on his own," Michael said. "Whose to say he'll come at all?"

Michael Davitt had voiced the thoughts that Egan could not bring himself to say aloud. It left him chilled. "Corydon trusts him. That has to be enough for us."

"Aye," Keelin said, taking a short piece of twine to tie up the bundle of powder. "Let's not go lookin' for trouble, Michael."

The one armed man shifted uncomfortably. "I'm lookin' to stay out of trouble, Keelin. If he don't come, what then?"

"We keep goin'," said Colin Tyrrell from the shadows. "If we're to have a risin' of the people in Ireland, we can't let Tom Kelly or the Holy Father himself, stop us."

Egan stood. "All right then. You all know what's expected of you. We get there, get it done and we're out before dawn. Who takes O'Leary and them home?"

"My team," said Darby Callaghan. "We slip the clothes on them before we leave the parade ground and lose ourselves in the countryside till we can get to Scotland and out from Stranrer."

"When we leave in the mornin'," Egan said, "Tully's goin' to ground the key to this place. Them that's usin' the house later, look for the key top stickin' up somewhere round the door. There'll be no talkin' once we leave here so if you have questions, ask them now."

No one spoke.

"Get some sleep then. Three o'clock'll come early."

"Willie," Tully whispered, "relieve Pat. Keep your eyes open."

The man nodded and left.

"Your bombs finished?" Rory whispered to Keelin.

"Aye," she yawned, tying up the last package.

"Come here, then." He pulled her into his arms and leaned back against the wall. In minutes Keelin was asleep, her head on his shoulder, her fingers threaded between the buttons of his shirt.

Sleep wasn't so easy for Egan. Knowing Michael Davitt had had the same thought about Tom Kelly worried him. He had met Kelly twice, both times with Jimmy Stephens. Kelly was one who had immigrated to the United States and fought for the North during the American Civil War. He came back to Ireland, as many Fenians had, but he arrived as an American

Colonel and searched out Jimmy Stephens. Somehow he had made himself an important part of the Brotherhood. He went back to America and when he returned, he brought high ranking American Fenians with him. Instead of setting up headquarters in Ireland, as everyone thought, he stayed in London, "To keep an eye on the Lioness," he had said.

Egan slept, but fitfully. It was nearing three when he shook Rory. "Time to dance," he said.

"Aye," Rory murmured thickly, his arms tightening around Keelin to wake her. She smiled sleepily as he knotted his new red scarf around his neck.

The men stirred at Egan's order. Those in charge of placing the bombs tucked the bundles inside their shirts. The last man out was Tully Linnehan who closed the door and grounded the key.

Frozen dew crunched beneath their feet, mingled with the creaks and groans of trees and out-buildings to vanish from the sleeping memories of those in nearby houses. A dog barked. Stars, like diamonds sprinkled on black silk, winked in a moonless sky offering only the dimmest light. The air was sharp with the scents of damp wool, cold ashes and fear.

In minutes the vast shadow of Chester Castle became a menacing truth as it rested peacefully on the banks of the River Dee. As Dob Quinn had promised, the iron gates were uncoupled but he was no where in sight.

At Egan's nod, Colin Tyrrell slipped inside and sprinted along the grass that met the southern wall. From the corner of the forbisher's workshop, the guardroom was visible. He took a moment to study the sentries' walking pattern. The one closest to him would be easy. He crept from the cover of the building, the thin rope wadded in his hand. He waited in the shadows at the end of the patrolled path. With a jerk and twist, Colin tightened the garrote around the man's throat. The musket dropped first. Colin took the keys and dragged the body out of his way, then crouched in the darkness to await the other guard who would surely come looking.

The others, like nebulous phantoms, sped to their assigned places and distributed the bombs as planned. Tully Linnehan's team tied a cord outside the door of the officer's quarters, just five inches above the top step. When the bomb blew, Tully hoped to see every British officer lying on his face in the gravel, an easy mark for Fenian fists and clubs.

Dob Quinn had said the guards would be lax but no one expected to see some of them sound asleep at their posts on the wall.

Keelin winked at Rory, clutched her skirt and beckoned to those assigned to her. One man kept watch while she and three others dug and planted their bombs, secured the fuses and vanished behind the bushes.

A guard sneezed, cleared his throat. The invaders didn't breathe as the sound of boots and hardware scraped over the stone. Silence again.

Egan squinted toward the north wall. Everything hinged on Kelly's bomb. Wait. He knew Keelin would hold out for Kelly's blast before setting off her bombs at the Half-Moon Tower. Would Rory?

Egan felt for his pistol. He'd never killed another human being and didn't want to now, but he couldn't help wondering how it would feel. Bile rose in his throat. His gut tightened. What had Ma said? '*People are for lovin' . . . Kill their evil ideas . . . not them that has them.*' He moistened his lips. It was too late for that now . . . too late. It was past time!

The smell of rain glutted the air. Where was Tom Kelly's explosion?

Egan looked at Rory. The muscles in Rory's jaw quivered, his eyes flashed, demanding action. Egan tried to quiet him with a raised hand. Give Tom more time. Nae! Damn, him! Rory mouthed. Wait! Egan answered.

Colin Tyrrell appeared at Egan's' side. He held up two fingers then drew them across his throat.

Egan nodded.

Rory struck a match, hid its glow behind his palm. He looked from Colin to Egan.

Rory was right. The time for waiting had passed. They had to find the prisoners and get out. The longer they waited the less likely surprise was on their side. Go! Egan mouthed and Rory touched the flame to the fuse. The faintly acrid odor wafted upward as the tiny flame sputtered toward the gunpowder bomb.

"Kill it!"

Egan twisted to see Dob Quinn at his elbow. "What the hell are you doin' here? You're supposed to be at the gate!"

"Kill the fuse! Quickly, now!" he demanded in a scratchy whisper.

"Tis too late!" Egan seized the little man's over-sized lapels and yanked hard, glared into his face. "Spit it out, damn, you!"

"They got word we was comin'!" Dob answered, pulling at Egan's hands.

"How? Who?"

"How do I know how or who?" he grunted. "What I do know is they've filled the bloody guardroom with wee Irish orphan Buachaillís! O'Leary and them aren't here. They never was!"

"That's a lie! Who told you that?"

"I listen where it does the most good, Egan O'Shea!" Dob's jaw was set. He managed to wriggle from Egan's grasp and sat back on his haunches to rub the new wrinkles from his lapels.

"So what are we to be doin' then?" Egan asked angrily.

"Get out quick . . . while you can."

"Like hell," Collin growled. "I just killed two sentries. Nobody leaves until this is finished!"

Rory was incredulous. "We come to make Ireland felt in this bloody hell-hole and I mean to do it!"

"And if what he says is true?" Egan rasped. "Are you willin' to be hurtin' or maybe killin' Irish kids?"

"No . . . But there's no kids in the Half-Moon and the fire's near got it now!" Rory turned his temper on Dob Quinn. "You told them, didn't you, you toothless, little bastard!"

Egan's glare forced Rory back. "We've no time for that! Find Keelin and get out!"

"You'd best be leavin' yourself, Egan," Dob repeated with a cautious glance at Colin. "They might not know we're here yet. But count on it, they'll be keepin' the Buachaillís here till they're sure we'll not strike."

"If you knew this, why did you open the bloody gates?"

"I fixed the gate before I knew." Dob paused. "I just learned about the Buachaillís from a notice I found on the ground by the armory."

Without hesitation, Dob withdrew the folded, dirty poster from his inside pocket and thrust it at Egan.

"Why would they do a thing such as that for God's sake?" Egan hissed and handed the paper to Colin.

"Think, man!" Dob said. "By Fenians killin' Irish kids we'd set the whole world against us and maybe think twice about takin' the fight onto British soil again."

"Damn them!" Egan whispered, his hands curling into fists. "What about Kelly's team?"

"I don't know. I never seen them," the little man said, his leathery face breaking into another one-toothed grin. Had Egan not known better, he'd have thought Dob Quinn an idiot.

"And the gates, you bastard?" Colin said.

"Open." Dob looked up. The sky was clotted with heavy clouds. "Rain won't come in time to douse the fuse, but it'll raise the Brits soon enough."

"And what of you then?" Colin growled, "Crawl back into the hole in the ground where you come from, you damnable little mole?"

"I'm no mole," Dob bristled, "I'm a patriot."

The powder hissed noisily and, with a yawning roar, it erupted in earsplitting thunder, smoke and flame. The ground rocked. For one frozen moment they stared at each other then scattered as soldiers spilled from the barracks onto the parade grounds, jerking up suspenders, yelling, cursing, some with muskets, some with sabers.

Tully Linnehan's men fought the officers back until someone shouted: "Fire! Fire!"

No one knew if the words were an order or a warning but flashes of gunpowder flared from atop the walls and the hot whisper of musket balls sprayed the quadrangle. Soldiers lit lanterns and Fenians shot them out. Glints of white gave away soldier positions; their undershirts making perfect targets. But it was the slashing hack of the sabers that unnerved even the most fearless among them and sent them running for the gate.

"E . . . Egan!" Kevin Burke sat on the ground, grasping his bloody arm. Behind him the dim silhouette of a soldier raised his musket. Egan's pistol was in his hand before he realized he'd reached for it. He fired. The man's hands flew to his head as he dropped to one knee and fell face forward.

"Kevin! Take me hand! Come on, lad, before they lock us in!"

Kevin struggled to his feet. Egan put his arm around him. "We got to hurry, Kevin," Egan cried. "'Tis but an hour till dawn."

Townspeople, some with torches, still in their nightclothes, swarmed outside the castle walls, hampering the Police. Shots barked out above their shouting. The stench of gunpowder riveted the air in heavy, choking waves. In the midst of the torches, Egan took off his coat and removed his shirt. He wrapped the shirt tightly around Kevin's arm. He had to stop the bleeding. It would surely lead someone to the old cottage.

In the chaos, no one seemed to see the two men as they hurried through the dark streets and down the road toward the safety of the abandoned meeting place. Half way there it began to rain.

Desperately, Egan searched the mud for the key that Tully had grounded and finding it, opened the door. "Get inside, Kevin," Egan gasped.

Once inside, Kevin dropped to his knees and Egan dragged him into a dry corner and propped him up, lit a candle and sat next to him. For a moment he closed his eyes, unable to believe what had just happened—and what hadn't.

"Great God Almighty!" Kevin groaned and clutched his arm.

"I'm comin'," said Egan and, getting himself to his knees, he secured the candle to the edge of the table in a fresh puddle of wax.

The thin, quivering flame brought the wound to life. A saber had sliced Kevin's right upper arm, severing his biceps.

"How is it?" Kevin asked weakly, his eyes shut.

"You'll not be choppin' wood any time soon, I can tell you that." Egan strained to see something in the fusty house with which to clean Kevin's wound and stop the bleeding. "Where's that damn whiskey?" He lifted the candle. The sickly light flickered on the bottle. "Half full," Egan said with relief. He uncorked it with his teeth and filled his mouth, letting the heat of it trickle down his throat. "Here," he said, tipping the whiskey to Kevin's lips. "Tis all we got. Take a drink and I'll use the rest to clean your arm. Tis goin' to burn like bloody hell. Are you up to it?"

Kevin took one swallow, then another. "Are you sure we should be drinkin' this? I mean, after what you said about havin' clear heads?"

"Aye," Egan said. "That was for Rory. You know how he can be."

Kevin nodded. "Might I be havin' another wee drop then?"

Egan gave him the bottle. "One more. I don't want to be here if the P.C.'s come buggerin' about." He didn't want to worry Kevin about the

Police Constables who, by this time, must be searching for the Fenians who had challenged Chester Castle. And he didn't want to tell him that if they were found, they would hang.

He searched out a clean section of shirt and ripped it away, dribbled whiskey over it and wiped the edge of the wound before pouring the liquor directly onto the raw, swollen flesh.

Kevin cried out and collapsed. Egan tried to close the gaping slit but could do no more than wrap it in whiskey-soaked layers of his dirty shirt.

"I hope we get home in time for Keelin to sew you up," he said and held his breath at a sudden scratching on the door. He hurriedly finished Kevin's bandage and crept toward the sound. Rain besieged the cottage and dripped maddeningly inside. He gritted his teeth, tried to hear. The scratching came again and he cursed his own fright as he fumbled to reload his pistol. If it were a P.C., he'd blow him straight to hell. Yet, why would the police scratch like that? Surely they'd come bursting in like a herd of bulls. He took a deep breath and reached for the door.

"Ahhh, God in Heaven!" Egan said, relieved at the sight of Tully Linnehan. "Tully, why the hell was you scratchin' like an auld byre cat?"

Tully was huddled on the ground, his head against the doorpost. His eyes fluttered open, blinked the rain away. He looked up at Egan and offered a frail blood-stained grin. "Give a friend . . . a hand?" he asked, his voice grating.

Egan crouched in front of Tully. "Where are you hurt?"

Tully laughed thickly and spat a mouthful of blood into the mud. "They killed me, Egan. But I'll not die . . . in front of them."

"You're not dead, you fool Irishman! But the rain's likely to drown us both if we don't get inside. Here, lean on me."

Tully threw his good arm over Egan's shoulder. Egan braced himself and stood. Inside, he helped Tully to the floor and put an old cushion beneath his head. He lit another stubby candle from the first one and moved it above Tully's body. He found three bullet wounds; one in the right leg, near the groin, one in his chest and one in the lower abdomen.

"Who else got away?" Tully asked, coughing.

Egan shook his head. "I don't know. So far, tis just you and me and Kevin. I sent Rory and Keelin out first, but I don't know. You?"

"Pat and Willie made it, I think." Tully turned his head and spat blood onto the dirt floor. "Last I seen, Colin and Darby was fightin' back to back."

"What about Michael?"

Tully shook his head. "I never seen him." He opened his eyes and squinted at Egan. "There's a bloody traitor in with us, lad . . ." he said, pulling himself up with handfuls of Egan's coat.

"I know. Lie back now. You need to rest. We'll be leavin' at dark."

"You get him, Egan," Tully gasped. "You get him for . . . me! You . . ."

"I will. I will," Egan promised, peeling Tully's fingers from his coat and laying his hands alongside his body. "Ahhh, Tully . . ." He fought the tears and crossed himself then made the sign of the cross over Tully's chest and gently closed the eyes of his friend.

He patted Tully's shoulder and went to check on Kevin. He was asleep, breathing easily. There would be no pain until he woke.

The candle sputtered its last and Egan lay next to Kevin waiting, hoping for sleep that would not come. The faces of his friends swarmed before his eyes. Who wouldn't make it home besides Tully Linnehan? Had anyone been captured? Who was the traitor? Tom Kelly? Rory thought it was Dob Quinn. Why hadn't anyone else come to the house?

Egan's blood turned cold. The traitor knew about the house. Had he informed the police about that also? Worse, he didn't know how long they had been there; one hour, two?

"Kevin!" Egan shook him and went to peer out the window. For the first time he was grateful for the downpour and the lengthened nights of early spring.

"Kevin, lad! We got to get out of here!" he whispered sharply.

Kevin groaned and reached across himself to his arm. "I can't move me fingers," he said hoarsely.

"Don't worry about that now. I'm goin' to tie your arm up and pad it good so it don't bleed any more. How do you feel? Can you walk?"

Kevin cleared his throat noisily. "Me head feels like the bees just found a new home but," he groaned as the pain worsened, "I'll walk if I have to. Where are we goin'?" he asked, his breath coming in halting gasps.

"Home, I hope."

Kevin used the wall to help himself to his feet. "Let's go."

Egan led him through the dark house past Tully's body. He opened the door, the road looked clear. He took Kevin's good arm and they went outside to meet the rain.

Since Egan was sure the ferries were being watched, they had but one way home; past Chester Castle, down to the River Dee. It would take days to get back to Drogheda but he had no choice.

Tall trees cast stark shadows across their path even in the dead of night as the deluge drenched them.

"This way," Egan said, turning Kevin down the hill toward the river. Just short of the bank, under the protection of the trees, Egan stopped. "Sit here till I come back."

"Aye," Kevin gasped, sliding to the soggy ground beside an oak.

Egan stole along the bank in the shadows. He had to find a boat.

Dogs barked, whined and went back beneath porches and fishing docks to get out of the rain. The only two boats he saw were beached and too big for him to push out into the water without help. Going any farther down stream would be foolish. Kevin shouldn't be left alone any longer. Egan jammed his fists in his pockets and turned back. There it was!

"God be praised!" Egan murmured and wondered how he could have missed it. The row boat rocked silently beside a small pier. He crept into the water, released the bow line from the cleat. Rain had formed a puddle in the bottom and Egan smiled. The boat was empty and watertight.

He walked along the bank pulling the boat behind and managed to lift two oars from the first of the larger, beached boats. He used one oar to tether the boat to the shore while he went for Kevin.

"Kevin!" he whispered. "Ahhh, for God's own sake, man. Where are you?"

He heard a moan from lower down the hill.

"What the hell are you doin' here? I left you up there, safe."

Kevin groaned loudly as he sat up. "I slipped."

"Shhh!" Egan warned. "The weather won't have kept all the P.C.'s at home tonight. Come on, up with you. I got a boat."

Egan managed to get Kevin to the boat and laid him down in it.

"Did we all get away, then?" Kevin asked, his voice growing weaker.

"Nae," Egan said and paddled out into the center of the Dee where the current was strong and would carry the small boat to the Irish Sea.

The rain slacked off and morning dawned fiercely cold. The two men shivered awake. They were soaked and Egan's first decision was to find dry clothes and something to eat. He counted the money in his pocket; less than five pounds and he needed at least two for the ferry home.

"I'm goin' to beach us on the north bank where there's more cover," he told Kevin. "I'll go lookin' for what we need. Besides we have to get to the Mersey. There's no ferry's runnin' from the Dee, home."

Kevin nodded vaguely, his eyes shut. Egan saw perspiration on Kevin's face. He would have to clean his wound again soon. A fever meant infection.

Egan hauled the row boat as far aground as he could with Kevin lying in the bottom. "Back quick as I can," he said and climbed the bank.

A weak sun peeked from behind dark clouds. "Eight o'clock, maybe," he said.

The dull clang of the cowbell was unmistakable. Egan watched three cows head for a white-washed barn and he followed in the high grass.

A stout woman was already there, holding the barn door open. She called each animal by name and as the last of the stanchion bars closed, Egan headed for the house. It was reasonable, he thought, that if there were children, they would be doing the early morning chores, so the house should be empty.

He slipped into the kitchen and helped himself to a handful of floury baked scones. In the larder, his nose led him to a cured ham and he cut several chunks from it, dropping them into an empty egg basket he picked up from the table. He dumped a small bowl of apples onto the ham. From the bedroom he chose dry trousers for himself. They were tight but long enough. He yanked on a pull-over and a brown woolen coat. The sleeves were short but it fit across the shoulders with room to spare.

"These'll never fit a man the size of Kevin," he said openly. "But these will," he said, smiling at the long skirt and shawl. He grabbed stockings, an apron, a cap, a shirt and stuffed them into the basket too.

"Come now, wee puss." The gentle voice of a woman sounded near the door. "Can't have you in the byre. You'll be stepped on sure as I'm . . ."

"Ahhh, God," Egan mouthed. Tis the woman with a bloody cat! He pressed himself to the far side of the chifforobe.

"I was sure we put that egg basket on the table. Here now, Miss puss. Stay inside. Must have taken it with me and forgot." She laughed at herself and closed the door.

Egan finally breathed again. She'll be back for this damn basket, he thought and quickly poured it's contents onto a coverlet and drew all four corners together. He tossed the basket onto a chair and, with his eyes on the door, looked for anything he could use as bandages. On a side board, he discovered a small bottle of witch hazel and a pile of towels behind which stood a jug. He pulled the cork, sniffed. "Medicine," he said and smiled.

He searched for a razor to shave Kevin's beard but found none.

He opened the coverlet, put most of the towels and the witch hazel on top of his other acquisitions. The kitten jumped onto the table and attacked the ham. Egan jumped. "Damned little beast!" The frightened cat leaped to the sideboard, knocking cups off hooks and scattering doilies. Hurriedly, Egan counted out one and a half pounds in shillings, which was all he could spare. He left the money on the table and looked out the window. The barn door opened. He swung the coverlet full of food and bandages over his shoulder, grabbed the jug and ran for the cover of the reeds where he dropped to the ground, turned to watch where the woman went. At first she stared at the open door then entered and came out again with the egg basket being careful to close the door tightly behind her.

"Thank God cats don't talk," he said under his breath.

Kevin lay shivering in the boat. He was unable to answer Egan when asked if he could eat and he felt hot to the touch. First things first, Egan thought. He soaked a towel and laid it across Kevin's forehead then did his best to get the wet clothes off him. "You'll be mad as a scalded dog when you see your new clothes," he said. "But I could do no more'n this."

By the time Kevin's arm was cleaned and bandaged and he had eaten, it was past mid-day. Gradually, he became more lucid as the day warmed. Egan sank the boat and let the oars float down stream. To his surprise,

:tter that had followed Egan lay on the doorstep of Rory's little house
:da, his sad brown eyes seemed to look behind them for someone
ve but he alone was the only sign of life. Neither Rory nor Keelin
question both of them thought: Were they the only ones to escape?
built the fire while Keelin searched the pantry for potatoes
s. She fried them in salted butter and a bit of vinegar. Rory pulled
wn from the top shelf and poured whiskey into two glasses.

you think I should be cookin' up more . . . just in case?"
ed, her voice low, hopeful.

nodded. "I'll help you."

peeled and sliced and Keelin cooked. It filled the time and gave
ething to talk about but as the sun went down, they became less
that anyone would arrive to eat it.

dog whined outside but would not come in.

finished his second glass of whiskey. "Come on," he said. "Let's go
l do no good waitin' up or tryin' to coax that silly dog inside."

" she sighed. "Can we leave the curtains open . . . in case? Just so
w that someone else got home?"

walked to the window, pushed the curtains aside then stuffed
rf brick on the fire. "That'll do it," he said.

lay awake in the darkness a long time, saying nothing for there
ng to say, and again they cried.

worried about Siobhan," Keelin said, catching her breath and
r eyes. "She's so young and now with Colin . . . gone what will
her?"

ll keep an eye on her best we can. Tis her ma needin' us more
n'."

he couldn't present Kevin Burke to the world in broad daylight.
a man his size might be taken for a woman and that was their
e. Kevin was willing and Egan was glad, for it would have taken
to carry one of Kevin.

Kevin accepted the woman's clothing as a necessar

his own clothes be worn underneath; wet or no

Waiting was always hardest and it would be

leave the cover of the river brush. They filled

and talking about how the rising had been ru

besides Tully Linnehan, wouldn't come home a

Kevin into the skirt and blouse then they climb

the barn where they hoped to find a horse and

Egan left Kevin in the late afternoon sh

the house, tried the barn door. It was locked.

"Kevin," he said, returning. "I can't get in

I could never get a horse and cart out. Can you

Kevin looked at him and nodded. "Tis n

legs."

Even at the slow pace Egan set, Kevin tir

get to Liverpool was to take to the road and he

Rory and Keelin stopped briefly at Clogherhea

man they knew for sure would not be coming bac

his family. It was hard, but knowing that Colin d

among them was even worse. Rory was convinced

didn't argue. As Rory's wife, she had to support h

They didn't stay long in the Tyrrell's hou

they should. Siobhan had sunk to the floor in

beside the table, stared at the pair of them loo

no idea where she was.

Rory promised to come back to help i

the window shutters that swung crazily by

you alone," he promised.

As they retreated from the house Siobh

grabbed Keelin and pulled her close. He didn

stop either. He finally caught his breath and th

Drogheda and the familiarity of home.

The red

in Drogl

else to a

asked th

Ro

and onio

the jug

"D

Keelin a

Ro

Ro

them so

confiden

The

Ro

to bed. I

"Ay

they'll kr

Ro

another

The

was noth

"I'r

wiping h

happen

"W

I'm thin

Egan kne

By night

only cha

two of hi

At dusk, as Kevin slept in roadside bushes or deserted houses or barns, Egan scoured the closest gardens for food. He found little. It was time to plant again. From his place among the weeds, he was surprised to hear the lively voices of children. He craned his neck to see them playing in the twilight with an old but serviceable bathchair. While three of them rode inside the three-wheeled, wicker, tub-like contraption, the fourth pushed. Egan knelt in the weeds and watched. The clanging of a bell sounded and the children abandoned their toy.

"Wait!" Egan called, bringing the three boys and a girl up short.

"We have to go, sir, didn't you hear the bell?" the eldest said, crowding the smaller children behind him.

"Is that your bathchair?" he asked.

"No. It's just for us to play with. Why?"

"Well then, how much do you want for it?"

"How much what?" the boy asked.

"Quid. I want to buy it."

"Are you joking? It's auld. We play in it."

Egan mentally added up the money in his pocket. "Will you take five shillin's for it?"

"Five shillings!" The boy looked at the others who pulled on his shirt sleeves. "Five shillin's . . . *each?*"

Mentally Egan choked then he nodded and pulled the money from his pocket. Four little hands stretched out before him and he plopped the money into their palms.

"Thank you, sir!" they called, turning toward the sound of the bell.

The bathchair was bent, had one squeaky, wobbling wheel and several broken wicker strands, but Egan was elated as he pushed the newly purchased vehicle toward Kevin's hiding place.

Kevin hadn't shown fever in the last two days but his recovery would accelerate if he didn't have to walk.

"Kevin!" Egan called hoarsely. "Kevin. Wait til you see what I spent all of twenty shillin's on."

A muted rustling in the dim undergrowth led Egan to him. Kevin wasn't nearly as interested in the bathchair as he was in the handful of shriveled carrots and turnips that Egan pulled from his pocket.

After they ate, Egan helped Kevin into the chair and covered him from the eyes down with the shawl and took to the road in the dim moonlight.

"This thing jiggle's me giblets," Kevin complained.

"Ahhh, go on," Egan said. "Let your giblets jiggle. Tis better'n havin' them dangle from a rope! Just steer us to Liverpool and remember when we get there to keep your mouth shut and covered."

They spent another day hiding in the English countryside. Every minute was a worry but the longer they took getting home, the better their chance of not finding Constables guarding the ferries.

Egan used the witch hazel purchased from the old woman's kitchen to clean Kevin's arm. The wound had started to heal and that concerned him. If they were too late, Keelin would have to recut it before she sewed it shut.

They made up two of the eight passengers on the last ferry to Dublin from Liverpool. The tattered bathchair and the scarf around Kevin's face drew questioning glances.

"She always wears that in public," Egan explained, "ever since the mule kicked her."

It seemed to be enough for no one inquired further.

The ferry pulled up to Dublin pier early in the morning and Egan pushed the bathchair down the plank. Kevin's hairy knuckles appeared from beneath the shawl, gripping one side.

"Not a word," Egan whispered through the high wicker behind Kevin's head. Once on the dock, Egan played at adjusting the shawl until everyone had gone. Then he wheeled his cargo into the nearest alley where Kevin chose to discard his female clothing.

"I love me Grandmar, but I don't take to dressin' like her," he said.

"Are you sure you're feelin' all right?" Egan asked, concern for his friend's failing voice.

Kevin nodded. "Can we keep the cart?"

"Aye," Egan said, grinning, "for a while."

The thirty miles to Drogheda took them directly past the Martin farm. He knew they couldn't stop.

"Too bad," Kevin said.

Egan shrugged. "I'll see Maire later. How are you feelin'?"

Kevin turned so he could see Egan pushing behind him. "I can keep goin' as long as you can." He grinned. Exhausted, they spent the night in the same familiar barn that Egan used on his trips to see Maire.

In the middle of the next afternoon, the red Setter announced their arrival.

"Ahhh, God be praised!" Keelin said, crossing herself. "You must be half starved." She loaded the table with food and drink.

"Get your sewin' basket," Egan said, patting the dog. "Some bloody Queensman tried to slice off his arm."

Kevin dropped into a chair, his face pale as cold ashes.

"Who else is home?" Egan asked Rory through a mouthful of food.

"Pat and Willie got in last night. Michael came this mornin' with Moran and O'Casey. They said they saw ten or twelve others." He bowed his head. "Darby Callaghan didn't make it . . . Colin neither."

Egan put his fork down. "Tully Linnehan got it, too. The bastards killed him three times over."

"Ahhh, God," Rory sighed. "Know anythin' about the rest?"

Egan shook his head. "They'll turn up. I think Corydon was with Kelly and them. Have you heard from Dob Quinn?"

"That ruddy little traitor! He'd better not show his face here!"

Egan sat back, wiped his mouth. "Don't go condemnin' Dob till you've got more proof. Michael Davitt vouched for him. That's good enough for me."

"I don't need more proof. A nod is as good as a wink to a blind horse and me eyes and ears are still workin'. How many of us have to die before you'll believe he should be shot for the traitor he is?"

"Rory, please, love," Keelin interrupted as she started scraping Kevin's wound with a poteen-soaked rag. "Leave off Dob Quinn. I'm with Egan on that." She smiled at Rory. "Help me now. This is really goin' to be more'n either of us can stand. Get another jug. If I'm to stitch this wound, Kevin's goin' to need a bellyful."

Egan watched Rory wrinkle his nose at the weeping gash. Everyone but Kevin understood that his arm would remain useless to him for the rest of his life. But Kevin wouldn't have believed it had they told him.

Rory got the jug and refilled Kevin's glass but he refused to drink alone. Keelin threaded the slim, arched needle that Kevin himself had designed and made for her. She unrolled a pallet and blanket for him and waited.

"What are you goin' to call your dog, Egan?" Kevin asked.

Egan shrugged. "I'm thinkin' we'll call him, Padraig, if he decides to stay."

The dog barked.

"Padraig, indeed," Keelin muttered sourly. "'Tis a crime, callin' an orange dog after Ireland's own Patron Saint. You should be ashamed."

Kevin lifted his glass. "May the Lord keep you in His hand, and never close His fist too tight on you."

They emptied their glasses and Rory poured more. He grinned as he offered another toast. "May you live to be a hundred, with an extra year to repent!"

It was Egan's turn. He stared into the glass of clear liquid then raised it to Kevin. "Here's a health to your enemies' enemies."

"Aye," Kevin said and drained his glass again. "Are you thinkin' of goin' home to the Boggeragh's, Egan?" he asked.

"And how did you know that?"

"I seen it on your face these many days. Go in the mornin'. Stay as long as you dare. Rory and Keelin'll care for me." He looked at Rory who nodded back at him and poured the glasses full again.

"St. Padraig was a gentleman," Rory said, his eyes bright, glass lifted, "who through strategy and stealth, drove all the snakes from Ireland, here's a toastin' to his health; but not too many toastin's lest you lose yourself and then, forget the good St. Padraig and see all them snakes again!"

Egan took charge of the jug. He poured drops for himself and Rory and they watched Kevin slip into a drunken stupor.

"Bring him over here and lay him down," Keelin said. "Rory, love, prop his arm over this." She had taken an empty jug, laid it on its side between two rolled blankets to have a solid surface on which to sew. She put her knee in Kevin's palm and with the tip of a spoon, carefully scraped away the last of the scab until fresh blood flowed from the wound. "Hold him down," she said and both men anchored Kevin to the floor.

He jerked some, moaned and cried as Keelin forced the needle through the tough outer layer of skin. Each new puncture brought more blood and more nonsense and tears from Kevin.

"Was I to tell you to quit your blather, t'would do no good, I'm guessin'." Keelin said as she knotted the thread and went on to the next stitch. "Poor lad. Tomorrow his head's goin' to be hurtin' more'n his arm. That much poteen would put down a horse."

Egan felt sick to his stomach. Keelin sat in a puddle of blood. There couldn't be any more if they had cut the arm off.

"Keep him still!" Keelin ordered. "I'll be sewin' his arm to his cheek for God's own sake."

Thirty-two stitches later, Keelin poured poteen over the wound and bandaged it with strips of clean linen. For what it was worth, it was done.

"Get washed and go to bed," Rory said to Keelin. "I'll clean this up."

Egan got a blanket from the trunk in the bedroom and covered Kevin, said good-night to Rory and made a pallet for himself. The dog curled up at his feet. As he fell asleep he heard Kevin weep: "Here's health and long life to us. The woman of our choosin' to us. A child every year to us. Land without rent to us. And, God willin' . . . may we die in Ireland!"

9

"The older the fiddle, the sweeter the tune."

Egan didn't stop to see Maire. The longing to see his family drove him south into the Boggeragh Mountains of County Cork. It didn't matter that it rained or that some nights he and Padraig found no warm place to sleep. It didn't matter that his feet hurt when there were no carts going his way. What mattered was getting home. Again his mind traveled back to the famine that had taken baby Francis before he was four months old; Marian had died soon after and there had been no trace of Hugh since he left for England.

As he walked up the familiar hillside road, he was amazed at how things had stayed the same. The few trees were taller. The moss covered stone fences were more settled. The black-faced sheep ignored him as they had always done and the mud was in the same places.

Atty O'Shea stood with her back to him, hanging clothes on a line in the mist, her white hair wisping from the long pins that tried to hold it in place.

"Ma?"

She turned cautiously. A slow smile spread over her face as she dropped the drawers back into the basket and grasped her skirt front. "Egan!" she cried. "Finn! Finn! Egan's home!"

Mother and son met in a flurry of tears and kisses. Finn dropped his loy and bounded over the young plants. "Egan! Egan!" he called and raced up the path from the garden patch scattering chickens in his wake.

They strolled, hand in hand, into the cottage, out of the light afternoon mist. "I see you've got a new friend there," Atty said, nodding at the dog.

"Aye," Egan said and petted Padraig's head. "He's become a good friend. Do you mind him bein' here?"

"Not if you're friends." Atty filled the tea kettle and put out a loaf of fresh baked fadge and sweet butter while Finn lit the lanterns and built up the turf in the fireplace.

Egan watched them. When he had been home two years ago, they hadn't looked this old. His ma's hair was completely white now. The joints of her fingers were thick, twisted and the blue of her eyes was washed of its brilliance.

His father's dark auburn hair was still thick, curly, streaked gray and nearly white at the temples. His broad shoulders, stooped from the years of famine, made him look older than his sixty years.

"Have I grown another head, lad?" Finn asked.

Egan chuckled. "Nae, Daddy. I was just thinkin' how much I wanted to be like you."

Finn patted his son's shoulder. "And I, you. You're doin' now all the things I'd like to have done with me life and couldn't."

"Couldn't, is it?" Atty said, pouring three cups of tea. "More like *didn't*, I'd be sayin'. I don't remember tyin' you to a post to keep you here."

"Ahhh!" Finn grumbled. "Don't go payin' attention to that, Egan. Tell me what the Brotherhood's doin' now. Are we any closer to tossin' them damn Orangemen from Irish soil?"

Egan shook his head and smiled sadly. He lifted his mother's hand from her apron pocket away from her rosary beads.

"No politics, Finn," Atty said, holding Egan's hand. "Let's hear about the boy." She sat between them. "Is there a colleen in your life?"

"Aye," he said, grinning.

"Her name?"

"Maire . . . Maire Martin."

"And where does she live? What does she look like? Are you goin' to be bringin' her here sometime?"

Egan took a deep breath as he gathered all the lovely things that Maire was. "She lives north of Dublin and she's pretty as Summer. Her hair is bright as polished copper and her eyes are like green fields in the mornin'. God willin', I'll be bringin' her here soon."

Atty gazed at him. "Are you goin' to be marryin' her, love? The church is small but tis lovely all dressed up in Spring flowers."

Egan laughed. "That's all she talks about, but with me in the Brotherhood and all . . ." He shook his head.

Atty sent a stinging glance at Finn. "You never mind them. Your da's filled your head with that nonsense since you was a tyke. If you love this girl, marry her. The Brotherhood be damned!"

"Atty!" Finn admonished. "You mustn't be sayin' things like that. The Brotherhood is all that stands between us and total British rule. You can't be wantin' that. We already pay our bleedin' tithes to the damned Prods. You don't like that much, if I recall!"

"Wait! Wait!" Egan said. "I don't want to be sendin' you two into opposite corners. I come home because . . . because I need to be here for a while. I need to have somethin' that's sane in me life. I can't stop dreamin' of the way things were before . . ." Egan couldn't speak any more, the knot in his throat forbidding another word.

The puffs of turf bricks punctuated the long silence. Atty placed her hands on Egan's arms. She could feel him tremble beneath her fingers and her eyes filled with tears.

Finn cleared this throat. "How long can you stay, lad?"

"A few days, Da, if. . . if you have room for me."

Finn looked stunned. "If we have room? We've waited these many years for you to come home. Stay as long as you can. Can't you see? Just look around you, tis help I'm needin' here. So . . . so I'm hopin' you can stay a decent amount of time, though I won't be keepin' you if you have some business up north."

Egan tried to smile.

"Don't be proddin' the lad, Finn. I'm thinkin' he's tired to the bone." Atty patted his hands and stood. "Come, love," she said and led him into the dark, little room he had shared with Hugh.

There was only one bed there now and his mother cleared it of hand made quilts and braided rugs. She had Finn push boxes of old IRISH PEOPLE newspapers that he had saved into the far corner. The pile of old clothing she had torn into strips were pushed onto the floor at the foot of the bed.

Finn stood behind them holding the lantern. Atty fluffed a down pillow and sacked it, dropped it onto the narrow bed. She shook out a quilt and tucked it down beside the wall.

"Now," she said, "if you'll be sittin'." Gently, she pushed her son onto the bed and lifted his feet, untied his shoes.

"Ma, you don't have to be doin' that. I'm not a baby."

"Egan O'Shea," she said sternly looking into his tired silver-blue eyes, "for as long as we'll be livin', you'll be our little boy." She went back to her task. "And there's no shame in that. Now, loosen your belt and lay your head on that pillow."

He stood and gathered his mother into his arms and the tears just came.

As Atty and Finn left the room, Padraig entered and lay quietly beside the bed.

For the next three days Finn and Egan worked together; whitewashing, nailing, strengthening, hoeing, laughing, talking. Atty watched them, listened to them. Her eyes brightened at the sight of them together. She wished Egan could stay forever, never go back to the life he must be leading with the Brotherhood.

"Ahhh," she chided herself, watching the two men in the garden. "If wishes was horses, all the beggars would ride." Atty rubbed her hands down her apron. "Lie down, you silly auld dog," she said and went inside to start the mutton stew and bake more fadge.

"Come, lad!" Finn called across the garden patch. "Put down that bloody loy." He shot a sidelong glance at the house then motioned for Egan to hurry.

"What's wrong?" Egan asked, bounding over the rows, drawing Padraig behind him.

"Shhh! Sure'n you don't want your ma to be seein' this now." Finn rolled a large stone over revealing a hole in the ground as big as a bucket. He thrust his hand in and retrieved a crockery jug, lifted it to his ear and sloshed it. "Ahhh, tis enough."

"Enough for what?"

"Enough to share, o'course. Don't be tellin' me you don't lift a jug now and again," Finn said with a trace of disappointment.

Egan shrugged. "Now and again," he said with a shy grin.

"Ahhh, that's a good lad. There's not an Irishman alive, or dead, who can't be enjoyin' a taste of good Irish whiskey." He pulled the cork with his teeth and spit it into his hand. "I'd not believe it."

"But, Da, our work's not done."

"Work, lad," Finn said seriously after another quick glance at the house, "is always there. Look around you. The damned stuff never goes away. But a jug is a wee touch of heaven, and tis not always full. A man needs to take the time to win back what he lost by workin'!" He patted the crockery with gentle, dirty hands.

Egan smiled and mopped the sweat from his forehead on his shirtsleeve. "Tis nice to know you've not changed, Da." He couldn't help the little laugh in his voice.

Finn placed the cork in his shirt pocket. "Lord knows I try to remain the same, but the years are eatin' me up." He tipped the jug to his lips then handed it to his son.

Egan sipped.

"We got to be movin' from here. Tis too close the the house."

Egan and Padraig followed Finn. There was a curious joy inside Egan as he strode beside his father. He was suddenly a man in the eyes of the man he most admired. A smile overtook his face and he thought he stood a little taller.

They jumped the eastern fence and leaned their backs against the cold rocks. The valley stretched before them and a south wind blew down from the mountain. In the shelter of the fence they emptied the jug and talked of the Brotherhood. Finn learned about Rory and Keelin, Dob Quinn, Colin Tyrrell and Kevin Burke's near miss at Chester Castle.

"Did he live?" Kean asked.

"Aye, Da. He lives. His arm is useless but he lives."

"And you," Kean said, "how are you? What happened to you there when the battle broke out?"

Suddenly the air became sharp and heavy like inside a dead chimney as Egan remembered what he'd done to save Kevin's life. It was hard for him to breathe, hard to raise his head or open his eyes.

"Are you all right, lad?" Kean asked, all at once concerned for his son.

Egan nodded without a trace of conviction. He looked into the blue eyes of his father. "I never . . ." He swallowed hard as his stomach lurched. "I never . . . killed a man before but I had to . . . He . . . he was goin' to shoot Kevin. I couldn't let . . ."

Padraig crawled into Egan's lap as if he knew.

"Killin' is hard no matter when or where it comes or how important the reason is and I wouldn't be countin' you much of a man if it didn't trouble you." Kean's wide hand rested on Egan's shoulder. "But we're truly in a war for our lives, Egan and I'm so proud of you for doin' your part. Still, there's blood in war and people die. You saved your friend's life. That's reason to be proud; not to go braggin' mind you, and not to go losin' your head over it. You done your duty and that's the fact."

Egan forced his fingers into his auburn hair. "You're right Da. I know you are but I can't stop seein' him spattered in his own blood . . . fallin' to the ground behind Kevin." Tears brimmed on his lower lashes and finally dripped from his chin to the ground.

"We've all seen things we'll not forget. We just have to live long enough to make them stop comin' round so often. Do you understand me, Egan?"

Egan wiped his face and nose on his shirtsleeve. "I do." He managed to clear his throat and send a weak smile in his father's direction. "I do."

"So, tell me lad," Kean said, trying to lighten the situation. "What are the bloody British up to now? They don't come into the Boggeragh's and news of the big world travels on a snail's back."

Egan breathed deeply and set his voice. "Same as always, Da." His jaw tightened. The silvery blue of his eyes turned cold as steel. "They've taken Habeas Corpus from all of Ireland so they can arrest us now and not tell us why or how long we'll be gaoled. Protective Custody they call it. What they do is keep us in custody till they've protected the life from us!" He paused to let his statement take root. "They're still tumblin' cottages in Ulster. All it takes is a Constable's say so and down they come leavin' families homeless and hopeless."

"Them bastards!" Finn growled. "How can any Irishman dance to that divil's tune?"

Egan shook his head, his forehead furrowed as his memory overflowed with sound of the protestant festival. "The worst is July when Ulster goes Orange and marches day and night to the poundin' of them God-forsaken Lembeg drums that don't stop till . . ." Egan flushed crimson, suddenly realizing that his fists were full of grass that he'd pulled up and wrung dry. "Well," he sighed, dusting his hands, "tis not a place to be Catholic, that's sure."

Finn growled, "One day the brave boys of Cork will make a noise that'll sound all the way across the water to rattle Victoria's teeth. I swear it!"

Thick clouds rolled slowly along the western horizon. The sky turned dark. "We best be getting' back." Finn groaned as he raised himself to his feet. "How's your money holdin' out? You able to work?"

Egan shrugged. "I do a bit of this and that; carry hods, do some barberin'. The Brotherhood does the rest."

With arms around each other's shoulders, they walked back toward the cottage. Wind whipped around them and thrashed the long grasses that grew on the hillsides. The clouds thickened as they took up their loys from the garden. The milk cow bawled at the barn door. Padraig barked.

"Past her time," Finn said, squinting at the sky.

"I'll do the milkin', Da. Tell Ma I'll be in soon."

Finn nodded. He stood a moment beside the door and pushed both hands through his hair. "I smell of poteen. Sure'n Atty'll be on me again like green on grass."

In the barn, Egan leaned his head against the cow's flank. The warmth of her and the whiskey in his belly nearly put him to sleep as he squeezed the constant, monotonous streams of milk into the wooden bucket. It felt good to be home; almost as if he'd never left. He closed his eyes and saw again how Finn touched Atty, how he looked at her sometimes, as if he couldn't get enough of her. "Ahhh, Maire," he said. "Will we ever have a place of our own? Is Ma right? Can we marry in the church anyway?"

He stripped what was left of the milk from the cow's udder and turned her loose. Rain began to fall before he reached the house.

"I suppose you've been at the jug too," Atty said not looking up. "Tis a good thing that what goes into a man don't make him wicked, but what comes out of him."

Egan pressed his lips together, put the bucket on the table and glanced sheepishly at his father.

"Best be strainin' that and puttin' it in the back room," she said. "Supper's waitin'."

"Aye, Ma," Egan said. Even with the reprimand, he felt warm, wanted. He hated that he had to leave in the morning.

"Brotherhood business?" his mother asked.

"Aye," Egan nodded. "But I've made up me mind about somethin' you said, Ma. I'm goin' straight to Maire and ask her to be me wife and when it's time, I'm goin' to bring her here . . . home, for good."

Atty smiled. "And when will it be time, love?"

"Don't go pushin' the lad," Finn said. "'Tis enough he's comin' home with a wife." Finn's eyes met Egan's. There was a knowing in them and a pride that each felt in the other.

"Would it be too much to be goin' down the road with me tomorrow, Ma? I'd like to say good-bye to Grandfar and Marian and wee Francis."

Atty smiled at her son even as she twisted her well worn apron in her hands.

In the warm morning sun, Finn stood in the doorway of the cottage holding Padraig back and watched as Atty, dressed in black and Egan in his leaving clothes walked down the road. Over her shoulder, he could barely see the wild flowers she carried.

"Twas Grandfar called me home," Egan said softly, his hand on his mother's elbow as they walked.

She nodded. "I thought as much. He's been crowdin' me own dreams too . . . and you," she said, "you bein' the one he favored and all."

"Do you think he'd be proud of me, Ma? Now, I mean."

"There's no doubt of that. I'm thinkin' he's real proud of you." She stopped to face him, her eyes cloudy with tears but she was smiling as beautifully as Egan had ever seen. She sniffed and blinked the tears away. "Are you rememberin' your rosary, love?"

"Not always," he confessed.

"You mustn't forget it . . . it bein' who you are and all." Wordlessly, she placed her rosary into his palm.

At first he thought to give it back and then his fingers closed around the beads. "Aye, Ma," he said as they continued toward the graves.

"You must be teachin' your own children, you know," she said finally. "You can't be treatin' them like the Proddy heathens treat their children . . . not givin' them what they need to be keepin' them civilized. Goin' about killin' us and each other . . ." She clicked her tongue. "I'm havin' a hard time understandin' them. And them callin' themselves, Christian. It don't seem right when there's so much vengence in them."

"I know, Ma. With their British sympathies, I don't even try to understand them."

Atty sighed silently. He hadn't taken her meaning. "I don't think they're really Irish," she said, "I'm thinkin' they're probably Scotsmen of some evil strain. Do you know what I mean? They're always and forever fightin' each other." She glanced up at him, her brow furrowed wondering if he understood her thinking.

They came to the graves and after the weeds were pulled and the flowers placed, they meandered back to the house, each trying in their own way to put off the inevitable. But, none the less, it came and Atty stood with Finn, his arm around her shoulder, watching as their last child crested the hill and vanished from their sight.

10

"Many an Irish property was increased by the lace of a daughter's petticoat."

AIBREAN (April)

"Maire? Maire Martin!" Peg called from the doorway. "I'll swear to you, Luke," she muttered with a slow, intense shake of her head. "That girl can find more places to hide when I'm wantin' her. You might try callin' her yourself. She's probably down the hill, wanderin' about."

"I'm thankin' you Mrs. Martin," Luke MacSweeny said and tipped his cap before moving off in the direction she had indicated. He changed his grip on the handful of drooping flowers and rubbed his other palm down the pantleg of his gray suit. Releasing the tight shirt button at his throat, he called, "Maire. Where are you, Maire?"

Mountains of white clouds lingered in the pale sky. A light breeze rustled the oak leaves in the clumps of trees that grew on the gentle downward slope. Luke picked his way around huge granite stones, cracked and pitted by time. He finally saw her standing like a figurehead on the bow of an enormous boulder. Her back was to him, her hair and skirt blowing freely in the wind, her hands locked behind her.

He called.

Maire turned, her smile fading as she did. Ahhh, Egan, she thought, are you never comin' back?

Luke walked around the boulder. It had been over a month since he had seen her in Dublin. His heartbeat quicked. His palms were sweating. "I brought these for you." he said, thrusting the flowers at her.

She accepted the wilting roses without a word of thanks. "I thought you'd forgotten about me, Mr. MacSweeny," she said coyly.

"Not for a minute, Miss Martin," he whispered, his eyes drinking her in.

"Would you be findin' it in you to help me down from this . . . rock?"

He raised his arms to her waist and she leaned toward him, her hands on his shoulders, the flowers in his face. Gently he lifted her to the ground but couldn't make himself release her.

"And are you intendin' to kiss me, then?"

"Aye," he managed, before his lips brushed her cheek, she turned her head and walked farther down the hill.

Confused, he took a deep breath and followed. "Are you not glad to see me, Maire?" he asked, watching the sway of her skirt.

"I am . . . I suppose . . ."

"You suppose?" He walked down to her. Her behavior surprised him, but everything about Maire Martin surprised him. "When I last saw you, you kissed me like . . . like . . ."

"I don't recall," she said quickly. "'Twas a long time ago."

Luke sounded worried. "The other man's been back?"

"Maybe," she smiled and shrugged, knowing Egan hadn't been back in over a month. Her eyes strayed to her fingertips as she absently plucked at the rose petals.

"Maire," Luke said, taking her by the shoulders. "I know it's been a while but, sure as rain falls you can't forget what happened between us. There was somethin' real and you know it. Can you be lettin' it go so easy?"

"Lettin' what go?" she asked, innocently.

Luke took her face in his hands and looking into the depths of her green eyes brought his mouth close to hers. She closed her eyes in anticipation of his kiss yet he came no closer, forcing her to stand on tip toe to reach him.

"Damn!" she fumed. "I'll not have you teasin' me!" She stalked determinedly up the hill.

He caught her arm and pulled her around slamming her into his chest. His voice darkened. "And I'll not have you teasin' me!" His mouth came down on hers, hot and furious until her arms rounded his neck and she returned the kiss.

Luke was elated. He felt the curves of her body against him and longed to run his hands over every inch. But he would not . . . not this girl. Her lips were soft, yielding and it was getting hard for him to think as her fingers moved in light circles on his neck. "What are you feelin' inside, Maire?" he asked, his voice a rough whisper.

"I'm not sure . . ." she said breathlessly.

"Is this what love feels like, then?"

"Love?" Maire stiffened slightly. "I . . . I don't know."

Luke held her as she cuddled next to his chest. It was hard to keep his hands from roaming. Why did he care so much about this girl? She was everything he thought he hated. She was disloyal, unthinking, distracting, profane, and a general bother. And she was everything he wanted: Beguiling, beautiful, profane, willful . . . wonderful.

She drew back, her eyes soft. With her fingertips on his jaw, she drew his head toward her, her parted lips pink and quivering as if suddenly cold. His arms tightened around her as he drew her against his body, feeling breasts and hips and the curve of her waist in the palm of his hand. Her lips moved beneath his and she became all there was in the world.

Egan thanked the cart driver who let him and Padraig off on the roadway between Maire's house and Dublin. He shifted his pack and glanced at the sky. It was hours before dark and he could make it to the Martin farm easily before then. This time he would go to her door. After all, his intentions were honorable so he should have nothing to fear from her father, no matter how he felt about the Fenians.

He dusted his coat and looked at his dirty shoes. I'll have to be cleanin' up when I get closer, he thought. "It won't do to go in lookin' like a tinker . . . not on a day as important as this, eh, Padraig?"

The dog barked, wagged his tail.

Egan took out his flute and walked in time to his own music, imagining what Maire would say when he finally asked her to marry him in his church in the wild Boggeragh mountains. Why, she'd throw her arms around his neck and squeeze the daylights out of him! "Egan, love, tis about time!" he said, laughing.

Egan found himself actually looking forward to meeting Kean Martin again. The first time hadn't been so bad, though Martin had intimidated him, simply from the aspect of age and intelligence. It was the next time, when he'd spoken of his Fenian views, that had set the man against him. How could an Irishman accept the oppression of British Rule in any form? Well, he would suppress his Republican feelings for now and except for Maire, he'd have no opinions at all.

At one of the clear runnels that splashed across the road, Egan washed his hands and face, combed his hair, cleaned his shoe tops. He shook the dust from his coat and cleaned it, hoping the spots would dry before he reached the farm. "Come, Padraig," he said. "We've got somethin' important to be doin' this day."

The road from Dublin was mostly uphill but Egan didn't notice his cramping calves until he rounded the curve onto the Martin property.

He sat on a stump in the shadows to rub the kinks from his legs where he could see the house, less than a hundred yards away. "Lie down, Padraig," he ordered the dog. "Be still."

Maire's little brother, Bobby, walked out of the barn leading a dark, saddled horse. Chickens scratched the ground around the cottage door. A hog squealed. Kean Martin walked into the sun, heading for the sty, with a bucket in his hand.

Egan was comfortable in the shade, watching his future in-laws but he couldn't help wondering where Maire was. Visions of their last meeting warmed him. He could smell her hair, feel her kisses, her naked breasts. He looked at his empty hands almost expecting to see her there.

Peg Martin came from the house. She shook a small rug free of grit. "Maire!" she called. "Maire Martin!"

Egan heard a faint answer travel on the wind.

"You and Luke come back to the house now. I made some tea."

Luke? Egan didn't remember that name and he watched the house.

Maire and a stranger strolled hand in hand over the hill. She carried lifeless flowers that drooped around her fingers and though he couldn't see her face clearly, he supposed he saw her smiling at the young man. Egan's jaw quivered. Unconsciously, his whole body trembled. What was going on? Who was with Maire? Surely it wasn't the old man from Dublin that her father had picked for her.

Padraig growled. The hairs stood up along his backbone. "Hush," Egan ordered. "We can't go bargin' in. We'll wait to see what happens."

Egan moved farther back into the trees. Every minute seemed an hour. The sun was a molten mass when Maire and the stranger, leading his mount, walked toward him from the house. As they came closer, Egan studied the man beside Maire. He was tall, lean, dark, young, handsome and worst of all the two of them were very familiar with each other. Egan sank back into the shadows and listened.

"I'll be back soon," Egan heard the man say, putting his arm around her waist.

Egan gritted his teeth, seethed.

"I'll be waitin'," Maire said almost too soft to hear. But her bright smile told him more than words.

The young man scooped her up in his arms till only her toes touched the ground. The kiss he gave her was more than friendly.

As Egan watched them, his anger turned to despair.

Maire walked, hand in hand, with the man to the road where he mounted his horse and trotted south toward Dublin. She stayed until he was out of sight. Her smile turned into a long sigh.

"Well, that was a pretty picture," Egan said coldly, his upper lip curling over each word as she bumped into his chest.

Maire clutched her throat as she steadied herself. She didn't know whether to be coy, afraid or demanding. "Egan, love," she said showing her surprise, hoping he would forget what he must have seen in her sudden sincerity. "Where is it you've come from? You nearly scared me heart into stoppin'."

"That's too bad. I come from there," he nodded toward the shadows.

She swallowed and minced away from him, her skirt swishing from side to side. "Had I known you was there, I'd have acquainted you with . . . *cousin* Luke."

"*Cousin* Luke," Egan mimicked with a grim smile.

"Aye," she said nervously. "We haven't seen him in awhile . . ."

"And why is it that I've not heard of *cousin* Luke before?"

She struck a defensive pose, her fists on her hips. "We've not talked about a lot of things, Egan. And I've decided somethin'," she snapped, feeling herself suddenly in control. "I'll not be waitin' under the oak for you to be showin' your face at your bloody pleasure. We'll be speakin' of my pleasure from now on." She turned and stamped away, knowing he would stop her.

Egan caught her arm and spun her around. Her eyes flared like sparkling green gems at the sight of his raised hand.

She blinked. Her face tightened and she thrust out her chin, held her head higher. "You'll be strikin' me but once, Egan O'Shea!" she hissed. "You're not me husband, nor me father and I'll not be treated like the pub wenches you're used too!"

For the first time Egan heard steel in her voice. He dropped his hold but his hard eyes never released her. He wanted to yell at her, shake her head off! He glared at her, hatred in his eyes. Why couldn't she just tell the truth? Why did she have to make such a mess of it?

Maire stood her ground, knowing that if Egan had slapped her, she deserved it for lying. She fumbled with a loose thread inside the pocket of her apron. Setting Egan against her was the last thing she wanted. Why was she so confused? With Egan here, he was the only man she wanted, but when Luke kissed her, she couldn't think of anyone but him. She wished she could tell Egan the truth about Luke but she had lied already. If she told the truth now, Egan would surely know her for a liar. Ahhh, damn! I hate the both of them alike! Maybe not Luke . . . *maybe*.

Maire looked at Egan cautiously. "You shouldn't be sneakin' up on a person . . ." she said, filling the silence. "Tis enough to be scarin' them into an early grave." She raised her eyes to meet his.

Egan looked beyond her to the road. His joy had been stolen, his confidence diminished, his love for Maire sank to its lowest ebb. "I have to be goin'," he murmured and turned away.

"You just got here." The pained expression on her face found its way into her voice.

He turned back. "I've been here longer than you think."

"When are you comin' back? I haven't seen you in such a long time. I don't want to be arguin' with you. I love you."

Egan ignored the tears in her voice, grabbed his pack and slung it over his shoulder. "Come, Padraig," he said.

"Egan!" she pleaded. "What am I to be doin' till you come back?"

The torment on his face didn't prepare her for his answer. "Wait for cousin Luke . . . like you told him you would. You'll not be lonely, Maire Martin. As for me, you're not worth me time." He walked away. What had he been thinking of anyway? It was plainly against the rules for a Fenian to marry. He must have gone bats for a while, that's all. It was good that he had come to his senses. At least there was Luke to thank for that. He laughed miserably.

In the safe darkness of the forest, he looked back. Like a lost lamb, Maire stood where he had left her. The sun shone on her coppery hair, giving her the fragile appearance of an angel with a golden halo. His eyes drank her in. Finally, she lowered her head and turned away, becoming a hazy shadow that shrank into the distance, floating from his teary gaze. "Damn you, Maire . . ." he said, wiping his eyes, "for makin' me give promises to me ma and da, makin' me need you more'n I should, then doin' this!" His voice became a wretched murmur through his clenched teeth. "But I'll not play your fool . . ." He turned north toward Drogheda knowing that he'd just made the most difficult decision in his life.

The month crept by for Egan. Only twenty men had returned from Chester Castle of the twenty-seven who had started out. Five of them were known dead. Two were still missing.

Kevin's arm wasn't healing well and he used it as an excuse to go to his grandmother's farm. Rory sent Keelin to see her mother, saying that it would do her good.

Egan worked like a madman. He whitewashed the house inside and out. He dug up the entire garden patch and fixed the fences, put new hinges on the gates. At night he brooded and drank. He saw Maire's hair in the sunset and the ocher gleam of candles; the rose water she wore wafted through the window from the wild rose bush; the plates they ate from were cool, white, smooth as her skin. His mind was so full of her his bones ached and he was unable to speak of her for fear of trembling.

Rory tried to understand, thinking that he might act the same way if Keelin vanished from his life. "God Almighty, Egan," Rory finally said. "Are you goin' to work yourself to death or are you goin' after Maire?"

Egan looked up from his glass. "Neither."

Rory skidded a chair up to the table. "The hell! You don't talk anymore for her twistin' your mind into ropes that could hang you."

"I don't think about her anymore . . ."

"Tis a real shame, Egan. Most Irishmen are fair liars, but you don't have the knack." Clicking his tongue, he shook his head in disgust. "Why don't you tell me what's in your head. A man don't give up a colleen as fair as Maire Martin without good reason."

"I have reason!" Egan shouted. "Damn good . . . *reason* . . ."

"Well, what is it? Friends talk, damnit!"

Egan turned away.

Rory ignored Egan's rejection. "I'm thinkin' that you should do what me and Keelin did in Manchester."

Egan turned around, reached for the poteen.

Rory held the jug down. They're eyes met.

"All right," Egan sighed. "You'll sit there and pop if you don't tell me, so go ahead. What did you and Keelin do in Manchester?"

Rory grinned as he poured the home-made whiskey into Egan's glass. "We married," he said casually.

"You know that's against the rules!" Egan said, stunned by Rory's confession. "A Fenian don't marry. We want no widows. You know the bloody Orange lords are hangin' us daily for doin' no more'n breathin' and it don't matter that Keelin . . . What the hell are you grinnin' at? You look like a gnat that swallowed a goat!"

Rory nodded. "I did, in a manner of speakin'."

"What are you talkin' about? Did you marry her or not?"

"I said I did. Keelin and I married each other. No priest. No church. No bother . . . in a pub." Rory's face broke into a reckless grin. "We done it alone. Well, not *really* alone. The pub was near crawlin'. We said the vows and she wears my ring, well, the Brotherhood's ring . . . the one we use for cover."

"That's not legal," Egan said. "No one would believe that!"

Rory smiled slyly. "Keelin does."

"And you?" Egan asked.

"Aye. And me. Who knows how long this set-to with Queen Vic will go on? We been fightin' them for more'n five hundred years. What makes us think it'll be over in a month or a year . . . or another hundred years? I like a good fight as much as the next man but in a hundred years, Egan, I'll be damned tired. As for the rules . . ." he shrugged. "I know there's good reasons for them, but when I'm with Keelin, there's a couple of good reasons to be breakin' them!" Rory cupped his hands in the air around imaginary breasts.

Egan shook his head and smiled awkwardly. He knew those feelings. He'd had them enough as he'd lain alone. There had been other women in his life but Maire was wrapped around his heart, she filled his soul. "And you're sayin' that I should be askin' Maire to do that . . . with me."

Rory shrugged, spread his hands. "Why not? Has she never asked why you've not wanted to marry her before now?"

Egan nodded and sipped his drink.

"Well, then? Unless you can tell me why you shouldn't . . ." Rory studied Egan's face. "Look. The law don't have you married. The Brotherhood don't have you married. Only the two of you know it. To Keelin and me, why, we're as bound to each other as if there'd been a priest, witnesses and Holy Mother Church there to see it."

Egan stared into his glass. "There's another man," he said roughly. "I saw them together and she lied to me." He downed the whiskey, poured more. "He's closer to her own age . . ."

"Ahhh! Age stinks! If you love her, get her back!" Impatiently, Rory stood, his chair tipping to the floor. "Me da used to say, 'You'll never plow a field by turnin' it over in your mind.'"

"That's all fine to be sayin', now, with me up to me rump in Fenians!"

"So what?" Rory blared. "It don't mean nothin' that she was with another man. It don't mean nothin' that she lied to you. It don't mean nothin' that you're, what, ten years older? And it means even less that you're up to your arse in Fenian's."

"I'd not be able to trick her. Maire's too smart for shenanigans."

Rory righted his chair and straddled it, his arms leaning carelessly across the back. "Shenanigans is it? I'm tryin' to give you back the woman tis plain to see you can't live without and your callin' it shenanigans? I never, till now, took you for a fool, Egan O'Shea!"

"A fool, is it?"

"Aye. A bloody, sightless, dimwitted fool! And if you want me keepin' this sudden opinion of you, don't let me tell you how to go about reclaimin' her!"

Egan leaned back in his chair, folded his arms across his chest as if to hold his anger inside. "I'm listenin'," he said.

"That's better, now." Rory paced the room like a Prussian Field Marshall. "You know that place by the oak you told me about? Go there. Leave somethin' that she'll know is yours."

"I have nothin' like that."

Rory threw his hands in the air and rolled his eyes heavenward. "Then leave a flower or somethin'. Anythin' that'll catch her attention so she knows you've been there."

"Should I leave a note then?"

"Ahhh, Jaysus, Maire and Joseph and the wee donkey, too," Rory sighed scornfully. "When it comes to love, I truly question your Nationality. Nae. No notes. She's got to be left wonderin'. She's got to be left thinkin' about you. Your problem is that you've got a mind for leadin', but not for lovin' and I'm not sure I'm doin' Maire any favors by puttin' you two back together!" The painful look on Egan's face caught Rory by surprise. "Just do as I tell you. Everythin' will be fine."

"When you married Keelin in the pub did . . . did you . . ."

Rory stopped. He didn't blink as he looked drolly at Egan. "Not right away," he said. "We waited till we got back to our digs."

Egan laughed with Rory until tears flooded down his cheeks. He rubbed his eyes with the heels of his hands then rested his head in his palms.

"You're too drunk to be goin' anywhere now so best get some sleep," Rory said with a yawn. "I'm hopin' things'll change by mornin'. Even the dog thinks you look like a dying duck in a thunder storm. You've got to go to Maire, man. You can't go on like this. I'm thinkin' of headin' back to Clogherhead for a couple of days anyhow to help the widow Tyrrell. Leave Padraig with me." Rory reached across the table and finished Egan's drink. "I'll tell you one thing, sure. If a stranger come pluckin' fruit from my tree, I'd not be mopin' round here. I'd break his bloody arms . . . then I'd fence me tree."

11

"The believer is happy, the doubter is wise."

Maire Martin lay on the hard mattress listening to the gusting wind outside her window; wind that bent the tree enough to scrape against the side of the house. Bobby's light snore in the bed across the narrow space between them was an irritation but she was too tired to do anything about it.

The clouds had been swept away by the wind and moonlight bolted through the flapping curtains of the loft bedroom scattering silvery stains across the foot of her bed and over the floor. She rolled over. "Shut up, Bobby!" she said in a half-whispered yawn. "You could wake a tin whistle."

Another sleepless night was building up. She was angry and depressed, miserable and sorry. She had been short tempered with everyone and she had kicked the sow more than once lately.

The face of Egan O'Shea was stamped on each eyelid and when she closed them he was there saying that she wasn't worth his time. "Damn, you! I am so worth it! Everyone says so. If you was worth you own salt, you'd be knowin' that, you great stubborn fool!" Maire punched her pillow and flopped over onto her back. "And you shut up, too!" she said, pressing her hands over her ears to shut out the wind that whined and moaned through the branches of the oak. "Ahhh, Egan," she wept, "you've got to be comin' back to me. I don't love Luke, I promise . . . He's just a . . . he's just . . . oh God help me he's . . . wonderful." The blanket helped muffle her sobs but it couldn't stop her tears.

Bobby yawned. "Why don't you stuff a rag in it and go to sleep, for heaven's sake?" he mumbled, pulling the covers over his head.

"You'd best quiet yourself, Bobby Martin," Maire sniffled angrily, "or I'll boot your backside up between your shoulders, you nosy toad!"

"Aye. Then I'd look just like you . . ." He turned over.

Maire's shoe glanced off the wall and rolled to a stop in the moonlight.

The butcher store in Dublin was choked with late day customers. A smiling MacSweeny wielded the hacksaw and the wide butcher knife while Roddy weighed the pieces, wrapped the meat and took the money.

Luke entered from the back door, another half mutton carcass on his shoulder, his apron red with blood. The side of meat was hefted to the ceiling where Luke rammed the iron hook through the hock. He held it in place for a moment, stopped its swing and tugged down to secure it before covering it with a fresh sheet.

The sun was nearly set. Soon the customers would be gone, then they could eat supper and Roddy would be sent to bed. That's what Luke waited for. He wanted to speak privately with his father. He had kept it to himself long enough. It was all he could think about. Maire Martin must be his wife. There was no other way. He couldn't sleep or eat and being away from her was like punishment. He would spend the rest of his life making her happy and just being able to see her smile would make him content as long as he lived.

After supper MacSweeny settled himself in the chair with a heavy sigh as he uncorked his jug of punch. He poured some for himself and a little for his son. Nervously, Luke drained the glass.

"This must be important," the elder man said, grinning.

"Aye," Luke said, staring at the empty glass. "I . . . I'm seekin' your blessin', Da. I'm goin' to be askin' Maire Martin to . . . to be me wife."

MacSweeny nodded thoughtfully and poured more liquor into Luke's glass. "She's a pretty one, Luke," he said with deliberate slowness. "Pretty girls are sometimes scared of blood . . . and butcher stores are full of it. Have you talked about this . . . together?" He eyed his son over the lip of his lifted glass. "Or have you decided this on your own?"

Luke sipped. Their blue eyes met. "Nae. I've not talked of it with her yet. I wanted you to know first and tell me what to do . . . me never doin' such a thing as this before."

"I see." MacSweeny studied the grim, handsome face across from him, watched the tapping fingers.

"Are you agreein' with me then? I don't want you to be unhappy, Da, but I . . ." He took a mouthful of whiskey and let the heat of it settle him before he went on. "I have to be tellin' you, I'm havin' trouble stayin' away from her," he said with a shy grin and finished the rest of his punch.

His father's brow furrowed as he glanced again at the empty glass in front of Luke. "Aye. I could tell somethin' was growin' in your bonnet." Smiling, he leaned across the table. "Or in your trousers."

"Nae, Da!" Luke frowned harshly at his father's wide grin. "'Tis not that at all . . . well . . ." He struggled, a twitching smile lifting the corners of his mouth. "Not totally . . . anyway."

MacSweeny's belly laugh filled the house.

Luke's embarrassment mushroomed. "You'll be wakin' Roddy," he said in an angry whisper, "and I don't want to be explainin' to that wee clúrachán!" He pushed away from the table and stood, his chair skidding over the worn boards.

"That *wee clúrachán* probably knows a bit more than you think he does. Might be he could teach you somethin' you could use on your weddin' night." MacSweeny's eyes flashed with soundless laughter.

Luke turned away, his head falling to his chest. He sucked in a deep, tortured breath and let it slowly escape.

"Ahhh, lad! Don't be hasty with your auld da. I been waitin' for this to happen. Let me enjoy it!"

Luke walked back to the table. "Are you of agreement, then?" he asked, worried, his eyes pleading.

MacSweeny shifted in his chair. He brought both forearms to his knees and looked sincerely into his son's face. "Don't marry her because she's comely as a rose or ugly as a thorn. Marry her because she'll be a good wife to you— give you sound, strong sons to stand with you, here . . . when I'm gone."

"Ahhh, Da," Luke said, "you'll be here a good long time."

A wry smile creased the older man's face and he looked pensively into his own bare glass. "Aye," he said softly and poured the punch again. "When will you be goin' to tell her what's on your mind then?"

"Tomorrow, if you'll not be needin' me round here for the day."

MacSweeny's generous smile glistened in his eyes. "Here's to Mrs. Luke MacSweeny. A finer man she could never hope to have in her life . . . or her bed." He lifted his glass and winked at his son.

AIBREAN (April)

"Not another word, girl!" Kean Martin shouted. "You've the voice of a fish monger and the tongue to match! What Luke MacSweeny sees in you, I'll never know! But he's asked to marry you and by the livin' God, marry him you will!" Kean slammed his fist on the table.

Kate screamed and toddled to Peg. Bobby sat against the wall, his eyes wide, his mouth shut.

Tears spilled down Maire's cheeks as she stood before her father. Mulishly, she lifted her head, not bothering to wipe her face as she cleared the sobs from her throat. "And . . . and when's this all to be takin' place?"

Kean glared at her. "When he says so. Are you understandin' me, girl?"

Maire nodded in outward obedience. "Can I be goin' now?" she asked with as much dignity as she had left.

"And where is it you think you're goin'?" Kean demanded.

"Outside," she said, choking on the hostility she squelched. "Where I can breathe!" She grabbed her shawl from the peg by the door and wrapped it sloppily over her head and shoulders.

"Well, while you're breathin', do some thinkin' and make it about a weddin'!"

She drew in a deep breath and held it. Sobs were rising again. She nodded curtly, unable to speak.

"Back before dark," Peg added softly, "remember the cow needs milkin'." She wished she could comfort Maire and tell her that she understood. But that would have to wait just as the speaking of her mind to her husband.

The door closed behind Maire and she ran, blinded by tears, to the oak. Strange feelings mounted within her, twisting, choking the life from her. The fury was for her father, not for Luke. She had never taken orders well and her father had stopped giving them, until now.

She sank into the old leaves and new grass beneath the tree, weeping. Her stomach churned, making her sorry she had eaten supper. "Wish I could go up the ladder to the loft, pack me things and go. Was I a lad I'd be doin' just that!" she sniffed and rubbed her sleeve under her nose.

Luke had overwhelmed her with his proposal and, in a simple way, she did love him. But being commanded to marry him left her cold as winter rain. Everyone had smiled as they left the house, leaving the two of them alone. Luke's deep blue eyes fairly simmered with love when he said; "Maire Martin, I come to ask for your hand in marriage. I promise to love and care for you and keep you all me life." He held out his hand. "Will you be me wife, Maire?"

Whatever words she had stuck in her throat and when he knelt at her feet and kissed her hands, it was more than she could bear. "Ahhh, Luke," she said, mortified, "stand up. You can't . . . you can't kiss me from there . . ."

Somehow Luke took that as a yes and when her family came back inside there was a celebration that stunned her.

Now she was out under Egan's oak, alone. Angry, she searched for something to throw and pricked her finger on the thorns of a newly cut rose. "And just what are you doin' here?" Furiously, she lifted the flower and crushing its petals, threw it aside then sucked the blood that bloomed on her thumb. "Now who'd go droppin' roses here?" She pinched the flesh and watched the blood swell into a small globe. Her eyes drifted back to the flower that was as red as the blood that dripped from her finger.

"Bobby?" she ventured. "If you're hidin', you'd best come out, or I'll beat you to raggins when I catch you!" Uncertain, she inched closer to the tree.

Another rose sailed through the air, falling next to her. She gasped and scrambled to her feet. The bushes in front of her rustled. "Who's there?" She turned and started to run back to the house but someone caught her and before she could scream, Egan pulled her tight to his chest. He looked at her for a moment letting her recognize him before he pressed his lips against her cheek. What he had seen happen with Luke the month before, wouldn't matter after tonight . . . if she said, yes.

"Ahhh, Egan" she whispered, her voice taut, doleful, "thank God you've come!" She clasped her hands around his neck and her lips met his in a desperate kiss.

His heart raced with joy as he felt her need. Once again she had made him whole.

"Marry me, Maire Martin," he said softly, breathing the words again and again across her forehead and down the side of her face to her lips again. "Never let me try to live without you again. T'would be better if you killed me right out."

She was breathless. She poured herself into the feel of him and the sweet smell of roses that clung to him. Her anger evaporated, leaving no room for hatred or sorrow . . . or Luke. Joy swept through her, heating her blood. Had anyone ever felt the way she did when she was in Egan's arms? "Ahhh, Egan me darlin', aye . . . aye . . . I'll marry you, love."

His hands roamed down her back, over her buttocks molding her against his body.

"When?" she asked. "Where?"

"Now. This minute. Come with me."

Maire glanced back at the house and then at Egan. The sun reflected in his eyes and she could do nothing but follow him. They walked, half ran, down the gentle slope away from the house.

In a rocky hollow that Egan used for shelter sometimes when he came to see Maire, he stopped. "I'm askin' you again. Marry me. Right now. Right here with no one to throw flowers or weep."

Maire looked around. "But we've no priest. No one ever married proper without a priest."

"I know someone who did."

"Who?"

"Can you tell me who married Adam and Eve?"

Maire crossed herself. "Why, God Almighty, o'course."

"Would you let Him marry us?"

Confusion spread across her flushed face. "I don't think that's the way it's done any more, Egan. That's why God made priests. Maybe He thought that one weddin' was enough for Him. And He's probably forgotten how . . . it bein' such a long time and all." She crossed herself again.

Slowly, Egan rubbed her arms, letting the friction warm her as their eyes met. "All we have to do," he said, his gaze intense, "is know that God's angels surround us as we say the vows, just like Adam and Eve did."

"Who did?"

"Adam and Eve."

"But . . . I . . ." Maire was more than confused, she was terrified.

Egan lifted her chin and kissed her. "The day when I saw you with, that . . . boy, I was comin' to ask you to marry me. I wanted you then, and I want you now— now that I know I'll be dyin' without you . . . Ahhh, marry me darlin'!"

His lips were soft, demanding, dissolving her will. "We belong together. You know it and I know it. Marry me and no one can tear us apart. Not now, not ever."

His kisses smoldered through her as he spoke.

"I . . . I want to believe but . . ."

Egan held her, caressed her. "Believe it, Maire. Believe *me!*"

Snatches of her father's angry words came back to her. Damn! she thought, let him marry Luke himself! "Aye, Egan, I believe . . ."

Egan took her shawl and placed over her head carefully. "Stand still," he said. "Wait for me." He ran further down the hill and returned with a small bouquet of wild spring flowers, took one and tucked it into her hair so that it peeked out from beneath the shawl then he handed her the rest. "Every bride needs to carry flowers."

They faced each other in the last of the sun's splintered rays, holding hands, speaking vows, each taking the other for better or worse, for richer or poorer . . . unto death.

"I'm sorry I have no ring for your finger yet, Maire. But I'll get one. And a house to be sure. Till then you'll have to be stayin' here with your folks and keepin' our secret."

Maire nodded, snuggled against his chest as they sat on his coat in the grassy nook. "Was this a game for you, Egan?" she asked warily.

His arms enclosed her. "Nae, Maire. You're me wife just as sure as dew in the mornin'; as if there had been a priest and a hundred witnesses."

"Truly?" The shawl dropped to her shoulders.

Egan sensed her hesitation of his sincerity. "Aye, love. Don't go thinkin' this wasn't real or true. I've loved you for an age. You know that's truth."

"And I've loved you," she said as she played with the buttons on his shirt. "Are you sure there were angels around us?"

"Absolutely."

"Is this what freedom feels like?" she asked quietly.

"*Freedom*," Egan said, interlacing his fingers with hers. "I think so. In a way we've been set free." He lifted their hands and kissed hers.

"Do you know why I was out by the oak?" she asked.

"Thinkin' of me, I hope."

"Aye. I was. And, because me da has arranged for me to be marryin' . . . someone else."

Egan's contented expression fled. "Who, that auld man in Dublin?"

Maire nodded then shook her head. It wasn't right to lie to your husband. "Nae. A lad from Dublin."

"That Luke fellow?"

She swallowed and set her jaw, waiting for what he might do when she told him. Get it done, girl, she heard the voice in her head say. She whispered softly, "Aye . . ."

"It don't matter, now, Maire. You can have but one husband." His lips brushed hers and his bitterness toward Luke sifted away as chaff in the wind when her fingers came to rest in the hair on his chest. "Let me love you, Maire." His voice was deep, rich with the sound of earnest longing. "Like a man loves his wife."

"Will I look different to you, then?"

Egan captured her face with his hands, kissed her softly. "You'll look like a woman who's loved beyond measure."

Maire slid down on the coat, her green eyes commanding his lips to hers. "Aye," she sighed, aching with feelings she didn't understand.

The Martin bedroom was dark except for the sliver of moonlight that speared through the narrow split in the curtains.

Kean tossed.

Peg lay quietly, sadly beside him, her eyes open as if she could see her own past stir before them. The image of Conor O'Gill's powerful, sweat-shined body stood above her, naked to the waist, and his words made soft echoes in her brain. "I'm goin' to make love to you, Peg . . . and you're goin' to be lovin' me back . . ." Gooseflesh covered her as fingers of memory caressed her skin. That same day Conor gave her five gold guineas and seven ancient Scottish coins to hold for their marriage. He had earned them across the water building houses and gardens for an English gentleman, he'd said. One week later she spent two whole guineas on bundles of flowers for his funeral. Her face was wet. Tears after so long a time? She brushed them away. What would her life have been like had Conor lived long enough to marry her?

Kean grunted and flopped over. "Still awake?" he asked thickly.

"Maire's not home. Ahhh, Kean, I wish you hadn't been so hard on her. She's just tryin' to make a place for herself in the world. I'm thinkin' maybe we shouldn't force her to marry Luke MacSweeny. It could be a great mistake."

Kean rearranged his pillow. "A bigger mistake is to be waitin' for that houligan O'Shea to come round again. Who knows what he could talk her into? With the MacSweeny lad she'll be well taken care of. You saw what kind of business MacSweeny does at his butcher store. Maire'll be well off some day," he yawned, "you'll see."

Peg sighed, the darkness hiding the toss of her head. "Aye," she said submissively. "But in the meantime, she's out there in the dark, and I'm frightened for her."

Kean slipped his arm behind Peg's neck and pulled her head onto his nightshirted chest. "Ahhh, don't go borrowin' trouble now, Peg, darlin'. She's probably in the byre all nice and warm in the hay and we'll be seein' her bright and early for breakfast."

"I hope you're right. I hope she hasn't run away or somethin', her bein' so high spirited and all."

"That's not high spirit, Peg; tis plain bullheadedness. The girl wants her own way no matter what and, aye, we've spoiled her badly but when push comes to shove, she'll be givin' in. She knows who's boss."

Peg pulled away. "Ahhh, damn, Kean! You'd not know spunk if you fell in it! She's a young woman . . . did you hear what I said? *Woman!* She's not a child to be ordered about anymore. I'm sorry for goin' against you, but you can't be makin' decisions that should be hers or . . ." Peg stopped. She had said too much.

"Or what?"

Her voice shook and Kean strained to hear her. "We'll be losin' her. I love her and I know that you do, too. She's full of fire, that one, and she'll go away from us. I don't want that to happen. I want our children livin' round us . . . and our grandchildren."

"Now, now, don't go to worryin', Peg darlin'." Kean consoled. "I'll talk to her tomorrow. Maybe I was a wee bit hasty tonight—" He withdrew his arm, yawned again. "—but only a wee bit mind you." He pressed a kiss on her forehead and turned over.

Peg lay staring at the black ceiling. Tomorrow. She hoped tomorrow wouldn't be too late.

The sun rose in a clouded sky. Egan stretched and blinked awake. Maire was up on one elbow, watching him.

"You're beautiful," he said, twirling a copper ringlet around his finger. "I want to wake up to your beautiful face every mornin' of me life."

"I feel beautiful today. Mrs. Egan O'Shea tis a grand thing to be." She kissed him, feeling his overnight growth of beard.

"Forgot me razor. Next time I'll remember," he apologized and rubbed his hand over his chin.

"I suppose I'll get used to it." She sighed, laughing at the pitiful face he made. "I've got to be gettin' home. Ma will be frantic for me."

"And your da?" Egan said, wrapping his arm around her neck and pulling her close.

"Aye, him, too. I'll likely be dancin' to the tune of a switch, I'm thinkin'. I have to go."

"Not until . . ."

"Until what?"

Egan smiled as he lifted the blanket.

"Are we to be doin' that again then?" she asked innocently.

"Aye . . ." His voice became a whisper as he moved closer. "Just one more time."

He pulled her head down to kiss her, taste her, tease her and whisper her name again and again.

Never had she heard it said with such devotion. Silently, she prayed that what she had done . . . what *they* had done, was right in God's sight. But how could this be wrong?

It was well into the afternoon before they discovered that they were hungry for something more than each other.

"All I have is this," Egan said, pulling a small chunk of cheese and a stale scone from a niche in the rock. "Ahhh, damn!" he said as he unwrapped it. "The bugs got it."

"Wouldn't be a proper outin' without them. Give it here." She reached for the cheese. "I'll fight them for it," she said brightly.

They sat up crosslegged, facing each other. Egan watched as she dusted the insects from the hard cheese. "You're not goin' to be eatin' that now, are you? There's no tellin' what else they've been treadin' on."

"O'course I'm goin' to eat it. Everybody knows that bugs that come to private outin's have feet kissed by faeries. Why, their toes are cleaner'n yours or mine."

Egan laughed.

Maire broke the cheese and gave him the biggest piece. He put it to his lips and watched as she brushed an insect from her breast. The thought of leaving her nearly paralyzed him.

The weak afternoon sun glinted through the clouds, shining in her scattered hair. Her green eyes glistened when they rested on him. What more from life could he ask than to be with Maire, naked in the April sun, unashamed, unafraid, uncomplicated and yet more complex than he could express.

He cleared the raw emotion from his throat. 'I'll be comin' back more often now . . . so that we can be together."

Tilting her head, she looked at him and smiled. "Together has an all new meanin' don't it?"

He reached for her and she pulled away. "Ah, ah, ah," she said shaking her head slowly. "No more of that. We'll be here till they find our bones." She giggled when she said it.

"Aye," he said, grinning.

She lifted her face to the sky and leaned in to kiss him.

"Ahhh, Maire, I wish we could tell your ma and da we're married."

She quickly came alive. "O'course we can! Sure'n you don't want them to keep on with plans for me marryin' Luke MacSweeny do you?"

"Aye. For now."

"Are you mad?" She looked up into the heavens. "Have I given meself to a madman, then?" It was obvious to Egan that she rejected the entire thought. "You can't be meanin' what you just said. I'm thinkin' we've gone too far round the bend to be keepin' it a secret! Besides, you should've heard what ma said about what me virginity costs. *Lord save me!*"

"It'll only be for a short time, Maire, darlin'. We'll have to pretend for a few weeks, that's all. Just till I can get you a ring and a home of our own."

"And what if it's decided that I'm to marry Luke next week?"

"Ahhh, Maire Martin . . ."

"Maire Martin O'Shea!" she corrected.

"Aye, girl. And I also know you can talk the birds from the trees. Don't be tellin' me you can't talk the likes of your da and Luke—what's-his-name, into anythin' your mind thinks up."

Her crooked, adolescent smile broke the tension. "Well, all the same, I wouldn't be takin' too long, was I you. Just because we're married don't mean I'll be acceptin' feeble excuses or waitin' forever, now."

Egan slid closer. "You are made of thunder and lightnin', aren't you?"

Maire laughed and buried her head against his neck.

"If I could have stayed away from you, Maire, I would have. I'd have never come back after . . . after seein' . . ." His voice broke and he paused to gaze sadly across the fields. "But I can't stay away, Maire love. You're the air I breathe. I can't live without it—or you."

She drew closer to him, her breasts crushed in the hair on his chest.

"I can't be livin' without you either," she said softly. "Don't be away long when you go this time."

Egan looked past her to the ebbing sun. Back before dark . . . He had to be back, too. Why? He couldn't remember.

O'Shea, he chided himself, straighten up! Shake out your thoughts. There are others who count on you.

"Egan?" she whispered, her lips moving against his ear. "Where is it you've gone? Your eyes are lookin' past me into somewhere that's far away."

She melted into his hands. He could hardly believe how he hungered for her.

Maire gazed into his eyes so deeply she thought he might weep. "Is it for what we've done? Are you sorry we married as we did? Oh, Egan . . ." She grabbed her clothes as if they would run away by themselves and yanked on her drawers and blouse.

He suddenly became aware of what she was doing. "Maire love, where are you goin'? What's . . . ?

"You think we've done wrong. I can see it on your face. I have to go home."

"Nae," he said softly. "Come, lie with me once more before we leave . . . so we can remember this day with the joy it deserves." He lifted his hand to her and pulled her to her knees before him. It was but an instant before the fear and disappointment left her face and they became one, swaying, moving slowly in a rhythm as old as time. Nothing was as important as that moment because, for them, nothing else was . . .

Egan played a jaunty tune on his pipe as he walked down the long shadowy road that would take him back to Drogheda. In the five days of the week he had been gone, Maire had made a new man of him and he was happier than he could ever remember being. He wanted to share it with someone and he hoped that Rory would be there when he reached the house. Keelin might be there, too. She would love to hear about the *wedding*.

Then again Rory might still be at the Tyrrell's. Colin's ma deserved more than a short visit and a wave goodbye. Perhaps Kevin would be back from his grandmother's farm. He would enjoy hearing about Maire, too. It was, after all, Kevin who kept encouraging him to go to her and avoid the sting of the faeries.

12

"The best way to keep loyalty in a man's heart is to keep money in his purse."

The little house in the Drogheda hills was awesomely quiet. The door and windows were shut up tight.

"Looks like I'm by meself for a bit," Egan said. "Maybe Corydon's been here and left a note about what's really goin' on with O'Leary and them." The thought itself quickened his pace.

A sickening odor came from somewhere around the house. Egan touched the door handle and the muscles of his neck tightened. He stared at his rigid hand then took a step back, his gaze roaming over the front of the house. No one in their right mind would have left all the windows shut on a hot, muggy day like this.

He stood there a moment longer breathing in an odor he'd only smelled once before at the slaughter house outside Cork.

"Kevin!" he called. "Kevin, Rory, Keelin! Anybody here?"

Shadows grew together. The promise of rain floated on the air. Twilight fluttered in on faeries wings and Egan's mind drifted back to the faery stories his grand father used to tell him when he was a wane but somehow they all came back at once in a jumble of voices and visions. He covered his face and gripped his hair, pulled until it hurt. He turned from the door and walked away, stopped to gather his thoughts and remember just who he was and what others expected of him before he went back.

A smudged reddish stain smeared the cottage threshold and nearby the broken beads of a rosary lay crushed into the ground. "Kevin's," he said, bending to retrieve them.

A nearby crow cawed.

Egan jumped, laughed nervously at himself. He made up his mind to find the source of the odor later. He pushed the door open. The stench hit him full in the face. The door bounced back as it struck against the wall. He pushed it again and it stood open. The dark interior gaped before him. He covered his nose. His heartbeat echoed in his ears keeping time with the maddening drone of flies. The house was steeped in the reek of stale blood and butchered flesh.

Egan's skin crawled. Beads of sweat spread over his forehead. He tried to speak but had to clear his throat. "Kev. . . Kevin are you in here?" Egan called weakly, clinging to the rosary. "What's your rosary doin' in the dirt? Anybody?" Slowly, his eyes adjusted. He spun quickly out the door and stood with his back against the outside wall, his eyes closed, his pistol in hand. He took some rapid breaths and turned back. His nostrils filled with a salty nauseating stench. A shadowy, broad shouldered figure was seated in a chair, his back to him.

"Kevin, answer me!" Egan called in a choked whisper. "What are you doin' sittin' in the dark like some kinda bat in a cave? Are you feelin' all right?" The question was ludicrous and he knew it. "Ahhh, Jaysus! Sweet Mother 'o . . ." The words escaped his lips in heavy moans.

The truth crushed in on him. The man was tied to the chair. And worst of all, it was Kevin. Blood was spattered over the floor and walls. Egan shuddered a near silent scream. With shaking hands, he threw open the windows. Both lantern's lay broken. He lit a candle. The room came to dull, eerie life. Except for the slaughter house, Egan had never seen so much blood in one place. He stood like a mudlark in the piercing silence. "Ahhh, Jaysus! Jaysus, God!" he stammered, lifting the light to Kevin's face. He hardly recognized the swollen, fly eaten features. The milky eyes were nearly eaten out and most of the nose was gone. Covering his mouth, Egan ran outside, fell to his knees. He wretched until there was nothing left in his stomach and even as he wept and prayed not to go back inside, he knew he would. Finally, on unsteady legs, he stood, locked his jaw and took several deep breaths before entering. He went to the bedroom and got a quilt. "Get away from him, damn you!" he shouted at the busily biting flies as he covered his friend. "Who done this, Kevin?" he groaned, wiping his face on the sleeve of his coat. An answer was not long in coming.

Soap and water wiped the blood away but no amount of cleaning could erase Egan's memory. On the wall, circled in Kevin's blood, was the red hand print of Ulster Loyalists. How did they know this was a Brotherhood house? Of course, the traitor. *The traitor!* Suddenly, Egan realized he could no longer see and the sound he heard was that of his own sobbing. Kevin Burke was dead and in the most hideous way imaginable. Nothing could change that. If only he hadn't gone to see Maire. If only Kevin had stayed at his grandmother's. If only . . .

The night was the longest of Egan's life. He crouched in the corner behind the door, his pistol cocked. If they came back, he'd be ready for them. They'd do no more damage here. In fitful spells of sleep and sobs he was startled awake by howling wails of wind. The Banshee, he thought and watched the ghostly spirit sweep through the sky foretelling death and searching for the lost souls of dead men. Egan rubbed his neck in an effort to wake himself fully. The curtains smacked against the walls. It was all a dream. But he was yet folded in the same corner and the body in the chair was still across the room from him. That part was no dream. The whole place smelled foul and outside rain assaulted the thatched roof behind waves of wind. The room turned white as lightning fingers struck the ground and split the sky open. Thunder, like a fired cannon, answered with a mighty *CRACK* and Egan shuddered. With every flare his stomach lurched and he felt as if his empty belly would turn itself inside-out.

At the first gray light of dawn, after saying a stream of "Hail Maire's" for his friend, Egan began to search for clues. He steeled his nerves and gently peeled away the blanket.

Kevin must have come back right after he had left to go to Maire's for he had been dead several days. His face was a chalky blue where it wasn't bruised or laid open.

"He must have been beaten senseless before . . . before . . ."

The bullet hole in Kevin's temple was encrusted with yellow fly eggs. A shiver raced through Egan. He cleared the bile from his throat and started again. There had to be something besides bloody shoe prints all over the floor and the rough circle in the corner with the single hand print. "The Red Hand of Ulster," he said bitterly and it matched the taste of ashes in his mouth.

Finally, Egan measured the shoe prints. None of them were Kevin's for there was no blood on the bottoms of his shoes. From the measurements, he surmised there had been three men. "It would take more than two with guns to bring down the likes of Kevin Burke, even with one useless arm," he said with a momentary smugness that dissolved into despair. He could take no more and went outside into the leftover wind and drizzle, grabbed the shovel and began to dig. "Why Kevin?" he shouted at the sky not thinking there would come an answer. "Were the buggers after Rory?" Egan said absently, ". . . or me." He lifted another spade of earth and threw it onto the growing pile. "Who's the bloody traitor?" he cried and threw himself into the work of grave digging until he dripped with sweat and his muscles screamed in pain.

In the gray afternoon, Egan stood wearily beside the mound of Kevin's grave, lost in memories of his simple friend, distraught that there could be no wake, no funeral. Dying in springtime contradicted nature. He had always thought that, but it hadn't stopped Grandfar or his cousin Liam or his sister, Marian or Kevin from dying in the face of the contradiction. He felt sick again. The hand-hewn cross at the grave's head tilted in the west wind. He knelt and pressed pebbles in and round it until it stood firm.

"So little," he murmured, thinking of the clues he had been able to gather during the past several days of scrubbing and cleaning. "We'll get them, Kevin," he promised angrily. *"Aye,"* he imagined Kevin saying.

Inside again, Egan smoored the fire, added a bloodied turf brick and watched it sizzle into a blaze, listened as the blood hissed. He scrubbed his hands from the elbows down then filled the tea kettle. Still in shock, he settled into a chair at the table, wrapped his arms around his shoulders and rocked himself as he studied the whitewashed walls of the little house that he had always thought of as a safe place. He remembered the hours of scouring so most of the blood was gone, except for the three whole shoe prints on the floor and the hand mark on the wall that he had saved to show the rest of the band when they arrived. He had also washed the towels and blankets and hung them in the wind. Kevin's broken rosary was hung over the cross above the bed. The rope that had tied Kevin lay coiled on the table. Most of the odor that had clung to every corner of the place was gone but still Egan left windows open as if it could clear the foulness from his mind.

He sipped some tea. Nothing else would stay down. Dark halfmoons colored the skin beneath his eyes and he doubted he would ever really sleep again.

"Hello the house!"

Egan threw the door open at the sound of Rory's voice and Padraig's high-pitched bark. "Thank God," he sighed, gratefully. "Keelin with you?" he asked when Rory entered.

"Nae. She'll be comin' in a day or two. Light a lantern, will you now?" He wrinkled his nose and watched Padraig sniff at the place where Kevin had been murdered then, whining, the dog found the foot prints and growled. "What's been going on here? The place smells like the cat died and since we don't have a cat, I'd say our house was used as a dumpin' ground." He pulled off his coat and cap before dropping into the nearest chair.

"You didn't see it then?"

"See what?" Rory asked, catching the heaviness in Egan's voice. "What's been goin' on? Why the hell are you sittin' in the dark?"

Egan swallowed hard and took as deep a breath as he dared, fearing the control he had been able to achieve would be spoiled. "Somebody's murdered Kevin."

"What?" Rory said, an incredulous bent to his voice.

"Right there, where you're sittin'. The grave's to the side of the house."

Rory bolted from the chair, stared at it. "You can't be meanin'. . . *dead.*" His face paled.

"Cold as a wedge."

"Why? Who?"

Egan pointed at the wall.

"A message from Ulster?" Rory said, hardly able to believe what he heard or what he saw. "Newcomb and them from Belfast?"

Egan shrugged. "When I found Kevin, he'd been dead for days. I put together an idea or two and saved some of his blood." He nodded toward the wall and the floor. "They left that, too."

Rory looked at the rope as if it were alive.

"It won't harm you now." Egan lifted one tightly wrapped end.

Rory's eyes narrowed. "They could still be near then?"

"I don't think so. I been here these last eight days. I'm thinkin' they done what they come for and left. Did you tell anybody besides me that you was leavin' here?"

Rory shook his head. "Only Keelin. I said somethin' to Kevin but—."

"'Tis good to have you home," Egan said tightly, his eyes welling.

"Aye," Rory said behind an uneasy smile. "Sorry it wasn't sooner for your sake. You look like you've not slept in a month of Sundays."

Egan offered a weak gesture of indifference. "Now that you're here, maybe I will."

With a glass of whiskey raised in salute, Rory paid his respects at Kevin's grave. Memories of the soft-spoken giant and some regrets filled him and tears fell untended. He emptied his glass, knelt and crossed himself.

The dark of the new moon closed in around them and Egan was glad he didn't have to spend another night with his pistol in his hand.

In the late morning, Rory fried up some boiled potatoes and cabbage in leftover pork fat. "Are you not goin' to eat then?" he asked, surprised to see Egan put on his coat.

"Ahhh, nae . . ." Egan said slowly. "I'm needin' some . . . air." The smell of grease nauseated him and he needed time to think. "I'll come back." He closed the door behind him.

The sun was warm and welcome after the storm. The wind had stilled. Dark clouds crowded the horizon but contented itself with drenching the west. Egan walked pensively down the road, his hands in his pockets. His mind was a clutter of questions that he had to sort through . . . alone.

It was dark when he returned.

"I was gettin' worried for you, Egan," Rory said. "Where've you been?"

"Walkin'. Get the bottle. We've got a lot of talkin' to do."

Candles burned well into the night as the two men sat solemnly at the table each turning a small glass of poteen in his hand.

"I still say t'was Dob Quinn led them here," Rory growled.

Egan sighed hopelessly. "Take another look at the footprints, for God's sake. There's none of them that small."

"You think it was a Constable's bunch then?" Rory asked, not quite sure of all that Egan had told him. "And you're sayin' that they came for me, not Kevin?"

Egan rubbed his eyes. "I'm not sure of any of it. Newcomb and his Proddy bunch are feared of leavin' Belfast, you know that. I don't think our traitor would have a rope like that one. Look at it. Only a Parliament-paid Constable or a some damned Ulster Lord would be havin' one as grand as that."

"And there was three of the bastards," Rory said, his hand moving thoughtfully over his freshly shaved chin. "They go nowhere alone."

"I'm thinkin' that they probably had a warrant, which is why Kevin would let them in without runnin' or blowin' their heads off."

"Aye . . ." Rory's eyes bored into Egan's. "What's to say they won't be back? We don't know if they got what they come for, especially if what they wanted was *me*."

"Or me. Or maybe they did want Kevin, though I can't see why. He wasn't a leader. He was a runner." Egan shook his head and drained the punch into his empty stomach. "As stupid as they are, they're not ignorant of the Brotherhood and what we mean to their rulin' of Ireland. Looks like they found, or was led to this house. For whatever reason, they pegged it for what it is. If Kevin gave us up before he died, they'll sure be back. If he didn't," he shrugged, "they might come back just to see what's goin' on now or they might think that what they did would scare off the divil himself." Egan's brows lifted. He refilled both glasses. "On the other hand, they might have left Kevin as a warnin' that they can do what they please and they're sayin', *'you're next'*."

Rory nodded. "What are we to be doin' then, Egan?"

"I don't know. That's all I'm sure of." Egan put his head in his hands, raked his fingers through his hair. "Jaysus, I wish Jimmy was here."

"Well, do you have any thoughts? Any ideas?"

"I'd like to call a meetin' of the lads but I doubt they'll come."

"They have to know what happened to Kevin. If we can't be findin' exactly who done this, we can make them all pay!"

Rory didn't wait for Egan's order. He threw on his coat and left the door open on his way out. The grapevine would be put in motion the next day.

At the appointed time, behind blanketed windows, Rory Kilcullen's little house bulged with angry Fenians. Avenging Kevin Burke was their top priority.

"And what the bloody hell did they think we'd do when we found what they'd done to one of our own?"

"They're pigs, the lot of them!"

"They deserve all we'll give them!"

"Blood'll run, I swear. And it won't be Fenian blood this time!"

"Aye!"

"Aye!"

Egan let them rave. Men who had laughed at Kevin and called him a simpleton only days before, today made him a hero. But what they spoke reflected his own bitterness, though he knew revenge, by itself, made a weak premise for striking at the heart of England.

Egan pulled a chair to one side of the room and stood on it. "You all know now what happened here," he began, his voice strained. He pointed at the red hand print. "We intend to be strikin' back where it'll hurt. I've decided to take the fight to Ulster."

The room buzzed with approval. "What's the plan, Egan?"

"I had thought of blowin' the walls out of the Constable's office in Drogheda, but they'd think we could do no more'n that. 'Tis time lads," he said softly, "that wee Queen Vic tasted her own tears. We can't impress her by killin' her soldiers so we'll be goin' after what'll make her bleed instead. We're goin' to put our mark on Prince Albert."

"What are you sayin', Egan?" Rory asked. "Auld Albert's dead these five years."

Egan smiled. "Aye. And auld Vic is still wearin' her mournin' black and buildin' him a clock tower to stand in the middle of Belfast. We're goin' to knock it down and paint Kevin's initials on every brick!"

"Aye! Aye! Aye!" The muffled cheers spread throughout the room.

Egan raised his hands for silence. "They'll know then we don't take lightly what they done to our brother, Kevin Burke!"

The room silenced at a light tapping on the door. All eyes turned toward Rory.

"Aye?" he said, watching Michael Davitt pull a pistol from his belt.

"Rory?" It was Keelin's voice.

Everyone breathed again.

"Look who I found on me way back," she said, entering with J.J. Corydon. "Why was the door locked? I didn't know there was a meetin' tonight."

Everyone reached to shake Corydon's hand while Rory took Keelin in the bedroom to tell her about Kevin.

"How could anyone do such a thing?" she asked tearfully.

Rory shook his head. He simply held her. "How are your folks?" he asked.

She nodded through her tears. "They're fine. They was glad to see me."

"Did they ask about me?" he asked, trying to cheer her.

Keelin lay her head against his shoulder and sobbed. "Hold me, Rory. I need you so."

Egan pulled Corydon aside and told him what had happened in the house before he came. He was shocked to hear about Kevin but he had news of his own.

"They've split up O'Leary and them," he said. "They did it long before we challanged Chester Castle but they let nobody know it. I've found a man who's in a place to give us all the information we want . . . for a price."

"Aye," came the knowing response.

"Who is this man?" Egan asked.

"I can't give that away," Corydon said. "He'll talk to nobody but me. You can't blame him for lookin' out for his own neck."

"And his own purse!"

"At our expense."

Corydon shrugged and found a chair to sit in. "That's it or nothin'." He released a miserable sigh and raised his eyes to Egan. "Tis your call. I didn't make the rules . . . he did."

"Is he a Brit?"

Corydon nodded.

"How will you know what he tells you is true?" Egan asked.

Corydon leaned forward, rested his forearms on his knees. "He's an auld man. He's lost two sons in Belfast. He wants England out of Ireland as much as we do. Our ace is the fact that he's got two more sons in the army and he don't want to lose either of them to an Irish bullet. He figures with the money we give for what he knows, he can bribe one of the commissioners to keep the boys he has left out of harm's way."

Egan nodded. "Tis up to you then," he said to the men. "We'll vote. It'll be whatever you decide. J.J. can't vote on his own idea. I only vote if there's a tie so talk about it now."

While the men considered, Corydon motioned Egan aside. "I'd not go blastin' about on the Albert Clock. Maybe what happened to Kevin, God rest him, can be used to our advantage. Whoever showed them this house and killed Kevin might be shown up for a fool or a traitor to them by us doin' nothin'. They expect us to take revenge. But if we don't . . ." He waited for Egan to figure it out on his own.

"They'll not trust him again, thinkin' that he led them into killin' an innocent man . . ." Egan rolled the thought over in his mind. "Aye. Tis good. Why not let them kill him for us."

Corydon smiled, nodded.

For the first time since he had sat by the fence in the Boggeragh Mountains with his father and the jug, Egan laughed. He told the men what he and Corydon had spoken of and what was decided. Not all were happy, but all agreed . . . for the moment.

After learning how much money the informant wanted and by when, the men voted and Corydon's idea was accepted by all but four votes.

"I'll go to Dublin and see about the money," Egan said, "and meet you back here in a month."

Corydon agreed. "That should give the auld man time to find out exactly where O'Leary and them are and what we can do about getting them out. When you get to the print shop for the money, you must say one thing: *TIR na nÓg.*"

When the men were gone, Rory pulled Keelin onto his lap. The house was quiet as a grave. The dog whined.

Keelin patted Padraig's head. "Givin' him such a noble name and him bein' orange." She turned her head back and forth slowly, clicked her tongue.

Rory smiled. "You'd rather he was green, I suppose."

Egan skimmed his hand over the dried blood on the wall.

"I want that left," Keelin said, watching him. "I don't want any of us forgettin'. Never."

"Aye," Rory said. "It'll stay." He pushed Keelin up and said to Egan. "We're goin' to bed. Will you be here in the mornin'?"

Egan nodded.

Alone in the light of a candle, Egan emptied the poteen jug. He lay down on the pallet, his head swimming and dreamt of Maire.

"Jaysus, Egan," Rory complained. "If you don't stop pacin', I'll have a floor with a bloody trench runnin' through it!"

Egan raised his hands to his head, covered his eyes. "Where's Keelin?"

"Outside, plantin' flowers round Kevin's grave. Why?"

Egan dropped his hands but didn't answer.

Rory tried another tack. "How's Maire? You did go to her, didn't you?"

"What?" Egan scowled, annoyed that Rory could be so removed from the heaviness of the last fortnight.

"Did you ask her to marry you?"

Egan turned, shoved the curtains aside to look out the window, hide his face and brush at the sudden flow of tears. "Aye."

"Well?" Rory asked. "Did you? Did she? Are you?"

"Did we, are we, what?"

"Married, you fool?"

"Aye," he answered, the corners of his mouth curving into a sudden dreamy satisfaction.

"So that's what's wrong with you. How many days did you have with her after . . . alone, I mean?"

"One night and half the next day."

"That's all? Jaysus, I'd be ready for the loonybin, too. Go on back. You'll never plow a field by turnin' it over in your mind, remember? If you have to, bring her here."

Egan faced him. "Aye. And we'll all share the same wee bed, I suppose." Rory gave him a puckish grin.

"You're too fae for me," Egan said. "I'm goin' for a walk. Come, Padraig."

A strong breeze blew Egan's hair and he smoothed it back. The sun rested on the hill to the west, its shimmering rim caught his eye as it sank slowly behind the darkening hills of County Meath. He picked up a stick and threw it. The dog retrieved it and dropped it back at Egan's feet. He threw it again. Padraig never seemed to tire of the game. "Tis all the same, isn't it, lad," Egan said quietly, turning the chewed stick over in his hand. "We're just like you, Padraig. We're chasin' after a stick called freedom that'll never be truly ours; in our lifetime anyway. And we'll carry their teeth marks in our hearts and on our skin forever." He threw the stick again and watched Padraig bound down the hill in the twilight. "Ahhh, God," he moaned. "This'll never be done with. They'll blame us and we'll blame them till we're off to killin' each other again."

He longed to feel Maire in his arms but could not wash Kevin Burke from his mind and now he had to go to Dublin for money to pay an informer that he'd never seen much less met. He sat alone in the moonlight, his head in his hands.

"Look at him, Rory," Keelin said, "sittin' up there, playin' with that silly dog. I don't know how he's keepin' his mind in order."

Rory moved up behind Keelin. He pulled her collar away and kissed the warm flesh of her neck.

She sucked in her breath as the heat of Rory's kiss rushed down her spine. "How can you be so thoughtless when your best friend is so tormented?"

"Thoughtless is it? Let me tell you, I was thinkin' all the time."

"Ahhh! You know what I mean!"

Rory looked past Keelin to the figure framed in moonlight. "He's too serious for his own good. Did you know that he and Maire married . . . like us?"

"They did?" Keelin took Rory's face in her hands and turned suddenly serious. "Well, tis all the more reason you shouldn't be blind to him. He's feelin' the weight of what Jimmy left to him. He feels the ruin of Ireland and he can do nothin' about it and now he's got a wife who knows nothin' about the Brotherhood. Tis up to you to back him up, take some of the weight off."

Rory pulled away. "I'm not blind, damnit! I'm just not goin' to be losin' me mind over it. Not even for Ireland! Don't you know yet, Keelin, we're free as we're ever goin' to be . . . with a few exceptions."

"Aye! Like them that rot in prison for doin' no more'n lovin' their own country! Like Kevin Burke who lies dead beside your own house! Like Jimmy Stephens who . . ."

"*Enough!*"

"Enough is it? I'll be tellin' you what's enough, Rory Kilcullen! Enough is not a drop of Orange in Ireland! Tis Home Rule! Tis makin' our own laws without interference from any other king, queen or country in the world. Tis Ireland for the Irish with not one British boot on it. That's what's enough!" Keelin's eyes flashed with a light that Rory had rarely seen. "Why is it you stay in here with me when he needs you so much out there?"

Rory didn't answer. Angrily, he grabbed his coat and the door slammed behind him.

Keelin gazed out the window and smiled. The two men she loved most, besides her own dear father, sat side by side talking about the things that mattered. She arranged the table then readied herself for bed.

When the two men came back into the house they found two chairs at the table, a fresh jug of poteen and two glasses.

Rory sat and reached for the jug. "She wants us to talk."

"Drink is more like it," Egan said, shedding his pullover.

"Ahhh. She thinks we don't understand each other at all."

Egan raised his brows and his glass. "To Keelin," he said.

"You're sayin' she's right, then?"

Egan smiled.

"If you're thinkin' I don't know what you're goin' through, Egan, you couldn't be more wrong. I feel it too. I just don't let it suck me dry. I take things as they come and I don't worry about them when they're done."

"It looks to me like you're playin' some joke, Rory, and you only get angry when nobody laughs."

Rory leaned both arms on the table. "It is a joke, Egan. But the British are the only ones laughin'. They've got us by the short hairs here. Even some of our own are turnin' us in. Look at Maire Martin's father. He thinks you're a houligan of the first order and that the Fenians smell of Irish blood. If he knew for sure who you are, he'd have you swingin' over Kilmainham's front door by your thick neck, tomorrow, with you're wife lookin' on! We're locked between us and them and they're both unbeatable. Tis all a joke, Egan, can't you see that?"

"They're not unbeatable, Rory. Not if we keep at them. We'll wear them down if it takes forever."

Rory poured more poteen. "That's what it'll take all right, for bloody ever."

"Aye," Egan sighed and slumped back in his chair.

Surprise and fascination spread over Rory's face. "You think so, too?"

Egan nodded. "I do."

"What the hell are we doin' riskin' our lives tryin' to blow up castles or clock towers then? Why aren't we settled in makin' love to our wives and raisin' babies, gettin' drunk at the pub on Fridays?"

"I don't know," Egan murmured, "but I'd best be findin' out before I catch an English bullet in me back. What I do know is that Jimmy Stephens left this in me lap with no plan to follow and I'm damned tired of tryin' to figure it out for meself. All I want to do is get O'Leary and them out of prison, then they can have it or give it away. I want to go to Maire and put a ring on her finger, take her back to the Boggeraghs and live like a human bein' . . ." He gulped the whiskey. "I'm tired, Rory and I have to go to Dublin and convince them bastards who raise the money to give me five-hundred-pounds to give to Corydon to pay a man I never met on the say-so of someone who . . . Ahhh, never mind." He laid his head on his folded arms and closed his eyes.

Rory stood and finished his drink. "Go to Maire tomorrow. Stay as long as you like. Me and Keelin'll go to Dublin. You know Keelin; give her the chance and she'll make you believe that rain's just the drippin's of a cherry tart. They'll be beggin' to give her the quid."

Rory grabbed a folded quilt from beside the fireplace and placed it around Egan's shoulders before he went into the bedroom, dropped his clothes and slid in beside Keelin. His hands found the softness he wanted and he pulled her into his arms. In her sleep, Keelin wrapped a leg over him, her fingers spread through the hair on his chest.

In the morning they found a note from Egan. *"Gone to Maire",* was all it said.

Egan stopped for the night in the shelter of the barn he had stayed in many times before on his way to and from the Martin farm. Padraig stretched out beside him in the hay. Egan was thankful for the warmth of the big red Setter. He was more than tired. It should have been easy to sleep but it wasn't. Familiar faces floated behind his eyes, one becoming another as he tried without success to wipe them away. Kevin Burke's curly hair and wide smile paled, overlaid by the rotting remains tied in the chair. Dob Quinn's leathery leprechaun features sprang to life in an impish grin that spread over his face like a wave over still water. Rory and Keelin appeared together like circling gulls. Their worry shown clearly. They whispered. He couldn't hear. The faces of O'Leary, Luby and Kickham flashed thin, weary, waiting. And Maire . . . beautiful, copper-haired Maire. Her creamy face turned up to him, her pink lips eager for his kiss.

Tomorrow.

Padraig yipped in deep sleep. Egan was tossed by the restless dream. He couldn't stop marching around Richmond prison. He was like Joshua at Jericho, and when the prison walls ruptured more than O'Leary,

Luby and Kickham tumbled out. There were fifties, hundreds, thousands of Irish men and women who spilled from the splitting sides.

A shaft of sunlight inched over Egan's eyes and he awakened to the sound of milk squirting into a wooden bucket. Padraig licked his face. Egan hushed him. He had neglected once again to ask permission from the family who owned the barn, but he had never slept this long before. Quietly, he lay back waiting for the sound to stop.

The barn door creaked and closed. Egan and Padraig edged toward freedom. They would have to make a run for it. Egan peered out the door. An old woman struggled under the weight of the milk pail. White hair shone above the scarf that had slipped from her head to her shoulders. Egan stopped. She was much like his ma . . . older.

"Top of the mornin', Mother," he said cheerfully. "Can I be of help to you?"

The old woman nodded, unsurprised. "I was wonderin' when you'd be wakin' up, lad. This bucket gets heavier as I get aulder." She smiled at him. The whistle in her speech breezed through the spaces left by missing teeth. "Bring the milk and your dog. I'd wager he's hungry, same as you." She stepped carefully over the threshold of the dark, thatched cottage.

"You . . . you knew I was in your byre?" he asked, embarrassed.

"Aye," she answered, rummaging through the small pantry. "'Tis not your first time in me byre neither . . . nor the dog. You used to come alone, though."

Egan watched her slice ham and take a round loaf of soda bread from the oven. She dropped the knife, groped around the floor for it.

"Can I help?"

"Nae. I been helpin' meself for on to seventy years."

"How long have you been blind?"

"Ahhh!" She shook her head. "Can't remember. Eyes don't mean so much." She raised her face and smiled again. "So long as you don't go changin' things round."

"Me name's Matty Burke," she said. "I don't want you leavin' till I know yours."

The name leaped out at Egan, leaving him chilled. "Egan," he said, "Egan O'Shea, from the Boggeragh mountains in Cork."

"I hear that's a long ways away from here," she said to the clang of pans.

"Aye, Misses. Tis far."

"Is that where your goin' lad?"

"Not today. I'm goin' to see me wife, Maire. I miss her terrible."

"And why is she not with you?"

"She's a captive, so to speak. She still lives with her family until I can take her with me."

"Ahhh," Matty said with a nod. "She's young then."

Egan could hardly grasp the old woman's perception. "Aye," he said softly.

Matty nodded and placed a plate of eggs, ham and thickly buttered soda bread on the table before him. "Eat now," she said and dropped ham scraps to the floor for Padraig.

Egan stayed longer than he had planned as he listened to Matty Burke talk of her grandson, Kevin, and how Egan reminded her of him. "Comes when he can," she said with a round shouldered shrug. "Twas only a short time ago he was by. He couldn't stay, though."

She shuffled about her own work while Egan fixed buckets, chairs, the doors, anything he could see needing repair.

"He's a Fenian, you know," she went on. "Ahhh, the lad makes me proud, fightin' for Ireland the way he does. Showed me the wound on his arm. It'll make a fine scar."

Egan wiped his sweating forehead. "Aye, Misses," he said and twisted the wire tighter around the worn strips of wood that made the old bucket waterproof again. "Now you have two pails." He placed it on the table in front of her.

She found the knotted wire, felt it. "I'm thankin' you, lad. You done good things for me. I'll be sayin' an *Ave* for you, sure."

She was quiet for a time and Egan saw a question form on her wrinkled face. "You're a Fenian, too, aren't you, lad . . ."

Before Egan could answer Matty continued.

"If you see me Kevin, tell him to come and stay longer next time. A body gets lonely. Tis bad I miss him. I've been alone these many years and he's the only son of me only son who's now gone from a British bullet."

She drew a resigned breath. "Ahhh! Tis the ravin's of an auld woman. You're wantin' to be off, so take your dog and go. Just be comin' back now and again."

"Aye, Mrs. Burke. I'll be back." He leaned over and gently hugged the rounded shoulders, called Padraig and left before his heart broke.

"But Ma," Maire pleaded. "You don't understand. I can't marry Luke. He's a nice lad, but . . ."

Peg lifted the basket of eggs with her right hand and placed her left hand on Maire's shoulder as they walked to the barn. A light wind stirred the budding trees. "Oh, I understand all right, love. I know what it's like to think that you're in love."

"Think? Ma, I knew you'd not understand." Maire walked ahead of her mother into the barn's dark interior. She hoisted forkfuls of hay into the stalls. Hollow pods floated about her hair, settled around her shoulders.

"Sit down, Maire," Peg said. "Tis time we had another talk."

Maire turned at the tautness of her mother's voice and followed her to the milk bench.

"Aye, Ma. Are you all right?"

Peg nodded and smiled. She patted Maire's hand. "I love your father," she began.

"I know," Maire agreed. "That's plain enough to see, though sometimes I wonder how you . . . Never mind."

"Good." Peg took a deep breath. "But there was a man before him; a man who was strong and handsome. He worked in Dublin and sometimes in England. He was a builder." Peg looked at the surprise on Maire's face. "Oh, don't be so shocked. I wasn't born married to your da, you know."

"I . . . I'm sorry, Ma. I just didn't think . . ."

Peg smiled. "Course you didn't. You had no reason to." She gazed dreamily into the square of light that intruded through the door. "His name was Conor O'Gill. And I did love him. I was your age . . . older than a girl and not quite a woman. And Conor loved me. Against my father's wishes, I would sneak from the house to meet him."

"Ma! Not you!"

"Aye, that I would. I loved Conor more that I feared your Grandfar's lash, you see; and, the time's I shared with Conor was full of laughter and plans and all the things that young girls love. Lots of teasin'; lots of hopin'; lots of kisses . . ." She smiled warmly. "Lots of . . . things. We was always afraid of bein' caught but that only made it sweeter. And then one day . . . one day . . ." Peg's voice trailed away. She turned her head, cleared her throat.

"Aye. Go on, Ma," Maire urged, worry edging her voice.

"One day . . . he wanted more and told me so," Peg squirmed, a bit nervously. "And I was frightened, I can be tellin' you that. But when he looked at me . . . I knew it was no use. I loved him, you see."

"And . . . did you . . . ?" Maire's eyes became round with wonder, "give him more?"

Peg pressed her lips tightly. She looked into the green eyes of her daughter. "Aye," she said in a tone so soft she hardly heard it herself.

Maire slumped back against the wall as if she'd been slapped.

"Don't go to takin' it so hard, Maire, girl. He was a lovin' man and he had more to do with you than you know."

"What could a man like that . . . One who would take advantage of me own ma!"

"Now who is it who can't understand?"

"Tis different!"

"Really?" Peg asked.

"Aye. It is . . ."

"You mean tis different because we're not talkin' about you?"

Maire shifted uncomfortably and turned on her mother. "Who would have thought that me own ma would . . . would . . ."

"Would what? Love a man enough to lie with him?"

Maire turned her face away. "Oh, Ma, that's disgustin'!"

"Sure and you don't mean that, Maire. If it's so disgustin', why do I feel a wee bit of forgiveness seepin' through your burnin' cheeks?"

Maire straightened and sighed. Unexpected tears flooded her eyes. "Because . . . because . . ." The tears fell in silent, shining streams. How could she tell her mother about Egan? She couldn't . . . not yet.

It had only been a month since he'd gone and he'd been so definite about keeping their marriage a secret.

Peg's arms closed around Maire. The girl's tears moistened her mother's breast while Peg choked her own tears back. This was harder to tell than she'd thought.

Maire pulled slowly out of Peg's embrace, sniffing and wiping her face on her apron. "I'm so sorry, Ma . . . I just didn't. . ."

"Tis all right, darlin'," Peg said, pushing the coppery hair from Maire's face. "Tis all right."

"So what does this . . . Mr. O'Gill have to do with me?" Maire sniffled, settling herself against her mother's side.

"Everythin'. You see, when I met and married your da . . . you was already here."

"How could that be?"

"Well, you see, Conor and I was goin' to be married and then one day a friend from his work came and told me that he'd fallen from a great height . . . and died." Peg sighed sadly. "You were already on the way and . . ."

Maire pulled sharply away as the truth hammered home. "Then, Daddy isn't . . . he isn't . . ."

"Ahhh, Maire. He's your da. Any mindless fool can father a child, but it takes a man who loves and cares to be a daddy. And Kean Martin is all of that. Never once has he mentioned that you weren't his own flesh and blood. He took us in and cared for us when we was shunned by others. He's a good and wonderful man, Maire, and he loves you. That's why he want's you to marry Luke MacSweeny. You'll be well off some day. You'll not have any of that with the O'Shea lad. Your daddy's sure that he's part of the Fenian Brotherhood. Those men are not allowed to have a wife, darlin'. They're tryin' to win a hard war with precious few victories, but he's chaff in the wind. You'll not be knowin' where he is or what he's doin . . . or who he's doin' it with.

"Now, when Luke and his father come this evenin', I want you to be civil. I want you to listen to your da. Often times I've wondered what kind of life we'd have had if Conor had lived, but I know that I'm happy with your da."

Maire nodded. She had forgotten about Luke's coming this evening. How could she face him, pretending to be his intended, when she was already Egan's wife? Her mind reeled under the weight of what her mother had just told her. Would she be able to mask the lie? She had to pull herself together, meet Luke and his father with a smile and a pleasant "how-do-you-do", and pray that Egan would arrive soon with a ring for her finger.

"Maire?" Her mother's voice intruded.

"Aye, Ma?"

"Are you all right, darlin'? I wouldn't have told you if I thought you couldn't manage." Peg was suddenly worried by Maire's silence.

Maire took Peg's hand in reassurance. "I'd like to be alone for a while if you don't mind."

Peg kissed Maire's forehead. "I don't mind. I know it must be hard but, I don't want you to be makin' the same mistake I did."

Maire nodded vaguely. Mistake. Mistake. What mistake? Conor O'Gill? Was he the mistake? If he was a mistake then, was she too a mistake? She walked out of the barn and down the hill through the oaks and boulders to the place she'd married Egan. The clouds in the west became heavier and darker then a light mist fell. It hadn't been a proper winter at all and it seemed she wasn't a proper person either. She found herself laughing and weeping bitterly. Who was she? Was she Maire Martin? Maire O'Gill? Or was she simply Maire, the bastard daughter of Peg Martin and a dead man?

"Ahhh, God!" she cried to the heavens and fell to her knees. She wept until her head ached. It was as if she walked the hills sound asleep, for until she felt the cold raindrops washing her face, neither time, nor place nor family had meant anything. Shocked, confused for a moment, she stood twisting her apron, feeling the rain.

"Damn!" she scolded herself. "*Luke!*"

Grasping her skirt in both hands she lifted it above her knees and ran. What could they be thinking, her being gone so long?

"Damn!"

Gasping for breath, she approached the house. The MacSweeny wagon stood in the drizzle. Maire stopped to push the hair from her eyes then walked briskly through the door and bounded up the ladder into her loft bedroom, ignoring the jarred looks from her family and guests.

Shivering, she stripped her wet clothing off and stepped over them to pull on a dry skirt over her damp bloomers. The comb flew through her hair and with a knowing twist, pinned a knot to the top of her head and held it while combing the rest of her wet hair down her back.

She pinched her cheeks and smoothed her eyebrows, took a deep breath, checked her blouse buttons and descended the ladder. Disappointing her mother and father tonight would be wrong, no matter what.

"I know I'm late. Please be acceptin' me apologies, Mr. MacSweeny," she said pleasantly, extending her hand to the older man.

"No apologies needed, Miss Martin," he smiled. "Though we was worried and you did come in lookin' like a drowned rat."

Nervous laughter pulsed around her.

For a moment Maire counted the cracks in the floor. "Aye, I did that," she smiled timidly and lifted her gaze to her mother. "I'm all right, Ma," she said in a near whisper.

"I know you are, darlin'."

Kean cleared his throat. "Would you two care to be lettin' us in on what you're talkin' about?"

Peg turned to her husband and smiled broadly. "Nae. Tis between mother and daughter." she said and moved to the stove where water boiled for tea.

Luke's silent admiration of Maire was unmistakable and his blue eyes followed her every move.

Kean instructed Bobby to light another lantern as the day waned. Then the boy took a place in the window seat beside Kate.

The talk soon turned to the forthcoming wedding. Maire's heart pounded as the date was set. She felt Luke's warm hand on her shoulder and she turned to see his bright, handsome smile gazing down at her.

"You've been quiet tonight, Maire," Luke said. "Are you not happy with the date? Would you like it sooner?"

Maire nearly gasped. "Oh, nae! The date's fine. Just . . . fine."

The talk and laughter continued, though Maire heard none of it. Ahhh, God! she thought. What was she to do if Egan couldn't claim her before then? Her brain swam. Noise from the men's voices buffeted her. She heard something about the MacSweeny's staying the night in the byre and Kean saying they'd stay in the house, that he and Peg would give them they're bed and they'd sleep in the byre.

Maire stood. "Ma?" she cried weakly and sank to the floor.

She felt cold, wet rags on her forehead and heard muddled sounds swimming over her. She was in someone's arms and then she was in the dark. "Ma?"

"Aye, love. I'm here. You've had a busy day, I'd be sayin'. What with our talk in the byre and no supper. Then comin' in all wet and the weddin' and all."

"Where am I?"

"On me bed. Daddy brought you in."

"Ahhh, God, Ma. I'm sorry." Her hands flew to cover her eyes.

"Are you goin' to be sick?"

Maire shook her head. "I'm all right, truly."

"You poor child." Peg's cool hand moved over Maire's forehead. "Your hair's still wet, girl." She removed the hairpins. "Kean," she called, "bring some broth."

A moment later Kean entered and handed the warm cup to Peg. "What happened? Is she sick?" The worry in his voice pierced Maire's heart and she began to cry.

"Nae, Daddy," she wept, clutching his hand, pulling him down beside her. "I'm fine, really."

Kean's big arms slid around her. He drew her up and rocked her, the whiskers on his face pressing into her cheek as Egan's had done. Her arms wound around his neck and she cried, not knowing exactly why.

Peg stood in her bedroom, hands on her hips, her head tilted to one side as she studied the blue and white linen dress Maire wore.

"Ahhh, darlin' tis lovely. You make that dress come to life. Now if only you would do the same."

Maire flounced down from the stool and dropped onto the bed, the wedding dress billowing around her. "I'm not sure I want to be goin' through with this, Ma. Luke's a fine boy but . . ."

"But what? Is it still the O'Shea lad?"

Maire nodded. She couldn't look at her mother so she stared out the window at the rain.

"Tis just *the willies*, love. Every bride gets them. Tis fear of losin' somethin' you never had. It'll go away after the weddin'." Peg stuck the needle into her apron bib. Her voice was sure and firm as she pulled Maire to her feet and helped her back onto the stool.

Maire turned slowly feeling not unlike a sacrificed lamb as her mother stitched the wide hem. She shuddered inwardly looking at her naked finger. Somethin' I never had, indeed, she thought. Ahhh, God, please bring Egan back with a ring for me! Tis been so long since I seen him. I'll say me prayers every night and do seven, nae, twenty-one Hail Maire's everyday, Lord. I'll be a good wife, I promise. I'll wash and scrub and cook and I'll not complain. What about Daddy? He'll disown me, sure. Ahhh, don't let that happen while You're fixin' up the other. I'll do as many Hail Maire's as You like only . . .

"Maire!" Peg called louder, jerking on the hem. "You're not listenin'. Pick up your feet girl. Turn! Turn!"

Maire jumped as if her mother had heard her thoughts. "Aye, Ma. I'm turnin'."

Everyday had been the same since Luke left. The dress took up all their time and Kean was happy to spread Maire's chores between himself and Bobby while she was busy with her mother. He hummed all day long. Saints above! Maire thought, he's drivin' me bats!

The next afternoon the humming stopped long enough for Kean to announce: "Maire, darlin'! Come, look who's here!"

Peg hung the dress in her bedroom and pulled the closet curtain closed. "Go on girl. Didn't you hear your da?"

Maire walked outside to see Luke leading his horse to the barn.

"Hello, Luke," she called coolly.

"Is that all I get?" Luke asked as he pulled the saddle from the gelding's sweating back and hanging up the bridle. Walking to her, he placed his arm around her shoulder.

"You two must have lots to be talkin' over," Kean said, waving them away. "I know you don't have a lot of time, Luke so . . ."

"I'm thankin' you, Mr. Martin."

Kean nodded and went into the house. The door closed on Peg's impatient voice and Kean telling her that Maire would be back soon.

"You're busy then," Luke said, his arm tightening around her.

"Aye. The weddin' dress. Would you like to see it?"

"Why don't you surprise me?"

"That's silly. If you don't like the dress now it'll be a wee bit late to go changin' what's done when we're at the church in Dublin, don't you think?"

"I'm sure I'll like it. But if you want me to see it, then, I will . . . when it's finished."

"'Tis nearly done now. There's only the buttons and loops left."

"Let's go under the tree. I just rode the last two hours in this drizzle." He headed for the oak over the lip of the hill.

Maire stopped. The thought of sitting under Egan's tree with Luke was somehow the same as betraying him. "Wouldn't you rather go into the house?"

"Nae. Is somthin' wrong?"

She looked up into Luke's soft eyes, unable to hide her distress. "Nae. Nothin's wrong," she lied nervously. "I just don't want to go all that way. The byre's warm and we can talk there." Smiling, she tugged at his arm.

Luke's eyes veered from Maire to the barn. He tried to read her intentions but it was, as usual, useless.

"Now isn't this better?" she asked with some relief.

Weak shafts of light lanced through the few cracks and the open doors offered little in the way of light.

Luke backed her against the wall, pinning her with his arms. "And why did you want to come in here, Maire?" he whispered.

She shrugged. "Da said you wanted to talk. 'Tis dry in here." Her voice was so low she hardly heard it herself.

"Kiss me, Maire," Luke said, bending toward her trembling lips.

She turned her head, dipped under his arm and walked away. "I don't think we should be doin' that, now that we . . . we're to be ma . . . married, do you?"

"Aye. I do." He walked toward her, smiling.

She shivered as he neared. Nothing in her would obey. She didn't know if what she felt was fear or desire or something worse. He was too tall, too handsome, too much in love with her. Her heart danced in her chest. She hated herself for allowing him to touch her and even more, she hated that when he kissed her, she kissed him back.

"Ahhh, Maire," he murmured against her temple. "I do love you dearly. I'd marry you today if I could. When I feel you next to me, all I want is to have you for me own."

He sounded so much like Egan she struggled to separate the two. His words slurred through her mind, leaving her weak and confused. Was she really married to Egan or was . . . Of course she was. She'd given herself to him, hadn't she? She couldn't have two men. Ahhh, God! she thought panic-stricken, what kind of woman am I?

Suddenly Luke swung her up into his arms and carried her deeper into the barn, deeper into the darkness.

"What are you doin', Luke?" She could feel the pounding of his heart against her side and the warmth of his lips on her throat.

He placed her gently on the hay in the far stall. The sweet, spicy scent of dried clover hovered around them. Dim light slanted across Maire's face and he looked down at her, his eyes glazed as if drunk. Slowly, he lowered his head and his mouth brushed hers. He drew back and watched her tongue roll over her lips as if she were tasting his kiss. His body ached for her. His sense of right ebbed as his eyes followed his hand down the roundness of her hip.

She felt his need, but what shamed her was her own desire.

His warm hand slipped over her blouse to the buttons. One by one they opened and her breasts burst free. His mouth touched the white flesh, jolting her. She didn't stop him and her body longed for more. All at once she was crying uncontrollably. Shocked, he drew back and pulled her up into his arms. "Ahhh, Maire, love, I'm sorry. Forgive me. I didn't mean to be doin' that. I just . . ."

His misery was unmistakable and she wasn't sure she didn't enjoy it. Pushing out of his arms, she sat back and brushed the tears from her cheeks, the bars of light playing across her breasts. "Would you be buttonin' me up now, Luke . . . please?"

He fumbled with the buttons and loops as he tried vainly not to touch the flawless skin beneath his fingers. How could he be so unthinking; taking advantage of this pure girl. Ahhh, but she was so . . . so perfect . . .

Maire tingled from his touch but she gritted her teeth to make sure he never knew it. Still she was disappointed when the last button fit through the loop and his hands dropped away.

Silently she pulled the hay from her hair and clothing.

"Let me do that," he said softly as if it were penance.

She nodded, sniffing for effect, touching her hand lightly to her mouth to hide the smile that pestered its corners. Her eyes were glassy with tears conjured up as if by magic and she stared into his saddened face.

Why am I doin' this? she asked herself, appalled by her own actions. This isn't what I want . . . is it? Use things, love people. Wasn't that the way it went? Confusion. Her life had turned into a tangle of confusion. Why can't Luke be a friend, she thought. Someone to talk to. Someone to confide in.

She leaned against his shoulder, her hands lying limply in her lap. "Be me friend, Luke," she whispered helplessly. "Please, just be me friend . . . for now." Her eyes filled with genuine tears.

"I'm your friend, Maire," he said, his lips moving in the coppery waves of her hair. "I'll be your friend, darlin', for always."

No you won't, she thought. Not for always. The bitterness of it rushed through her like a storm releasing itself in uncontrived sobs.

Afraid that someone would hear, Luke raised her chin, his hands holding her face tenderly as he pressed his lips to hers. Her arms went around his neck and she returned his kiss with every ounce of energy left in her.

They fell back on the hay. Luke felt her hand moving slowly up his inner thigh and he moved to accommodate her.

Terrified, she continued, unable to pull away, more from curiosity than anything else. Feeling the mound beneath his trousers, she slipped her hand behind his belt, down into the warm secrecy between the fabric and his flat, hard stomach. There it was. Would he be like Egan or different? Who would know? Who would tell? Gently, she squeezed.

"Maire? If you're in here, Ma wants you now!" Bobby's voice rang through the barn like a scream from the Banshee.

Maire yanked free. For a moment she stared with disbelieving eyes at her hand and then at Luke. She rose unsteadily to her feet. "Ahhh, God, Luke, what was we doin'?" Her eyes were wide with fright as she turned and ran.

Luke sat there for a time, stunned that she would do what she'd done and then run from him.

Maire burst through the door of the house, breathless.

Peg caught the befuddled girl in her arms. "Maire! What happened? Where's Luke?"

"I . . . I don't want to see him, Ma. Not for a while. Please?"

Peg took her by the shoulders and gently shook the fright from her face. "What did he do to you?"

Maire's gaze steadied. "Nothin', Ma. He didn't do anythin'." She bowed her head and tears of confusion spilled from her eyes in wide, lazy streams. "'Twas me, Ma," she sobbed, reaching for the comfort and security her mother always offered.

Peg held her. "What do you mean, it was you, darlin'?"

"I did a horrible thing, Ma," she wept.

Peg lifted Maire's chin and looked into her daughter's teary, green eyes. "I want you to be tellin' me what you did that was so horrible. I mean you didn't cripple him or anything . . ."

Maire shook her head. "I don't think so."

"Well, then?"

The girl turned out of her mother's grasp and flopped into a chair. "I . . . Ahhh, Ma! I can't tell you. I mean tis not . . ."

Peg's eyes bored into Maire's. "Not what?"

"'Tis not . . . fittin' . . ."

"Well," Peg sighed. "I can't be helpin' you or Luke if you don't talk to me. Now what is it?"

Maire swallowed. "I . . . I touched him." Her voice thinned to a choked whisper.

"Ahhh," Peg said vaguely. "And just where did you touch him?"

"In the byre, Ma!" Maire said incredulously.

Peg shook her head. "I mean . . . It don't matter. I have the picture and I'm not likin' it. I'll have to be sendin' Bobby with you two after this. I don't think your chastity is goin' to be safe till after the weddin'."

Maire burst into a fresh round of tears and slumped at the table. This damned wedding was ruining her life! She was Mrs. Egan O'Shea and that's the way she wanted it. The rest could go to the bloody divil with her blessings. Twas all pretending anyway. She sat up, determined to tell her mother everything. "Ma, I need to be tellin' you somethin'," she sniffed. "Tis important. Will you hear without yellin' at me, now?"

"I'm listening, girl," Peg said, picking up her needle again.

Maire sat up straight, her hands folded tightly on the table as if in prayer. "Tis about Egan O'Shea. You see, he came back a while ago and I met him . . ."

The door opened and Kean entered with Luke. The words in Maire's mouth stuck to her tongue. Her first inclination was to climb the ladder to the loft, but she sat rigid, hardly able to breathe. She could feel Luke's warm gaze and a chill pulsed through her.

"Luke tells me that you two had a good talk in the byre about the weddin'," Kean said smiling. Then he looked closer at Maire's face. "What's wrong with you, girl? You're not goin' to be sick again, are you?"

"Nae, Daddy," she said quickly, rubbing her cheeks.

Peg glanced at the two young people. At first she smiled to herself, remembering, then her smile faded as Maire's words concerning O'Shea finally sank in. I'll talk to her later, she thought. Right now she needs to be with Luke.

"Luke has to be leavin'," Kean announced. "You'd best be sayin' your good-byes."

Maire sent a distressed look at Peg who ignored her and smiled at the quiet, handsome young man. "Good-bye, Luke," she said, turning back to her work. "Give our best to your father and brother."

"Ma?"

"Do as your da told you, girl."

Maire shoved the chair back under the table so hard it rocked. She grabbed her shawl and stamped outside. Damn! she thought. I should have kept me mouth shut for all the good it did me in there! "Come on, Luke!" she demanded, striding toward his horse. "I suppose you'll want him watered before you go." She jerked the reins and led the patient gelding to the watering trough.

Thoughts darted through his mind as he watched her. God! What a girl this is! Am I ever goin' to be makin' any sense of her?

Leading the animal back, she kept her eyes trained on the ground and handed the reins to him. "Good-bye, Luke," she said sharply and turned to leave.

He caught her arm, pulled her back. "Why are you angry, Maire?"

"Because . . . because what happened, never should have, that's why. I asked you to be me friend, not . . . not . . ." She glared at his hand on her arm. "Let go of me."

"Will you stay for a minute?"

"Nae!"

His grip tightened. "Then I'll hold on."

"All right, damnit. I'll stay."

"I don't understand, Maire. What's wrong? Why have you changed?"

"What's wrong? You silly fool, I put me hand . . ."

"I know where you put your hand, Maire," he interrupted quietly, quickly glancing around. "I want to know why you ran away?"

His eyes were overwhelming her again. She bit her lip to keep her senses. "Ma . . . She wanted me. Bobby said so."

"Then you're not afraid of me?"

Her hands went to her hips. "Afraid of you?" she snapped. "I'd sooner be scared of a mouse in the thatch!"

"Good."

"But," she said with some hesitation, "I don't want you doin' what you did to me in the byre any more."

"What I did? For God's own sake, Maire! What would have happened if Bobby hadn't . . ."

"Don't you go twistin' things, Luke MacSweeny!"

Luke's intense gaze softened and he put his arms around her waist, drawing her close. "What do you like, Maire Martin?"

"I don't like anythin'," she grumbled, pushing at his solid grip.

"So," he said with a twitching smile, his arms locked around her. "You're not afraid of me but you don't like anythin'."

"That's not what I said . . . is it?"

"Aye," he nodded.

"Well, you know what I mean." Her heart pounded again at his nearness. "Don't you think tis time you went . . . home?" she asked timidly. "It will soon be dark and you'll be late. Your da will go to worryin' . . ." Her words were chosen wisely but she couldn't seem to catch her breath.

Luke's smile faded as his hold on her tightened. "I can feel your heart," he murmured. "Tis beatin' for me. You're wantin' me just like I'm wantin' you . . . and don't say different."

She tried to pull away. "Don't be silly," she said, her fingers moving slowly up his arms. "I want you to be . . . goin' . . . home . . ."

"Wherever you are is home, Maire." His eyes wandered desperately over her face, settled on her mouth.

"Ahhh, damn, Luke. I don't want to be doin' this," she said, giving in. Her fingers finally met behind his neck and she allowed herself to enjoy his kisses.

"When I come back, Maire, will you be touchin' me again?"

She smiled at him, her eyes closed. "Ma said she's goin' to be sendin' Bobby with us from now on."

"We'll just have to play hide and seek then, won't we?"

"Aye . . . aye," she whispered, kissing him again.

Maire watched Luke step into the stirrup and mount the horse. He bent, touched her hair and kicked the gelding to a gallop.

That night in her room, sleep shunned her as if it knew what she'd done. The tree scraped at the side of the house as if to scold her. She tossed fretfully, finally sat up.

What was she to do about Luke? Though she'd tried to put him off, it only seemed to encourage him. And his kisses . . . What was she to do when he kissed her? His lips were warm, soft, eager and the need she felt from them was more than she could discourage. In fact, she *loved* them. She dreamt about them and all the colors that exploded around her when she felt them. What's to become of you, girl, she thought with a sigh. Like it or not there's two men in your life, Maire Martin or Maire O'Gill or whoever you are! There's one that you have and one that you want and it'll take God Almighty, Himself to sort it through. This would be a long night . . . a long, *long* night.

Egan watched the farm from beneath the old, wide spreading oak. A tantalizing aroma wafted down the hill from the house and his stomach growled. He searched for Maire's father but he didn't seem to be around, and that was good. "Ahhh, damnit!" he whispered to the red Setter sprawled at his feet, "I forgot to get a bloody ring!"

With no evidence of Kean Martin about, Egan wiped the mud from his shoes on the damp leaves and shook out his coat and cap. Glancing over his shoulder at the house, he spat in his palms and smoothed his hair back, replaced his cap and strode to the door, Padraig at his heel.

"Good day to you, Mrs. Martin," he said, tipping his cap when she opened the door. Her surprise didn't go unnoticed and Egan smiled. "And to you . . . love." His words were soft, caressing as his gaze fell on Maire.

Maire found no voice to answer. She stood trembling, the wedding gown clutched in her hands.

Egan turned again to Peg. "And where might Mr. Martin be?"

"In Dublin," she said haltingly. "What is it that you want?"

Egan's eyes met Maire's and for a knowing moment he touched her entire body from where he stood until, embarrassed, her gaze dropped away and she lifted the gown to cover her cheeks.

"I . . . ah, I was hopin' your husband would be here. I have some business I was wantin' to discuss with him."

Peg managed a weak smile. She wadded her apron front. Her eyes darted uncomfortably from one of the young people to the other. Surely, he didn't mean to ask Kean for Maire's hand. "Here I am, forgettin' me manners," she reprimanded herself. "I just cooled a tart. Would you care for some and tea?"

Egan's eyes touched Maire again. "Aye, Misses, I would." His fingers skimmed Maire's arm as he followed Peg to the table.

She poured one cup of tea and cut a slice of apple tart, placing it in front of him. "What kind of business did you have in mind, Mr. O'Shea?" she asked slowly, her voice full of suspicion for, what she knew of this young man, he was not what he seemed.

"Are you not joinin' me?" Egan asked, filling his fork.

"Nae," Peg replied. "'Tis too close to our supper time."

"Does Maire cook as good as you do, Mrs. Martin?" His gaze left his fork and darted between the two women.

"I suppose she does. Why?"

"'Tis nice to have the girl you love bein' a good cook too, that's all," he said and took another mouthfull.

Maire leaned weakly against the wall and waited for what kind of explosion would come next. Her hands blended into the paleness of the dress as her color drained. Was he going to tell after all?

Peg looked from Maire to Egan. "There's to be a weddin' soon, Mr. O'Shea. Maire's goin' to be the bride of Mr. Luke MacSweeny from Dublin . . . not you." Peg's voice was controlled and smooth. "I'll not have you turnin' her head now."

Maire raised her eyes to the ceiling. Her breaths were short, shallow gasps. Unknowingly, she crossed herself again and again while praying she wouldn't faint.

"I know that Mrs. Martin," Egan said, calmly wiping the corners of his mouth with his fingers.

Maire's attention dropped back to earth.

"She's told me that. But just because there's a weddin' comin', it don't change the love I have for her. Nothin' could be doin' that."

Peg softened. "I wouldn't be countin' you much of a man if it could," she said. "But I won't have you tryin' to change her mind."

"I won't be doin' that. I doubt I could be changin' anythin'."

Maire gasped, threw the gown to the floor and ran from the house.

"Maire!" Peg shouted after her.

"I'll stop her!" Egan grabbed his cap and raced after Maire, capturing her in the gully, down the hill, beyond the oak.

"Aye."

"At the trial . . ."

"At the trial."

Rory's dark eyes sparkled with excitement. "By God, we can do it!"

Egan bent over the table as he spoke in jubilant tones. "The first thing we've got to be doin' is gettin' Michael and Dylan here to set the plannin' but we can't use the usual ways of callin' a meetin'."

"Aye," Rory agreed. "What about sendin' Keelin to County Mayo for Michael. Tis a ways but she's up to it and no one would suspect her of any wrong doin'."

Egan agreed. "You know," he said thoughtfully, "Dylan lives in Mayo. Might Keelin fetch them both?"

"Mayo's a big place. Does Dylan live close to Michael?"

"Not far . . . maybe fifteen, twenty miles, I'm thinkin'. I'll find out tomorrow. And while she's gone I've got to go into Dublin to *visit* the print shop." Laugh lines chased themselves across Egan's face and burst into a full grin that met Rory's loud laughter.

"Shhh!" Egan cautioned. "You'll be wakin' Keelin."

"And she'd be lovin' it," Rory whispered.

At evening, Maire sat uneasily in the damp, musty thatched cottage. It smelled of soured milk and stale grease and she wished Egan hadn't left her there. Silently, Matty Burke's bent frame shuffled between the stove and pantry. Finally, she placed a heaping plate in front of Maire.

"W . . .would you be havin' a lamp, Misses?"

"I forget things like that, I do. Whether there's light or dark, tis all the same to me," Matty chuckled. "Before I sit, is there anythin' that's missin' from me table?"

Maire looked around in the dimness. "Without the lamp, I can't be tellin' you that, Misses."

"Aye," Matty said and brushed past her to the door where she lifted a dusty lantern from an old cluttered sideboard. Soon the room was filled with a warm shadowy light.

They crossed themselves and ate. Maire was surprised at how good the food was.

Matty's friendly acceptance had put Maire quickly at ease, but she was astonished by the filth. Dirt was thick in the corners. Cobwebs, weighted by grease, hung in wild profusion above the stove. Though the insides of kettles and pans were clean their outsides were caked with grime. And though Maire had often seen mice in the fields and the barn, she'd never shared a bed with one.

"The mice don't bother you? In the house, I mean," she ventured.

"Mice?" Matty said, rubbing a sleeve over the dribble of food on her chin.

"You hear so well, I thought you must have heard them too."

"Is that what that is. Well, now, we'll have to be gettin' a mouse catcher in the mornin'. Can't be havin' a guest of your importance sharin' a house with mice now, can I?"

Maire laughed. "Important am I?"

"Ahhh, aye, girl. Young Egan is me friend and havin' his wife in me auld house is an honor."

Maire was glad that Matty Burke couldn't see her blush. It was the first time anyone had called her Egan's wife.

Maire spent her days with wash pail and brush and within two weeks the little cottage was nearly spotless. She suspected it was the smell of lye soap that left her nauseous in the mornings and was grateful when the days drew to a close. Her evenings before a turf fire with Matty were becoming familiarly comfortable and though she managed to fight her homesickness by day, at night she longed to see her mother and father and baby Kate. By now even Bobby's teasing would have been welcome. And when Matty spoke of her grandson and Egan . . .

"I miss him so much," Maire said forcing the tears back. "Where does he go? What does he do that takes him away for so long?"

Matty caught the anxiety in her voice. "I know, love," she sighed. "Is that why there's no ring on your finger, Maire?"

Though the old woman couldn't see, Maire hid her hands in her lap. She said nothing.

"I understand. Where have you two been livin' then?"

"I've been at home. Egan comes whenever he can."

"Oh . . . "

That one word was so full of meaning, Maire had to explain. "Oh, no, Misses. Egan and I are married, tis just that he had no ring at the time but he's goin' to bring one to me soon and then I won't have to be livin' with me folks you see and . . ."

Matty scooted back in her chair, her milky, wandering eyes made Maire squirm.

"So your ma and da don't know about this marriage, is that so?"

Maire bowed her head. "Aye, Misses," she said softly.

"And you've been here all this time without them knowin'."

"Aye, Misses." Maire's voice was almost a whisper as she undertood the reprimand.

"By this time, your ma must be half out of her mind with worry for you, girl."

"I know but . . ."

"What would you be doin' if your own wee colleen had gone off with someone you didn't know?"

"They know Egan, really."

"I'm guessin' they don't approve of your young man."

Maire wanted to ask if Matty was truly blind. "I know they're worried but . . . but they want me to marry someone else. I can't go back . . . I just can't! I have to wait for Egan."

"Just the same," Matty said, "When Egan comes back, I'll explain about our talk. He'll understand. He's like me Kevin that way. He'll know t'was the right thing for you to be doin'. If your folks know him, like you say, they'll see why you ran away and be happy just to see you're home."

"What makes him go away for so long? I can't stand it!"

"Me Kevin's the same. I'm thinkin' tis somethin' in their bones or worse, somethin' in their hearts." The old woman rubbed her fingers over her eyes. "I'm tired, Maire. You'd best be getting' some sleep for goin' home tomorrow, for that's what you'll be doin'." She stood from her chair and shuffled away from the table.

Maire sat for a long time staring at the orange and blue flame that dwindled in the lamp. What would Ma say when she saw her again? It hadn't been an easy time when she'd left but nothing was easy anymore. And what about daddy? she thought. He'll hate me sure. I just wanted to be with Egan and he left me here with an auld woman I never met before, workin' me hands dry and he's not even here to see what I've done for her. Ahhh, God! Leaning her elbows on the table she threaded her fingers through her long, copper hair. The lamp sputtered out and she was left alone in the dark with her thoughts.

Egan rocked back in the chair and waited. The room above the printer's shop was small, musty with the stark aroma of wet ink. He got up and went to the window. The shutters were latched.

"We take no chances," the man wearing the visor said upon entering the room. "We lost a man last month to one of Newcomb's paid killers."

Egan turned, nodded. "We've had the same. I've come for the money that J.J. Corydon promised. "

"And did he say what it was for?"

"Aye," Egan said. "He did."

"Well?"

"Well, what?"

"I can give you nothin' without the word he gave you."

Egan frowned then smiled. "*TIR na nÓg*," he said.

The man removed his visor and went to the safe in the corner of the room. "The damned Brits have intercepted the last two deliveries from O'Mahony in New York, so . . ." He spun the dial and in seconds he extracted a pouch. "This is enough punt for the first meetin'. We can give no more until we know the information is good and we get another package from America."

"I understand," Egan said. He thanked the man and tucked the pouch safely away in his money belt.

Kean Martin paced. The unshaven beard and red-rimmed eyes emphasized his inability to rest. He was on edge and young Bobby kept his distance. Peg cried all the time. She blamed herself for Maire's going. Little Kate played quietly most of the time, by herself or with Bobby. It was almost a if she knew and understood the family's stress.

Nights were the hardest.

"You're sure she left with that O'Shea houligan?" Kean asked again, sitting across from her.

Peg nodded and pushed another spoonful of porridge into Kate's open mouth. "He was right here in me own house. When he left, I thought he was gone but he wasn't. He told me that he loved her. I should have seen it comin'. Why else would he walk in here, bold as Queen Victoria, and say such a thing as that and to me for God's sake? Damn him anyway!"

Kean leaned on the table, covered his eyes with the heels of his hands. "'Tis all because of him, then."

Peg had heard the same words from her husband for over two weeks now. Tears filled her eyes once more. Would this ache ever go away? Would she ever see her daughter again, with or without Egan O'Shea? Her family had changed more than she could have guessed. Bobby was lifeless, silently obeying orders from her and Kean. Her free time was nonexistant. Kean had forgotten his pipe and the sweet fragrance of blended tobacco no more filled the room after supper.

Suddenly Kean lifted his drooping head. There was a tinge of excitement that brightened his deep, sky blue eyes. "'Tis the same as kidnappin', Peg. I don't know why I didn't think of it before now!"

Kean was infused with a new energy at the thought. "By God, tomorrow I'll be goin' to Dublin to get the Constable after him! He'll not get away with stealin' our Maire, and her betrothed at that!"

Peg stared at him. "But she went with him of her own will. How can you . . ."

Kean rose from his chair. He wasn't listening. "Then, by God, we'll move the weddin' date to the end of next month. That should give her time to settle down after the Constable brings her home and by that time, everyone will know the name of Egan O'Shea for the kidnapper he is!"

"Oh, Kean, that might . . . Maire would hate . . ." Peg covered her mouth. He hadn't heard a word she'd said. Egan was no kidnapper and she knew it. She'd seen them together. Had it been herself and Conor and faced with a wedding she didn't want she might have run away, too. "Watch Kate, Bobby," she said softly and went outside in the last of the sunlight leaving Kean to mutter alone.

She walked to the oak. The leaves beneath the old tree were crushed. *A bed for lovers?* she asked herself. Moving back up the hill, she looked again over the gradual edge, down into the shadows in the gully. A sudden warmth settled in her depths as she remembered Conor's hot kisses, his rough working hands. "How I miss you." The words she formed in her mind slipped softly from her lips.

"Peg, darlin'," Kean called. "What are you doin' down there?"

She turned to see him coming toward her and she sighed deeply. "Feelin' the end of the day, I suppose," she lied.

Kean walked down the hill, put his arms around her. "You're cold," he said.

She shook her head. "Worried maybe. If Maire comes back to us she'll be different you know."

Kean pressed a kiss on her temple. "I know. I'm just hopin' that Luke MacSweeny will still want her."

Incredulous, Peg pushed out of his embrace. "You want her to be goin' through with the weddin' even after this?"

"Don't you? I mean, that much couldn't have changed . . ."

"Ahhh, Kean . . ." Sharply Peg released her breath as she gave up her challenge, dropped her head onto his shoulder in surrender.

He drew her close again. "You'll see. She'll be glad to be getting' back home and Luke will look good to her after all this, I'm tellin' you."

Kean took her hand and they walked slowly back to the house. Tomorrow would be another difficult day . . . especially for Peg.

At sun rise, Kean harnessed Winnie to the cart. First he would go to the Constable then to the MacSweeny's. With luck, he'd be home before dark. Peg stood in the doorway and watched, her arms folded over her chest forming a useless shield. There was a sickness in her heart for Egan O'Shea.

In the dark of early morning, Keelin sat on the edge of the bed running a comb through her thick black hair. "Don't be doin' that now," she said affably as Rory reached around her naked torso.

"Then don't be sittin' here like that in front of me." Rory's voice was deep, playful.

"Like what?"

"All bare and lovely. You know how I hate it."

"Aye," she teased. "I know all about that."

"So what do you intend to be doin' about it?"

Keelin leaned back across his chest, turned over and snuggled in. "Now then," she whispered, "what do *you* intend doin' about it?"

He turned her toward him. His loving gaze sifted through the pale blue of her eyes into her heart. "Tis a pixie you are, Keelin Bonner Kilcullen and I'll love you till the day I die . . ." He gathered her into his arms and pressed his body into hers.

Roosters crowed announcing the sun as Keelin and Rory lay content in each others arms.

Keelin stretched. "When is it you want me to go fetch Michael?"

Rory yawned. "Egan said day after tomorrow would give us time enough. And don't worry about Dylan. I'll go after him. He's achin' to be after some Fenian business."

Her fingers moved softly through the hair on his chest. "I'm . . . thinkin' that after Manchester, I don't want to be doin' this anymore." Her voice questioned him and she waited uneasily for his thoughts.

"And what would you rather be doin' than fightin' for a free Ireland?"

She was quickly up on one elbow. "Tis not that that's not important, only . . ."

"Only?"

"I just . . . I . . . I want the things other women want. I want a home, Rory . . . and a family."

"What's wrong with this place?"

"Ahhh, Rory, tis is a bloody meetin' hall. Every Fenian knows it and uses it as his own. I want a house where we belong, just you and me . . . somethin' I don't have to share unless I want to."

"Should I be tellin' Egan to go, then?"

"Nae. Egan's like a brother to us."

Rory pulled her down next to him and smiled. "All right, love," he whispered, twirling a strand of her hair through his fingers. "I know what you're sayin'. We'll talk to Egan after Manchester and we'll train someone else to take our places to do what we do."

"You're meanin' that, truly?" she asked anxiously, up on her elbow again.

"Aye. I mean it. I'm twenty-five-years old. 'Tis time to be gettin' a real life goin' . . . with you. When I was younger I looked to the Brotherhood because there was excitement in it, but you're all the excitement I need and that's sure." His eyes searched Keelin's round, smiling face. "I'm thinking that we've outgrown the Fenians, you and me. What do you think?"

"Oh, aye," she agreed excitedly. "Except for special occasions, of course."

"Of course."

Balding Chief Constable Crippen bent over a long, glossy desk at the Police Station in Dublin. His wide, red face shone as if the same substance had polished both.

Kean Martin stood, cap in hand. He waited his turn behind others who, like him, had already fixed their names to official documents after they had explained their grievances. He went over and over what he would say to the Constable. O'Shea wouldn't get away with this! Not this time. He was a houligan and a scroundral and not fit to be anyone's son-in-law, much less his. Maire was precious. True, she was strong-willed but she'd make a good wife for Luke and nothing would destroy this opportunity, no matter what he had to do.

"Martin! Kean Martin, to the desk!"

He moved forward. The desk was higher than he first thought.

The Constable's red-veined hazel eyes peered over square spectacles. He forced a finger between his neck and stiff collar to loosen it before he spoke. "Well?" he asked. His voice was gruff, his pen poised above the document Kean had signed.

"I've . . . I've c . . . come to report a kidnappin', your honor," Kean stammered, twisting his cap, awed by the formality and activity of the place.

"Who's been kidnapped?" the man asked in uninterested tones.

"Me daughter, Maire . . . She . . ."

"When?"

"I . . . I'm beggin' your pardon, your honor?"

Crippen cleared his throat. "Mr. Martin," he condescended, "I am not a judge. I'm a Constable, so you can refain from calling me, *your honor*. Now, when was your daughter kidnapped?"

"About two weeks now, I think . . ."

"Two weeks? You've waited *two weeks*? How old is this girl?"

"Seventeen, your . . . S . . . seventeen."

"Are you sure she didn't run away?" Crippen's fingers fluttered in the air.

"Ahhh, no sir. Maire wouldn't run away. She's a good girl. About to be married, she is, to a butcher's son."

Crippen struggled to keep from rolling his eyes. He smiled stiffly. "Do you have any idea who might have kidnapped her, Mr. Martin?"

"Aye. I do." Kean stepped closer to the desk and whispered hoarsely. "'Twas Egan O'Shea from Cork who took her."

Constable Crippen motioned to an indifferent officer who stood beside the desk with pad and pen. "Mitchell," he said, "put Egan O'Shea on your list. See if there's anything in our files about a man by that name."

"From Cork," Kean added.

Mitchell touched his hairline in a weak acknowledgement of authority and left the room.

"Is there anything else that you can tell me about this situation, Mr. Martin?"

"Aye, sir. We'd like for you to be findin' her before her weddin' day . . . if you please."

Constable Crippen nodded patiently. "And when would that be?"

"The last Sunday of next month. We've all ready changed the day once and we'd not like to be changin' it again . . . *sir*."

"We'll do our best. Now, if you'll take a seat over there with the others, we'll see what our files say about the man you mentioned."

"Aye," Kean nodded. "I'm thankin' you, sir."

Kean sat in the empty chair below the row of high windows and waited.

After the long line diminished, the room was plunged into a muted hum as each person anticipated their second call to the big desk. An hour later Kean still waited. Thinking he'd been forgotten, he approached the desk and rapped the top lightly.

Constable Crippen looked peevishly over his square spectacles. "Was your name called?" he asked.

Kean shook his head. "I was thinkin' that an hours time was enough to find Egan O'Shea in them files, I was thinkin' . . . sir."

Crippen's finger's searched through the stack of dogeared papers before him. "You're Martin," he said coming across the complaint bearing Kean's name.

"Aye, I'm Martin."

"Mitchell!" Crippen hollered, silencing the low drone that hovered about the room.

Mitchell returned, his arms full of folders and dropped them in a neat pile on the desk.

"Anything in there about O'Shea?" Crippen asked.

"Who?"

"O'Shea." He raised his brows and waited for a response. "*O'Shea*, Mitchell. *O'Shea*. Is the name in those folders anywhere?"

"I didn't see it but you can look if you like, sir."

"Great God," Crippen murmured and reached for a file. "Good help in this town is like finding another who can walk on water."

Kean stood quietly at the corner of the highly polished desk watching. The thought passed through his mind to ask if he could help but vanished as the small eyes peered over the spectacles again.

Crippen closed the last folder. "Not a word, Mr. Martin. I'm sorry. Without a file on this man, there's little we can do except get the word out and have all the Constables on the look out for your daughter."

Kean's heart dropped but a new thought brought a more definative way to get Maire back. "I'm not surprised," he said. "A Fenian brother would keep himself pretty clean, wouldn't he?"

From the gasps he heard, Kean knew he had the attention of the entire room.

Crippen's finger snapped the tight collar button. "What did you say Mr. Martin? "

Kean's face grew solemn. "O'Shea's a Fenian, sure as I stand here and he's got me daughter."

As the room broke into a rush of activity, Kean smiled inwardly as he felt the noose slip around Egan O'Shea's neck.

"Don't move Mr. Martin. We have some questions for you."

Kean assured Crippen he would stay where he was. "I only want him for kidnappin' me daughter . . . that's all," he said with a sudden jolt of remorse. "Just for the kidnappin', mind you."

Kean spent the next two hours in a room telling an artist what Egan looked like and a stenographer everything else he knew about the man. He signed more papers. Food and drink was brought in for him. The sky was streaked with evening red when he reached the MacSweeny home.

"Well, bless my soul, tis Kean Martin! Come in, come in."

As Kean stuffed his cap into his coat pocket, MacSweeny dragged him inside.

"Take a load off," the butcher said pointing to the quilt-draped sofa. "Luke! Roddy! Company's come!"

The sparse living quarters, to the side of the butcher store, was as clean as three males could have kept it. Kean sat and leaned his forearms on his knees. "I need to be speakin' to you, MacSweeny . . . alone for a bit."

The butcher moved closer when Kean's voice level dropped.

"Sounds important. What is it?"

"Maire's gone. I've got the Constable out lookin' now."

"Where did she go? Have you heard from her?"

"I don't know where she is. She was kidnapped by that O'Shea houligan and she's gone. Don't tell Luke yet. Let the Constable do his job. We don't need to muddle this up. I just thought you should know."

"Tis serious, then."

"Aye. Serious as a funeral. The Constable said he'd have a force out at me house tomorrow mornin' to set out lookin' for them."

MacSweeny's big hand covered his jaw as he thought about what he had just heard. He walked to the open rear door and glanced about.

The boys were nowhere in sight. "I'm glad they didn't hear me call them," he said. "I don't know what Luke will think about this."

Kean's gaze held tight to the butcher's. "You don't think he'll want to stop the weddin', do you?"

"That'll be up to Luke. He loves Maire, truly but . . ." MacSweeny came to stand beside the sofa. "How long has she been gone?"

"Not long. We just found out ourselves," he lied. "Though we did wait a couple of days to see if she was able to get away and come home on her own." Kean gathered his thoughts. "God knows where he's taken her. We're so worried, MacSweeny . . . for her life and all. Who knows what a Fenian might do to a strong minded girl like *our* Maire. Was he to look cross wise at her why, she'd scratch his eye out!"

MacSweeny dropped into his overstuffed chair. "A Fenian, you say. A member of the *Brotherhood*? Are you sure, Martin?"

"As sure as anyone can be. What they'd be wantin' with her I'll never know. But, the Chief Constable said they'd be puttin' all the other cases aside to find that houligan and get Maire back to us. Which brings me to tell you Peg and I have decided to change the weddin' to the last Sunday of next month. Just so Maire can have a chance to settle down from her ordeal." Cautiously, Kean examine the other man's face. Would he believe and accept the hurried words or would there be a need for more half-truths?

"You're sure they'll find her, then?"

"Aye. They'll find her," Kean affirmed, relieved. "You know the Constablary, when they get started on somethin' they're like a dog with a bone."

MacSweeny nodded slowly. "I don't think I'll tell young Luke about this right now. I'll wait a time and see what happens."

"Good," Kean said with a brisk smile. "Tell him she's had a touch of fever and puttin' the weddin' back will be good for her. He'll understand. Just don't let him come out to the house while all this is goin' on. I don't like lyin' to the lad, but as you can see for yourself . . ." He spread his hands and shrugged.

MacSweeny sat staring at the far wall. His head bobbed slowly as he listened to Kean's words.

"I'll have to be goin' now," Kean said. "With the Constable comin' in the mornin' I'd better be there."

"Aye."

Kean let himself out.

The Martin farm was a beehive of activity. Peg supplied hot tea to subdue the chill of early morning for the seven Constables who arrived.

Peg shook her head. "Why do they all choose to speak at the same time?" she murmured to herself.

Bobby was captivated. Though he was in charge of Kate, he missed nothing. Sitting on the corner of the low porch, where he could see the barn and far down the road as well, his lively blue eyes took in every move made by the officers.

"And you, lad," the officer in charge said. "What would you know about this man, Egan O'Shea?"

Bobby shrugged and shifted Kate to his other knee. "Nothin' much," he said. "Only . . ."

The Constable's thick brown brows raised.

"Only that he came round here sometimes to see Maire."

"Was she ever angry with him?"

"All the time."

"Why is that?"

The boy lifted his shoulders again. "I don't know. I thought she liked him."

"Was he ever mean to her, or you?"

"Nae. He hardly ever came to the house though. Maire and him would talk sometimes by the auld oak, there," he said, pointing. "I don't think he liked me Da very much."

"Why's that?"

"Nobody ever said, so I don't know."

"Did you ever hear O'Shea . . . or your sister, mention the Fenian Brotherhood?"

Bobby shook his head.

The man grinned, tousled Bobby's hair and left to meet with the other uniformed men. Bobby knew they were talking about him because they would glance back at him from time to time as the man related what little he'd been told.

Peg walked up behind him. He turned to see her smudge a tear with the hem of her apron.

"What's wrong, Ma?"

She shook her head and smiled painfully. She bent to take Kate from him. "Tis wrong, Bobby," she whispered. "Tis all wrong, what we're doin'."

"How do you mean, Ma? Maire's gone and Daddy's got the Constables for gettin' her back. Isn't that right, Ma? Isn't it?"

"Tis time to do the milkin', Bobby. The bucket's in the kitchen."

"Ahhh, Ma. That's Maire's job."

"Aye. Do you see her anywhere? Your da's been doin' it for her. Now it's your turn. Now go. Do a good job this time."

"Aye, Ma."

Bobby did as he was told although he kept an eye and an ear on the activity of the police.

Peg entered the safety of her house and closed the door on the words and bustle just beyond her front porch. She stripped the tiny girl for her bath, tested the water in the tub she had placed on the side board and watched her youngest laugh and splash the water with chubby little hands. She dried Kate with a warm towel, dressed her and laid her in the corner on a pile of blankets, protected by a gate of smoothly finished spindles.

An hour later the yard was empty and Kean came inside and sat at the table, smiling. There was a glint in his eye that Peg hadn't noticed before. It was the look of a hunter who had finally cornered his prey.

"She's not home, yet," Peg murmured adding fresh water to the kettle.

"Aye, true, but O'Shea is on his way to becomin' a bad memory, he is. We'll not be troubled with the likes of him for long."

"I thought they'd gone out to find Maire. Remember, our daughter's missin'?"

"They are. They are. But gettin' their hands on O'Shea . . ." Kean rubbed his palms together.

Peg sat, fidgeting with her apron. "What will that do for them?" she asked. "And what will happen to him, Kean? You know what we're doin' is a bald-face lie. *Maire went with him.* He didn't force her."

"Ahhh, Peg, don't you see, me darlin'. The only way I could have them come was to tell them that she was kidnapped by a Fen . . ."

The truth was out. He hadn't meant to tell her but it was too late.

"By a *Fenian!* Damn, Kean Martin," she seethed. "That could cost your immortal soul! If they find and hang that young man, it'll only be because he loves our daughter, for *nothin'* else!"

Her green eyes flashed with anger as she waited for his answer.

"There's no need to be speakin' to me like that, Peg. I did what I thought you wanted. And, by God, the man *is* a Fenian! You heard him yourself that night he came here to see Maire. He sat right where you are now and said it himself by speakin' out against the British crown the way he did!"

"Well now, I've never taken a likin' to British rule, meself!" she snapped. "And I'd just as soon have Home Rule, too! Now, what does that make me? Are you goin' to accuse me of bein' a Fenian or an Irish patriot?"

"What's all the noise about?" Bobby asked, entering with a full pail of foaming milk. "Can you not hear Kate wailin' away?"

Peg rushed to quiet the tiny girl. "We was just havin' a discussion," she said to reassure him though the strained look on his face told her she'd failed.

Kean stood and pushed the chair under the table. "I'll be back for supper."

"You've not had breakfast. Where are you goin'?" Peg called after him.

Kean shut the door behind him.

"What's wrong with Da?" Bobby asked hefting the heavy pail to the table.

"I said somethin' that I shouldn't have, I'm thinkin'. I'm thinkin', too, that the next few days are goin' to be hard ones for us." Peg fixed her eyes on her son, took his chin in her hand. "Be on his side, Bobby," she said, her gaze on the closed door. "He's goin' to need someone on his side."

"Michael!" Egan shouted grasping the tired young man by the shoulders. "I was beginnin' to worry about you two."

Keelin dragged chairs out from around the table. "Tell me about your trip."

She rubbed her eyes and forehead.

Egan stared at her. "You've come a long way. Why don't you go lie down while Michael and I do some talkin'"

She nodded wearily and left the room.

"Did somethin' happen out there, Michael? She's never looked so used up."

"Nothin' out of the ordinary and for a lady who's goin' to be a mother I'd say she did quite well especially walkin' all that way when no rides come along."

Egan's face mirrored his surprise. "You can't be serious."

"I'm serious as a tooth ache. I picked her up twice from a dead faint. I even had to go to the Constable's office in Longford for help once. Scared me out of a year's growth. When she found out where I'd gone she was mad as a scalded cat, I can tell you but," he shrugged, "I didn't know what else to do. I thought she was sick and that was the closest place to be getting' help that late at night."

"Does Rory know, you think?"

"I couldn't be guessin' that. Rory's the father, then?"

"That's *Mrs.* Kilcullen in there," Egan admonished. "Make no mistake about that."

"I didn't know."

"We should let Keelin tell him, don't you think?" Egan said in a rough, cautious whisper.

"Aye. Knowin' her temperment as I do now, it wouldn't be safe stealin' that thunder from her."

"I know tis still early, Michael, but I've got a pallet on the pantry floor and you're welcome to it if you'd like to rest before Rory and Dylan get here. We'll talk about what we're doin' then."

"Aye," he yawned. "We haven't slept for two days, tryin' to make up the lost time. No wonder Keelin looked so tired . . . she is."

"Tis good that Rory went after Dylan. I thought Keelin could go but Rory thought better of it."

Michael stretched, rolled his shoulders.

"Did Keelin tell you why we need you?" Egan asked as he took a blanket from the chair by the door and handed it to Michael.

"She talked of Manchester Courthouse and the trials of O'Leary, Luby and Kickham. Nothin' more."

Egan nodded. "When Dylan and Rory get here, we'll go over everything. Get some rest, now."

A mild rain washed the twilight when Rory and Dylan burst through the door.

"Tis a noisy pair you are," Egan reprimanded. "Keelin and Michael are restin'. Quiet down." "Ahhh, they're here. Keelin's all right?" Rory asked wiping his rain-damp face on a thinning flannel.

"Aye. Keelin was . . . not feelin' well but she's sleepin' now. She'll be fine in the mornin', I told Michael we'd wake him as soon as you two got here."

Dylan draped his wet coat on the back of a chair and sat down with an exhausted sigh. "I could use a hot cup of tea," he whispered and ran his hands over his upper arms.

Egan placed the kettle over the fire. "Tis good to see you, Dylan," Egan said. "Tis been a long time."

"Aye, it has. But I'm back for good this time."

Rory slid the curtain aside to peek in on Keelin. "She's a beauty, that one," he said proudly. "Ask her to do anythin' and tis as good as done."

Egan grunted absently. "Just wait until you hear what she's goin' to be doin' now . . ."

"Did you say somethin', Egan?" Rory asked.

"Nae. Talkin' to meself again. You get that way when you're left alone as much as I am."

"Well then, you must've had time to figure out what we're to be doin' when we get to Manchester."

"Aye, I have." Smiling, Egan set the cups on the table and went to wake Michael.

"Has Corydon come round yet?" Rory asked.

"He'll be here in the mornin' sometime."

"You have what he wants?"

"I do."

Dylan looked bewildered. "Rory said there would only be the five of us."

"That's fine," Egan assured him. "Corydon's found an informant in England but he needs money to make him talk. That's all. He's got nothin' to do with what's goin' on at the Manchester Courthouse."

Peg Martin drew her shawl back up over her shoulders. She sat outside on the stool by the front door, a needle in her hand and worn clothing in her lap. Though it was cool, the cloud-laced, late afternoon sky gave better light by which to mend than the protected dimmness of the house.

Kate sat at her feet on a blanket, pulling and chewing on a rag doll that had once been Maire's. Squawking birds scattered in the trees and flapped into the air as soaring stones from Bobby's accurate aim clunked against the branches.

"Don't you have somethin' useful to be doin', lad?" she asked, a thorny edge to her voice that Bobby had come to recognize as normal since Maire was gone.

"All me work is done, Ma."

"What about the turf?" she said, her gaze drifting over to the wheel barrow full turf bricks. "Grab the bricks and stack them proper. Get it done then talk to me about havin' nothin' to . . ." The words caught in her throat. Her heart pounded so hard it made her ears ring. "Maire," she breathed. "Thanks be to God!" She wanted to run to meet her like the father in the story of the prodigal son but that wouldn't be right . . . not now. Where were the Constables? Shouldn't they be with her? Aye, but they weren't. Did it matter? Where was Egan? Had she run away from him? Nae. Not after what she'd seen of the two of them. She forced herself to look away and, through blurry eyes, continue mending.

"Ma, look, tis Maire! Ma! Can you not see her?" Bobby gasped and let two bricks slide from his fingers.

"Aye, lad, I see her."

"Are you goin' to just sit there like you don't then? Aren't you glad?" Bobby rubbed his suddenly sweating palms up and down the sides of his trousers.

"Aye, I'm glad. Go to her."

Bobby jumped to a full run. "Did the Constables find you?" he shouted, breathlessly in her face.

"Constables?"

"Aye. Daddy got seven Constables to go lookin' for you. They came runnin' when Da said you was kidnapped."

"Kidnapped."

"Aye," he said, running circles around her. "That's what they said. Asked a lot of questions, too, they did. You look all right," he said, looking her over. "Did he whip you or anythin'?"

"What? Of course not! How do you think of such things?"

"Well, if I was goin to be kidnappin' someone, that's what I'd do . . . maybe."

"Good God. Bobby Martin, you're mad as a box of frogs! Why I missed the likes of you I can't be guessin'. Is Da home?"

"Nae. He goes out everyday lookin' for you. I'm glad you're back. Now maybe they'll stop yellin' at each other and I won't have to milk the cow." He ran on ahead to kneel beside Peg. "She's all right, Ma. He didn't whip her or anythin'. I think that Luke will still want her. She looks pretty good."

Peg stared at him, unable to curb her smile. "Where did you get the idea that he wouldn't want her?"

"I heard you and Daddy talkin', you know. You said somethin' about her bein' spoiled or soiled or . . ." He scratched is temple with his forefinger. "I can't remember exactly."

"Well, I'll thank you to forget whatever you thought you heard. It had nothin' to do with you."

Maire stood several feet away, waiting, but Peg's eyes never lifted from her mending."

"Hello, Ma," she said softly.

"Hello, Maire. Are you home for good or just for now?" Peg's voice was soft but curt.

"I . . . I don't know that, yet."

Peg drew a deep breath and finally looked at her daughter. "I see. What are you goin' to be tellin your father about where you've been?"

"I don't know that yet either."

"What do you know, Maire?"

Maire began to cry. "I . . . I know that I missed you more than I thought I would and . . . Da. I thought . . ." She dropped to her knees beside her mother. "I didn't mean to cause you trouble. I just wanted . . ."

Peg stopped mending, drove her needle through her apron bib. She smoothed the copper waves on the bowed head. "I know what you wanted, girl. And did you get it?"

Maire's whole body shook as she wordlessly clung to Peg's lap. A brisk gust of wind prompted them into the house. Peg handed the mending to Bobby and guided the toddler through the door. Maire dropped Peg's hand to scurry after the doll before it was blown away. For a moment she stood in the wind clutching the familiar toy then she grasped her skirt front and ran into the house.

Peg filled the tea pot with hot water and placed it on the table. "Are you hungry?" she asked as detached as possible.

"Aye. A little."

"Sit."

Maire closed her eyes and smelled the familiar aroma of oat cakes and jam.

Bobby sat next to her and watched the growing strain between the two women. He'd said all that he had to say earlier. He knew his mother was delighted to have his sister home, but she was so distant. He didn't understand the thin conversation and he knew that Maire wanted more of a welcome from her mother. Perhaps Da could straighten things out when he got home. But, he always came home tired and cross. Bobby shrugged, placed his hands between his knees and waited for the storm.

As hungry as she was, Maire picked at her food. "Are you terrible angry with me, Ma?"

"Aye. Tis glad I am that you're home and unhurt, but angry is the best word for your leavin' the way you did. I prayed for you all the days you were gone, that God would help you find your way home so we could be a family again and I give Him praise that you're here now. But, aye, I'm angry."

Maire sniffed and rubbed the back of her hand under her nose. "I'm sorry, Ma. I'm truly sorry for not gettin' word to you where I was. Egan left me with a nice auld woman who took good care of me. She . . ."

Peg held up her hand in a sign to stop. "Well, isn't that lovely. You left your da and me here to worry ourselves sick over you while some strange, auld woman takes *good* care of you." Peg's tone was as hard as Maire had ever heard. "What you don't know is before long the whole of the British Empire will be thinkin' that Egan O'Shea is a kidnapper and a Fenian to boot. They've got drawings of his likeness Maire, lots of them. They'll search for him until they've made him fruit for the gallows. That's what you're runnin' away has done. I don't think that's what you wanted, girl, but that's what you got!"

Horrified, Maire stared at her mother, unable to speak, nearly unable to breathe. "Ahhh, Ma!" she finally gasped, tears pooling in her wide, green eyes. "You can't be meanin' that. You can't!"

"Oh, I mean every word, I do. To convince the Chief Constable to start lookin' for you, your da turned the OShea lad in for a Fenian. They'll not stop their huntin' just because you *escaped* from him and you're safely back home."

"But, I'll explain to them! I'll . . ."

"You'll what? Tell the world that you ran off with a man who's a known enemy of the Crown just because you wanted him to bed you?"

"Ma!" Maire cried, glancing sharply at Bobby. "Stop it, Ma . . ." She buried her face in her arms and wept.

"Egan O'Shea is a dead man, Maire. Get used to it. He's dead and gone! And you'd best be prayin' to God that Luke MacSweeny will still have you because he's your last chance, now!"

"Roddy!" Luke called from the backdoor of the butcher store. "Saddle the young mare! And don't be wastin' time about it!"

His father grabbed his arm. "Luke, you can't be goin' out there, now. I didn't tell you about this to make you a mad man. You've got to be waitin' just like the rest of us. She'll be found, lad. Everything will be all right, you'll see."

Luke shook his father's big hand free, stripped to the waist and dipped into the pail of fresh water to wash the mutton blood from his arms. "You should have told me before now! I'm not a lad anymore, Da, and I don't want to be treated like one, especially by you!" He rushed into the house. "Roddy! Bring the mare!"

MacSweeny knew he couldn't stop his son. "The Martin's were afraid that if you knew, you wouldn't want her anymore."

Luke yanked a clean shirt from the dresser, met Roddy at the store front, swung aboard the skittish sorral. "I'll have her all right. And when I catch the bastard who kidnapped her, I'll break his scrany neck!"

"Luke! Luke!" His father called after the lunging animal. "Come back here!"

"What's goin' on Daddy?" Roddy asked, confusion spreading across his young face. "Why was Luke in such a hurry? He didn't even button his shirt or take his coat."

MacSweeny sighed heavily and wiped his hands slowly down his apron. "Your brother has a great problem and I don't think he'll be able to solve this one."

"Is it that girl, Daddy?"

"Aye, lad. That it is . . ." MacSweeny said, sighing through his words

Roddy pursed his lips, his head rocked up and down in firm conviction. "I could've told him she was goin' to be a problem."

"And how would you be knowin' that?" MacSweeny asked, his gaze still on the road where his eldest son had vanished.

"Since the first time she come here . . . I could tell. She's a fae one and just too pretty."

14

"Promise is in honor's debt."

As the spiney orange fingers of dawn shredded the night sky, Keelin stood at the crest of the hill behind the little house in Drogheda staring out across the sea, the big red setter at her side. Her jumper was pulled tight against the cold morning air. She turned as the dog's wagging tail announced the man behind her. She smiled and reached for his hand.

Egan put his arm around her and squeezed. "Michael told me about the baby," he said softly, kissing the top of her head. "Does Rory know?"

She shook her head. "Nae. I don't want him knowin' yet. After Manchester, then I'll tell him. Promise me you'll not say a word."

"Done," he said as he became aware of her troubled profile in the pale, expanding glow of the new day. "Sure and you don't intend to be goin' with us now?"

"Aye, I do." She turned to face him displaying a counterfeit calm. "You need me. My part in all this is easy enough and without it nothin' will go."

"We'll change the plan, then."

Keelin smiled again. "Tis a good plan, Egan. Tis workable and many will be thankful for it."

"I hope so, Keelin."

She stretched her arms around his waist. "Has Corydon come for the money yet?"

"Aye. That's when I saw you out here."

"He didn't come in?"

"Everyone but us is still asleep and he was in a hurry."

"Did he say anythin'?"

"Aye," Egan said.

"Well, out with it."

"He said that Kelly and Deasy have been arrested and they'll be on trial, too."

"In Manchester?"

Egan nodded.

"Was J.J. sure?"

"He sounded sure. He said he was."

"Did he say what they was arrested for?"

"Possibly for tryin' to bomb Chester Castle but, he wasn't positive."

"That might have been why Kelly's bombs never went off," Keelin said. "Will J.J. be part of our mission at Manchester, then?"

"Nae. He knows nothing about it. Besides, he's got business with the informer in London."

"What about Kelly and Deasy then?"

Egan shrugged loosely, "If they're found guilty they'll more'n likely be sentenced to time in Clerkenwell same as the others unless they're sent to a different prison."

"But what if they're let off. Who'll take them and how will we . . . ?"

"I know, love. There's lots of questions we'll have to find answers to."

They watched the quiet, shimmering ball of sun rise higher in the blue-white sky. In seven days the five of them would leave from Dublin for Manchester to await the outcome of the trials.

"When will you tell the lads . . . about Kelly and Deasy, I mean?"

"Later. I'm thinkin' I want to know more before I give them somethin' else to worry about."

Keelin nodded and took his arm. "I'm thinkin' you should tell them sooner."

"Come, girl," Egan said "Time for breakfast."

Keelin let him lead her past Kevin's grave where she crossed herself and walked on to the house.

"One day me Maire will be havin' a baby . . ." he said in a near whisper.

Keelin elbowed him in the ribs. "Why, you auld cushion," she laughed. "Some hard-hearted Fenian leader you are, talkin' so about wee babes. Are you not the one who's supposeed to have shot off kneecaps and tarred and feathered innocent Irish girls for just talkin' to the British Bulls?"

Egan couldn't help laughing. "Is that what I'm supposed to have done? Who in the world ever said that?"

Keelin stopped. "Jaysus, Egan, you don't know?"

"Know what?"

"Michael and I heard many frightenin' tales about what the leaders of the Fenians do to them who stand in their way. We laughed but there are those who believe it and . . ."

"Did they call Jimmy Stephens or me by name?" Egan asked, a worried frown creasing his forehead.

Keelin thought for a moment. "Nae. Not that I can remember but whoever is branded a *leader*, won't have an easy time of it in the courts, I'm thinkin' . . . when it comes his time."

The entire day was spent in waiting for the hours to pass. Keelin patched one of Rory's shirts by an open window. Rory teased her and played with Padraig. Michael and Dylan caught each other up on the news from east and west and Egan slept.

After the evening meal, they talked again about Manchester.

"I'm wishin' we could just pinch off their bloody heads!" Rory expressed graphically.

"No violence, now," Egan cautioned, sending a quick glance at Keelin. "You know how they improve on the truth as it is. We have to be givin' them nothin' to be tellin' at all."

"Aye, Egan," Dylan stated tapping his fingers lightly on the table. "I agree. No blood, especially ours."

Michael grinned. "The way you have it planned, Egan, I can see no reason for anyone to panic, even the guards."

"That's what I'm hopin'." Egan replied. "So we take the van after it passes under the train tressel at Hyde Street.

"Who's on the inside at the courthouse, Egan?" Rory asked.

"Just Willie. He's been there for the last week keepin' an eye on things. He'll be lookin' for us."

"Good," Rory said.

"Go over it again, Egan," Keelin said. "We need to be hearin' it again and again until it happens easy."

She rose and stood behind Rory, her hands resting on his shoulders.

"First," Egan began, "we arrive at the courthouse and separate. If they're let off, we'll make ourselves known to them and take them home. If they're sentenced, we follow the prison van until it's one day out of London. With them bein' so close to Clerkenwell, the guards shouldn't suspect a thing. As a matter of fact, they should be pretty close to bein' asleep from the lack of activity.

"Rory and Keelin will be travelin' together bein' sure to change their clothes to somethin' different every day. Some days you'll be ahead of the van some days behind but you'll always know exactly where it is.

"Michael and Dylan and I will follow the van from the woods or other streets."

"How many guards did you say there'll be?" Rory asked.

"Should be five. One for each of us, except for Keelin."

"Why not me?" Keelin asked, her fists on her hips.

"That's the only change. After the van is stopped and the guards are under our guns, I want you to be gettin' the keys and open the locks. Get everyone out. Remember, there may be more than the three we want. Take them all down the road, out of sight, and wait for us. Start them changin' their clothes."

"Aye, Egan," she agreed.

"Dylan, your pistols are good in either hand so you'll be holdin' two or three guards."

Dylan nodded.

"Michael, you and I will disarm our guards if they're armed, and tie their hands with their own belts then force them into the van . . ."

"Best be silencin' the yell out of them, too." Rory said.

"Aye. Keelin, remember to take enough gags with you as well as the other things you'll be bringin'. One wad in their mouths and one to tie around each of them so they can't spit it out."

"Aye," she said.

"Rory," Egan continued, "I want you to cause a short distraction."

"Where? What kind?"

"Any kind. After the van's been stopped, I want you to take the guards minds off what's actually happenin' for a few seconds. Can you do that?"

"The timin' will have to be perfect."

"Aye. That's why I'm choosin' you."

"I can do it."

Egan turned back to the rest of the men. "Whatever Rory does should be givin' us just enough time to take them down. We'll tie and gag them then put them in the back of the van and slap the horses on their rumps. They'll be at Clerkenwell before mornin' and we'll be scattered through the countryside.

They'll by watchin' the western ports so we'll have to be leavin' the country through Scotland and France."

"I've always wanted to see France," Keelin winked.

"Why not?" Egan said. "You and Rory take Kickham with you. Go through London to Dover and across to Calais. Get a boat from there down the Channel to Cork."

"Why Kickham?" Rory asked.

"You'll be needin' someone who can speak French."

"Are we really goin' to France, then?" Keelin cried, fascinated by the prospect.

Rory pulled her onto his lap. "You said you wanted to and there'll not be a better time than this."

Egan smiled at Keelin as she wrapped her arms around Rory's neck and kissed him. Suddenly he missed Maire more than he could stand. "Michael," he said dragging his gaze away from the two he envied. "You and Dylan get to Scotlnd with Luby quick as you can. Take the ferry from Portpatrick to Belfast."

Michael grinned at Dylan. "Best leave your rosary at home, lad."

"Aye. And here I am with nothin' more orange than me hair," Dylan chuckled goodnaturedly.

"Now, do we have enough quid?" Egan asked.

"Aye," Rory answered.

"Good, spread it out now among us."

"Get the purse, Keelin," Rory said and she left his lap, entered the pantry and retrieved the money.

Rory divided the coins, leaving just enough behind for emergencies when they returned.

Egan stood. "Go over the plan together at least once a day and don't write one word of it down anywhere. I'll be meetin' you in Dublin at the boat in six days. Oh, one more thing," he said, glancing at Keelin. "Corydon told me that Kelly and Deasy have been arrested and they'll be on trial with, before or after, the others. If that's true, we'll have to take them, too. Michael, if that happens, they'll be goin' with you and Dylan." He grabbed his coat and left.

"Where's he goin' this time of day?" Dylan asked, turning in his chair to see Egan close the door behind him.

"To Maire of course," Keelin said softly, looking into the dove-gray depths of Rory's dark eyes.

The sorrel mare slid to a shuddering stop in the Martin's front yard. The sun had long ago turned the sky over to the stars as Luke banged on the door.

Kean anwered. "L . . . Luke!" he sputtered. "What are you doin' here, lad?"

"I come to see Maire. Where is she?" he demanded, pausing only long enough to catch his breath before pushing his way into the house.

"She's in the loft, Luke," Peg answered in hushed tones as she shut her bedroom door behind her. "She's asleep. You'll have to wait until . . . "

Luke broke for the ladder and was in the loft before either one could stop him. It was dark. He fumbled around the slanting walls and tripped over stray shoes. "Maire," he called softly, hoping desperately for an answer. "Where are you? Are you here?"

He heard a low moan and the rustle of bedding by the wall below the single window. He pushed the curtains aside. "Maire?" He pulled the covers away and saw Bobby so he threw them back again.

"Maire?"

"Ummm?"

Below, Peg clutched Kean's arm keeping him from following. "Leave them alone," she whispered. "It may be the only way of gettin' them together . . . ever."

"But tis not proper, Peg . . . them up there . . . *alone*, with Bobby and no one else," he warned.

Peg shot him a sour look of disapproval. "And what do we know of *proper* any more, Kean? Do you want them married or not?"

"Aye, but . . ."

"Oh, shut up! Listen."

Slowly Luke's eyes adjusted to the dimmness. He knelt beside the other bed and eased the blanket from her shoulders. Her hair fanned out like the sunset across the white pillow and he ran is fingers through it, sifting it's satiny strands. There she was. Perhaps it was good that he hadn't known she'd been gone. It didn't matter now anyway. She was home and if he had to, he'd guard her every minute until the wedding. Even with being put back a month, the wedding was so close now, just ten days away. Nearly everything was ready. He had the ring; the beautiful gold band that was his mother's. His only suit had been cleaned and pressed so it looked almost new. They would stay with his father until their new house on the outskirts of Dublin was completed. The money he had set aside to pay for his long dreamed of journey to France and England was of no importance now. Only Maire mattered and their life together. All of the money was gladly used up; gone to buy building materials. And every spare minute he had was spent on finishing the home he'd soon share with her.

In the sparse light that filtered through the window above her bed, he watched her sleep, mesmerized by her deep, even breaths.

What had happpened during her ordeal? As long as she was all right, and she seemed to be, it was of no consequence. The love he had for her was strong enough to cover anything and he made up his mind that he'd never ask about what she'd gone through.

He bent to kiss her cool cheek.

She stirred, smiled, turned toward him. Her eyelids fluttered sleepily as she saw Egan before her and raised her arms to him.

Luke slid to his knees, pulled her onto his kneeling lap and held her. "Ahhh, Maire," he sighed, "I love you so much, me darlin'. Are you well? Are you hurt?"

At the sound of his voice, Maire's eyes snapped open. She was sleepily confused. At first, she was back at Matty Burke's house, then her own room took shape around her. The arms that held her were not a dream. Slowly, she drew back from the broad chest that supported her.

"Luke," she said in surprise.

"Aye, love."

She moved back onto the bed, her eyes wide, her hands still in his. "What are you doin' here?"

"Me da said that you'd been kidnapped. I had to come. I had to know. And when they catch that dirty . . . so-and-so, I hope they break his neck before they stretch it!"

"Don't be talkin' such things. You don't know what you're sayin' besides, I'm not kidnapped an . . . anymore. I was never in any danger and I'm home now."

"So I see," he said smiling. "You won't blame me for worrin', now, will you?"

"I suppose not." Exasparated, Maire drew the blankets up under her chin. Her eyes darted around the small, dark room. "Where's Ma and Daddy?" she asked, suddenly unnerved.

"Down there, in the kitchen listenin', I'm thinkin'."

Relieved, she agreed. "Should you be up here, then?"

"Probably not. But, I had to know you were really here." As he spoke his hands moved slowly up and down her arms,

Maire felt the love he had for her. Everything will be all right, she thought, as long as he doesn't kiss me. When he kisses me, I lose me mind and I don't want that.

Luke's hand moved to the back of her head.

Her heart raced. "Don't," she murmured.

"Don't?"

"I mean, not yet . . ."

Luke sat back on his heels trying to understand. Why wasn't she throwing herself at him? Too many things had passed between them. Too many kisses. Too many promises. "How long have you been back?" he asked.

"Yesterday," she offered weakly.

"Ahhh, Maire," he sympathhized, "was it awful then?"

"Aye."

"Luke," Kean's low voice sounded. "'Tis time you came down now."

"I've got to be goin', Maire. Won't you kiss me good-bye?"

Maire cringed knowing what would follow if she permitted such a kiss. "Go now," she said. "I'll be comin' down behind you."

He took her hand and pulled her hard against him. "I love you," he said, his lips warm, moving against her cheek. "I'm not sure how but you've captured me soul and tis all I can do to not take you away with me now."

Maire couldn't speak. She could hardly breathe.

"We're comin', Mr. Martin," he said and brushed his lips over her finger tips.

She swallowed back the feeling of dread that grew inside her. The meeting with her parents and Luke had to come sometime. Perhaps, because of the hour it would be a short one. They'd talk about the wedding of course. She thought she'd been lucky enough to have missed it, but thanks to Kean, the wedding day had been changed so she hadn't missed anything . . . anything except being with Egan.

She watched as Luke descended the ladder. When she was finally alone, she sighed heavily, her face in her hands. Then, gathering all her reserves, she swung her legs over the edge of the bed, pulled on her robe and followed him.

"Come here and sit, girl," Kean ordered.

Peg placed cups of steaming tea of the table and sat across from Kean, next to Maire. If nothing else, this was going to be interesting and she wanted to be between them should Maire and Kean *have words*.

Luke sat close to Maire. He sipped at his tea.

"Would you care for somethin' stronger, lad? Kean offered.

"No, sir. Tea is fine."

"How was your ride from Dublin, Luke?"

"I honestly don't remember, Misses."

Maire drew a quick breath and let it slide out between her teeth, sick to death of all the sweetness. "Well?" she asked sharply, "are we just goin' to sit around bein' nice all night or do we really have somethin' to say here?"

Kean's brows raised. "Aye, girl. We have somethin' to say. We all want you to know that we love you and tis glad we are that you're home. Your weddin' is barely ten days away and I'm thinkin' that we should be doin' some plannin' right now as to what's goin to be happenin' then." Kean's face fairly beamed.

"Aye," Luke said with a wide, eager smile.

Peg leaned back in her chair. "The weddin' dress is done and the veil."

Maire glanced at her mother, closed her eyes and pressed a sigh through her teeth.

Kean glared at Maire. "Thank your mother, Maire, she worked hard on that."

"Thank you, Ma," she said, her voice cold. Though they could force her to be Luke's wife they could never take Egan out of her heart. She would be his whenever he wanted her. Egan O'Shea would always be the part of her that Luke could never touch.

"Now, I'm thinkin'," Kean went on genially, seemingly satisfied with Maire's shallow response, "that we should all leave a day or two early. Tomorrow I'll ask old Toolis to come by and feed the animals and do the milkin' and gatherin'. If I tell him he can keep the milk and eggs he'll be here all the earlier."

Peg nodded, a grin twitching one corner of her mouth as she returned Kean's good humor.

"You'll be stayin' with us, o'course," Luke insisted.

"Aye. If tis all right with your father, Luke," Kean stated. "If not, we'll stay at the Inn. No need to burden him with five extra people to work around and feed."

"Twould pleasure him greatly, I promise you. We'd love to have you." Luke's eyes fastened on Maire.

"Well, then, tis settled." Kean's open hands smacked his thighs with the finality of the decision. We'll leave here two days before the weddin' then, just to be sure everythin's done and ready, and stay with your father." Kean's attention shifted to Peg. "Does Bobby have anythin' decent to be wearin' to the weddin'?"

Peg smiled. "Aye. I've just made a new pair of trousers and the coat is almost done."

"And what about you?"

Peg shrugged. "I'll be wearin' somethin' you can be sure of that."

The conversation droned on. Maire couldn't understand their enthusiasm. They laughed and carried on, telling each other who they had invited and who would give the best gifts.

Father O'Reilly was ready to do the honors and a nun would place flowers from the garden in the Church and two little girls from the convent school would throw rose petals before the bride as she walked down the isle.

Maire yawned.

"Ahhh, you're right, girl," Kean grinned. "Tis late. You'll be stayin' the night?" Kean asked Luke.

"I'm surely wishin' I could but I left Da in such a muddle I'd best be getting' back. He'll be needin' help in the mornin'." Luke shoved his chair away from the table and stood.

"Tis a good lad you are, Luke MacSweeny," Kean said and extended his hand.

"Thank you, sir." He shook Kean's hand then turned to Maire, took her by her shoulders, bent and kissed her cheek. "Good night, Maire," he said softly, his eyes probing deeply into hers.

She smiled, blinking his gaze away. "Good night, Luke."

Egan sat back in the chair, the rising sun behind him. "When did she leave, Mrs. Burke?" he asked.

"Ahhh, Egan, don't get things confused. She didn't leave, I sent her. I sent her home." The old woman put a finger to her chin as she tried to remember exactly. "I sent her . . . three days ago, no four. Four days. When she told me that her ma didn't know where she was, well . . . I know how I feel when I think of me Kevin, and it hurts, lad, not knowin'," she sighed as she spoke.

"She should be home, then, "Egan murmured. "I hope she faired well at night, alone."

"I'm sure she's fine. I prayed her all the way there. I want you to understand why I sent her. Mothers are strange people, Egan. They always feel that they need to know about their children. Not *all* about them, just that they're safe. Aye, lad, women are quite different from men that way and when they become mothers . . ." she shook her head, "they become even more peculiar."

"Aye," he said with a nod. His thoughts turned to Keelin. Though she was the same she was somehow different, too.

"Well then, you take me meanin' lad, why I had to be sendin' her back to her people?"

"Aye, Misses."

"Will you be goin' after her then?"

"Aye, Misses."

"Here then take this." Matty handed him a pile of oat cakes rapped in a kerchief. "Share these with that big oaf of a dog."

He kissed her on the forehead and left.

The forest was clear of morning fog. Sun streaked its way through the oaks, the yew and juniper. Magpies squabbled above him as he played the never ending stick game with Padraig. Then from the corner of his eye something flashed on a nearby tree. White. Paper. Curious, he went to see. His heart sank as he saw his face and his name.

"A kidnapper," he whispered. "Me. Ahhh, God." He ripped the poster from the bark and stuffed it in his pocket. He'd straighten everything out when he reached Maire in the evening. It was time to tell the Martin's everything.

"Damn! I forgot to get a ring again," he said in a self berating tone. Suddenly he had to see the paper again. There was something that crept back into his memory. He drew it slowly from his pocket, almost fearfully. He straightened it. It was there all right. At the bottom in perfect script:

Member of the outlawed Fenian Brotherhood. Wanted for crimes against the British Royal Crown.

"God Almighty!" Egan shouted. He glared up through the tangle of branches to the pale patches of blue. He crossed himself slowly. "What am I supposed to be doin' now?"

In his journey to the Martin farm, Egan ripped three more posters from trees, cramming them into his pockets. He felt dazed. It was all so preposterous. Who did this? Kean Martin of course, who else? "Crimes against the British Crown," he repeated, hotly. "Well, they've seen nothin' yet, damn them! Damn them all!"

He reached the house in time to see a man on horseback gallop away. He moved in closer, the dog at his heels. Through the window, he could see Maire climbing the ladder to the loft. Kean Martin loosened his belt and tugged at his shirt as he went into another room. Peg cleared cups from the table and washed them, turned them over on a towel, took the lantern and followed her husband.

He was too late to see Maire. How he ached to touch her. He walked toward the oak. The prospect of sleeping alone in the leaves again was not a pleasant one. When he reached the tree he turned around and stared back at the house through the overlapping layers of blue moonlight. I wonder if they've barred the door? he thought. I wonder if I could . . . "Now, wouldn't that be a foolish thing to be doin'?" He shook the likelihood away and settled down beneath the tree as he'd done so many times before, lifting his collar against the chill that was to come. "Well Padraig, at least tis not rainin'."

In less than an hour heavy clouds smothered the moon and the first drops of rain spattered the dusty leaves above him. He awakened with a start.

"Damn!" he rumbled. There was no place to go but the barn. He passed the house and looked through the uncovered windows again. Maire was so near. Hesitantly, he tried the door. It opened. Martin keeps this well oiled, he thought, thankful for the silent access. They'll put me in the loony bin for sure! His heart was racing. He turned to the dog and raised his hand.

Padraig whined but sat. He closed the door and pulled his shoes off. As silently as he could, Egan tiptoed up the ladder, taking two rungs at a time. There was no light. He stood on the landing and listened. Bobby's light snore sounded above the rain off to his right. Slowly, he moved to his left in the unfamiliar surroundings. His shins touched the edge of what he guessed to be Maire's bed. He lowered his hands and ran them lightly up the blankets, over knees, buttocks, breasts, shoulders. Then gently he clamped his had over her mouth and kissed her cheek.

Frightened, Maire jerked awake, tried to scream and pull away but he held her fast and whispered in her ear. Then he released his hand and pressed his lips to hers. Her arms swung up around him and as she kissed him she thought that telling anyone about what happened to her this night would be a foolish thing, for no one would ever believe it.

"You're wet," she whispered.

"'Tis rainin' out there." His lips touched her face and shoulders.

"How is it you're here?"

"The door was unbarred. And earlier, I saw you through the window. You can't expect me to see you and not come to you now, can you?"

She shook her head. "Have you come for me, then?"

"Aye. Later . . . and to make love to you now." His voice impatient with longing. "And in the mornin' I'm goin' to be tellin' your ma and da all about us. I'm tired of hidin' the truth. I want them to know that we're married so there's no more nonsense with that Luke fellow."

"You can't tell them, Egan love. You can't be here in the mornin'. Promise me you won't," she pleaded.

"Nae, Maire. I can be here. And I will."

"But it'll do no good. Don't you see, we're goin' to go to Dublin in a week. They'll have me married to Luke in Saint Michan's Church the day after and . . . "

"Like bloody hell they will."

"Shhh!," she warned. "Daddy will wake and be off to the Constable with you. You don't know what he did."

"Oh, I know what he did and he'll have to be undoin' it." He stripped off his wet clothing as he spoke.

"Let me talk to him first," she spoke urgently. "I'll tell you what he says. Ahhh, please, Egan. I love you. I don't want you hurt."

He lifted the covers and slipped in beside her on the narrow bed. "I have business in England that can't be waitin' for you to talk to them. I'll be back in time and, so help me God, you'll be marryin' nobody!" He pulled her roughly into his arms and kissed her as if to brand her as his own.

Her warm hands slid down his cold body, feeling the tenseness in him relax at her touch.

He tugged at her nightgown, lifting it away from her legs, freeing him to roam her warm, milky skin.

The feel of his lean body against hers left her breathless. "If Bobby wakes up," she gasped, "we'll be doin' lots of explainin'."

"Aye." His voice was soft. "Maire, darlin', let me in."

He eased above her, his kisses destroying the last of her prudence. Her bed had never creaked until now. Surely, her parents would wake and find them! Egan would be killed and she would be thrown out into the rain! She tried to listen for footsteps but Egan's insistent kisses persisted, igniting ageless sensations that reeled through her, sweeping all conscious thought away, heating her flesh with passions that defied time and place.

Soon all she heard was her own muffled cries that burst into a brilliant rush of energy that jolted her, subdued her, consumed her, leaving her weak and totally mystified.

"Ahhh, Egan . . ." she purred and nestled against his chest, lost in the last delirious remnants of stolen passion. His strong, even heartbeat sounded in her ear lulling her into a deep, contented sleep.

Egan lay quietly beside her, unwilling to move, unwilling to leave. What would happen if he stayed? The Martins would learn they had no right to make his wife marry another. They'd learn that he loved Maire as he loved Ireland. They probably wouldn't believe a word he said. They might hide her away or send her where he'd never find her. Maybe she was right. "But for Chester Castle, I've killed no one," he murmured, his arms closing around her, "but Luke—whatever the hell his name is, will die before havin' this girl . . . I swear to God."

Long before dawn Egan struggled into his damp clothing and shook Maire. Sleepily, she raised her arms and he held her. "I should be stayin', you know," he whispered.

"It frightens me to think of what would happen if you did."

His fingers threaded her hair as he cupped her cheek in his palm. "They need to know about us, then no weddin' will be takin' place. Will you tell them?"

She nodded and wondered why she didn't tell him that her mother already knew. "I'll . . . I'll tell the priest at St. Michan's," she whispered.

"That's my girl." He kissed her, slipping the tip of his tongue along the closed line of her lips.

"More," she rasped, clutching at his coat sleeves.

"Later . . ." he promised. "Now I'm off to the Boggeragh's."

"The mountains?"

"Maire," Bobby moaned in his sleep, "shut up you noisy bird." He turned to the wall and covered his head with the blanket.

Egan nodded and grinned as Maire gripped his coat. Gently he removed her hand, kissed her palm. "I'll see you soon, love," he whispered.

She held her breath as he descended the ladder. The door clicked open and shut. A dog barked. Strange, she thought. We've got no dogs round here. When finally she could breathe again, she remembered Egan's big red Setter and turned over to settle into the warm memory of her secret.

15

"Put silk on your goat and it's still a goat."

MI LUNASA (August)

Finn O'Shea yawned, stretched, shoved his shirt into his trousers and tightened his belt. The smell of fresh scones greeted him when he walked into the kitchen. Patting Atty's backside, he reached for one. "'Te!', *Hot!*"

"Amadan', *Fool*," she said in the Irish and smiled at him. "'An bhfuil ocras ort?', *Are you hungry?*"

"'Nil'." Finn grabbed the milk bucket. "The cow's at the byre. I heard her bawlin'."

Atty nodded. The water on the fire was ready for the washing and she hefted it to the tub outside. It didn't take as much time or water as it once had when the children were at home. Only Egan was left now and him with the Fenians.

Nothing got easier. Her shoulders ached with age and the joints of her knees grated when she walked, but the tub needed filling.

Finn came from the barn with the milk and stopped to help Atty wring soapy water from a blanket. Though he said nothing, he knew it pained her now to do the things she had done for a lifetime.

Morning mist still covered most of the garden-patch but there was something odd in it and Finn squinted to make it out.

Atty turned to look where Finn pointed. "'Fear', *A man . . .*" More than that, the man was working the patch and a big red setter romped beside him.

Atty dropped the blanket into the tub and hurried down the path that led to the garden. For a moment Finn thought to get his shillelagh but then he could only watch as his wife threw herself into the man's arms. "Egan!" he said under his breath. "'Tis Egan!"

They stood as one in the melting mists with the fragrance of newly turned earth in their nostrils. The colors of morning shimmered, blending together with liquid ease.

In the cottage, Finn lit the lamps and threw the windows open. Atty pushed the bowl of small tawny apples aside to put tea and scones on the table.

Egan watched them move things about to make him comfortable. He knew if he tried to speak, the lump in his throat would choke him so he drank the tea and listened to the familiar voices.

"'Ar mhaith leat tuilleadh tae?' *Would you like more tea?*," Atty asked.

"'Ba mhaith,' *Yes (I would)*," he said softly and pushed his cup across the smooth, age-polished table.

"'Conas ta tu?', *How are you?*" Finn asked.

Egan smiled and nodded. "I've not heard this much Irish since I was a tyke. Have you taken it up for good then?"

Finn glanced at Atty. He shrugged lightly. "We just fell into it, I suppose. When we was younger, 'tis all we spoke, and now . . ." He shrugged again.

"'Tis all right," Egan said. "I like it."

"How long can you stay this time?" Atty asked.

"A little while."

"Good. Are you a Fenian still?"

"Aye, Ma."

Atty sighed. "I worry for you, lad." She glanced at Finn and fearing an argument, changed the subject. "You still have the dog."

Egan patted Padraig's shoulder. "He's good company."

"What ever happened to the girl you was tellin' us about?"

Egan cleared his throat. "I . . . I married her, Da."

"And you didn't bring her with you?" Atty sent a sad and somewhat worried glance at Finn. "Sure'n you didn't leave her alone."

"Ahhh, nae, Ma. She's with her own people. It . . . it was hard for her to be gettin' away just now. I'll be bringin' her soon as I can."

The place hadn't been repaired since his last visit and for the first time Egan took in the full measure of his father; the stooped shoulders, the squinting eyes, the gnarled hands. I never dreamed you'd get auld, Da, he thought and for the next few days Egan busied himself nailing, whitewashing, hoeing, harvesting and keeping Padraig from chasing chickens. His da still kept one jug of poteen in the barn and one down below the rock fence. They talked and drank and sang together. Egan played his tin whistle for the first time in months. He knew his ma was aware of the jugs but she didn't say anything, allowing Finn to have his secret. She hummed a lot and went more often into the patch to visit, often surprising the men with cups of fresh cold buttermilk and butter-filled scones. It was a time of little rain and much sun; a time of peace.

"You'll be goin' tomorrow, then?" Finn asked.

"Aye."

Atty went into the bedroom and returned with a small quilt. "Take this for Maire when you go. Tis but a wee thing. She could be usin' it for the first babe." She placed it on his lap. It was thick and soft, made of dark wool and pale cotton lace, here and there a patch of green velvet.

"Tis lovely, Ma."

"Would you be havin' another tune in you, lad?" Finn asked.

"Aye, Da." The tin whistle fell into his hands with ease and the gentle music of, "My Maire of the Curling Hair" swirled about them as Finn and Atty sang over and over:

"Wake, linnet of the osier grove!
Wake, trembling, stainless, virgin dove!
Wake, nestling of a parent's love!
Let Moran see thine eyes.
Me Maire of the curling hair the laughing cheeks and bashful air,
a bridal morn is dawning fair with bluses in the skies.
Me love, me pearl, me own dear girl, me Mountain Maid arise."

"What's wrong with you, girl? You've been off your feed ever since you got home." Peg said, dipping the long fork into the bubbling pot.

"I . . . I don't know, Ma. I'm feelin' strange."

Peg dropped the meat back into the iron pot. She felt Maire's forehead. "There's no fever but you're sweatin' like a docker. Go outside."

Maire barely made it past the door before everything in her stomach came up. Peg rushed after her, catching her as she crumpled to the ground.

"Kean!"

Maire awoke in her mother's bed.

"How do you feel, love," Peg asked.

"Better." She tried to sit up. "Me head aches."

"No wonder. You have nothin' left inside you, now." Peg turned to leave. She stood just outside the door. "I'm gettin' things ready to wash. I've not seen the rags from your monthlies lately. Have you . . ." Peg stopped, a speck of dread flickering across her face. "It don't matter. Rest a while. I'll be back."

Maire lay her head on the pillow. She crossed herself. I'm bein' punished for Egan's comin' to me bed, I know it! Tears fled her eyes and dampened the blanket she had pulled up to muffle the sound. I've felt poorly ever since Matty Burke's. Maybe I ate somethin' bad. Ahhh, Egan, I wish you was here. I need you so . . .

Peg put the armful of dirty clothes on the kitchen floor. "Maire, darlin', why are you cryin'? Do you hurt somewhere?"

"Aye, Ma," she wept, her voice faint, dismal.

Peg sat beside her. "Well? Where? I can do nothin' if you keep it to yourself."

"I can't . . ." Maire turned away and drew her knees to her chest.

"I'm your ma, girl. Sure'n you can tell me anythin'," Peg said, patting Maire's shoulder.

"Ahhh, Ma, tis me heart that hurts more'n anythin' . . ." Before Maire could stop, the whole story of Egan's night time visit spilled out with the tears. "And that's all," she sobbed.

"All?" Peg cried, shaken. "You're lucky your da didn't hear him. He'd have loaded that auld blunderbus and put a hole through your young man big enough to drive a team through. I told you before, the two of you speakin' of vows of marriage outside the Church means nothin'. Tis the witnesses that give you courage to go on when you think the love is dead. Sayin' vows to the wind is a fool's wish, a faeries promise!"

"But it wasn't to the wind, Ma. Twas to each other."

Peg spun away, arms folded. "How could you have allowed him into our home much less into your bed?" she asked uselessly. "Why would you rob me of a real weddin' for me first born?" She blinked back tears.

Maire bowed her head. "I let him in because he's me husband, Ma."

"Husband be damned! What a mess you've made of things." She wanted to strike her daughter and at the same time, she longed to smooth back the silky, copper hair that tumbled about her child's troubled face. "I don't know how to tell your father," she finally said.

Maire shuddered. "You can't be tellin' Daddy, Ma!"

"And what am I supposed to do, then? Let him go on thinkin' you're ready to be the wife of Luke MacSweeny? I think not."

"But Ma," Maire pleaded, "he'll hate me and . . ."

"So you wed Egan for yourself and you mean to wed Luke for your father?" Peg threw her hands in the air. "It don't work that way!"

"I know, Ma. I'll always love Egan. But," she sniffed, "I can't hurt Daddy. I need some time to think."

"What are you thinkin' he'll do when he finds out about you and Egan? And he will! Things like that don't stay buried. They spring up like snakes in Eden!" Peg's voice shattered Maire. "I know what your plan is, girl, and it won't work. You can't have Luke and Egan, too. Not for a minute. You'll love one and hate the other and make three people miserable all their lives!"

"And who might the third one be?" Maire asked, trying not to cry.

"You, you little fool. You, that's who." Peg rubbed her neck and sighed. "God help you, Maire. You're just past seventeen and your life is thirty years in ruin."

"You won't tell Daddy, will you Ma?" Maire begged.

"We'll see. I'll be thinkin' on it, be sure of that." Peg twisted her apron. "Sometimes I wonder whose daughter you are."

Maire watched her mother walk away. Could it be that she really did want both Luke and Egan? Was that possible?

For days Peg and Maire hardly spoke. Maire existed on weak tea and stale soda bread. Kean complained, "I'll not be givin' a gatepost to MacSweeny's son," and insisted she eat. Peg kept her close, watched her carefully, prayed daily that she wasn't with child. But her heart sank as Maire's hand continually went to her abdomen.

"What's the matter now, girl?"

Maire sighed, dropped into a chair. "I don't know," she muttered. "Some times me stomach just . . . rolls."

Peg held her breath. "Let me see," she said, forcing the words.

Maire's hands dropped away allowing her mother to feel her belly.

"Seems quiet enough now."

Maire pressed her hand over her mother's. "There it is. Feel it?"

Peg sighed, sadly. "Aye, Maire. I feel it."

"Is it serious, then?" Maire's green eyes widened as she searched her mother's sullen face.

"I'd say that it is, love. And I was prayin' hard it wasn't so."

"What, Ma? What's wrong with me?" Her face paled.

"Nothin'. There's nothin' wrong. Tis just a baby."

Maire's jaw dropped. "Ma, stop teasin' . . . That can't be, I mean, it can't!"

"Aye, girl, it can. A baby's in there sure as turf burns. Is Egan O'Shea the only man you've lain with?"

"Ma!"

"Answer me." Peg didn't blink. Her eyes were hard as steel.

Maire nodded.

"I can give thanks for that much anyway," Peg sighed. "You can't be doin' what you must have done, Maire, and not be payin' the piper. You've seen the horses mate and the cattle. It works the same way."

"But tis not the same! Not at all!"

Peg raised her brows as if to ask the difference.

"Well, tis not!" Maire wailed. "We're not animals and Egan was not perched upon me back!"

Wearily, Peg rubbed a hand over her eyes. "Maybe not, but it comes to the same thing. You're goin' to be havin' a wee babe and believe me, Luke'll know tis not his. Tis certain you can't marry him now."

Maire paced the kitchen as a light rain tapped against the window pane. She had heard all the names women were called who had babies without husbands: loose, wanton, trollop, whore—on and on. And where was Egan, anyway? Why was he never around when she needed him? The time was so short! They were to leave for Dublin soon. Maire glared at her mother, her eyes wild. "Tis all the more reason I have to marry Luke. I'll tell him it come early! I'll tell him . . ."

"And when your baby looks like Egan O'Shea?"

"Damnit, Ma, it'll look like me!"

"You have it all tallied out, then . . ."

"I have." She stared out the window at the old oak where she had secretly met Egan so many times.

"I wouldn't be you, girl . . . not for all the wishes I could get from a faery caught in me hand. I raised you to be a good wife but I'm feelin' sorry for young Luke already. You'll be the seed in his tooth for as long as you live."

Maire turned from the window. She set her jaw and glowered at her mother. "Nae, I won't!" she sobbed and ran down the hill to the oak.

Maire sagged into the leaves. She tried to sort through the feelings that battered her, smothered her. Luke waited in Dublin. He was a kind man, a loving man, who kept nothing from her. A girl should be glad to be Mrs. Luke MacSweeny. But what of Egan? He was such a mystery, appearing as if by magic and disappearing the same way. Where did he go when he left? What did he do? He told her nothing. Was her father right? Was Egan one of those stupid Fenians wanted by the Crown?

The baby rolled and, amazed, Maire caressed her stomach. She found it all a bit hard to believe. Whatever happened now, the baby came first. What kind of life would Egan give his child? Ma had said that he'd be hanged, sure; that Luke was her only hope. "Ahhh, God, Egan, I love you so. You promised that I'd never marry Luke. But Daddy said I would. And Ma . . . Ma feels sorry for the lot of us."

Now Egan was gone again and Luke simply waited for her, knowing she would come. "Aye," she sighed, "I'll come." To do anything else meant disappointing the man who had loved her first. She would take her wedding dress and go to Dublin and smile while the flower in her withered from thirsting for Egan O'Shea. The baby probably would look like him, just to haunt her for the rest of her days.

Maire pulled herself up against the tree's rough bark. She was soaked, but the passing early autumn shower went unfelt. Her hair clung thickly to her scalp and rain washed away the tears that washed her face. She bent to pick up the dead stem of a wild rose. A thorn pricked her finger. Blood rose in a round red globe just as it had before.

Dublin's quay was nearly empty and shrouded in thick fog. Unseen waves slapped the pilings. Hungry gulls abandoned the air, content to waddle about the wharf in search of food.

Rory and Keelin leaned on the smoothly-worn railing. Michael and Dylan purchased their tickets and walked toward the city.

"Leavin' Ireland's always a sorrow," Keelin said against Rory's shoulder. "At least this time we're goin' together and comin' home through Cork. I've not been to Cork, have you?"

"Nae. Egan says tis lovely and County Kerry, too. We'll do some sightseein' if we can. Go round the ring maybe."

Keelin smiled broadly and snuggled closer to him trying to block out the cold. "When does the boat leave?"

"Not until the fog lifts I'm thinkin'."

"Any sign of Egan?" she asked.

"Not yet. I'd not be worryin' about him. He'll be along."

"Do you think he's seen the posters?"

"I hope not. Egan's no kidnapper."

"You don't really think he took Maire, do you?"

Rory shook his head. "If he did he'd have brought her to us, now wouldn't he?"

"I suppose . . ."

Rory's arm tightened around Keelin in a comforting squeeze. "I don't know what they was thinkin'. And who pegged him for a Fenian?"

"I'm wishin' I knew. That's the scary part, isn't it?"

"Aye, love. That it is."

Dockers pushed loaded carts through the swirling fog, up the planks onto the ship then returned to repeat the journey again and again.

People queued up at the ticket window and luggage was heaped onto the carts and pushed aboard.

The insipid sun was no match for the clouds that fell around them in a fine, chill mist.

"There's Egan," Rory whispered.

A Constable strolled the docks.

"What's he doin'?" Keelin asked cautiously.

Their eyes followed the Policeman who moved from one person to another.

"He's got a poster," Rory said.

"Egan's?"

"I don't know."

They moved closer. They couldn't see through the fog and the noisy workmen made it impossible to hear. Finally, pulling Keelin behind him, Rory bumped the officer.

"Ahhh, sir, I'm sorry," he said.

The Constable looked from Rory to the picture and said: "No harm. No harm." He straightened his uniform. "Would you have seen this man in your travels?"

Rory took the poster and stared into Egan's face. "Nae."

The Constable handed the paper to Keelin. "You Misses?"

Keelin looked at the picture and shook her head. "A strange lookin' man," she said softly, forcing the Constable to strain to hear. "A dark one by the looks of him." She turned to Rory. "Did we not see this man in Galway a month ago?"

Rory took the poster again and peered at it. He rubbed his chin. "Could be. But the man we saw had a girl with him."

The officer brightened. "Where in Galway?"

"Was it Clairenbridge?" Rory asked her.

"Nae. I'm thinkin' it was Athenry . . . by the Abbey." Keelin's attention turned again to the Constable. "We can't be sure o'course," she hedged, "but it does look like him. A bit darker than this though with curlier hair."

The Constable took out a pencil. "Would you recall the day?"

"Sometime the middle of last month I'd say," Rory told him.

The Constable touched the edge of his hat and left.

Keelin's eyes sparkled above the glove that hid her smile.

"For a bit there, Mrs. Kilcullen," Rory complained tartly, "I thought you was describin' me."

"I was," Keelin giggled. "Let's find Egan."

Egan walked along the railing looking out to sea. Rory moved up beside him.

"Where's Padraig?" he asked offhandedly.

Egan smiled. "When I found out he liked me da's chickens more'n he should have, I left him with a young lad in Dublin. He said his father was a butcher. Can you think of a better place for a dog? At least he'll have food and the boy likes him."

"How did you come upon the likes of him?"

"On Halston Street . . . at St. Michan's."

"What was you doin' there?"

Egan looked soulfully at his friend wishing he could tell him all the sorry details. "Prayin'," he said.

Keelin stepped between them. "There's another Constable on the dock," she warned.

The men turned, leaned against the rail. Egan pulled his wool cap down over one eye. The officer passed a poster.

"Damn!" Egan hissed and turned back to the sea.

"You know then," Rory whispered.

"I know. I have a whole pocketful of the damn things! I'll be glad to get to Manchester and away from this! I wonder if Willie's been able to learn more about the trial."

Rory glanced at Keelin, his face betrayed his concern. "I know you mentioned Willie at the meetin' but I thought it would be just the five of us," he said. "When did Willie come on board?"

"I met him in Dublin when I was comin' back from the Boggeraghs. He was leavin' for Manchester anyhow so he's been there a while now. Like I said before, he'll keep an eye out for us and let us know what to expect." Egan stepped away from the rail. "I'm sorry I failed to tell you all of it. Me minds been jugglin' a hundred things lately."

"I'm glad he's with us. I like Willie. He's a good man." Rory breathed deeply of sea air, patted Egan's shoulder and moved toward the Constable.

"Nae, love. Let me," Keelin said and pushed past him, walking purposefully toward the official.

She struck up a serious conversation with the man and guided him over to Rory and Egan. "Look, Johnny," she said to Rory. "'Tis the same man, isn't it? The one in Galway, I mean."

They played the same game. Egan's heart thudded in his throat when they thrust the picture at him.

"You remember him, Paddy, don't you? He was the one at the Abbey with the pretty girl." Keelin turned again to the officer. "I'm sure it's him, though he's darker than this picture shows. May I be keepin' this, your honor?"

The Constable grinned. "Aye, Misses. There's plenty more where this one came from."

Egan felt his legs turn to water. "Am I a dead man, then?"

"Not as long as Keelin keeps sendin' them to Galway."

The voice of the ship's purser burst above the crowd. "Show your boardin' passes for the Emerald Sea! Boardin' passes!"

They waited while children, carefully guarded by parental hands, were herded up the gang plank. Satchels and packages were shifted to other arms as the purser reached to puncture each ticket.

Keelin preceded them onto the ship and within minutes the sailing tug had pulled the ferry into open water where her own canvas bellied out in the wind.

The floor of Manchester courthouse was cluttered with onlookers. Smells of wool and rose water, hair tonic and oiled wood were carried aloft on clouds of pipe smoke.

"Heard anythin' yet?" Willie asked Egan in a strained whisper.

"Nae. You?"

Searching through the mass of people to the dais, Willie frowned as he shook his head. "I've been here more'n four days already. Corydon said O'Leary's trial was supposed to be first."

Egan scowled. "Corydon's here? Somethin's wrong. He was off to London, not here."

Egan looked bewildered. "When I saw him last he said he was on his way to London." As he spoke, Willie's face expressed his questions.

Egan was silent. Why was J.J. here? Did one of the team tell him? Did it matter if they did? In the end it must be a coincidence. Perhaps he had business in Manchester before he went to London.

"What's goin' on, Egan?" Willie asked, his brow furrowed.

Egan shook his head as if to eliminate his thoughts. "Did J.J. tell you about Kelly and Deasy?" he asked.

"Nae," Willie said, "What about them?"

"J.J. told me they were arrested and they'll be on trial today as well as O'Leary and them."

"Ahhh, Kelly's on the list for this afternoon. I never thought it was Tom though." Willie moved back into the crowd. "I'll see what else I can find out."

Egan silently counted two days until Maire's wedding. If the courts didn't try O'Leary, Luby and Kickham today, he'd have to risk something else. His stomach churned. Would he stay and rescue his friends or would he leave them to rescue Maire?

"Egan! Egan O'Shea!" The hoarse, familiar whisper came from behind him in the crush of people.

"Dob Quinn! God Almighty! What the hell are you doin' here?"

"I was wonderin' the same of you. If you're here for O'Leary and them, go home. They've flown like feathers in the wind."

"What are you talkin' about? How do you know?"

"J.J. Corydon."

"And how would he be knowin' that?"

Dob smiled his tiny-toothed grin. "Corydon seems to know a lot more'n we give him credit for."

Egan grasped Dob's lapels, lifting him off the floor. "What did he tell you?"

"That they're bein' brought here with Tom Kelly and Tim Deasy in a police van and they're on their way here now."

"Hush!" a portly woman ordered. "I came to see this trial. Please take your business elsewhere!"

Egan glared at her and she shrank back. He released Dob Quinn. "If you've got somethin' to say, say it. I got no time for the likes of your bloody games!"

Dob brushed his sleeves, smoothed his lapels. "'Tis no game, just a warnin'. Don't be makin' trouble here. Things are bein' took care of, so don't go tryin' to help. Sure as hell's hot, somebody'll die."

Before Egan could say another word, the little man retreated into the mass of larger bodies. Egan pushed his way outside to Keelin and Rory.

"I don't understand," Keelin whispered anxiously. "What does it mean, 'they're on their way here in a van?' I thought O'Leary and them was here already. You told us about Tom Kelly and Tim Deasy, but…"

"I don't trust anythin' that bloody little Clúrachán says!" Rory hissed. "How did he come to be here anyway?"

Egan glanced back at the courthouse. "Who knows?"

"Well, what now?"

"Damnit, Rory!" Egan growled. "How the hell do I know?"

Keelin took Egan's hand. "I'll find out. You two stay here."

Egan's eyes met Rory's in apology. Why didn't just one plan go right? The men they had hoped to free could be anywhere by now. What had Dob Quinn said? *Flown like feathers in the wind*? With suspension of Irish Habeas Corpus a retrial, anywhere, was at British whim.

The Martin family cart, packed with most of Maire's belongings, arrived at the MacSweeny store and residence at early evening.

"Maire!" Luke called and ran to lift her to the ground. He didn't notice her shallow smile or how lightly she touched his taut shoulders.

Peg watched them sorrowfully. The men slapped each other on the back with loud greetings. Roddy and Bobby hefted the baggage and dragged each piece into the house. Two-year-old Kate struggled to get out of her mother's arms when she saw the dog.

"Was your trip a good one then?" Luke asked, guiding Maire from the wagon to the house.

"Twas fine," she said, her attention also on the big red setter. "Whose dog?" she asked. "I've not seen him here before." Her anxious eyes met those of her mother who offered a glance of closed, simmering patience.

"Roddy!" MacSweeny blared. "Get that good-for-nothin' dog out of here, now. He don't belong in the house!"

Luke gave Maire a quick hug and whispered, "Roddy's watchin' him for a man he met in Dublin. He'll soon come back for him."

Padraig's dark, playful eyes settled on Maire. He whined, tried to pull away from Roddy's grip. "I'm tired, Luke," she said. "Where am I to be sleepin'?"

He grinned, reddened. "In me own bed, if that's all right."

She stopped. "I . . . I don't think . . . I mean, is it proper?"

"I'm not goin' to be in it, love," Luke laughed. He pressed his lips to her temple. "Not tonight, anyway," he whispered. "Hungry?"

She couldn't shake the quivering smile from her lips. "Just tired," she managed.

Luke led her to the small, converted storage room that served as his bedroom. The dog broke away from Roddy and followed, but Luke turned him back with a sharp glance at his brother who dragged the animal toward the back door. "At least there's no loft to be climbin' into tonight," he teased.

Maire sat on the edge of the wide, newly constructed bed, obviously built for two. The fading smell of fresh paint and the fragrance from the vase of wild flowers was a pleasant mixture. "Nice," she said, fingering the lace that spread across the blue quilting.

"Ma," Luke said. "I watched her make it. Lots of things she made'll be yours when we leave St. Michan's."

Maire forced a smile and nodded.

"Well, then," Luke said, lifting her bag to the bed, "did you bring all your things?"

"Almost . . ."

Luke grinned, his eyes filled with love. "We'll go for the rest after the weddin'. Not havin' everythin' here'll make it easier when we move in to our own house. Tis near finished you know."

She couldn't help smiling back at him. "Are you goin' to show it to me tomorrow, then?"

"I think I'll keep it a surprise," he said, teasing. "Tis me weddin' gift to you."

"Tis a big gift, Luke. I have none for you."

"Ahhh, Maire, you gave me the best present of me life when you said you'd be me wife. I want nothin' more." The broad smile again filled his eyes. "Use that side of the chest. I cleaned it out and put new paper in. You can sleep now, if you like. I'll be in the Best room. If you need me, just call." He tipped her chin and as he brushed her mouth with his, he pulled her against him and his lips rocked over hers gently, then as if they had always belonged to him alone. Her fingers dug into his biceps and even as she tried not to, she kissed him back. Abruptly, he released her and was gone.

Stunned again by his kiss, Maire watched the curtain fall shut. This was going to be harder than she had imagined. Ahhh, God, Egan, she thought, where are you and why's your dog here? Are you out there watchin'? If you are, you'd best fetch me quick for I don't know what to do when Luke kisses me. He unravels me like a loose thread. Where are you, you fool?

Sighing, she pulled her clothes from the satchel. Sure'n I've got to be seein' the priest. What good will that do? He won't listen. He'll be just like Ma. I don't care. I want to see St. Michan's before the weddin' anyway. The weddin' . . . She sank onto the bed, her shoulders rounded with the weight of a problem she saw as unsolvable. "Damn, Egan," she said under her breath. "Your dog is here! Where the bloody hell are you?" I'll tell him they forced me . . . that I had no choice. That'll do it. That'll have to do it!

Her hands worked independent of her mind. Clothing fell into drawers without thought as she struggled with the presence of Padraig and the absence of Egan. "What can I do?"

In the Best room, MacSweeny held his glass out to Kean. "To Luke and Maire!" he said as the glasses tinked together.

"Aye," Kean replied. "And to many healthy babes!" He winked at Luke and sipped the whiskey.

Peg rose stiffly from her chair. "If you two are goin' to be congratulatin' yourselves all night, I'd like to be gettin' the children settled. Maire said she wants to go to St. Michan's tomorrow."

"But, Ma," Bobby protested. "We just got here. Can't we stay up longer? Tis not like there's work to be doin' or anythin'."

"We've been here long enough. Tis time for you to sleep!"

Bobby groaned again.

Kate sat at Peg's feet and lay her head on the floor, her thumb in her mouth. "Will you look at that now?" Peg said accusingly. "Mr. MacSweeny, I think tis time our boys was in bed."

MacSweeny shrugged. "Roddy," he bellowed. "Up you go."

"But, Daddy!"

The stern look above MacSweeny's highly waxed mustache sent the boys scuffing from the room without another word.

"Now you two can toast yourselves sick if you like." She picked up the little girl and went into the main bedroom. "Good night, Luke."

"Don't mind her," Kean apologized. "With the auldest girl marryin', she's off her feed, that's all."

MacSweeny remembered the first time he'd been exposed to Kean's wife. She hadn't been in too good a humor then either. He hoped Maire's temperament would be better . . . for Luke's sake.

"Maire's all settled in, then?"

"Aye, Da," Luke smiled. "As much as I can, I'm thinkin'."

"That's a good, lad," Kean said, clapping the young man's shoulder. "Me Maire's a lucky girl, she is."

Luke grinned. "I'm the lucky one, sir. There's not another like her."

"She's a beauty, I'll say that," MacSweeny put in.

"Aye," Luke agreed. "I'll be sayin', good night now, Da. Roddy and I'll get up early to tend the stock so if you and Mr. Martin would like to be layin' in . . ."

MacSweeny slapped Luke on the back. "You know, Martin. God never made a better mortal than the one I'm givin' your daughter."

Kean lifted his glass in salute. "We couldn't do better."

Luke climbed into the loft beside the two boys. Moonlight ran through the curtains in long streaks of silver light. He lay on the thick downy mattress, arms folded behind his head, eyes shining in the moon's reflection. Maire was finally here even if she did seem a touch standoffish. No one could take her now. He'd won. Somehow he'd erase that other man from her memory. He turned over, closed his eyes. I'll love him out of you, he thought, smiling, that's what I'll do.

Peg tossed. The bedroom was flooded with moonlight. Kean was still with MacSweeny, no doubt drinking himself into a stupor. She leaned across the bed to close the curtains. Tomorrow would dawn all too soon. Did they expect her to make breakfast? Nothing had been discussed. What would Maire do tomorrow? Would she be able to go through with the wedding now that she carried O'Shea's child? And poor Kean thought that everything was perfect and it couldn't be worse. And just how the divil did that dog . . . ? They never went one without the other. With him here, Egan couldn't be far behind. Peg heaved a sigh and drew the blankets to her shoulders. She rubbed her tired eyes. "Ahhh, God in heaven, if we ever needed a miracle, we're needin' one now. What can I do?"

Maire decided that Luke's small bedroom was a cozy place as she unbuttoned her bodice and draped her clothing over the chair. She stood before the long mirror, looking at her naked torso. Her hands moved over each tender breast and down her abdomen. Maybe Ma was wrong about the baby. After all, she hadn't felt any movement for a while. Maybe she had just been a wee bit sick for a time. She shrugged and reached for her nightgown, then paused to take one more look in the mirror. Before settling into Luke's bed, she pressed her hands over her stomach. There was the fluttering. She breathed a half-yawn, half-sigh. "What am I to do?"

Dawn stole silently through the windows into the house. Luke groaned as he shifted his weight on the flattened down-filled mattress and opened his eyes. He lay there a moment adjusting his limbs on the uncomfortable pallet, thinking how much nicer it would have been to have slept in his own new bed. Then he pulled himself upright and rubbed the sleep away.

"Roddy!" he whispered sharply. "Roddy, up with you now."

The boy rolled over and sat up. "Is it mornin' already?"

"Aye. Get your clothes on."

The air outside was dense, heavy with the scent of moisture. A low sky swelled darkly and ragged flashes of far off lightning illuminated the gray underbelly of the clouds.

Luke glanced toward the west. He judged there was more heat than fury in the discharges and if the storm came as far as Dublin, it wouldn't last long.

"Stop playin' with that infernal dog and get to the animals!" Luke ordered above the dull coughs of distant thunder. "I can't understand why Da lets you keep him anyway."

"He's a great dog, Luke. Watch." Roddy picked up a stick and threw it. The big red Setter lunged forward scattering the sheep.

"Now look what you done!" Luke said. "That dog'll set them off and we'll be spendin' the day chasin' woollies. Just between you and me, Roddy MacSweeny, I got other plans!" He turned back to his work. "Where did you say he come from?"

"A man asked me to keep him while he was gone, that's all. I got him at the Church when you sent me to see Father O'Reilly about them wee convent girls. He's a great dog, Luke. Really."

"He's a nuisance!" The muscles of Luke's upper body bulged as he hoisted fork-loads of hay into the mangers. "He's goin' to be causin' trouble round here. I can see it comin'."

Padraig stopped playing the stick game with Roddy and took his prize to Luke, dropping it at his feet.

"Away with you, you houligan," he said.

The Setter lay down, his head on his paws, his round brown eyes following Luke's every move.

"Looks like he's wonderin' why you don't like him," Roddy said.

Luke strained under heavy buckets of soaked mash and turnips for the pigs. He poured the slop into the long trough ignoring the sharp smell that erupted from the ankle deep mud of the pig pen. "Tis not that I don't like him, it's just that I'm thinkin' a dog in a butcher store is not a farsighted thing to do."

Padraig inched closer as Luke's voice softened. "What's his name, anyway?" Luke asked.

Roddy shrugged. "Tricks, I think. I don't remember exactly."

"Did the man say when he was comin' back?"

"He'll be over the water a few days, he said. I'll take him back to St. Michan's tomorrow."

Padraig pushed closer to Luke until his head rested on Luke's thick leather boot.

Luke smiled. "Well, then, tomorrow we lose a dog and gain a wife. I'd say that's more'n a decent exchange wouldn't you?"

Roddy scowled. "I'm not thinkin' that at all! I'm thinkin' I'd like to be keepin' him."

"Keep this dog! Are you bats? First, he belongs to another. Second, a dog in a butcher store is madness. Third, you don't even know his name for sure. Ahhh, nae, Roddy, tomorrow you take him back like you promised. Now, get to work! Listen to The Pair. Hang some oats on them before they kick out the stalls!"

Roddy mumbled under his breath and turned to care for his father's matched pair of thoroughbreds. He patted his thigh and Padraig came running.

Peg squeezed from beneath Kean's heavy arm and leg. She checked Kate and covered her then pulled her own robe tight to close out the early morning chill and combed her hair before going into the kitchen. Quietly, she stuffed the stove with tinder and kindling from the box on the floor beside it, lit it then put on the kettle for tea. One cupboard after another creaked open as she sought flour and soda, salt and caraway seeds. A short time later two round, floury lumps of bread were shoved into the cast-iron oven.

In the back porch pantry she found a covered crock of butter. "Needs salt," she murmured upon tasting it, startled to see MacSweeny filling the doorway.

"Didn't mean to frighten you, Misses," he said, his face creasing into the usual grin. "You didn't have to be makin' breakfast, but tis glad I am you are. Tis eight long years since this kitchen's been graced by a woman fair as you."

Peg had thought she'd forgotten how to blush. "I'm thinkin' fairness has nothin' to do with it, Mr. MacSweeny," she said with a softly disconcerted laugh, staring again at the crock she carried.

"Ahhh, nae, Misses. Tis a beauty you are still. Make no mistake. And Maire's the spittin' image of you."

Peg drew a quick breath. "There's more to Maire than the eye can see, Mr. MacSweeny. I hope in a years time she's still beautiful to you." She grabbed a flannel, folded it and opened the oven door. The aroma of baking bread drifted through the kitchen.

MacSweeny's mystified gaze examined her for a moment, then he left the house to help the boys with their chores.

By mid-morning Peg and Maire had the kitchen cleaned of every crumb and cobweb, though they'd not spoken beyond the banalities of simple requirement except to mention the presence of Egan's dog. "Does it worry you?" Peg asked.

"I'd be lyin' if I said it didn't. But I can't help hopin' . . ."

"That he's close by?"

Maire dragged her cleaning rag along the window sill as she stared through the freshly cleaned pane. Roddy and Bobby played in the street with the dog while the men rocked and smoked their pipes under the dripping porch roof. Steam rose from the roadway and blinding rays of sun reflected off the cobblestones.

"He's not out there, girl. I doubt he'll come for that dog at all."

"He'll come, Ma," Maire whispered. "I just don't know when."

Peg felt her shoulders droop as low as her spirit. "Give me that rag and fetch Kate. She should be awake by now."

"Aye, Ma."

Peg took the cloth and watched Maire disappear into the bedroom then went to the open front door. "Don't be gettin' wet, Bobby," she called, cleaning rags in hand. "We're leavin' for the Church soon and I'll not be havin' to change your clothes before we go."

"Ahhh, Ma! Why do we have to go?" the boy complained, throwing the stick again. "I want to stay. Look at the dog. Isn't he grand? Don't he remind you of . . ."

"Aye, lad," she interrupted. "Grand."

Kean stretched. "Ahhh, Peg. If Maire wants to go to the church, why don't you let her go with Luke and leave the rest of us out of it? Where are the two lovebirds, anyway?" he yawned.

"Maire's carin' for Kate at the moment and . . ."

"That's not right, Peg," Kean said with a wink in MacSweeny's direction. "Maire should be carin' for Luke, not a squirmin' handful like Kate."

"She might as well be gettin' used to it." Peg turned to go back into the house. "She'll have to learn soon enough."

"What's that, Peg?"

"Nothin'," she replied and stood in the doorway. "Aye, Kean," she said softly. "I'm thinkin' you're right."

Kean groaned, leaning forward to lift his weight from the chair. "Right about what, love?"

"Sendin' Luke with Maire . . . alone."

Kean smiled and kissed Peg's cheek. "I'm glad you're seein' it my way. I'll hitch Winnie and they can take our cart."

Winnie's hooves clacked over the cobblestones. The towers of Trinity College gleamed in the distance and the music of tin whistles and drumming bodrhans seeped from the walls of nearby pubs. The shadowy waters of the River Liffey came into view as Luke turned the cart onto Essex Quay. They crossed the Liffey over Grattan Bridge and headed up Capel Street. Luke pointed out more of Dublin's sights.

All Maire could do was nod and smile apathetically. Luke shrugged off her seeming lack of interest. Everything in their lives would change tomorrow.

He turned the cart down Little Britain Street to Halston where, behind an ivy-covered iron fence, Saint Michan's Roman Catholic Church lay nestled in a mound of late summer flowers and trees embellished with yellow leaves.

After Luke tied Winnie to the fence, he rang the bell at the gate and led the way into the darkly cool Sanctuary. He dipped his fingers into the brass pan of holy water in front of a bank of burning candles, crossed himself and genuflected.

"Ahhh, Luke MacSweeny," Father O'Reilly said cheerfully as he closed the door of the ornately carved confessional. "What a nice surprise. You're not here to be married are you? Good heavens, have I got the day wrong?" He lifted the linen pallium from his shoulders, kissed it and tucked it into his pocket.

Maire watched both men phlegmatically as Luke assured Father O'Reilly his memory was still intact and listened to the father's quiet voice tell them the banns had been read the past three Sundays and no one had come forward to object to their marriage.

Maire looked hard at the priest. Though she didn't know what she had expected, Father O'Reilly was certainly not it. His hair and brows were as white as his surplice, yet there was not a wrinkle on his face. Deep blue eyes twinkled above a wide flattish nose and he was short, not so much as an inch taller than herself. His hands were cool and soft as cotton when he greeted her. She stared at him, waiting for him to look away, then uncomfortably, she withdrew her hand and walked slowly down the center aisle toward the alter.

"Do you like St. Michan's?" he called after her.

She turned. "It'll do," she said, her voice resounding clearly against the vaulted ceiling. "I suppose there'll be a bigger place than that," she pointed back at the confessional, "for me to be waitin' . . . before."

Luke smiled. Maire was her old self again.

"Aye," the priest replied. "Would you like to look at it now or wait until you come tomorrow?"

Maire shrugged. She had challenged him as she challenged every man and this one hadn't squirmed at all. "Now," she said.

Father O'Reilly led them outside and turned toward a cottage to the left of the sanctuary. The room they entered was light and spacious with unusually tall windows and padded furniture. A long, wide mirror hung on the far wall.

"If it's rainin'," Father O'Reilly said, "I'll have Sister Maire Tyrone bring you to the alter without goin' outside. All you need to worry about is young Luke here who'll, no doubt, be shakin' in his boots."

"Aye," Luke laughed.

"Father," Maire said. "I have somethin' on me mind. Can we talk together . . . alone?"

"Of course." He turned to Luke and asked him to excuse them for a moment.

Luke nodded and winked at Maire as he closed the door behind him and walked back to the Church.

"I can see you're troubled, Maire. Come, sit here."

She folded her hands in her lap and pressed her lips tightly.

Father O'Reilly reached to cover her hands. "Is it that bad?" he asked.

Maire nodded. She took a breath, stared down at her shoe tops. "I'm needin' some advice . . . maybe more like help. You see . . ." She raised her face to him. "Ma said . . . "She swallowed hard, her voice shrank to a whisper. "Ma said there's a baby inside me."

The priest couldn't hide his shock. "How does your Ma know that?"

"Ma knows things," she said, stunned that he would ask.

Father O'Reilly gathered his senses. "Well, let's start at the beginnin', Maire. Who's the babies father? Is it Luke?"

She bowed her head and swallowed back tears. "Nae. Tis Egan . . . Egan O'Shea. I love him, father, and me da turned him in for a Fenian and I don't know what to do. Da says I have to marry Luke . . . but I'm married to Egan. We done it ourselves sayin' the vows and comin' together and makin' the promises . . ."

The priest caught his breath and collected his words. "Does your da know about the baby?"

Maire shook her head, her copper waves catching the light like a halo. "I love Luke, too, I do. I can't help it. I know I could make him a good wife but . . . I know, too that I'll be dreamin' of Egan. What'll I do?" A sudden rush of tears overwhelmed her. She sank to the floor in front of him and wept.

Father O'Reilly smoothed her hair lovingly. "You're not the only one this has happened to, Maire. Sit up and we'll talk." He lifted her from the floor and offered his handkerchief.

Maire took it, wiped her face and nose. "Ma says me life is in ruin and there's no fixin' it but to marry Luke and forget Egan and that Luke will know this little one inside me is not his and he'll hate me and I'll ruin Luke's life, too and Egan will probably kill him. Oh, God!" She grasped his hands "Will the divil take me?"

Father O'Reilly listened as Maire wept and sniffed, wiped her eyes and wept some more. "Maire," he said calmly, "You forget that you're not alone in this. Should you tell Luke? Yes, you should. But that's not the end. It sounds to me like this Egan is a bit undependable. I'm sure he loves you but you can't be married without the blessin's of God and the church and the support of your family and friends. No one is *really* married by doin' it themselves." He finally realized that Maire was naïve as a child about the whole situation. "I need you to know somethin' Maire and remember it all the days you live. Right now your life is in a tumble but it won't last and I'll be here to guide you when you need me until tis all resolved. And, you have to know that there's nothin' that God can't forgive. He makes all things new and He makes no mistakes. You are His child and He won't abandon you or your wee babe.

"The divil is liar from the beginnin' and a thief who tries to steal your soul and make you think you're worthless when the Lord Himself sent His Son Jaysus to make you His treasure. You're God's own treasure, girl. Remember that."

Maire smiled for the first time in days. "But what should I do? I don't feel like a treasure . . ." she said, her green eyes shimmering with tears.

"You must think about the baby. That is your most important duty now. Who will care for your child better, Luke or Egan? Consider each of them. I think you know what you should do and I will stand with you against anyone who questions your decision."

Maire stood and wrapped her arms around the priest. "Thank you," she cried even as she felt Egan slipping out of her life forever and, beneath her stomach, the fluttering began.

Rory wiped his forehead with the red kerchief from his pocket and tied it loosely around his neck. "When did Corydon find out about this retrial?" he asked.

Egan shrugged. "June. July. Why?"

"I don't know. Nothin' maybe. Seems strange they'd choose Manchester to retry them, that's all. He was here an hour ago. I should have asked him meself. Did you see him inside?"

Egan shook his head.

Keelin hurried toward them.

"What did you find out?" Rory asked.

"At least some of it's true. Kelly and Deasy was arrested on the tenth. They're comin' here now. I didn't learn a thing about O'Leary and them. They could be in the van, but . . ."

"Where's the van now?" Egan asked.

"They're supposed to be here by noon so it must be close, why?"

"Keelin, love," Egan said, confidence again in his voice, "do you think you could be startin' a mild disturbance?"

Her already round eyes became enormous. "And just what kind of disturbance are you wantin' now?"

"A big one. A big, loud one."

"When would you like this big, loud risin'?" Rory asked with a wink.

"Soon as I can find Dylan and Michael and Willie."

"Fifteen minutes, then?"

"Aye," Egan said. "Five days is more'n enough time to spend here with nothin' to be showin' for it. If you can persuade the Bulls round here to stop a noisy street fight, the rest of us can get the van. If O'Leary and them are there, we'll free them now."

"And Kelly and Deasy?" Keelin asked.

Egan laughed. "What the hell, them too."

"What about us after the risin's over?" Rory asked.

"I don't want you waitin' round that long. Start it, that's all. Then while the Bulls are busy, get out. Go on to Dover and get the ferry to Calais, just like we planned. If we find you, you'll be takin' Kickham with you, if not . . ." Egan shrugged, grinned.

"All right," Keelin said, "off with you then. This auld man and I have a scuffle to be startin'."

"Auld is it?" Egan heard as he went back up the courthouse steps to find the others.

"Are you ready, Keelin me darlin'?" Rory asked, holding her hands as they stood behind the tall well-trimmed hedges of the courthouse.

"Aye. But kiss me. If I'm goin' to be causin' a risin', I'm wantin' to know you love me first."

With a broad smile, Rory scooped her into his arms and kissed her eagerly. "When we get home, I'm goin' to . . ."

"Be a father," she said, "sooner than you think."

Rory stared at her, smiled, not quite believing. "When?"

"About four months." When he tried to speak again she pressed a fingertip over his mouth. "Let's be finishin' this," she said, "and then we'll take our baby and build a lifetime together."

He smiled and kissed her again. "'Tis a wonder you are, Keelin Bonner Kilcullen."

"Aye." A coy smile flashed at the corners of her mouth and lit her eyes. "Off with you, now."

They left the concealment of the hedges just as the sun sliced the clouds, thrusting shafts of warmth onto the busy street.

Rory climbed the courthouse steps. A dozen people loitered on the street and a dozen more near the court itself. They'll do for a start, he thought. He took a deep breath. "Is there an Irishman in the sound of me voice or anyone who knows what's goin' on in Ireland today?" he yelled in his best, but clearest brogue.

"Aye!" Keelin called from the street.

Some people passing slowed to listen.

"Are you aware that Parliament has extinguished the right of Habeas Corpus for Ireland as easily as snuffin' out the flame of a candle, leavin' us in medieval darkness? Do you know that Scotland'll be next and there's a true possibility that them pompous donkeys will roast all British subjects in the same fire?"

Keelin moved around the clumps of people. Many were simply curious, but the longer they listened, the more Rory's words took root. Soon the gathering neared fifty people, most of whom Keelin surmised were Irish. She moved, encouraging vocal responses by her own visible interest. "Tell us more!"

Then she stopped, turned to see a young girl on the outskirts of the crowd who had climbed on a wooden box beside a lamp pole. "Jaysus, Maire and Joseph, tis Siobhan Tyrrell," she said under her breath. "What's she doin' here?"

Keelin angled her way toward Siobhan.

Male British voices joined the clamorous din: "What are you talkin' about?" "What's goin' on?"

"Go home you crazy Mick!"

"Stop stirrin' up trouble!"

"Trouble's stirrin' all right," Rory shouted back. "And tis you in the pot. The problem is the broth's not hot enough yet, but it soon will be and by that time you'll be too numb to know you're about to be et!"

"Tis you who'll be et, you bloody . . ."

"Siobhan," Keelin called. "Get out of the street, girl. There's trouble comin'."

"I'm here and I'm stayin'," she answered. "I can help. I want someone to answer for Colin bein' killed."

"You'll find no answers here. For God's sake get away now while you can!"

"Let him speak!" a woman screamed over the crowd.

"Aye! Let him talk!" Keelin called. When she looked back, Siobhan was gone.

The crowd had doubled. People spilled out of Pubs, pints in hand, to hear better what went on at the courthouse. Some began to nod in agreement. Women put down their bundles and hushed their children. Now, Keelin thought, stir the kettle. Make them angry.

"If they can be yankin' rights from the Irish," Rory went on with sweeping gestures, "what makes you think they'll leave England be? One day you'll wake up and find that you have no more rights than an Irishman! Are you goin' to let that happen?"

"No! No!" The loud growing knot of people began to make themselves heard.

As Rory railed on, more spectators bunched around the steps. The big polished oaken doors of the courthouse opened and two English Bobbies, truncheon straps wrapped around their wrists, moved toward him. He edged away. "Are we losin' the right to be speakin' out in public now?" he cried, pointing at the silent officers.

From where she stood at the rear of the crowd, Keelin couldn't tell who started the row, all she heard was the whistle. Another whistle shrilled. Some onlookers fled as more Police arrived while others threw themselves into the confusion. Rory's voice lifted in the midst of the crowd, now well into the hundreds in number, urging them to fight for their God-given rights of speech and Habeas Corpus. A woman screamed.

Rory blocked the thrust of a swinging night stick and reached for his pistol. It was gone.

The crowd had become a shrieking mob, wildly frantic, striking out at the authority that tried to hold it back. Blood ran from gashed foreheads, cheeks, chins struck by careening truncheons wielded by the advancing armed authorities.

Rory shook off hands that grasped after him. In his attempt to reach Keelin, he shoved two Officers into the street, sending them sprawling, one of the helmets went flying. The Officer's head struck the base of a lamp post and Rory knew he would never get up.

"Keelin!" he called. "Keelin! Where are you?"

"Rory! Rory!"

"Run, Keelin! I'll find you! Run!"

From his vantage point at the second story window of the courthouse to the road where the police van had stopped, Michael Davitt asked, "Who the hell are they, Egan?"

"I don't give a tinker's dam who they are," Dylan answered. "What are they doin'?" He turned to Egan. "Could others have come for O'Leary and them?"

"Nae. There's somethin' goin' on here that stinks to high heaven." Egan took the binoculars out of Michael's hand, he looked around the van, through the foliage. Seeing nothing he gave the binoculars back to Michael and started down the staircase when he stopped and turned back.

"Michael!" Egan called. "Can you make out who's in the van?"

"Nae! There's too much goin' on. Did you hear a gun shot?"

"Aye! Where's Willie?"

"In the thick of it, I'd wager."

"Watch the driver," Egan said, grasping the handrail. "What's he doin'?"

"Runnin', if he's smart," Dylan whispered. "I've not seen such a donnybrook as this. How many do you count?"

"Twenty . . . twenty-five. If they're after . . . Wait! Look!"

The van doors opened. The body of a policeman tumbled to the ground, blood spilling from a wound to his face.

"There's Willie!" Michael said in a hoarse whisper.

Egan rushed back to the window, squinted to read Willie O'Brien's hand signals. "O'Leary and them aren't there. Ahhh, Jaysus, Maire and Joseph!" Egan touched Michael's armless shoulder.

"Maybe Corydon knows somethin' about this. Rory and Keelin are probably on their way to France by now."

"Let's go."

The mob crushed in on Rory. Men and women fought erratically, ripping, tearing while he dodged one blow after another. His small diversion had sprung too quickly out of control. He struggled through the furor he had created; sidestepping flailing fists, stumbling feet. At last he pushed to the outer edge of the masses where he could finally reach Keelin and make the run for Dover.

A pistol shot rang in his ears. He froze. A trail of white vapor lifted and hung on the moist air.

Though she didn't hear the volley, Keelin watched the smoke rise from the pistol barrel. "Rory!" she screamed, stunned by the sudden fire in her chest. Ahhh, God, she thought, this isn't supposed to happen! Where did the gun come from?

J.J. Corydon appeared before her. She grasp his arm for support, determined to stay on her feet. "J. . . ," she gasped. "Rory?" Corydon shook her hand free, stared into her startled face. "I'm . . . I'm sorry it had to be you," he said and slipped the still smoking gun into his coat pocket.

Keelin staggered. Blood bubbled through her lips, garbled her words. "This isn't supposed to . . . happen . . ." She dropped to her knees, her arms cradling her abdomen. "We was goin' h-home . . ." She toppled. Face down. Breathe! Once more! Once more . . . . . . no more . . .

People backed away in stunned silence leaving a human corridor through which Rory passed. One visibly shaken Policeman stood by, as if the three victims on the street needed guarding. When Rory recognized Keelin, the outside world vanished, taking with it its faces, its noises, its meaningless politics. He didn't feel the hands or hear the orders to stand back as he knelt to touch her. When he finally turned away from the blood that seeped from the black exit hole in her back, he saw the Bobbie. "Why?" he asked, his heartbreak turning to anger. "Who done this?" he roared. He was propelled beyond hurt, beyond reason and, without warning, he lunged.

The crowd gasped as the Policeman wielded his night stick in a practiced course. Blood spurted from the left side of Rory's face. He dropped to the street like a paving stone.

Dob Quinn met Egan, Willie O'Brien and Michael Davitt as they rushed into the confusion in front of the courthouse. "I'm hopin' you had nothin' to do with this Egan O'Shea," he whispered roughly, "because it'll be the end of you! It may be anyway!"

Egan looked out over the loud, angry, bleeding mob. "Jaysus! What happened?" he asked, seeing police drag bodies to one side of the street.

"Twas death you brought here, Egan. There's a Bull down. Sure'n someone'll pay for that. I don't want it to be you so run, the lot of you." He turned his attention to Dylan, Willie and Michael. "O'Leary and them was never here! I told him that inside."

Egan grasped Dob by the hair. "What do you mean, never here?"

"You been lied to all along. That's what I mean! Twas the work of J.J. Corydon. He's your traitor, you fool!" Dob struggled free of Egan's grasp. "Twas him fouled the raid at Chester Castle and him who got the lot of you here for Her Majesty's henchmen. They've got you're name, Egan and they'll be searchin' like never before. Now you best get yourselves home and stay out of sight or you'll all be meat for the birds over Kilmainham's gallows! And was I you, lad," he said to Egan, "I'd be hidin' forever. Corydon made sure you can't show your face again. I seen the poster and your likeness tis near perfect. Believe me, they'll not forget this day unless they hang you tomorrow. In two days there's a boat leavin' Liverpool for America. Tis the last freighter of the year and you'd be a damned fool to be missin' it. Go now before this quiets down and they see all your scrawny necks beggin' for ropes!"

Michael yanked on Egan's coat but he wouldn't move. "Where's Keelin and Rory?" he demanded.

"Who do you think them other two are?" Dob pointed at the street.

Men were covering the bodies with coats and tarps. All Egan could see clearly was the red handkerchief around Rory's neck and Willie O'Brien kneeling beside Keelin's body holding her hand.

"Go on!" Dob Quinn urged them. "Egan'll be right behind you."

Egan's vision blurred. The blood that ran between the uneven stones made him sick. He cried out but had no voice. He couldn't speak or cry or scream. Rory and Keelin lay on the bloodied street while the eyes of strangers probed and wondered about them; who they were, where they'd come from. He couldn't leave them. He'd asked them to cause a disturbance and they'd done exactly what he'd asked . . . as they always had. Whether he was hanged or not, he'd not leave them to be buried in a pauper's grave in an unknown place.

"Don't be thinkin' of stayin', lad," Dob said from behind him. "I know what you're thinkin' and I'll do what I can to see them laid out proper. Don't be killin' yourself for somethin' you can do nothin' about now. The honor's in livin' not swingin'." Small, stubby hands shoved at him. "Go, there's no glory here. Get on that boat, Egan. Your life's in your own hands . . . now, save it!"

Egan heard but when he turned Dob Quinn was gone. "God, forgive me," he gasped, crossing himself. Overwhelmed, he pushed shaking hands through his hair. Gooseflesh covered his body as he took one last look at the street and Keelin's dark hair that danced in the breeze from beneath the tarp. "If I do nothin' else in me life, Corydon. I'll see you hang!"

Egan's sudden hatred of John Joseph Corydon was invaded by a desperate need for Maire and, blinded by tears, he ran through the crowd away from Manchester.

16

"Do not mistake a goat's beard for a fine stallion's tail."

"Ma?" Maire called dismally as her mother turned to leave the bedroom.

"Aye?" Peg answered coolly, not moving.

"I know tis late but can we talk, Ma?" Maire's voice was small and lost. Her slender fingers moved back and forth over the lacy bedspread. "I know I'm not doin' what you'd like, but . . ." Her eyes raised to see her mother's rigid back. "But I can't help it if I love Egan O'Shea. And I can't help it if Daddy want's me to marry Luke MacSweeny. I'm not intendin' to hurt you or anyone," she sniffed, "but I'm goin' to be hurtin' somebody no matter what and . . . I'm on both ends. And you knowin' about . . . about . . ."

Peg turned to face her weeping daughter. "The baby?"

Maire nodded shamefully.

Peg sat next to her on the bed and took her hands. "Don't for one minute think that what's happened is the fault of that poor, innocent babe within you. Not for the space of a wink." Peg's words were scolding but her voice was like a poultice. "I know that I've been mournful. But tis only because I know what lies in front of you, girl. Make no mistake, when it comes time for this wee thing to be born, I'll welcome him, for you see, he'll be mine too, and loved as much as any."

"And if he's a colleen?" Maire asked, wiping at her face with an open palm.

"Especially if he's a colleen."

They sat for a moment in the shadowed stillness of the room, each wishing there was more to say and knowing that there wasn't. When Peg left, Maire pulled the thick comforter back and slipped into the cool bed. It would be her last night alone and she spread her body crosswise, taking up the entire space. Then she curled into a ball and cried.

Luke met Peg at the bedroom door. "Is she all right?" he asked anxiously.

"Aye," Peg nodded, and offering nothing more, went to sit beside her husband. Somehow, Kean was more handsome than he'd ever looked to her. She wanted to touch him, hear his voice, surround herself with the security he, so unselfishly, offered.

"Well," MacSweeny wheezed as he bumped through the back door, his sleeves and shirt-front soaked. "I finally got them two roughnecks cleaned up."

Frowning, the boys walked in behind him in white nightshirts, their hair dripping.

"Off to bed with you, now," MacSweeny ordered. "I told you you'd be spotless as two sacred lambs for the weddin' and I meant it!" He flopped into the leather chair. "Them are two rare birds, I can tell you. They near drowned me!" He turned to Luke. "And how's the groom doin'?"

Luke smiled awkwardly.

"Anxious, uh, lad?" MacSweeny's brow lifted, he grinned and straightened himself in the chair with a loud groan. "Well, you won't be seein' her again till she walks down the aisle."

"I'll see her in the mornin', Da, when we leave."

"Nae, lad," MacSweeny said with a definite shake of his head. "You and me, we'll be goin' in the carriage, early. We'll feed the stock and leave before anyone else is up. Tis bad luck to be seein' the bride before the weddin'. Best you climb that ladder yourself now and get some sleep."

Luke was surprised that his father ordered him to bed but he bid good night to everyone and climbed into the loft, settling himself on the down-filled pallet. He listened as the Martins talked and watched long shadows weave across the ceiling then he turned over and tried to sleep. He tossed for hours, thumped his pillow and rolled.

The wind pushed at the side of the house. Luke jumped at the sound of the dog's single bark. Sitting up, he wrapped his arms around his knees. Perhaps a drink of water would help. He padded down the ladder in his bare feet, past Maire's room, through the kitchen to the back porch where he took a long drink from the cold metal dipper. With his eyes closed, he drew a long, deep breath of sweet autumn air. Retracing his steps, Luke stopped at Maire's curtained doorway. Da said it was bad luck to see her before the weddin', he thought, toying with the hemmed edge of the drape. Just once wouldn't hurt and she'd never know . . . no one would know. Besides, she was asleep. He drew the curtain aside and stepped into the room. Nothing was visible and he was sure his heart would strangle him if it didn't leave his throat. He stood, flattened against the wall as if frozen by the rustling of the bedclothes.

"Luke?" Maire whispered sleepily.

He thought his skin would fall from his bones as he answered, "Aye, love."

"Are you just goin' to stand there, then?" she yawned.

"I . . . I just come for a drink of water."

"There's no water in here," she said, adjusting herself on the pile of pillows.

"I . . . I know that . . . I just . . ."

"Just what?"

"I didn't know you was awake. I just wanted to look at you. How did you know I was here?"

Maire shrugged. "I don't know. I guess, I wasn't sleepin' too well meself. How do I look?"

"I . . . I can't see you to clear."

She sighed. "I can't see you either. Come here."

Luke's eyes grew wide. "I don't dare."

"Why not?"

"We . . . we're not yet married."

Maire groaned impatiently. "Damnit Luke, we will be. Do you want me or not?"

"Shhh!" Luke warned. "Course I do . . . but . . ."

Maire threw back the covers. Resigned to what her life was to hold from this time forward, she offered herself, willingly, unwillingly . . . it was all the same. She had Egan's child and no one could change that. What she had to do now was be a good wife so that Luke would take care of them both and when Egan came back from where ever he'd gone . . . well, that would be faced when the time came. Right now Luke was here and she had to convince him she loved him. "Luke," she said softly, her fingers finding his in the darkness. "You're wantin' me . . . like I'm wantin' . . . you." She led him, pulled him down next to her and eased her nightgown over her head. "Take that off," she whispered, tugging at his collar.

He paused but she insisted and his nightshirt fell to the floor.

Her hands explored his naked chest and met behind his neck. She heard his breath falter, then shudder from his mouth as she pulled him down beside her and pressed her body against him. She ran her fingers across his shoulders, down his torso and over his stomach. "You can touch me, Luke. I won't break," she whispered, drawing his hands to her breasts, "and kiss me. I want you to kiss me . . . and don't stop . . ."

Wind and salt spray stung Egan's face as he stood numbly at the ferry's bow. He had to get Maire in time to catch the ship for America. He didn't know where the others were. He was alone. Thoughts scattered like chalk dust from the black slate of his mind; from the famine and the loss of Grandfar and Marian and baby Francis to the trips to Cork and his ma's smile. From his da's tales of how his brother, Hugh, had vanished from their lives to his jugs of poteen, hidden behind rock fences and in the byre, to the hedge schools and the nighttime songs and stories of Ireland at her greatest. And there was Jimmy Stephens, Kevin Burke, Rory and Keelin. Rory's voice echoed, "Keelin and I married each other. No priest. No church. No bother. In a pub . . ."

Egan put his head in his hands but he was too tired to cry. He reached inside his coat and pulled out the tiny blanket his mother had given him. Why had he carried it all the way to England with him? He stared at it and realized that when Keelin died, their baby died, too. He mourned that as much as anything.

Breathing deeply, he looked out over the railing into the gray waves. Other passengers, bound for Dublin, kept their distance. He felt as if he were painted with the very color of death.

He reached his cold hands into his coat pockets. There, tangled in his fingers, was his mother's Rosary. "Ma," he whispered, "I wish…"

Keep your mind on Maire, he ordered himself stubbornly, feeling for his pistol tucked in his belt at the back of his trousers. Keep your mind on Maire and breathe or by all that's Holy, you'll use the pistol on yourself.

Peg put the last pin in her hair and picked up a cloth wrapped package.

"What is it you have there?" Kean asked, buttoning up his good trousers and reaching for his top coat.

"A sewin' case I made for Maire." Peg handed it to him.

"Ahhh, Peg, darlin,'" Kean said softly, moving the wrap aside. "'Tis grand. Every time she uses it, she'll think of you, and love you all the more." His arm tightened around her in a loving hug.

"Is everyone ready, then?" she asked.

"Aye. I seen to that."

Bobby and Roddy sat stiffly on wooden chairs. Maire stepped from behind the curtain, her dress in her arms.

"Have you got your good shoes?" Peg asked her.

"Aye, Ma."

Kean patted the small of her back as he guided her toward the door. "Come on, lads," he called, "Winnie's waitin'."

"Can the dog ride with us, Daddy?" Bobby asked. "The man'll be at St. Michan's to get him today."

"Long as he's clean and he don't make no trouble."

"Aye, Daddy!" The boys raced to the door and climbed on the cart urging the dog in behind them.

"Here, Maire," Peg said, "I want you to be wearin' this. The sky's lookin' desperate."

Maire twisted into the heavy coat and for a moment Peg left her hands on the girl's shoulders. Maire bent to touch her cheek to her mother's hand.

"I love you, Ma," she whispered.

"I love you, too, child."

They walked outside. Peg held Maire's wedding dress until she climbed onto the seat, then Kean helped Peg onto the back of the cart and placed Kate in her arms.

"Won't be long now," he said and winked at Peg.

Winnie groaned and puffed and sometimes slipped on the wet stones. Half way to St. Michan's, a fine mist began to fall from the charcoal clouds. Maire folded her dress and tucked it inside her coat.

Finally Winnie pulled the cart through St. Michan's open gateway and Kean helped the women to the ground. "Don't be long," he said with a broad smile at Peg. "This girl wants to be gettin' married."

"There's plenty of time," said Peg, giving him the toddler. "There'll be no weddin' without her. Be sure of that."

Kean turned the cart, tied Winnie to the post by the gate and pointed the boys toward the church.

"What am I to be doin' with the dog, Mr. Martin?" Roddy asked.

"Best leave him outside."

"What if he runs away? I'll be in trouble sure."

"All right. You two stay here until the man takes his dog or you see Maire comin'. Whatever happens first, you get yourselves inside and sat. And if either of you shows one speck of dirt on them clothes, I'll be havin' your hind parts for supper, understood?"

"Aye, Daddy!" Bobby giggled.

Kean raised a finger, his stinging glare causing loud gasps. "Don't be doubtin' me for a minute, lads. I'm serious as a boil on the Queen's royal bum."

Wide-eyed, they nodded in stiff unison and watched him leave so they could finally exhale.

A light glimmered through the long windows of the bride's room as Maire stood barefooted in her underthings waiting for her mother to slip her wedding dress over her head.

Peg knelt to start with the button and loop at the bottom of the bodice.

"I can do that, Ma," Maire said.

Gently, Peg slapped Maire's hands. "Don't touch nothin'. You should always start with the last button first. That way it comes out true." Peg glanced up at Maire's blushing cheeks. "I seen how you button. Tis seldom you get it right."

Maire sighed and held her hands away.

"Now," Peg said when she'd finished. "What do you think?" She turned Maire toward the mirror.

"Tis lovely, Ma."

Peg reached for the veil. "Ahhh, darlin'," she said, placing a crown of ivy and lace on Maire's freshly combed and pinned hair. "In the light, you're lookin' like a saint from heaven."

Maire took a critical look at herself in the mirror, her finger following the rounded neckline of her bodice. "Well, this saint's glad you moved the buttons. Another month and I'd not be able to breathe."

Peg smiled sadly. "Twould be nice if you loved Luke."

Maire paced the room, sat, stood, paced again. "I'll try. He's nice enough . . . and he loves me. That'll make it easier. I just don't know what I'll do if . . ." She looked fearfully at her mother. "Had Conor O'Gill come back, Ma, what would you have done?"

Peg sucked in a breath. "I don't know that, child," she said, turning to face the window and the vivid autumn colors in the rose garden. "What I do know is that I've grown to love Kean Martin with every part of me." She paused a moment then turned back to her daughter. "And if I was to hurt him, twould break me heart into pieces unfit for mendin'."

In a forlorn embrace, they stood for a long time looking into the misty, silent garden.

Egan bounded off the ferry after inquiring how long the passenger vessel would be in port.

The Pilot glanced from his pocket watch to the brooding sky. "Two hours. Maybe less if this comes real weather."

"Don't leave without me. I'll be back!" Egan called and ran.

The man waved him off and closed the pilothouse door on the drizzle.

Egan ran up the bustling streets of Dublin until his legs would take him no further. He leaned against a building and looked at the leaden sky, his lungs aching. Maire had said the wedding would take place at half-ten in the morning. There was yet time to get to St. Michan's before . . . If Maire had convinced the priest she was already married, she might not be at the church at all, but if she hadn't . . . that's what nagged him. If she hadn't succeeded, her father would have her go through with the marriage to *cousin* Luke.

"Damn him, anyway!" Egan gasped.

"Watch who you're damnin', lad," squawked a voice behind him.

Egan turned to see a small woman, shriveled from age and work and weather. "Is there a quick way to reach St. Michan's?" he asked.

The woman squinted at the sky as her tongue clicked over her gums. "St. Michan's Anglican or St. Michan's Catholic?"

"Jaysus, woman, Catholic!"

"Only if you was a bird, lad. Only if you was a . . ."

Egan ran on. The chimes of Dublin Castle clock tower tolled ten. Now it was a foot race against the coming storm and elapsing time. A saddled horse, tied in front of a house on a side street, caught his peripheral vision and he wasted no time analyzing right and wrong. "I'll bring you back, I promise!" he said and streaked away toward what he hoped was an empty church.

"Well," Maire sighed, "do you think everyone's come who's comin'?"

Peg glanced out the window again and nodded. "I'm glad we decided to hold the weddin' here, aren't you?"

"Aye. Lord knows, our little church wouldn't have been proper, what with all the MacSweenys in Dublin." Maire's green eyes grew round. "And where would we have put them all?"

"I don't suppose the byre would have done, do you?" Peg asked wryly.

Sister MaireTyrone tapped on the door and entered.

"So . . . how do I look?" Maire asked her.

"Like the bride of promise you are, Miss Martin," the Nun said. "The girl who was goin' to play the harp, your young man's cousin, I believe, isn't here yet, but he has decided not to wait. Would you like to be goin' in now, then?"

Peg stepped outside. "The rain's stopped. I'm thinkin' we'll use the path, Sister. Tell them the bride'll be there in a few minutes."

The Nun smiled and closed the door softly behind her.

"Now, remember, lift your skirt so it don't get wet," Peg said, bending to pick up the back of the dress.

"Can't we wait just a few more minutes for Livie to get here," she said. "You've never heard her play. She does it so . . ." The words stuck to Maire's tongue and she stood on the open threshold like a marble statue.

"I'll hear her play another time. Go on, girl," Peg urged.

"Ma?" Maire said, her tone shallow, breathless as she watched a horse slide to a grinding stop in the church yard. In the span of a wink, the rider cleared the saddle. He looked lost for a moment, then she heard Bobby: "Maire's in the cottage," he said and pointed. Roddy asked him about the dog, his arms around the neck of the jumping, barking Irish Setter. Thoughts ran like ink on a wet page in Maire's mind.

Peg followed her daughter's stare. "Ahhh, God!" she cried and pulled Maire away, pressed her body against the door to keep Egan out. She fell to the floor as the door was forced open.

"Maire's comin' with me, Mrs. Martin," he said coolly, taking the girl by the wrist. I mean you no harm, but I'll not see her wed to another." Sweat beaded Egan's upper lip. A two day's growth of beard shadowed his square jaw. His eyes were red with exhaustion and wild from running. The mist had molded his auburn hair into tight curls and his coat sagged unevenly.

"You'll not get away with this." Peg's voice shook with anger and fear as she pulled herself into a chair. "They'll hunt you down. Don't you know?"

"They won't find us." He looked at Maire. She was beautiful.

Maire shook free of Egan's grasp and dropped to the floor at her mother's feet. "Ahhh, Ma, don't you see? I have to be goin' with him now. I love him. What I'm carryin' inside, is his, Ma. I have the chance you never had. Let me take it. Please, let me go!"

Peg gathered Maire to her. "Do you know what you're askin'?"

Maire drew back, searching her mother's eyes for understanding. "Please, Ma. I have to go! I have to!"

"Hurry Maire! We've less than half an hour to meet the boat!" Egan said nervously, feeling the back of his belt for the pistol. "Let's go before they find out. I don't want to be hurtin' anyone!"

Maire glanced up at him and back to her mother.

"Here!" Peg thrust the gift she'd made into Maire's hands.

Maire kissed her mother's cheek. As they turned to leave, Peg took the veil from Maire's hair and forced her into the heavy coat. "I don't want you catchin' cold." She hugged her once more. "Egan," she said, her voice firm, unflinching. "I want you to take this and marry her proper this time." She twisted the wide gold band from her own finger and dropped it into his palm. "You'll be needin' this, too." She hoisted her skirt and took a small pouch from her petticoat pocket. "Tuck it in the package until you've time alone to look at it. Now off with you before I change me mind and scream for your father!"

Egan kissed Peg's teary cheek, grabbed Maire and ran. "Get in!" he cried as, hurriedly, he tied the borrowed horse to the back of Kean Martin's cart. He grabbed the reins and Winnie lunged through the gate, down Halston and Little Britain streets to Capal, across the bridge and east toward the waiting ferry. Padraig bounded after them, barking.

Bobby and Roddy stood in open-mouthed wonder. They looked at each other then ran into the Church. "Daddy! Daddy!" they both cried. "The man's back but he didn't take the dog. He took Maire!"

Wedding guests dashed behind Kean Martin, MacSweeny and Father O'Reilly. Kean ran to the bride's quarters. "Peg!" he called. "Peg!" His steps slowed to a wrenching stop as he entered the room where she sat her face in her hands, rocking, weeping. Dropping to one knee, Kean took her by the shoulders. "Peg? Are you all right? What happened? Where's Maire?"

She looked at him through wet, stricken eyes. Reached to him for comfort.

"Martin!" MacSweeny roared. "What's goin' on? Where's Maire?"

Kean's gaze darted from MacSweeny to Peg. "Well?"

"Egan O'Shea . . ." she said.

Maire clung desperately to the wobbling seat of her father's wagon with one hand and grasping her mother's gift with the other as Egan cracked the whip over the mare's straining back. The cart careened over the slippery streets, scattering chickens and children from it's path.

Egan glanced over his shoulder at the horse he'd tied behind. The side street was coming up fast on his right. Muted thunder growled in the distance. Time and weather were still his greatest enemies. The temptation to pass the street where he had borrowed the horse was immense . . . but he'd promised. "Hold on!" he shouted and yanked the right rein, turning Winnie up the road.

Pulling the cart to a creaking stop, he set the brake and leaped to the street, untied the horse and slapped its rump, and sent it wandering up the road. "Go home!" he cried.

"Egan! Are you bats? They'll be comin' after us, sure!"

As he leaped back onto the wagon, Padraig caught up with them.

"Damnit, Padraig!" Egan said roughly, "you'll be leadin' all of them to us. Shut up and get in!"

Kean took Peg by the shoulders. "Think, Peg. Where'd she go?"

With tears breaking her voice, Peg recited all she could recall.

"Great God Almighty!" Kean stood, his voice rising to match his height. "Why the hell didn't you call for me or fight him yourself? Did he have a gun or somethin'? Damnit, woman!"

"Gun?" MacSweeny said. "What's this about a gun?"

"I saw no gun!" Peg insisted.

"That goddamn Fenian!" Kean bellowed.

Outside, Luke cornered Bobby and Roddy. "Which way?" he asked, his eyes darting from one boy to the other.

"I'm not sure, Luke," Roddy said. "By the time I ran down the street, they'd turned the corner. I think they went toward the water."

Luke leaped into the nearest saddle and took off at a gallop. The boys could do nothing but watch in wonder at the pursuit.

"Where's Luke?" MacSweeny demanded of the boys who could only point.

"Luke's gone after them!" he shouted to the others. "And he don't know about the gun! Roddy, get in the carriage! Let's go!"

Horsemen, carts and wagons rushed noisily through the church yard gate and clacked down the street. Those left behind watched until all the men had vanished, then, as rain began to fall in earnest, they went back inside to wait and pray. Peg stood alone in the rain. "Take care of her, Egan," she said softly. "Hurry now! Hurry!"

Egan turned Winnie off the main road onto a side street.

"Where are we goin'?" Maire asked.

"They'll catch us sure, if we stay on the highway."

Laid out like a giant broken wheel with streets like spokes, Dublin radiated out in all directions. With his familiarity of the city, Egan knew to head east. He glanced toward the main road from the muddy little connecting street. Luke MacSweeny streaked past, followed by a parade of others, all heading toward the harbour.

"Ahhh, damn!" Egan said under his breath.

"What's wrong?"

"Didn't you see them? We just missed a mob of well-wishers. Our only hope now is to pray they don't spread out or see us usin' the side streets!" The whip cracked and Winnie sped down the narrow road where deep pot holes threatened the wagon and ate away at the precious minutes before the ferry left for Liverpool.

At the pier, Luke spun his horse frantically looking for Maire. He raced back and forth searching every avenue but saw no sign of her.

"Have you seen them, Luke?" his father called, jerking the matched pair to a frothing halt.

"Nae, Da. You?"

"Not a speck!" MacSweeny turned his attention to those around him. "Everybody spread out!" he cried. "They must be here somewhere!"

Men and horses scattered but MacSweeny held a tight rein on his prized dapple thoroughbreds. He thought that staying where he was, on the busy pier, might be more important than chasing shadows. He was right. "Roddy," he said, "stay back, out of sight." As soon as the searchers left the wharf, the Martin cart rolled to a stop not two-hundred yards in front of him. MacSweeny waited quietly while Egan helped Maire to the ground and watched them run toward him and the waiting vessel.

"Maire Martin!" MacSweeny called, his big voice booming, drawing the gaze of everyone on the docks.

Maire and Egan stopped momentarily, then Egan pulled her along behind him, trying to ignore the bellowing man.

"I'll charge you with kidnappin', you houligan! Turn loose of her!" MacSweeny moved his team swiftly to the edge of the pier, cutting Egan and Maire off just as the tug sailed into place at the ferry's bow. "Let her go! I'm warnin' you!"

"Go to hell!" Egan roared and pulled the pistol from his belt. "Move your wagon or lose a horse! What'll it be?"

"Don't, Egan!" Maire cried.

"Stay put, girl!" MacSweeny roared. "Luke's close by."

Maire's eyes welled. She wanted to scream. "I'm sorry, but I have to go. He'll kill your pair, don't you see?"

"Shut up, Maire!" Egan ordered, not taking his eyes from MacSweeny. "Go round and run for the boat," he told her, giving a gentle push toward the back of the carriage. "Touch her, auld man, and the horse drops," he promised.

Lifting her soiled hem, Maire did as she was told, giving a pained look at Luke's father as she passed. Once behind the coach, she ran, ignoring the ferry's purser who tried to collect the ticket she didn't have.

"Well?" Egan called to the butcher, his pistol still trained on the head of the nearest horse. "You can't stop me. I'll go round, under or over, so tell me what you want! Move your horses, or bury them!"

Padraig ran in circles, barking.

"The boat, Padraig!"

Again the dog obeyed the hand signal and ran up the plank.

MacSweeny began to sweat as he eyed the determined face and the cocked, unwavering pistol. Angrily, he yanked the team back and Egan ran for the ferry. The loading plank was gone. The sailing tug had started pulling the ship out to sea.

"Egan!" Maire called desperately as ear piercing thunder pealed above her.

At a full run, he leaped. All noise of the world vanished, only the hissing of wind filled his ears as he vaulted from the pier over the choppy, black waters to sprawl half on, half off the ship's deck where Maire and others pulled him aboard.

On the dock, MacSweeny howled at the top of his voice for the others.

"Where's Padraig?" Egan asked when he'd caught his breath.

"Sorry sir," the purser said, taking the tickets from him. "No dogs allowed."

Helplessly, Egan looked back at the pier. Someone had tied Padraig to a piling. He barked and gnawed wildly at the rope. Then he sat, whining pawing the air. For a moment Egan thought the dog would leap into the water and hang himself, then he saw the figure of a boy.

"That's Roddy MacSweeny," Maire said, sensing his distress. "He loves the dog. He'll take good care of him."

Egan leaned against Maire and the railing. Both his mind and body ached. He had acquired but one prize in all his life: Maire, and though she finally stood beside him, it seemed an empty victory without at least one friend to share it. All his friends were gone or dead and Padraig was only a dog after all.

"Ahhh, God . . ." He turned to Maire, unable to mask the pain that loss had drawn across his face. From stark exhaustion, he slipped to his knees and held on to her, knowing that without her, he was nothing.

Lightning shredded the northern horizon and a monstrous roll of thunder followed. The sky turned gray as charcoal and churned in giant circles above them. The tug's pilot signaled an early release of the ferry.

Most of the passengers had moved inside, away from the coming weather. Terrified, Maire watched Egan, afraid to let go of the railing, afraid God would have the sea sweep her away in retribution for abandoning Luke.

Breathless, she stared again at the diminishing pier where Luke's father was struggling to hold him back from the water.

"Maire! Maire! I'm comin' . . . I'm comin'. . ."

Tears streamed down her cheeks as she heard Luke's voice crying through the wind.

"Ahhh, God," she said, "what have I done?" And looking up to heaven, she gasped as the ferry's sails snapped and whipped with the fury of the gale, stretching full with the tarnished winds of freedom.

EPILOGUE

"I don't care what it costs!" Luke shouted in the fisherman's bearded face. "I'll pay all you want! Just take me to wherever that ferry's goin'!"

The man chewed on the end of his dead pipe. "Sorry, lad but no amount of punt is worth me life or yours. I can see how important this is to you but go tomorrow when the sea's calmer and the weather's not so desperate." He turned to seize his gear and the one salmon he'd caught.

MacSweeny watched his son from the wagon, knowing he had to let his boy deal with this on his own. All he could do was pick up the pieces when this was over.

Luke bent and grabbed his knees in frustration. He righted himself wiping the downpour from his face. "Tomorrow's too late, don't you see? He's a Fenian and he's stole me wife. She's in great danger. I'll not be able to find her tomorrow! *Please!*" he begged.

Shaking his head the fisherman replied: "Not today."

Luke snatched the man's lapels. "You don't understand, you damned auld fool; he's *stolen* her!"

"Well, now," he said, pulling Luke's hands away. "This *damned auld fool* is not fool enough to take you out there to die."

Disgusted with the old man, Luke stopped everyone with a boat and begged them to take him. They all pointed from the sky to the whitecaps on the water and told him, "Not today. Maybe tomorrow."

"Luke," his father called in an effort to comfort him. "There's no more to be done now except go to the Constable. I've found out where the ferry's goin'. Someone there will recognize that she's been kidnapped. Maybe she'll get away from him on her own and find her way back. Maybe we'll be seein' her sooner than you think. Maybe . . ."

"And maybe I'll fly to the moon on a pig!" he snapped furiously, his voice cracking under the weight of his grief. "She's gone, Da. You know it as well as I do."

The wedding guests straggled back too the church to pick up family and friends. Peg watched and waited for Kean in the bridal room with Kate and Bobby, her nerves raw, her eyes swollen, red from weeping. What if they'd been caught? What would they do to Egan who simply loved Maire so much that he'd do a crazy thing like this? And what would Kean be like if they'd gotten away and he discovered that she had given her wedding ring to Egan to put on Maire's finger? She sucked in a deep, desolate breath and held it as long as she could before she let it escape.

"Bobby," she said. "Take Kate into the church, please."

"Aye, Ma. Is Da comin' back with Maire?"

Peg shrugged. "Probably not. Go, take your sister. I have to wait here for your da."

The boy lifted Kate and her blanket and left Peg to close the door. Hours later she saw Kean drive Winnie and the mud-caked cart, still intact, through the open gates of the church yard. She ran out to meet him. "Well?"

"They're gone," he said weakly, "over the water. May that man rot in hell for this! I'll hound him till I draw me last breath! MacSweeny and I went to the Constable. The whole world is goin' to be lookin' for that houligan! You can be sure of that."

Peg covered her face with her hands and cried.

Kean jumped from the cart. "There, there, love," Kean said, taking her into his arms, holding her close. "We'll get her back somehow . . . someday."

But Peg didn't cry for the loss of her daughter as Kean thought. She knew that Egan would take care of her, wherever they went. She wept for the grandchild she would never see.

"I'll get the children," Kean said softly. "We're goin' home."

Though Luke took the earliest morning ferry to Liverpool he saw no one who had seen anything or anyone out of the ordinary. He stayed on the dock for three days talking to everyone who would speak to him. Still, he found no answers to his questions except that there had been a freighter that had left for America two days before.

The MacSweeny household was silent for days. Though Roddy hadn't mentioned it, he had looked forward to having Maire around. When she was there, there was a spirit in the house that he enjoyed and Luke was less like a boss and more like a brother to him. Now, he spent most of his free time with the dog and old Manus. And when he came home, no one asked where he'd been unless the smell of poteen was strong. Macsweeny took care of business as usual though his boisterous voice had mellowed somehow.

Luke did his job. He greeted the customers with cool politeness and answered their questions about his kidnapped bride and seemed to take their well-meant condolences in stride. At night, alone, he wept. It was at night that he was haunted by his father's words: *"Tis bad luck to be seein' the bride before the weddin'."*

Several days after the day he was to have married, Luke found himself on the stone fence where he had held Maire in his arms for the first time, just before they'd fallen off and rolled down the hill together. Padraig stood quietly beside the fence, below him. Together they looked out to the rounded horizon where the calm sea met the sky.

His mind was full of the last night he and Maire had spent together. How tenderly she'd touched him then, kissed him, loved him, urged him to make love to her and he did, gladly. He could still feel the softness of her body against his and her gentle hands moving down his shoulders over his bare back . . .

He shoved his hands into his pockets. The ring was there, as it always was. He took it out and stared at it, tried to slip it on his little finger. It stopped just beyond the first joint. He looked out to sea again and put the ring back in his pocket. The light breeze tousled his dark hair and his eyes filmed over with tears.

"Tis bad luck to be seein' the bride before the weddin' . . . Tis bad luck . . .
bad luck . . ."

Egan and Maire's story will continue in...

A STAND
for
TIR na nÓg

IN THE BELLY OF THE BLUE FISH

Spring 2017